Desirée's heart constricted as she spied Megan's tiny figure venturing out onto the frozen surface of Redd's Pond.

"Don't go any farther. Come to Mommy," she coaxed. But the two-year-old's chubby legs only propelled her closer to the pond's soft center.

"Oh, God!" Desirée screamed, scrambling to reach her daughter.

The added pressure was too much. Desirée heard the crackle just as her fingers locked onto Megan's snowsuit. She hurled the child toward the outer edges of the pond as the ice gave way, and Desirée plunged straight down into the freezing water.

Not like this! she thought. *She was going to die.*

As her head disappeared through the hole, she visualized Jacob's face.

ABOUT THE AUTHOR

"Perhaps the most interesting fact about myself
is the total absence of any creative ambition
until the age of thirty," says Ruth Alana Smith.
"But after years of savoring the written word, I
was struck by an inexplicable urge to string
together thoughts and words of my own." Her
readers are glad she did! In this, her sixth
Superromance novel, she once again brings to
life an innovative and challenging story line
that showcases the talent that had been lying
dormant for so many years.

Books by Ruth Alana Smith

HARLEQUIN SUPERROMANCE
158–THE WILD ROSE
208–FOR RICHER OR POORER
265–AFTER MIDNIGHT
311–THE SECOND TIME AROUND
356–SPELLBOUND
400–A GENTLEMAN'S HONOR

Don't miss any of our special offers. Write to us at the
following address for information on our newest releases.

Harlequin Reader Service
P.O. Box 1397, Buffalo, NY 14240
Canadian address: P.O. Box 603,
Fort Erie, Ont. L2A 5X3

Soulbound

RUTH ALANA SMITH

Harlequin Books

TORONTO • NEW YORK • LONDON
AMSTERDAM • PARIS • SYDNEY • HAMBURG
STOCKHOLM • ATHENS • TOKYO • MILAN

Published August 1991

ISBN 0-373-70463-1

SOULBOUND

CHAPTER ONE

IT WAS the Christmas season in Marblehead. Good cheer abounded in the quaint township nestled along the rocky Massachusetts coast. The narrow, winding streets were packed with people celebrating the oldest of traditions—the Walk Festival. Everyone who was physically able had turned out for the event. Not even the icy winds blowing in from the sea had dampened the communal holiday spirit. The staunch New Englanders merely bundled up more snugly and ventured out of their warm winter dens to join in the fun.

The Walk Festival was a weekend set aside each year for the townsfolk to slow down and get reacquainted with their neighbors—a time when Marbleheaders truly practiced "peace on earth and good will toward men." State Street and the sailboats moored along the shore glittered with twinkling Christmas lights. In the main square, young and old alike gathered to gasp at the lighting of the seventy-foot tree and blend their voices with those of the caroling chorus especially on hand for the occasion. But it was the children who squealed with delight at the sight of Santa Claus disembarking from a lobster boat, for they knew he had come to take down their toy requests and fill their tiny outstretched hands with candy canes.

True to form, the Malone family had also braved the minus-ten chill factor to join in the festivities. Luckily Jacob was a tall man, and his daughter was afforded an unencumbered view of the jolly, white-bearded fellow in the red velvet suit as she sat on top of her daddy's broad shoulders. She clapped her mittened hands together and squirmed excitedly.

"Nick, Dada!" she chirped.

"Yeah, sugar. I see him." Jacob grinned and shifted to get a better grip on the rambunctious two-year-old. Given her wriggling about and the bulky snowsuit she wore, it was not an easy maneuver. Megan was a handful even under ordinary conditions. Her first glimpse of the wonder of wonders himself—Santa Claus—had her jabbering and jiggling like a monkey. He cast a look over at his wife and winked. "Old St. Nick is a little stouter and shorter than last year, don't you think?"

She smiled and admonished him with a shake of her head. "You're such a cynic, Jake."

He reached about with his free arm and pulled his wife close against his burly warmth. "I know you only fake believing in the old boy in the hopes of getting a bigger and better present," he teased under his breath.

"I was weaned on myths, remember? Preserving and observing them is a long-standing custom of my family." Her eyes twinkled with mischief as she glanced up at him.

It still amazed Jacob how he could be absolutely mesmerized by his wife's gaze. Her eyes were a startling shade of blue—lavender blue—and at the most unexpected and sometimes inopportune moments, they would seize him and hold him spellbound. He'd been about to remind her that her family customs were far from the norm, but the glib reply melted from his lips the instant he connected with his wife's eyes.

She was so beautiful. Stunning, actually. It was at moments like this that he wondered how in the world he had failed to notice that fact when they first crossed paths a few years back. The old cliché about love being blind simply wasn't true in his case. Just the opposite. Before he'd met Desirée, he'd been blindly going through the motions of living the good life. Then she came into the picture and everything changed. A wrong—or in his case, right—turn onto an unfamiliar road one snowy night had deposited him at her doorstep, and his life had turned right-side up. Of course, if someone had predicted then that he'd end up marrying his shy and somewhat peculiar landlady, he'd have laughed in their face. Yet it turned out to be true, and it had turned out well. He was one lucky guy and grateful as hell.

A pair of woolly mittens clamped over his eyes and broke the spell. "Nick, Dada," Megan demanded, pointing in the direction of Santa Claus.

"Yeah, okay, sweetheart. Daddy's going to take you to see him. Hang on to your diapers a sec." He focused on his wife again. "Your daughter's in a big hurry for a personal introduction to Santa. How come you make the promises and I always get stuck with fulfilling 'em?''

She gave him a minxish grin. ''Because I have to open the shop and serve up wassail and good cheer to our neighbors and customers.'' Petite of stature, she had to stretch on tiptoe to kiss his cheek. ''Why is it that whenever she's being stubborn, she's my daughter, but whenever she's all sweetness, she's yours?''

His green eyes danced with devilment. ''Mmm, I really don't know why that is, but you do make an interesting point, Mrs. Malone.'' Bending his head to hers, he slickly stole another kiss. ''I'd love to stay and discuss it, but gotta go make ho-ho-ho!''

''Coward,'' she teased, laughing.

He stooped and tipped Megan toward her so that Desirée could plant yet another kiss on her cherry red nose.

''Bye-bye. Bye-bye.'' Once Megan mastered a word, she repeated it like a magpie. If she was particularly fond of the sound of it, she'd occasionally double the word for good measure.

Desirée waved as the two crossed the street and slowly made their way through the throng. She hated missing Megan's first encounter with St. Nick, but she was obliged to participate in a custom observed during the final Sunday hours of the Walk Festival. The grand finale was a parade led by Santa and the carolers up State Street into the shopping district, where the proprietors offered holiday refreshments to the crowd.

Since her own establishment was on the route, she needed to be on hand to host the open house.

She cast a longing look at her daughter's pink snowsuited figure bobbing above the sea of heads, then turned and made her way back to Old Town. Thank goodness she'd prepared ahead and had had the presence of mind to set up her refreshment table in advance. She'd already stayed too long with Jacob and Megan. She knew it was silly, but whenever it was necessary for her to be separated from her husband and child, even if only for a short while, she became unsettled.

Jacob had to commute to Boston a few times a week to practice law, and she'd learned to cope with that because there really wasn't any choice. But she missed him terribly when he was away from her and worried herself sick if he was the least bit late coming home. There was such a strong bond between them that even when they were apart, she could sense when all was not well with him. And Jacob seemed to know exactly when she needed him to get in touch by phone. He made light of the incidents, saying it was merely coincidental, but she knew better. She knew it was because they loved each other so deeply, so intensely, it was as if they were one.

Desirée reached the two-story frame structure that served as both her place of business and their home in a matter of minutes. She quickly switched on the lights, discarded her coat and mink earmuffs, then dashed about lighting the bayberry and pine-scented candles she'd earlier arranged throughout the shop. The Christmasy smells soon filled the downstairs quarters.

She'd spent hours setting out the decorations, and now she stood back to survey the final effect. Everything looked as she had planned. Scores of red and green tapers glowed welcomingly, and ropes of mistletoe and wreaths of holly lent a holiday atmosphere to the room. The end result was greeting-card perfect—traditional, cheery and cozy. Well, at least as traditional, cheery and cozy as was possible, considering the nature of her business.

The Magic Herb Hut was no ordinary business. Nor was its proprietress an ordinary woman. The store had been in her family for three generations. The wares she stocked and sold were of an unusual variety—potions, elixirs, amulets, magic stones, rare herbs, books of old lore and practices. Her clientele was a mixture of serious believers and curious tourists. Some folks came in just to get a glimpse of her.

Every now and then someone new would hear the old rumors still circulating about the Warren women. They would visit the shop only as an excuse to check out the current owner. They were so obvious and so in hopes of getting a close-up look at a real live, honest-to-goodness witch. Desirée never understood what it was they expected to find. An old hag with a wart on her nose, she supposed.

Long ago Desirée had reconciled herself to the fact that people chose what they wanted to believe, saw only what they wished to see and conveniently discounted anything to the contrary. She knew that people's opinions of her were not always shaped by her actions; they were more a matter of the other person's reaction to her ties to the Craft. She'd never denied or hidden the fact that her mother and grandmother followed the ways of Wicca. But neither had she ever professed to be of like mind. Nevertheless, it had been assumed that her ways were the same as theirs.

Before Jacob entered her life, her own neighbors had been divided in their opinions of her. A goodly number had signed a petition to try to evict her from her home and livelihood on the grounds that she violated town deed restrictions. If it hadn't been for Jacob's championing her cause at a special town meeting, she might have lost everything dear to her. He had argued so brilliantly in her behalf. He'd exposed the superstitious bigotry festering in Marblehead and had shamed the town's citizens into amending their attitude toward her. What a day that had been....

A soft smile curved her lips as she thought back on the ordeal. Even though it had been a difficult time for her, fate had intervened. For not only did she eventually win the battle to coexist with her neighbors; she had also won Jacob's heart. He was all she had ever wanted, more than she'd ever dared dream of having. That year she had risked her soul and dabbled in the mysteries in order to summon up her dream lover. When he'd materialized out of a snowstorm, no one could have been more flabbergasted than she. Even now, she was unsure how a novice such as herself had conjured up the power to turn her soul's desire into a reality. Beginner's luck, perhaps.

The faint sounds of the approaching carolers seeped into the shop and her consciousness. The unfamiliar noise also rousted her Burman cat from her snooze on the stairs. Mew-Sinh took stock of all the burning candles and sniffed the scented air in a bothered fashion. The ageless feline disliked anything that disrupted her routine, and she made her objections known with a whining meow.

"I'm afraid you'll just have to tolerate our visitors, Mew-Sinh." Desirée picked up the big cat and spoke soothingly as she petted her. "I'm wary, too, but we must get over our shyness. Jacob's right. People misinterpret. They think us aloof or just plain strange."

Mew-Sinh sprang from her arms, turned her fluffy tail on the notion of socializing and bounded up the stairs. Desirée stared after her, a bemused expression on her face. "Okay, so maybe it's an exercise in futility. You're always going to be aloof, and I'm always going to be considered somewhat strange," she said aloud. "But we have to try—for Jacob and Megan's sake."

A tinkling of a bell above the shop's door heralded her first visitor. Apprehension turned to relief when she saw Archie Hooper in the doorway.

"Yule tidings," he called out to her. Only Archie would be so thoughtful as to choose his words carefully, she thought. The old shopkeeper from across the street had remembered that in the Wicca tradition, the sabbat of the winter solstice was celebrated from the twentieth to the twenty-third of December. The sabbat was called Yule. Today was the twentieth of December. She doubted anyone else in town realized or respected the significance of the date.

"Merry Christmas, Mr. Hooper," she returned warmly, unable to address him by any name other than the one she'd called him since childhood.

He hurried inside and shut the door firmly, keeping out the cold wind. Peering over his fogged glasses, he gave her decorating efforts a sweeping glance. "You've gone all out," he noted. "You're going to make me look like Ebenezer Scrooge."

"Who?" she asked, unfamiliar with the Dickens classic.

"He was a character in a book who lacked the Christmas spirit," he explained.

"Oh," she answered, hoping she didn't appear stupid. Her mother had been more interested in imparting the mysteries of their ways than recounting the classics. "I'm sure your treats will put mine to shame."

He looked pleased at the compliment, which was no more than the truth. Year round, people traveled miles just to sample his muffins. Making and baking and serving muffins was not something he'd chosen to do, but a legacy he'd inherited. Like Desirée, he'd been more or less saddled with a family tradition. After sixty-odd years at having been stuck in dough up to his elbows, he no longer minded or thought much about what he might've done instead.

"Are you all set? Anything I can help you with?" he volunteered.

Mr. Hooper was always so nice to her. Desirée appreciated his kindness, but in the back of her mind she sometimes wondered why it was so. His attitude bordered on protective.

"I think I have everything under control." She tried to muster a confident smile.

Sensing her uneasiness, the old gentleman slanted her a gauging look. "A little nervous about socializing with your neighbors, are ya?"

"A tad," she admitted, stepping to the refreshment table and randomly rearranging the paper napkins and punch cups. "I suppose I'm being silly, but I do wonder sometimes whether people accept me because they've really come to view me differently or..." She stopped short of expressing her innermost feelings and turned about with a dismissive shrug. "It's not important. I don't know what's the matter with me tonight. I'm just in a funny mood. It's a nostalgic season. It makes one think on things past."

Archie intuitively understood her line of thought. "Times change. To an extent, people do, too, Desirée. Sure, there's probably some who'll never alter their opinion of you or invite you to Sunday dinner. And some who'll forever be lukewarm where you're concerned. But generally speaking, I think the town's made real progress in its attitude toward you. And it isn't true, what you're thinking. Granted, folks are fond of Jake. They respect him a lot. But he isn't the sole reason they're behaving more civilly toward his wife. Slowly but surely they're getting past their superstitious preconceptions. They're getting to know you as a person and discovering what I've always known—that you're a gentle and giving lady who deserves their respect as much as Jacob.''

He offered her a fatherly smile along with the friendly advice. ''It isn't going to happen overnight, Desirée. A century of suspicion won't disappear in a matter of a few short years. Be patient. You had a decent turnout for the Walk last year. More will come this year. You'll see,'' he predicted with an encouraging wink.

She walked to where he stood and hugged his neck. ''Sometimes I wonder why you bother to take such an interest in me, but I'm glad you do.''

He seemed to hesitate when answering her. Patting her cheek, he simply said, ''I've long been in awe of the Warren women. They're special. You mustn't ever forget that.''

''I much prefer being classed as special to being viewed as strange.''

''Some folks don't know the difference, that's all.'' His hand dropped from her cheek, and he drew back a step or two. ''Well, I guess I better head back across the street. Folks will be arriving any minute.'' He started for the door. ''It's going to be a long night,'' he said offhandedly.

"According to the almanac and the Yule myth, it's tomorrow night that's the longest of the year," she remarked.

He looked back at her and grinned. "Yeah, well, according to these aching feet of mine, it's tonight. I dread the long hours ahead. See you tomorrow." He turned up his coat collar and stepped out onto the shoveled walk.

"Yes, see you tomorrow," was her automatic reply. Her goodbye was lost on a whoosh of wind. Archie never heard her bid him adieu.

MR. HOOPER HAD BEEN right. All in all, the turnout at her shop had been larger than the year before. She felt heartened at the surprising number of folks who'd partaken of her hospitality, and by the time she was preparing to retire for the night, she was much too excited to sleep.

As Jacob lay in the poster bed, listening to her happy banter and watching her undress, his own weariness disappeared, and he began to entertain thoughts of making love to his wife.

"I really think people are starting to accept me, Jake," she was saying. "Three of the five board of selectmen and their wives stopped in tonight. Amazing, huh?"

Jacob was much more intent on the slinky slide of the crepe party pants down her shapely legs. "Mmm, amazing," he replied, anxious for her to slip under the covers so he could wrap himself around her delectable body.

To his dismay, Desirée dillydallied some more, vanishing into the bathroom and continuing to converse with him while she washed her face and applied moisture cream to her already baby-soft skin. "Doc Greely actually bought a pouch of my healing herbs. He said his bursitis had been dealing him misery lately and he wanted to give it a try. Can you imagine?"

What Jake imagined had absolutely nothing to do with herbs or bursitis. He had something of a rising medical emergency of his own to contend with under the covers. "It's getting awfully cold lying in bed all alone. C'mere and let's make body heat." He scooted over and patted her spot in the bed.

Desirée snapped off the bathroom light and came to join him beneath the cocooning quilt. She cuddled up and nuzzled his neck.

Jacob's arms encircled her, drawing her even closer against his aroused body. "You know that turns me on," he murmured.

"There isn't much that doesn't turn you on," she countered, slipping a silky leg between his brawny ones and gently nipping his earlobe.

He made a half roll, flattening her back to the mattress and positioning himself against her soft breasts. "I can't help myself. I just look at you and I want you." He seared her throat and neck with feather kisses, inching his way to the rosebud nipples straining upward toward the warmth of his lips.

A gasp escaped her as his tongue swirled and his hand dipped toward her stomach, then lower still to the velvet triangle between her thighs.

Jacob was at a loss to explain his never-ending desire for his wife. There were times when he was on fire for her—times when he made love to her in what could only be described as a fever. On those occasions it felt as if his body would explode into a thousand pieces if he did not fuse with her quickly, intensely, primally. His heart would thunder, his limbs shudder, his very breath leave him the instant he touched her, his mind no longer capable of rational thought. It wasn't unchecked lust, exactly. It was something more profound—a white-hot feeling unleashed from the very center of himself. He never knew when it might happen or precisely what to label it. Tonight was one of those times, and he knew from past experience that afterward he would not be able to express to Desirée what had caused him to take her in such a fury of suffocating emotion.

"I love you, Desirée." His voice was a ragged whisper as he glided his palms along the satiny length of her inner arms, then laced his fingers within hers. Pinning her hands overhead with the gentlest of pressure, he eased his erection inside her.

She could feel every muscle in his body tighten, feel the wild pounding of his heart, feel his expanding urgency fill her. In the stillness, in the dark, she became sensitized to the heady scent of Jacob's passion. It hung in the air, clung to his skin, and when she claimed his lips, she could taste it on his tongue.

He was like a heat-seeking missile locked on target. He adjusted to the slightest deviation in the course of their love act. Wherever she moved in the space of the bed, however she veered, he followed. He accelerated and soared. She writhed with pleasure. Her hips rose to meet him—a little higher and more possessively each time. His hips dived and drew up—a little farther and faster with every lunge.

They traveled forward through a galaxy of sensuality, suspended in a weightless, wondrous dimension, yet all the while moving closer and closer to the moment of impact.

"Come with me, Jake," she urged, her fingers gripping his so tightly that her nails left half-moon impressions in his flesh.

Their bodies heaved and collided in a climactic explosion. Jacob saw star-bursts as he fell limply on top of his wife. Both he and Desirée were covered in a film of perspiration, and neither had the strength to move or speak.

"My God," he finally rasped, rolling onto his back and staring into the inky darkness. His chest rose and fell in short, spent pants.

Desirée brought herself back to full consciousness. Easing onto her side, she traced the deep cleft in his chin. "Was it good for you?" she kidded.

"Good?" he croaked. "It blew my mind, not to mention various other vital parts." He reached up, cupping the back of her head and drawing her mouth down on his in a dreamy kiss. "If it got any better, Mrs. Malone, I'd be a bona fide sex addict."

She laughed at his silliness.

Jacob folded her within his embrace and rearranged the quilt over their entwined forms. They said nothing for a moment, enjoying the warmth generated between them.

"Jake?" she finally ventured.

"Mmm," he said sleepily.

"Do you ever get spooked about how happy we are? You know, the old saying about things being so good that it's scary?"

The question caught him off guard. He thought about it for a second, then voiced his initial reaction. "No. A time or two I've felt guilty about having so much going for us while others don't seem to be able to get it together. But scared?" He scooted deeper into the comfy mattress and nestled her head on his shoulder. "Nope. Never."

"I'm afraid sometimes," she admitted. "I love you and Megan so much that it borders on being selfish. Even though I know it's not right, that it's unhealthy for all of us, I hate it when I have to share you with the rest of the world. I keep remembering an incident when I was small and my grandmother scolded me about my possessiveness. Since I'd spent so much of my childhood alone, I was unaccustomed to sharing my toys. On one, rare occasion when some distant relatives paid an unexpected visit, I hid my favorite playthings in an old steamer trunk. Grandmother caught me in the act. She told me that being unselfish was the basis of love and that to be otherwise was to invite sorrow instead of happiness into one's life. The tone she took with me scared me so much I not only shared my favorite toys, but gave them to the little monsters. They really were terrors, Jake. To this day, I regret doing it. I never outgrew being possessive of the things I cherish or my fear of what awful fate might befall me because of it.''

"Grandmothers can be imposing figures, Desirée. I'm sure she only meant to coax you into sharing and had no idea of the irrational fear she was instilling in you." He played with her long copper hair as he reassured her, gathering up luxurious strands and then letting them sift through his fingers. "What do you think? That some powerful being is keeping a tally of how much happiness the selfish wench in Marblehead has accrued? You can't seriously believe there's a limit assigned to each of us, that if we exceed our allotted amount, it'll all be snatched away in a heartbeat. Come on, sweetheart. That ranks right up there with Santa Claus—one man flying around the entire world in a sleigh pulled by flying reindeer to deliver presents to only the good children. You can bet your sweet bottom those little monsters who came for a visit got a delivery that Christmas, the same as you. Nobody was keeping a list of who was naughty or nice."

"It's not the same thing, Jake. Santa's make-believe. What I'm talking about is real. I believe in the existence of an all-knowing, all-powerful force, and I'm convinced we are accountable for our actions,'' she persisted.

Both the conversation and Jacob's eyelids were getting much too heavy for him to deal with at the moment. "Maybe so, sweetheart." He yawned and gave her shoulder a dismissive pat. "Don't worry so much. I'm sure God, or whatever you call the force, understands our human quirks better than we do. Personally I think you're almost perfect," he mumbled groggily. "Definitely a nice girl." His head slumped against hers, and the next thing she knew he was snoring.

DESIRÉE EXPERIENCED a restless sleep. She awakened off and on throughout the night. At four o'clock, she finally gave up, deciding perhaps the soothing properties of some sassafras tea might arrest her insomnia. Climbing out of the bed, she sauntered into the kitchen to fix herself a cup.

Sensing his mistress's disquiet, Mew-Sinh came into the kitchen and stationed herself on the windowsill to keep watch.

Desirée simmered the roots for a bit, then poured the pale liquid into a cup and went to stand at the window. She sipped the steaming brew while gazing up at the night's sky. It was then she first noticed that the moon was in its last quarter—the waning phase. In the Wicca tradition, the time of the dark moon represented the ending before the beginning: the death before new life, the time of the ebb tide when the secrets of the shoreline were uncovered by retreating waves. When the moon was hidden, the faintest stars were revealed, and those with eyes to see could read the fates and know the mysteries.

She blinked and glanced down at Mew-Sinh. "It's not a good sign—a dark moon on Yule's sabbat." The cat pawed at the sleeve of her robe. "Darkness triumphs, time itself stops on the long night of solstice. One thing becomes another as the Wheel of the Year slowly turns," she quoted from the myth.

The gold-tipped fur around the cat's neck stood on end. Her ears flattened against her head and a guttural sound gurgled deep in her throat.

Desirée stroked the cat to calm its jitters. "Shh, Mew-Sinh. It's only a symbolic journey we envision." She looked back up, beyond the bare treetops to the sliver of a moon looming above. "Even so, it's eerie to imagine a soul's crossing over to the Summerland during the time of the dark moon. I never liked it as a child when mother spoke of Yule's meaning—the cycle of losing to gain, of passing through the longest night to be born again with the rising sun."

A chill crept over her. She shuddered and drank down a gulp of the hot tea.

"What are you doing up at this hour?"

Jacob's voice startled her. Her eyes were round when she spun to face him.

"You okay?" he asked, concerned by her pallor and the strange look on her face.

She didn't dare confide her worry over the dark moon or the approach of the long Yule night at twilight. Dawn had yet to break, and she was fretting over the sun's setting. Jacob believed she dwelled too much upon the myths and mysteries as it was. The old ways were not his way. He put no credence in such things as starlight vision, the channeling of energy, magic symbols or binding spells. Though he tried—truly tried—to be open-minded about Wicca's influence over her, he discouraged her from delving into it too deeply. It was fine for Megan to know of her mother's special background, but he did not want his daughter to be strongly impressed by Wicca practices.

Desirée knew and respected his feelings on the matter. "I had trouble sleeping and decided to fix myself some sassafras tea. I think it was all the excitement over how well things went at the open house." Half a truth, half a lie was preferable to upsetting him, she thought.

He nodded dully. "Coming back to bed?"

"In a minute."

He left her to finish her tea.

When Desirée finally did return to bed, she fell into an exhausted sleep. She did not hear the alarm or Jake as he puttered about getting ready to go into Boston. It was the first time in their marriage that he'd left without breakfast or a parting kiss from his wife.

CHAPTER TWO

"BYE-BYE. BYE-BYE." Excited at the prospect of going visiting, Megan would not hold still long enough for Desirée to tie the hood of her snowsuit beneath her chin.

Desirée scooted on bended knees, turning left and right with each swivel of her daughter's head. "Please, honey, hold still. Mama has to fasten your hood before you can go see Leigh Ann."

Megan's blue eyes gleamed brightly, and she stopped twisting her head for a split second. "Go Lee-lee's. Go bye-bye," she stated happily.

Desirée breathed a sigh of relief as she successfully made a bow out of the two ends of the string tie. "There! We're all ready—a little late, but at least we're on our way."

She stood up and glanced wistfully toward the wall phone. She had wanted to call Jacob at the office before they set out for Marilyn Estes's house. Though he knew of her plans, she still had an urge to pick up the phone and dial his number. She knew it was silly, but she just wanted to hear his voice—mostly because she longed to hear the parting endearment he always used: "Love you, babe."

But Megan was insistent on getting under way. She'd tottered to the door and was attempting to twist the knob. "Go Lee-lee's," she chanted in a singsong fashion.

"Okay, Mama's coming." Desirée gave up on the idea of phoning Jake. It was more important that Megan have ample time to play with her friend. She so looked forward to the trips to the Esteses. Marilyn's daughter, Leigh Ann, was only a few months older, and the two had a grand time engaging in make-believe and hijinks whenever they were together.

Desirée collected her tote bag, grabbed the stroller and placed her daughter in it. She lifted the padded chariot and bundled passenger over the doorstep to the sidewalk, checked to be sure she'd remembered to put her keys in the pocket of the bag and then set out on the respectable hike to Marilyn's.

It was a clear, cold day, and the stroller ride was not exactly smooth going. Several times en route Desirée was faced with the problem of unshoveled walkways and had to carry both stroller and toddler over the barriers of snow. As she huffed and puffed, her breath formed white clouds in the air. Megan thought the frosty whiffs quite amusing and tried to catch them in a mittened hand. Halfway to their destination, Desirée was beginning to wish she hadn't turned down Marilyn's offer to pick them up. The opportunity to get a little fresh air and exercise had seemed like a terrific idea at the time, but in actuality it was a bit more than she'd anticipated.

They made pretty good time until they reached Redd's Pond. Only a short distance beyond the frozen pool lay Gingerbread Hill, a picturesque residential area where her friend lived. Along the fringes of the pond, Desirée was pleasantly surprised when she bumped into an elderly customer of hers. Mrs. Doblinkov was a sweet old soul, though rather bumbling and fragile. It seemed odd to find her out and about on a such a chilly day.

"Hello, Mrs. Doblinkov," she greeted her.

The old woman lifted her babushka-bound head and squinted in order to make out the person who stood before her through a cataract haze. A broad grin lit up her prune face when she recognized Desirée. "My, my," she greeted. "Who have we here? This can't be Megan. She's grown so." Her gloved hand patted the child's back.

"It's been a while since you've been into the shop," Desirée reminded her. "How have you been?"

It was the wrong thing to ask. Mrs. Doblinkov immediately launched into a nonstop account of her recent bout with the flu and then proceeded to list the latest complaints she harbored against her landlord. Since Desirée had once saved her from imminent eviction by selling her a magic money root—and secretly stuffing a roll of bills in her pocket for added insurance—the old soul naturally assumed she'd be sympathetic. She was, but she was also taxed from her hike and trying to contain her energetic daughter within the stroller.

Mrs. Doblinkov seemed not to notice Megan's impatient squirming. Hungry for company, she droned on and on. Not wishing to appear rude, Desirée decided to allow Megan a little freedom. She lifted her daughter from the stroller and set her down on the snow-crusted ground, but it was difficult to appear interested in Mrs. Doblinkov's ramblings while trying to keep a close eye on the active toddler.

At first Megan stayed close, amusing herself by making tiny, heel-to-toe boot prints in the white powder as she circled around and around her mother's legs. Desirée watched in amusement until Mrs. Doblinkov reclaimed her attention.

"As much as I hate to consider it, I'm seriously thinking about relocating to a retirement village in Florida," the old woman informed her. "It's a hard thing to uproot yourself after spending an entire lifetime in one spot."

"I'm sure it is," Desirée commiserated. Megan crouched down and scooped up a handful of snow, bringing it to her mouth to taste. Desirée bent and brushed the white clump from her mitten, merely shaking her head. Megan got the message. Eating snow was a no-no, so she would have to find another diversion.

"I have so many good memories," Mrs. Doblinkov went on, not missing a beat and blinking back the tears. "But then, it's not the same anymore. My friends have dwindled away. One by one they've gone to their final rest or moved to a warmer climate. There's only

Annie left, and everyone knows she's half-daft. I can't impose on my son and his family. They've had their own setbacks. He's a contractor, you know. What with the economy being so bad, his business has fallen off drastically. And with two children in college, he's struggling from day to day just to make ends meet. Aren't we all," she said with a shake of her head. "And when you're on a fixed income like myself, well, it's a constant worry. You'd think at my age a person might get a respite from all the headaches, but it isn't so, dearie. Just last week I got a notice that my Harry's pension fund has run out. Who can afford to live on Social Security alone? I tell you, it's a shame how the elderly are treated today. Take that landlord of mine, for instance..."

Desirée suddenly realized she'd lost track of Megan. Her head jerked about, and her heart constricted in her chest as she spied Megan's daring little figure venturing out onto the frozen surface of Redd's Pond.

"No! Megan! Come back here!" she blurted out, tearing after her daughter.

Mrs. Doblinkov was startled speechless. She stood paralyzed, looking on as Desirée pursued her daughter onto the ice—sliding, almost spilling and repeatedly calling her name. "Don't go any farther, Megan. Easy does it. Come to Mommy," she coaxed.

The giggling two-year-old thought it great sport to have her mother chase her. Her chubby legs worked faster, propelling her closer to the softer center of the pond. In her haste, the child fell. She landed spread-

eagled on her tummy and skidded across the frozen
surface like a hockey puck to where the water was
deepest and the ice not as solid.

"Oh, God!" Desirée screamed, scrambling to reach
her daughter. The center ice had held under Megan's
slight weight, but the added pressure of Desirée's was
too much. She heard the warning crackle just as her
fingers locked onto the legging of Megan's snowsuit.
What followed occurred in a matter of a few seconds,
but it all seemed to happen in excruciatingly slow motion to Desirée.

She knew there was no time to spare Megan the
shock or the rough shove. She yanked with all her
might, sending her daughter hurling toward the outer,
solidly frozen edges of the pond where, God willing,
the feeble Mrs. Doblinkov could rescue her. She heard
another, sharper crack, and she felt the ice buckle and
splinter beneath her feet. As it gave way, she plunged
straight down into the freezing water. Instinct made her
thrust out her arms to try to break her fall. She was
able to brace herself sufficiently to keep her head and
shoulders above water level for an instant—just long
enough to see Mrs. Doblinkov fish Megan from off the
ice and pull her safely up onto the dirty snowbank
ringing the pond.

Her eyes welled with tears of relief. In that brief
moment she realized her lower extremities were already tingling with numbness and weighted like lead
from the icy water. She saw the gap in the frozen surface widening, and it became clear to her that she was

going to slip under in spite of her efforts to hang on. There wasn't anything to grasp but slick nothingness.

Dear God! This couldn't be happening! She probably wouldn't be able to find the opening again once she went through the hole. She'd be trapped under the ice. Already she was struggling for breath due to her fear and exertion. *Not like this!* she thought. Her eyes fixed on Megan in Mrs. Doblinkov's embrace. The old woman was hollering something, then in a blink she was hobbling off.

Megan, she silently mouthed. She knew she was going to drown before Mrs. Doblinkov could bring help. Any rescue attempt would come too late. Nothing short of a miracle could save her. *She was going to die.*

Panic rose inside her, filling her throat with a rank bile. She should pray. Her mind wouldn't function, and her lips shivered uncontrollably. She tried to heave herself upward. It was useless. Her body weighed a thousand pounds. Her arms started sliding, inching in across the smoothness.

She began to sink into the icy depths of Redd's Pond. At the moment her head disappeared through the hole, she visualized Jacob's face. The last thing she remembered before losing consciousness was the rainbow prism of sunlight refracting through the frozen layer above. Strange, her oxygen-starved brain noted, how beautiful yet how cruel death was.

Beneath the crystal prison of ice, it was cold, cold, cold.

"DID YOU HEAR? Isn't it awful!" Patsy James burst into the Mug and Muffin Shoppe like a human tornado.

Archie was convinced her shrill voice caused the silver fillings in his mouth to vibrate. He scowled at her. Patsy was always making a commotion of some sort or another. "What in the devil are you babbling about?"

"Desirée Malone fell through the ice over at Redd's Pond and drowned," she gasped, collapsing into a chair and sucking in deep mouthfuls of air. "I don't know how you couldn't have noticed all the commotion," she wheezed. "They called in one of those whirlybirds to life-flight her to Boston." She jiggled out her coat and motioned for him to bring her a cup of coffee.

Archie couldn't believe what he was hearing. His old ticker felt as if somebody's fist was squeezing it. "Slow down, Patsy, and tell me what you know."

"I just did," she said huffily. "Will you bring the pot over? I need to settle my nerves."

True to form, Patsy was more concerned with her own condition than with filling him in on Desirée's. Calm her nerves indeed, he thought, grabbing the glass pot and a mug and hurrying over to the table. A caffeine fix was the last thing she needed. What the hell! He'd give her a whole damn potful on the house if she'd get on with the story about what had happened at Redd's Pond.

"You say they life-flighted her to Boston?"

"Mmm." Patsy practically dove headfirst into the mug. Her unladylike slurps only heightened his irritation.

"Will you get your mouth out of that mug and give me the lowdown?" he snapped. "First you say she drowned, then you say she was flown to Boston for treatment. Is she alive or not?"

Patsy donned an indignant expression. "Well, how should I know? I didn't climb into the helicopter with her. Besides, I only heard about it secondhand. Marilyn Estes told me. That's where Desirée was headed when it happened."

Archie decided he was getting nowhere by grilling Patsy. He tried a different approach. Settling in a chair opposite her, he allowed her to divulge the details at her own melodramatic pace.

The tactic worked. Patsy began to fill in the missing pieces of the story. "She had Megan with her. They were supposed to be doing lunch at Marilyn's place. She stopped to talk with old Mrs. Doblinkov at the pond. While they were chatting, Megan got away from Desirée. The child went out on the ice, and Desirée chased after her. Somehow she managed to shove Megan to safety just in the nick of time. But then the ice gave way before she could scramble off herself, and she plunged into the water like a rock."

Patsy paused to take another swig of coffee. "Poor Mrs. Doblinkov. There she was with a crying toddler in her arms, a drowning mother in the pond and not a soul around. You know how slow she is. There's no telling how much time passed before she made her way to the street to flag down help. Packing Megan probably slowed her down even more. It was lucky two men in a power truck happened along when they did.''

"Lucky how?" Archie prompted. He hung his hopes on her mention of the timely appearance of would-be rescuers. Perhaps things were not as grim as Patsy had originally implied.

"Well . . ." She stretched her account of the tragedy and his nerves to the hilt. "They had one of those newfangled car phones and were able to call for emergency help. They also had the equipment—a rope and such—so that one of them could be lowered through the hole in the ice to fish Desirée's body out. I pity the poor fella who went in after her. Don't you know that water had to be freezing cold?''

Patsy had an abundance of sympathy for everyone but the victim herself. Though Archie knew there was no love lost between the woman and Desirée, he found it pathetic that she could not set aside her petty bitterness and show a wee bit of compassion under the circumstances.

"The way I heard it, she had no pulse when they pulled her out. The two men tried to revive her with CPR until the emergency team arrived and took over. Mrs. Doblinkov overhead one of the medical team radio ahead that the victim was unresponsive. 'Pupils dilated and fixed and patient still not breathing on her own,' '' she quoted verbatim. "That's what the medic said as they were loading Desirée up.''

The spark of hope within Archie refused to die. He prayed it was the same with Desirée. Perhaps there remained a spark of life—a chance that she might yet come around.

"What of Megan? Who's taking care of her?" he asked in a worried tone.

"Marilyn Estes has her for the present." For the first time since storming into his shop with the news, Patsy's demeanor became more sensitive. "Poor Jake," she said sadly. "What a terrible shock. And to be left with a small daughter to raise on his own. I know how hard that is. I've done it." Her eyes grew tearful. "Poor, poor, Jake," she reiterated.

Archie's own eyes stung. He cleared his throat and removed his bifocals on the pretext of polishing them on the hem of his apron. Poor Desirée, he thought. How afraid she must have been.

THE FACT THAT ONE has not received a parting kiss from one's wife is one of those small details a person tucks away into a far corner of his mind and doesn't think about again unless something happens to bring it to the forefront.

For Jacob the jolt came in the form of a phone call. The secretary he shared with three other lawyers at the ACLU offices interrupted him in the middle of taking a deposition.

"Sorry, Mr. Malone, but there's a call holding on line two and—"

Jacob cut her off impatiently. "Please tell whoever it is that I'll get back to them."

"I, uh, think you'll want to take the call," she stammered. "There's been an accident. It's about your wife..."

Jacob punched the blinking red button before she'd finished speaking. "This is Jacob Malone. What's happened? Who am I speaking with?"

"Betty Lazano, sir. I'm head of patient services at Boston General. I'm contacting you about your wife. She was life-flighted to our trauma unit about fifteen minutes ago. We think it's best if you come down here as soon as possible."

The voice on the other end of the line was eerily calm, noticeably grave. Jacob felt a numbness start to creep up his body from his toes to his throat. He wasn't sure he could respond. He swallowed hard. "What happened and how is she?" It was as if somebody else had asked the question.

"A near drowning, sir. Her condition is extremely critical" was the reply.

Desirée...a near drowning...extremely critical. He heard the words as though they were coming through an echo chamber. They made no sense. "I'm on my way." He dropped the receiver onto the cradle, rose dazedly from his chair behind the desk and started to walk from the room.

"Jake?" an associate called after him. "What's going on? We're in the middle of taking a deposition here! Where are you going?"

"The call was about my wife. I have to get to Boston General. They say it's serious." It was the best he could do. He didn't fully understand himself.

"Good God! Let us know, Jake." Noting that Jake was leaving without his coat, the shocked associate collected it from off the rack and thrust it at him.

"Thanks," Jake mumbled, not bothering to put it on. The outside cold was negligible compared to the icy fear coiling in the pit of his stomach.

WHEN JAKE FIRST ARRIVED at Boston General, he was kept waiting in a hall outside the trauma unit while the medical team worked feverishly to save his wife. Twenty, thirty, forty minutes went by before the double doors marked Staff Only swung open and a lanky man dressed in hospital greens stepped forth.

"Mr. Malone?" he asked, wiping an arm across his forehead, then extending a hand.

"Yes," Jake said brusquely, barely having the presence of mind to return the handshake. "How is she? Can I see her?"

"In a bit. We're moving her to the Intensive Care Unit. You can see your wife just as soon as we get her comfortably situated. Why don't we sit down over there. I'll be glad to discuss your wife's case at length and answer any questions you may have." He gestured toward a lounge area at the end of the hall that Jacob hadn't noticed before.

Jake moved automatically. Something about the doctor's cautious manner made him steel himself against the discussion ahead. He sank to the couch, resting his elbows on his knees.

"I'm Dr. Granger, head of the trauma unit here at Boston General." The surgeon arranged himself in an adjacent chair, looking over at Jake and sizing up his mental state with a long, unflinching stare.

"I can handle whatever you have to tell me," Jake told him, meeting his gaze levelly.

Dr. Granger broke eye contact. "It's not good, Mr. Malone. When our trauma team arrived on the scene, your wife was clinically dead. She had ceased breathing, and all of her vital signs were negative. It's estimated that she was underwater for at least five, and possibly as long as ten, minutes."

Jacob's own breath left him when Dr. Granger used the phrase "clinically dead." A glazed look came over his eyes.

"The two men who rescued her from the pond initiated CPR on the spot, and the effort was continued throughout the trip in and then here in the trauma unit. All of us literally tried to breathe life back into her. I won't go into the various aspects of the medical procedures we instituted. They're pretty technical. The bottom line is that the joint effort paid off. Your wife is now breathing on her own."

It was the first positive thing the doctor had said. Jacob's facial muscles relaxed a little. "Thank God," he whispered hoarsely, dropping his head into his hands.

It was at times like these that Eric Granger wished he had specialized in medical research instead of the field he'd chosen. He hated having to face the families of accident victims, especially when the margin of life for their loved ones was so slim. Most of his patients were unconscious or only semiconscious when he first treated them. Not so with the families. Their pain was acute and sometimes unbearable. He was supposed to alleviate suffering, not cause it. Yet sometimes that's exactly what his duties entailed. Like now, when he had to inform Mr. Malone of his wife's bleak prognosis.

"I don't want to mislead you, Mr. Malone, so I am going to speak frankly," he went on. "Though our attempt to resuscitate your wife was successful, she is in what we refer to as a 'profound comatose state.' In essence, what that means is, she's in a very deep coma—only a fraction removed from death itself. I am sorry to be so blunt, but I've found it's far kinder than raising false hopes."

Jacob sat back and fixed his stunned gaze on the doctor. "Isn't there a chance she could come out of it?" The possibility that his wife might never awaken again, might never be a part of his and Megan's life again—might be lost to him forever—was more than he could bear.

"So long as there's life, there's always a chance. However, the longer she remains in a coma, the smaller that chance becomes. I wish I could be more optimistic. To tell you the truth, I think it's a miracle of sorts that your wife responded to the resuscitation attempt.

I've attended many drowning victims. Not once have I been able to reverse the fatal effects on those who were deprived of oxygen for as long as your wife.''

''Desirée is an extraordinary woman, Doctor.'' Despite his brave words, Jacob felt as if a load of bricks had been dropped on him. It took a supreme effort just to force his body up from the couch and square his shoulders. ''You might say she has a supernatural strength.''

Dr. Granger thought he was speaking in the broader, everyday context of the word. Standing also, he placed a hand on Jacob's shoulder. ''We'll continue to monitor her closely. I've ordered more extensive tests. If there is the slightest change in her condition, we'll be aware of it immediately. When I get the results of the tests, we'll confer again. If you should want to speak with me for any reason, day or night, don't hesitate to leave word with the staff. They know how to get in touch with me.'' He dropped his eyes and removed his hand from Jake's shoulder. ''I'm sure you're anxious to be with your wife. The elevators are down the hall and to your left. Intensive Care is on the twelfth floor. The nurses will assist you there.''

''Thanks for all you did, Doctor.''

''I wish it could have been more.'' Eric Granger's beeper went off. He smiled apologetically, then returned to the sterile environment beyond the double doors.

JACOB KEPT a vigil at Desirée's bedside throughout the night. Usually the nurses strictly enforced the visiting regulations—one visitor for only ten minutes every other hour—but in his case, they made an exception. The entire staff was touched by the sadness of the situation. It was obvious to them Mr. Malone adored his wife. No one had the heart to tell him he must leave her side. They knew that eventually his shock would subside, but at the moment he obviously needed to touch her, talk to her, simply be near her. What a shame, what a pity, what a waste, the staff whispered among themselves.

Sometime around the change of shift at 11 p.m., he thought he saw Desirée's eyelids flutter, as if she were fighting hard to open them.

His fingers tensed around hers. "Desirée, I'm here. Come back, baby. Open your eyes," he implored her.

The next second there was nothing. Not a flicker of a response.

He turned on the call light for a nurse, who materialized immediately. "Yes, Mr. Malone. Is anything wrong?"

"Her eyelids moved. I know I saw it. It was only for a second, but..."

"It happens, Mr. Malone," she said gently. "A reflex action," she explained.

"She heard me talking to her," he insisted. "She's trying to respond."

The nurse understood the terrible strain he was under. She realized how desperately people in his position wanted to believe that their loved ones were aware of their presence and on the verge of awakening. Experience had taught her to be tactful.

"Perhaps, Mr. Malone. The mind is a complex thing. We know that the subconscious can absorb information while a person sleeps. There is data documenting instances where coma patients did have recollections of conversations conducted in their presence while they were unconscious. Every situation is different. In the cases of profound coma states, we just don't know if the messages get through or how much is actually understood by the brain. Of course, it's possible, and we encourage the family and visitors to converse normally and positively with the patient."

Jacob nodded, then returned his eyes to his wife's lovely, reposed face.

The nurse checked the thermostat control on the liquid heat suit and neck coil wound around Desirée's body. Her prolonged exposure to the icy waters had also produced symptoms of severe hypothermia. After making a notation on her chart, the nurse glanced back to Jacob. "How about I get you something to eat?"

He declined with a shake of his head. "A cup of coffee would be good."

"Sure," she said with a kind smile.

The lump in his throat swelled. He thought he would choke on his grief before the nurse left the room. No sooner had she stepped out of the room than his fingers curled around Desirée's and he brought her hand to his lips. He squeezed his eyes shut and brushed his mouth across her smooth flesh.

"We missed our goodbye kiss this morning, sleepy-head." His voice cracked, tears trickling down his cheeks. "You owe me one." His big shoulders shuddered. "Tell you what I'll settle for..." He sniffed back the tears. "It's all I want, all I'll ever ask for the rest of my life. Just give me a kiss hello, sweetheart," he pleaded.

Nothing.

He rested his forehead against the mattress and eased an arm over her still form. "I need you so much. Please, baby, please wake up and kiss me hello," he sobbed, rocking his head from side to side.

CHAPTER THREE

A SENSATION OF SWIRLING within a spiral—moving counterclockwise and following it inward—engulfed Desirée. The whirlpool in which she found herself took on the characteristics of the Milky Way—a myriad of stars slowly revolving around a shining nucleus far, far away. Except for the glittering spiral, there was total velvet blackness. Except for the whooshing sound of the wind in her ears, there was utter silence. The swirling motion carried her throughout the center, beyond the mystical North Star, out into a gray, souplike atmosphere where her forward momentum instantly stopped. It was as if she had been thrust inside a dense storm cloud and her body was now floating instead of whirling.

"Hello, Desirée." The greeting did not come to her in the form of a spoken statement; she heard it as a melodious vibration transmitted telepathically.

She peered into the gray gel, wary but curious. She could see nothing but a faint, shimmering bluish aura hovering a short distance away. "Hello," she answered timidly.

"You mustn't be alarmed. I mean you no harm. I come as a friend." Again the communication was telepathic in nature.

Desirée had no difficulty comprehending the message, but she certainly did not understand her circumstances. "Who are you and where am I?" she asked of the shimmering aura.

"My purpose is to serve you both as a companion and a guide." The bluish glow came closer. "As for where you are, well, that is not as easily explained. Those on the worldly plane sometimes refer to this place as the Denser Between Two Worlds or the Grayland. We simply prefer to call it a place of transition or the state of the veil."

Desirée was now totally confused. *Those on the worldly plane?* Surely that's where she was—or should be. Of course, she was acquainted with the state the aura mentioned. She'd become knowledgeable about it through metaphysical readings and the Wicca myths. But all of that had nothing to do with her. It pertained to those who were no longer mortal. She didn't belong here! She must be dreaming. Yes, that explained it, she rationalized.

"You are not dreaming, Desirée." The shimmering whatever-it-was intercepted her thoughts.

"Okay, fine," she said, growing slightly hostile. "Then it's a nightmare. I want to wake up. Can you arrange it?"

"Unfortunately, no," the aura answered.

Now she truly was becoming alarmed. "I don't believe this is happening! My mind is playing some kind of terrible trick, and you're part of it. You're evil and I want you to release me," she demanded.

"Nothing evil, either in thought or deed, can exist on the astral plane, Desirée. It is not I who holds you here, and it is not within my power to release you." The bluish glow moved still nearer to her.

"I shouldn't be here. There's been some awful mistake, and I hold you personally responsible," she lashed out.

The phosphorous energy backed away, its aura dimming slightly.

Desirée panicked at the thought of being stranded alone in the gray soup. "Wait! Don't go. I need you to tell me how to get back."

The aura's response communicated regret. "My mission was to assist your transition. My intentions were only good. But you are correct in assuming a mistake was made, and it is I who must bear the responsibility. I wish I could return you to the mortal world, but the power to do so belongs to only the Highest Force. I am only meant to guide you there."

Desirée sought more-complete answers. "You say there was an error made. What sort of mistake? I don't remember the details of whatever precipitated my coming here."

"Confusion is a common condition when in the state of the veil. That is why it is so named. Things will become clearer as we proceed on our journey. You will remember the details of what occurred. The mistake I made was to intervene too soon. Though the breath of life had left you, I did not take into account the medical advances on Earth and sorely underestimated the determination of those who attempted to save you.''

Desirée's mind was spinning with the information being imparted. ''What are you, exactly? An angel or something like that?''

''No. You do have a guardian angel, but lately she has had more than her share of charges to oversee. Another was in a crisis at the same time as you, so I was dispatched in her stead. There is a certain order, and I am, as you would say, on a preliminary step of an ascending ladder of knowledge and importance. I am a mere apprentice, learning yet and restricted to performing only simple duties. Because of a shortage of more-experienced angels, I was granted permission to assess your plight and a moment of very limited power that I was to use at my discretion. Your stress was great and, in my desire to spare you, I acted hastily. I jumped the gun, to quote an Earth expression. Now we have no recourse but to proceed according to the plan.''

''Hold on,'' Desirée uttered in bewilderment. ''Maybe I should wait here. I don't want to risk losing an opportunity to return by moving ahead. Couldn't you just go and do whatever is necessary in order to straighten out this mess?''

''I'm afraid not. We must adhere to the plan'' was the inflexible reply.

Desirée threw up her arms in exasperation. "What is this plan you keep talking about? And precisely where are we supposed to be going?"

"The first part of our journey takes us to the Divine Depot, where newcomers go through a short orientation process. From there we start upon the second length of the pilgrimage, traveling through the Remembering Realm. The third and last portion of our trek will take you into the Sphere of Light, and there you will encounter the Higher Force, who will decide whether you stay on this plane or return to your former life."

The names were foreign to her—Divine Depot, Remembering Realm, Sphere of Light. Come to think of it, even her phosphorous companion was an alien creature. The only thing she knew about it was that it was an apprentice of sorts, seemingly gentle natured, highly intelligent, yet certainly not infallible. In her instance, it had made a doozer of a blunder. "Can I ask you a personal question?" she ventured.

"Certainly."

"Were you once the same as me? Was your appearance altered after undergoing the orientation process you mentioned?" Even though she'd felt compelled to ask, she was half-afraid to receive the answer.

"You asked two questions, but I will gladly answer both," her companion pointed out. "No, I was never of the same form as you. I am not even from the same galaxy. The orientation process is nothing to fear. It will not alter your appearance. Its sole purpose is to broaden your concepts."

"Thank goodness." She breathed a sigh of relief. Another thought occurred to her to ask.

"I am neither male or female," the aura responded instantly. "There are no opposites of my kind. Both are encompassed in one."

"Oh," she said, finding it disconcerting that her every thought was known.

"You will be taught the technique whereby you can be open to telepathy while at the same time safeguard your private thoughts," her companion assured her.

It was all too much for Desirée. "I don't care about learning the technique. All I want to know is when and how do I return to my own world. If following you to Oz is the only road home, then let's start hiking."

"Oz?" the entity probed.

"I was being sarcastic," she explained. "Oh, by the way, what do I call you?"

"K.T." it answered.

"Well, K.T., lead the way." She decided she had no choice. She sure wasn't getting anywhere standing still, and even moving forward was preferable to the gray limbo in which she was presently stuck.

The shimmering bluish aura started to move in one direction, abruptly turned toward the other, then stopped.

"What's wrong?" she asked.

"I am attempting to get my bearings," K.T. informed her.

"You *have* done this before, haven't you?"

"Once," K.T. told her sheepishly.

"Just once!" she exclaimed.

"Do not worry. I think I remember the direction we must go."

"Somehow I don't feel very reassured, K.T." Hesitantly Desirée followed her guide into the unknown.

GUARDIAN ANGEL First-Class Alistair Mackey raced into the gold, onion-domed Temple of Wisdom and sprinted up the marble steps two at a time. He knew it was improper to interrupt the Fisherman's nightly meditation, but he was much too upset to give a flying flip. The onetime croc poacher, formerly from the outback, wanted an explanation, and he was in no mood to wait until morning assembly to get one. He shot down the hall and burst in on the Fisherman while he was in the midst of prayer.

"Sorry, Your Eminence, but I've come on a matter that won't keep."

The Fisherman mouthed an "amen," sighed and slowly raised his imposing figure from off his bended knees. "I've been expecting you, Alistair. Come, let us sit down, and then we will speak about what concerns you." Alistair's superior moved to a small sitting area, assumed one of the emerald velvet chairs, then motioned toward the agitated angel in a signal to do the same.

"I've been resting on me laurels quite enough, thank you anyway." The stubborn Aussie folded his arms across his chest and maintained his widespread stance.

"Ah, but you more than earned a holiday on Cloud Nine, Alistair. Your caseload has been enormous of late, and you've performed your duties admirably."

Alistair's huge ego was momentarily appeased by the compliment. "Just doing me job, but it's nice of you to notice." His R and R had been loverly—no worries, just lazy bliss. He'd returned refreshed and in a much better frame of mind, only to be smacked square in the kisser with the news that had sent him into a tailspin. "You know what's got me halo in an uproar?" he asked with a jut of his stubbled chin.

"Sadly, yes." The Fisherman's eyes clouded. "I would've sent word to you, but it all happened so fast, there just wasn't time."

"Me point exactly, Fisherman. What in the bloody hell happened?" The blasphemy burst from his lips before Alistair could check himself. Great! He'd done it now. He'd receive at least a score of demerits for talking potty-mouthed again.

The angel had a strong personal attachment and affection for the charges in question, not to mention a penchant for backsliding into bad mortal habits during moments of pressure. The Fisherman decided to be lenient—he let the infraction pass with only an oral admonishment.

"I know it came as a great shock to you to learn of the Malones' predicament, Angel Mackey, but crude words and unseemly behavior solve nothing."

Alistair donned a sheepish expression and acquiesced to his lofty authority by sitting down in the chair he'd been offered earlier. "I know, I know," he muttered. "It was me rattled nerves that caused me to pop off. Forgive me, Your Eminence."

The Fisherman nodded, then proceeded to enlighten Mackey about the unfortunate matter. "We cannot always foresee what will transpire on Earth, Alistair, especially in cases of sudden death. Desirée Malone's daily chart readings gave no indication that her soul was in danger. Her guardian angel was not remiss. She'd checked the computer analysis and found nothing unusual. Therefore she directed her attention on another soul who did, in fact, require her assistance."

Alistair shrugged. "Gilda keeps her wings to the grindstone. I wasn't pointing the finger at her."

"That's good of you, Alistair." The Fisherman rolled his eyes back in his head. Where did the angel come up with these phrases? he wondered. "Earth was in a turmoil yesterday. We had more going on than we could contend with—an earthquake in China, a messy skirmish in Palestine and a meltdown at a nuclear plant in America, not to mention all the usual chaos and crisis."

"Sounds as if you blokes could've used me help." Mackey had a tendency to think of himself as indispensable and slightly more competent than his fellow angels.

More reckless was perhaps a better description. When, oh, when, would he ever learn the lessons of humility and discipline? The Fisherman drummed his fingers on the scrolled arm of the chair. "Our reserve of angels was depleted, which is the reason an apprentice guide was dispatched to the scene of Mrs. Malone's accident. The guide was given a moment of limited power to use if necessary."

The Fisherman paused, reflecting upon the decision he had made. Had he put too big a burden upon the inexperienced apprentice? Yes, he had, but that was not the worst of it, he silently lamented. Why hadn't he thought to check K.T.'s past performance record before sending the eager entity on such an imperative mission? The last time K.T. had assisted a crossing, a search party had to be sent out to find the missing guide and new arrival. There just hadn't been time to review the reevaluation. It did no good to second-guess the decision after the fact. The emergency had called for immediate action. Besides, K.T. was an outstanding apprentice, except for a poor sense of direction, of course.

The impatient angel soon intruded on his superior's thoughts. "I'm a bit confused, Fisherman. From what I can gather, Desirée was brought around after her dip in the pond. She's alive on Earth—barely but alive nevertheless. So what's her soul doing up here with us?"

Good question, the Fisherman mused to himself. "After her rescue, Mrs. Malone's vital functions were arrested for a very long time, Alistair. She was kept alive by virtue of outside life supports. Her physical self had expired. It was her soul that was undergoing great trauma, trapped as it was between the earthly and spiritual planes. The apprentice believed the dire situation warranted intervention. Her soul was brought over prematurely—before the efforts to revive her were abandoned and she was pronounced dead down below.

"Now we are faced with a profound problem. What should we do about the matter of her soul? She lies in a deep coma, only a shell of her former self. Her chance of recovery is but a degree above hopeless. Do we return her soul to her body when there's a good chance she will go through the whole ordeal again—perhaps in a day or a week? On the other hand, do we dare keep the two separated indefinitely? To my knowledge, such a dilemma has only occurred a few times before. Certainly not often. I must admit that the complexity of the problem weighs heavily on me. I really don't know what is the right or more compassionate solution."

Mackey had never seen the Fisherman so troubled. Neither had he ever known him to be stumped for an answer. The mate always knew what to do. "It's a touchy matter, to be sure," he conceded. His thoughts turned to his own problems—namely, his charge, Jacob Malone, and how to help him through the sorrow of it all. "How's me boy doing?"

"As you might expect." The Fisherman shook his head. "He doesn't understand and he grieves deeply. He prays for a miracle. The days ahead will be difficult for him, Alistair. He needs you as at no other time in his life."

"Poor bloke. I'll be going to Earth for a look-see. I'll grab me a bit o' rations, then hop the next shuttle leaving the Cosmos." The guardian angel made a motion to rise from his chair, but the Fisherman put a staying hand on his arm.

"There is a detail I neglected to mention."

Alistair sat back down.

"Mrs. Malone's spiritual half has not yet shown up at the Divine Depot for the orientation process."

The hair on the back of Mackey's sunbaked neck prickled. It was a fail-safe warning device he'd learned to rely on during his heyday as a tracker in the bush. "She should've arrived there by now. Who's her guide?"

His superior hoped Mackey would be charitable. "K.T.-99 was assigned the duty."

"What!" Mackey sprang to his feet, his color going from ruddy to crimson. "Not that blue blob, or should I say boob. It's a running joke that the neon-twit don't know its left from its right or which way's up. What bloody fool sent it?" he ranted.

"I did." The Fisherman slanted him a steely look.

Alistair got a grip on himself. "Pardon my profanity. I forgot meself for a moment. But, Your Eminence, we can't have the little lidy's soul frittin' about with K.T. It's a big cosmos out there. I'm sure the apprentice is trying its best, but it lacks experience, not to mention direction. They could be swallowed up in a black hole—lost forever. I should go after them. I'm the best tracker you've got."

"Modest, too," the Fisherman mumbled under his breath. "If they have not been accounted for by the time of your return from Earth, I will send you to search for them. There is only a certain length of time at our disposal by which to rectify our mistake and re-unite Mrs. Malone's spiritual and physical aspects, if the Higher Force so deigns it."

"Then I should scrap me mission to Earth and set out now," Alistair persisted.

"Your primary duty is your own charge, Jacob Malone. No," the Fisherman said flatly. "You should see to him first."

"But he wouldn't mind. He always put his wife's interests before his own. He'd want me to do the same," Alistair argued.

The Fisherman stood. The audience was over, the matter decided. "You must have faith that all will work out as it is fated to, Alistair. Now, do as I say and go to Earth with my blessing." He placed a hand on the top of Mackey's head.

"Yes, Your Eminence." The angel was stubborn and outspoken at times, but he wasn't a blathering idiot. He knew when to keep his thoughts to himself and when to obey.

He was obliged to conduct himself in accordance with the principles of heavenly order. He knew better than to question the logic behind divine purpose. He knew, awright, but sometimes he found the by-the-book business of angeling to be a royal pain in the keister.

CHAPTER FOUR

THE ICU FLOOR WAS strictly off limits to children. The posted fact did not deter Jacob from smuggling Megan into her mother's room for a visit. The tiny trespasser registered on the closed-circuit monitoring system, but the staff preferred to ignore the scene taking place in Unit D. Viewing such a private moment was too much for them to deal with. It was evident by Jacob Malone's expression that his nerves were nowhere near as steady as his hands as he held his daughter up so she could kiss her mother's cheek.

"Mommy, night-night." Megan pressed a finger to her lips in an indication for Jacob to be quiet as he pulled her back to him. He clutched her close and fought to get a grip on his emotions.

Megan's tiny arms encircled his neck. Often she and her father would play a game called "gimme a hug." It started out with a small one and then progressed by stages—Jacob would squeeze her a little tighter each time and request a bigger hug in return. "Gimme a hug. Gimme a big, big hug. Gimme the biggest hug you got," he'd tease her. The game would climax in an enormous grunt from him as she delivered a mighty-mite hug. Though her daddy hadn't made his usual request, she sensed it was one of those gimme-the-biggest-hug-you-got times. Her face turned a deeper shade of pink as she squeezed her father's neck extra-tight. The sound her daddy made was different from his customary grunt. It was a funny noise from deep in his throat. What's more, his big arms coiled even tighter about her. Her head shot up, and she peered at him quizzically.

Jacob managed a shaky smile. "You want the ice cream I promised you?" he whispered, playing along with the notion that Desirée was napping.

Megan nodded enthusiastically.

He shifted her to his other arm and bent down to kiss his wife. Desirée looked so peaceful, so normal. Crazy as it seemed, he sometimes wondered if he would be better able to deal with his wife's condition if she had the appearance of someone only a step removed from death. But in fact, she looked incredibly healthy. As beautiful as ever. The sight of her made him ache. Over and over again, he kept asking himself the same question. *Why?* There was no answer, only a feeling of overwhelming frustration.

He brushed an errant wisp of Desirée's hair back into place. "I'll be back a little later," he told her. But his promise to return had no effect on his wife.

He carried Megan from the room, not bothering to hide his precious stowaway as he walked toward the elevators. Megan waved to the nurses at the desk. They smiled and waved back.

As they reached the elevator, Mrs. Pinshaw, the shift supervisor, abandoned her post at the nurses' station and strode purposefully in their direction. The woman was a Vietnam vet who ran the floor like a military operation. Jacob punched the call button. She'd probably want to have him court-martialed for disobeying a direct order. Mrs. Pinshaw surprised him by reaching into the pocket of her white smock and producing a red cellophane-wrapped sucker, which she offered to Megan.

"A sweet for a sweetheart," she said, patting Megan's head and shooting Jacob a meaningful look.

He was saved by the preemptive ping of the elevator arriving. "We thank you, Mrs. Pinshaw." He knew she understood his meaning, as well. Megan was already trying to suck the goodie through the wrapper as they boarded the elevator. "Only one treat at a time, okay, sugar?" Jake told her. But trying to wrest the sucker from the two-year-old's clenched fist was like trying to take a bone from a puppy. "We're going for ice cream in the cafeteria," he reminded her. "Let's save the sucker for later."

Megan refused to relinquish the goodie. A sucker in the hand was more tempting than a scoop in the cafeteria.

Deciding it wasn't worth squabbling over, Jacob merely sheared off the cellophane and let her lick away. Desirée wouldn't approve, but . . .

Jacob stared unseeingly at the blinking panel lights. Desirée was on his mind constantly. It wasn't fair to

Megan. Ever since the accident, he'd spent day and night at his wife's bedside, unable to focus on anything else but her. Today was Christmas Eve, and he would never have remembered if Marilyn Estes hadn't reminded him. The thought that he could have forgotten something so vitally important to his daughter had shocked him to his senses. He'd made arrangements for Marilyn to bring her to the hospital this afternoon so she could at least *see* her mother on this special day.

Jacob was grateful that everyone had been extremely giving of themselves—his parents, co-workers, neighbors and friends, especially Marilyn and Archie—but he couldn't expect them to shoulder the full responsibility of Megan indefinitely. She needed her father's attention. Unfortunately he was in no shape to supply the normalcy she required. Though he was doing his best to behave as if he were coping, in truth he was a basket case. He wasn't able to think or function. Mostly he just wondered how in the hell he was going to get through another day.

The elevator stopped on the ground floor. Jake blinked. He was surprised to find himself surrounded by people. He had been oblivious to the ingress of passengers at the lower levels and being sandwiched between the rear wall of the elevator and a dozen or so other bodies. As he flowed into the corridor with the stream of visitors and hospital personnel, he took stock of his daughter. She had almost polished off the sucker; the icky red remains were spread from ear to ear and dribbling down her chin.

He took the stick from her. As he deposited it in a trash barrel outside the cafeteria, Megan planted a kiss on him, smearing the sticky stuff across both of their faces. He almost scolded her for a natural display of affection but caught himself in the nick of time. "What a yummy kiss, but I think we should find a napkin and wipe the goo off your face," he suggested instead.

The lunch crowd had hit and the place was filled with wall-to-wall people and noise. Jacob wandered about for a bit, trying to spot Marilyn and Archie. Finally he located them at a table in a far corner. Leigh Ann was in the midst of devouring a dish of ice cream. Megan began begging for a taste of it as soon as they sat down. Leigh Ann was not in a sharing mood.

Seeing the exhaustion on Jacob's face, Archie quickly volunteered to go to get Megan a dish of her own. Jake did his best to keep his daughter distracted while Megan did her best to dodge his attempts to clean the red stickiness off her chin.

"Did you have any trouble with the nurses?" Marilyn asked as she tried to coax Leigh Ann into giving Megan a spoonful of ice cream to tide her over.

Jake re-wet the napkin in a water glass and wiped the remnants of Megan's candy kiss from the side of his face. "They pretended not to notice," he answered her.

Megan banged her spoon on the table, demanding service.

"Don't do that, Megan." He put his hand over hers. She flopped back against his chest with a pout.

Jacob slanted a look at Marilyn. "It isn't easy, is it?"

"You're doing great," she assured him.

Megan perked up when Archie arrived with the ice cream. All was perfect in her little life again.

Archie had also brought cups of coffee for the grown-ups. For a while the three of them sat silent. The absence of conversation only served to magnify the other sounds around them—people chattering, dishes clattering, Christmas songs playing on the Muzak. Somehow it seemed wrong that life went on and Christmas would come and go without Desirée being a part of it. All three thought it, but no one said it aloud.

"Any change, Jake?" Archie ventured.

He shook his head and took a swig of coffee.

Marilyn and Archie exchanged concerned glances. "I was thinking, Jake," Marilyn spoke up. "What are your plans for Christmas? Jim and I would love it if you and Megan would spend the holiday with us. You shouldn't be alone at a time like this, and it would certainly be better for Megan."

"My mother asked us to celebrate with them here in Boston," he explained. "To tell you the truth, if it weren't for Megan, I couldn't care less if..." He stopped himself. Just because he was in lousy spirits was no reason to throw a damper on everyone else's holiday mood. "How I feel isn't important. I do want Megan to have a good Christmas. Desirée would want it, too."

"Uh-huh, she would," Archie concurred.

"Last year Megan wasn't old enough to really appreciate the fun of setting out milk and cookies for

Santa, tearing through the presents Christmas morning and getting the drumstick at dinner. Desirée and I were looking forward to sharing the experience with her this Christmas. It was going to be great. The best Christmas ever, you know?''

They knew exactly what he was saying.

''But now . . . well, I'm torn. I want to make it right for my daughter, but I also want to be with my wife. I don't know what to do.'' He slumped back in his chair, looking off into space.

Archie and Marilyn really didn't know how to advise him. They could only imagine his dilemma. ''Maybe you can do both,'' Marilyn finally suggested. ''It's a custom of ours to wait until Christmas Eve to decorate the tree. Megan would have a wonderful time with Leigh Ann. After they go to bed, you could gather up her presents and bring them over to our house. You're welcome to spend the night, too. It'd probably be a wise thing to do, since I'm sure they'll be up at the crack of dawn to check out the Christmas loot. Jim has really gotten pretty good with the video camera I gave him last year. We'll videotape Megan's every move for Desirée to see when she's feeling better. You and Megan could easily make it back to Boston in time to have dinner with your parents tomorrow. Again grandparents want to be needed. You could leave her with your folks while you make a trip to the hospital to be with Desirée.''

Archie thought it sounded like a dandy solution.

Jacob was hesitant. "You've done so much already. I can't impose..."

"Nonsense." She brushed off his reservations with a flick of her hand. "Good friends are never an imposition. Besides, the children entertain each other. Please say yes, Jake. I feel so helpless where Desirée is concerned."

"I know. So do I." The muscles in his throat tightened. He didn't dare elaborate.

Archie knew he was fighting to retain his composure. "I think Marilyn's suggestion is a good one, Jake. Take her up on it," he urged.

"Yeah, okay," he agreed. "I really appreciate it."

Megan followed Leigh Ann's example—burrowing her face into the bowl and lapping up the last of the melted ice cream with her tongue.

Marilyn took charge of the two. Jacob couldn't believe how efficiently she managed to shove aside the bowls and wipe both faces clean in one, quick motion. Even more amazing, neither child complained.

"It's getting close to the girls' nap time. I think I should take them home. You look awfully tired yourself, Jake," Marilyn noted. "Why don't you ride back with us?"

"I'm fine," he lied. "I want to stick around awhile longer, but if you need a breather I can change my plans."

Archie chimed in. "I don't think Marilyn's the one who needs a breather, son. She looks considerably

better than you do at the moment. Have you gotten any
sleep at all over the last few days?''

"A few hours." Jake put on Megan's parka and
zipped it up.

"You're running on raw nerves, Jake. Desirée's getting good care. There's nothing you can do right now.
She'd want you to get some rest." Archie bent back his
head and took his measure through the half-moon
portion of his bifocals. Jacob's bloodshot eyes, drawn
face, and two days' accumulation of stubble made him
look as if he'd aged twenty years.

Jake ignored the old man's inspection of him as he
tied the hood of Megan's coat. "Be a good girl and
mind Marilyn. Daddy will be there soon," he promised. "Gimme a hug."

Megan was too sleepy to put much energy into it this
time.

Archie shook his head, sighed and stood up. "I'll
help cart the kiddos to the car. Then I'm going to park
myself in the lobby until you're finished visiting so I
can drive you back to Marblehead."

"It isn't necessary, Arch."

"Sure it is. In the condition you're in, you might fall
asleep behind the wheel. Take as long as you want. I
got nothing better to do." Archie swung Megan up into
his arms and marched out of the cafeteria.

Marilyn finished tugging on Leigh Ann's boots, then
gathered up her own coat. "We're all praying for her
recovery, Jake," she murmured when giving his hand
a squeeze.

"I hope God's listening." He was beginning to wonder.

"You mustn't lose heart."

He knew Marilyn's faith in a miraculous outcome was genuine, even if her words were unoriginal. Though he was frightened and discouraged, he certainly hadn't given up hope. "In the past few days I've lost a lot of other things—sleep, weight, track of time. But not hope." His jaw squared. "I refuse to believe she won't recover. Desirée has a strong will. She'll make her way back to me, and I'll be there waiting for her when she does."

Tears threatened to overtake Marilyn. She gave Jake a clumsy hug, then hustled Leigh Ann down the aisle toward the exit.

Jake sank back into the chair. He felt drained beyond belief. He wasn't sure he could muster the strength to go back upstairs to the Intensive Care Unit, let alone travel to Marblehead and participate in the festivities ahead. But he knew he must. He had to for Megan's sake and because Desirée would want him to follow through on their Christmas plans. Damn! It was hard, so terribly hard, to continue on as if life were normal when his world had been turned upside down and it felt as if his guts had been turned inside out.

He took a last swig of cold coffee and pushed himself up from the table. He felt shaky, but he managed to put one foot in front of the other until he'd covered the distance to the elevators. It was how he functioned now—doing what was necessary, moment to moment, one step at a time.

THOUGH ANGELS WERE invisible on Earth, Alistair Mackey's scent was not only detectable, but familiar to the old Burman cat. As Alistair roamed the deserted upstairs quarters of the red frame Georgian structure, Mew-Sinh followed at his heels.

Not yet acclimatized to the sub-zero weather, Mackey shivered and rubbed his upper arms. "Colder than ice, it is," he grumbled to himself. "I almost caught me death the last trip I made down here. Being guardian angel to Malone deserves hazard pay."

Mew-Sinh merely meowed and continued to prance along behind the angel as he made his way to the kitchen. "What say we have us a midnight snack, eh, puss?"

The Burman had not forgotten the angel's habit of late-night raids on the pantry. She paced expectantly from her food bowl to the pantry, awaiting a special treat. She remembered the generous portions of canned salmon Mackey had served up in the past.

"Let's take a look-see," he muttered, poking his head inside a cupboard. "There's a can of fine tuna for the puss and a bag o' those tasty fish crackers for me-self."

He opened the can of tuna and dumped the contents into Mew-Sinh's bowl. "There now. That should keep you busy and out of me hair for a bit."

Mackey plunked himself down in a chair, propped his booted feet on the table and crammed a handful of the goldfish-shaped crackers into his mouth. As he munched, he glanced about the room. It looked the same as it had a few years back. Nothing much had changed, except for the addition of the child's high chair in the corner.

"Poor little sheila," Mackey lamented aloud, stuffing his hand inside the bag and shoveling more crackers into his mouth. The guardian angel hadn't been on Earth an hour, and already he strongly felt the missing influence of Desirée. The house felt empty. He could only imagine what Jacob must be going through—how hard it must be for him to walk these rooms and see her at every glance, feel her in every square inch of the place.

Mackey suddenly lost his yen for goldfish crackers. He shut the bag and directed a disapproving gaze at the gluttonous cat. "Have you no heart? You should be ashamed. Loafing about and gorging yourself while your mistress is wandering around lost between two worlds."

Mew-Sinh paid no attention to him, continuing to devour the tasty flakes of tuna.

"At least a bloke knows where he stands with a croc," he grunted.

The tuna gone, Mew-Sinh sat back on her haunches and leisurely licked her chops. Since no one had bothered to feed her since the morning of the accident, the cat's only response was one of natural satisfaction. She was grateful for the meal, and even somewhat pleased for another presence within the house—no matter what variety of presence it might be.

Mackey, on the other hand, wasn't at all pleased about being reunited with the haughty fur-ball. The cat was always underfoot. A regular nuisance, it was. He was giving strong consideration to chucking the pest out into the cold night when the sound of someone entering the downstairs shop startled him.

A pair of heavy footsteps began the climb up the stairs. Alistair jumped up from his spot at the table. He hadn't time to switch off the lights. He barely had time to grab the cracker sack and hide it in the breadbox. At the last second he tried to shoo Mew-Sinh away as he stationed himself in a corner of the room. More than once on his first journey to Earth, the damn cat had drawn attention to his presence by its sniffing, mewling and meowing.

It didn't occur to Jake to wonder why the light was left on. Neither did it occur to him that Mew-Sinh might be hungry after several days of neglect. He had other things on his mind—such as collecting Megan's gifts to take over to the Esteses'. It was already after midnight, and he was supposed to return to Gingerbread Hill by 6 a.m. with Megan's Christmas booty. Though he was rum-dum from exhaustion, he was half-afraid to close his eyes. Tired as he was, he could very possibly sleep through Christmas—and maybe even New Year's.

He slid out of his leather jacket and dropped it on the counter. Pressing his palms hard against his aching eyes, he merely stood for a moment, trying to collect his thoughts. A drink would be good. A stiff one, he decided. Walking to the pantry, he rummaged behind the canned goods until he located a bottle of Scotch tucked away on the top shelf. He blew off the dust before opening it, poured a goodly amount into a tall tumbler, then added a splash of water.

Mew-Sinh watched the process with half-slit eyes and minimal interest. Mackey, who had eaten a pound of dry crackers and hadn't had a taste of spirits in ages, was suddenly overcome by a tremendous thirst. He could almost taste the smooth Scotch as it slid down Malone's throat.

No sooner had Jacob left the kitchen than the guardian angel made a beeline toward the bottle left on the counter. He knew it was against all regulations and that the Fisherman could very possibly be observing from on high, but his immediate desire for a wee nip of Scotch was greater than the distant risk of demotion. Since he didn't dare run the tap, he elected to drink the liquor straight. Just in case his insubordination might have slipped the Fisherman's notice, he concealed the Scotch in a teacup. He took a whiff, then a swig, closed his eyes and exhaled a silent "ah" as the Scotch glided past his palate.

Mew-Sinh went to check on Jacob's whereabouts. Alistair followed the Burman, taking great pains not to spill a drop of his pseudotea. The two of them finally found Jake in the parlor.

Alistair was immediately struck by the scene that confronted him. There was something eerie about it. The room was dark except for the dim twinkling of an ornament atop an otherwise bare Christmas tree. Jacob sat in an overstuffed chair, his gaze fixed upon the tree and his movements robotlike as he sipped the Scotch. A big, unwrapped box lay at his feet, the lid partially cracked. Another box, wrapped in bright red paper and tied with green velvet ribbon, rested in his lap.

Taking a seat in another overstuffed chair opposite him, Alistair scrutinized his charge. Between twinks of light, he noted that Jake's face was taut and his eyes pained as he stared unflinchingly at the flashing ornament. Intrigued, Mackey gazed up at it, too, only then noticing that the ornament was in the shape of an angel, or at least in the mortal perception of that heavenly image.

Why did people always think of angels as female, sprouting a pair of gilded wings? he wondered. Yet there was something unusual about this particular ornament. For once, no golden hair crowned the angelic head. This porcelain figure had copper hair, the same as Malone's dear lidy. How strong, he thought. It had to be a family heirloom or a special gift.

Whatever the case, Mackey knew it held special significance for Jacob. Malone was obviously visualizing his wife with its every twinkle. He was hypnotized by it. Hurting from it. Why didn't he look away? It was only a torturous reminder of an empty holiday, an empty life without Desirée. The Fisherman had been right. Malone needed special attention throughout these testing days.

Mackey took a gulp from his teacup as Jacob swigged from his tumbler. Mew-Sinh sniffed at the partially opened box on the floor, then pawed at the contents. In the process the lid slid off and the tissue paper separated, allowing Mackey a good look at the fur coat inside the box. Knowing his pelts, Alistair recognized it as sable. He assumed it was a gift Jake had intended to give Desirée for Christmas. Jake never even noticed Mew-Sinh's mischief. He just kept staring at the flashing copper-haired angel.

Alistair figured that the gift resting in Jake's lap was from his wife to him. It had her touch. Pretty paper, velvet ribbons. But he wasn't opening it. Maybe he wanted to save it until Christmas morning, Alistair surmised, although technically it was already Christmas morning. And then he knew the reason why the present went unopened. Jacob had no intention of opening it until his beloved wife was by his side. There was only one thing he wanted this Christmas, one small miracle during this season of giving—Desirée back in his arms, whole and well.

Mackey wished with all his heart he could make it happen this very minute. Sadly he knew it was impossible to spare him the long, agonizing, doubting days ahead. Desirée's soul was lost in the Grayland. Possibly for all time. He hoped not, for that would truly be a tragic blunder. The only thing Alistair knew for certain was that he'd do everything within his power to find her and, with the Higher Force's consent, unite the pair of them again. He felt useless tarrying here on Earth. Precious time was ticking away. Yet Jacob was so miserable. Half out of his mind with grief, he was. There was no telling what the poor bloke might do if left alone without heavenly guidance. What a bloody mess!

Mackey drained the last of the Scotch from the teacup and smacked his lips. Jacob couldn't hear him. Well, not in the usual sense of hearing. If the occasion warranted, Mackey did possess the power of whispered suggestions that would register in his subconscious. But considering his charge's present, near-hypnotic state, Alistair doubted Jake would notice if he materialized before his very eyes.

Jake's eyelids felt as if they were weighted with sandbags. His head slumped against the back of the chair, the dark silhouette of the tree blurring, then vanishing. The empty tumbler slipped from his hand and fell onto the hardwood floor with a dull thunk. The copper-haired angel no longer flashed before his eyes. Instead, she blazed within his brain. Jake Malone was fast asleep. Deep in dreams—crazy dreams where everything was all mixed-up yet made such wonderful, scrambled sense. Dreams about a copper-haired angel. Dreams about Desirée.

She was there with him in the parlor of their home, laughing and twirling about. She clasped the sable coat close to her and nuzzled her chin and cheeks against the soft fur.

"Oh, I do love it, Jake," she exclaimed. "But you shouldn't have done it. It's much too extravagant." Her words said one thing, but the joy on her face and the excitement in her voice said quite another.

Her long, kinky hair fell across her face as she bent forward to examine the luxurious fur from the ankle-length hem to the rolled collar. Fine golden threads were woven through the copper mane, and a wide, metallic gold band circled her forehead. How strange—Desirée seldom wore any hair adornments, except for a modest barrette or bow once in a while. He'd never seen her wear a headband. As she spread her arms wide and gave a last swirl of glee, he noticed the garb she wore beneath the fur—a filmy, white waltz-length gown, a Grecian-style creation that crisscrossed her bust and accentuated her small breasts. He knew all her nighties by heart, but he'd never seen this one.

Something about the picture wasn't right. It was and it wasn't Desirée standing before him. She did and she didn't seem like herself.

"Why are you looking at me so oddly, Jake?" she asked.

"Am I?" he said dumbly.

"Yes, you are. Do I look comical in something this glamorous?" Her smile faded.

"No, babe. Not in the least. You look terrific, just as I knew you would." And she did. Beautiful, barefoot and swathed in sable. Yet there was something nagging at him, ruining the moment—something he was aware of but not ready to accept.

Desirée came closer to him. "Thank you, darling." She eased onto his lap and slipped her arms about his neck. "For the lovely gift and the lovely compliment." Her lips touched his. Her kiss ignited a fire somewhere deep inside, and he experienced a hot, stinging sensation that moved from the inner to the outer regions of his body. The sensation was the same as the effects of a too-sudden thaw from a terrible chill. His entire body shivered and smarted. But why? he wondered.

And then it hit him. Desirée couldn't possibly be here in the parlor with him, curled on his lap within his embrace. Desirée was in Boston, in a hospital, surrounded by medical paraphernalia and locked within a deep, deep coma.

He jerked back.

Stunned, she gazed at him through wide lavender-blue eyes. "What is it?"

"I, uh..." He eased her from his lap and stood. He wouldn't, couldn't meet her gaze. Instead, he walked to the fireplace, picked up a poker and vented his frustration by taking a few mindless jabs at the logs.

She didn't attempt to draw near him, as though she knew it was wise to give him space. "Do you want to talk about what's bothering you?"

"I don't know what's going on here," he managed to tell her.

"Going on?" she repeated.

"Who are you?" he blurted. "You look, act and sound like Desirée, and God knows I wish it were her here with me, but it can't be." He put back the poker and turned to face Desirée's double.

"Why can't it be?" was all she said.

"Because my wife is lying in a Boston hospital in a coma, that's why!" he all but shouted at her.

"Then how do you explain me?" the vision replied.

Jake rubbed the back of his neck. "I don't know" was his baffled response. "I can't think straight. I'm tired and confused. Maybe I'm hallucinating or something. You're the spitting image of her, but I know it's not real." He turned his head away and stared at the embers in the hearth. "Maybe I'm losing my mind," he mused beneath his breath.

Soundlessly she moved closer and placed a hand on his shoulder.

He started at her touch, as if her fingertips had singed his flesh.

"There are those things that can't or shouldn't be explained, my love. Things meant to be accepted on faith. Things that defy description and dimension. What is reality anyway, Jacob? Isn't it different to each of us? Don't we define it according to our individual perceptions?" She gently took his hand in hers. "My hand is warm. You can feel substance when we touch. Would it be so if I were a hallucination?"

Confusion clouded his green eyes. "But you're not her," he insisted. "My wife can't be in two places at once."

"Logic has nothing to do with love, Jacob. It has always been and will forever be a mystery to explore." Her slender fingers cupped the back of his neck and once more drew his mouth to hers in a long, deep kiss.

He surrendered to his senses, shuddering and clutching the angel-vixen tight against his yearning body. "God! You do taste and feel real enough." He removed the sable from her delectable body. The fur dropped to the floor in a heap at her ankles.

Wordlessly she stripped out of the filmy gown.

For a prolonged moment, his hungry eyes drank in the naked image he so desperately wanted to be that of his wife. Except for the gold adornments in her hair, the lady was a perfect replica—every curve, each freckle was exactly where it should be. She was the sum total of all his most intimate memories of Desirée.

The greatest need he'd ever known overcame him. Logic and reason escaped him. It truly was a moment of mystery and anticipation. He couldn't resist her. His only thoughts were of making love to her—making love to *his wife*. Jacob picked up the fur coat from where it had fallen and spread it out before the hearth.

When he finally lifted his gaze to hers, the uncertainty had disappeared. She saw only fathomless desire within his glazed eyes.

Slowly she began to undress him, first his sweater, then his shirt, belt and pants. As she had said, her hands were oh, so warm, and he could definitely feel substance as she stroked him. Hurriedly he stepped out of his shoes and peeled off his socks. His breath actually left him for a second as she flattened against him and her mouth closed over his, her tongue making delicious swirls as her hips moved rhythmically.

His fingers slid through her hair and clutched a handful of silkiness. "I've missed you so much...so much," he told her in a husky whisper.

"I know. It's all right, sweetheart. Let me help you," she offered, sinking to the bed of sable and guiding him down with her.

The mystery of which she had spoken unfolded for Jacob as he made passionate love to the woman of his dreams during the early hours of the cold and lonely Christmas morning. She was warmth; she was substance to stave off the icy emptiness forming at the core of his soul.

"Desirée...Desirée," he murmured, burrowing his cheek against the soft swell of her breast and dwelling in the delicious afterglow of sensational sex. She cradled his head against her bosom. It felt so comforting, so lasting. "I was afraid I'd lost you forever. I didn't know how I could exist without you. I didn't want to."

"So long as we exist in one another's heart, nothing can truly separate us, my love. We are two souls bound forever." And as she spoke those words to him, the angel-vixen evaporated into thin air, leaving him sprawled upon a sable coat, buck naked and quite alone.

JACOB AWOKE with a jerk. His heart was hammering and his head spinning. His eyes darted left, then right, searching for his missing wife. He spied Mew-Sinh curled up and asleep on the other longue chair. He saw the box containing the fur coat on the floor at his feet. His gaze fixed on the bare Christmas tree and the still-twinkling ornament at the very top—the copper-haired angel.

Gradually it began to sink into his brain that the wonderfully vivid interlude had only been a dream. His troubled subconscious had manufactured what he had wanted so much to occur. And a fine job he'd made of it, too—explicit, enlightening ecstasy. He smiled sadly...*and none of it real.*

Jake propped his elbows on his knees and dropped his head into his hands with a sigh. "You have to pull yourself together," he mumbled to himself. "She isn't here. She never was. She was just a product of your imagination."

Mackey roused and stretched. He felt cramped. It took but a second for him to figure out why. Mew-Sinh had joined him in the chair while he slept and confiscated most of his space. He gave the pesky puss a none-too-gentle shove onto the floor.

Jacob got to his feet and glanced to his watch. "Damn! I'm supposed to be at Marilyn's in less than thirty minutes." He started to walk from the room, then stopped short. He turned back and unplugged the extension cord that lit the tree's only ornament. He paused for a moment and stared up at the copper-haired angel.

Then he uttered something nonsensical; at least to Alistair's ears it sounded a bit daft. But then, he'd forgotten what a significant part dreams had played in Malone's past. In the beginning of Desirée and Jake's relationship, his dreams were all that bound him to her. Though Alistair had forgotten, Jake had not. He could not simply dismiss the connection between his wife and the bewitching angel who'd visited him in his sleep. Maybe it wasn't just a dream, after all. Maybe it was significant. Somehow he did feel better for it. Comforted, in a way.

"Thanks for last night," he said to the porcelain figure with the golden headband and gilded wings. "Two souls bound," he mulled aloud. "Maybe so."

CHAPTER FIVE

ONE MOMENT THEY WERE traveling within the dense gray stratosphere, and then suddenly the cloudy veil lifted. K.T. informed Desirée that they'd stepped across into another dimension and were now at the place known as the Divine Depot, where all new arrivals were processed. The conditions here were a little more Earth-like but still very strange.

The sky was colorless—no sun, no clouds, just a boundless, glimmering sheet of crystal suspended above her head. The landscape was flat, bright, bland and bare. Desirée was stunned by what she beheld. She'd anticipated encountering a lush, green paradise. Instead, stretched before her eyes was nothing but spacious, even terrain, the makeup of which was the color and texture of pumice. Smack dab in the middle of the gritty field sat their objective—the Divine Depot.

Desirée's first reaction to the depot was one of disappointment. She'd expected to find something a bit more elaborate—a maze of archways, marble columns and gleaming spirals. To her amazement, it actually resembled an old-time train station. A circular platform made of an acrylic material circled one enormous building. The structure itself looked very much like an adobe mission. Strangely there was not a great deal of activity taking place. What she could only assume was the latest batch of immigrants either stood in line or sat on benches. Some were dozing, a few conversed quietly, but most were just patiently waiting their turn to be validated. Though Desirée found her circumstances bizarre, the most jarring fact to her was the multitude of other souls assembled there.

"My goodness! There must be a thousand people gathered here. Did all of them, uh, well, you know..." She still couldn't quite bring herself to say the word aloud.

"Yes, they have all passed over," K.T. delicately expressed what she could not.

She liked K.T.'s term better than the alternative one. "Did they all pass over at the same time?" she asked in wonder.

K.T. confirmed that that was so. "Yes. This is but a fraction of the daily arrivals at the Divine Depot. They come in hourly intervals."

"So many." Desirée could not believe her eyes. "I had no idea."

"You think only in terms of your small part of the galaxy. There are many planets and souls that exist beyond your comprehension. That is why the new arrivals are first brought to the Divine Depot. We wish for you to gain new insights in order to understand how the parts become the whole. You have lived with limited vision, limited knowledge, but your enlightenment process begins today." The blue energy form glowed brighter at the prospect of her initiation.

"How do they keep track of everybody?" She moved a little nearer to her guide. The last thing she wanted was to become separated from him. Even if her companion had the constitution of a blue lightbulb, he—for so she had come to think of him—was the only familiar presence amid this alien setting.

"A log is kept. On Earth you call those who handle such things census takers. We simply call him the Logger."

"*The* logger. I hope you're not implying that a single person is responsible for processing every new arrival? Good grief! We'll be here a year at least."

"You will see that things are handled in a much more efficient manner than what you are accustomed to on Earth. Your anxiety is unwarranted. Time is of no consequence in the Beyond," the entity communicated.

"Well it's of great importance to me. I have to get back home as quickly as possible. I'm sure someone must be wondering and worrying about me. Why won't you tell me about myself?"

K.T. did not lose patience with Desirée. Once again, he explained the reason for his silence. "It is not meant for you to know or recall the details of your life just yet. As I told you, the veil will lift completely when we enter the Remembering Realm. For now, you must be content with the insights imparted during the orientation process."

Pursuing the matter was a waste of time and breath. She'd learned by now that K.T. wasn't going to budge from his stated position. Try as she might to ream a clue from the apprentice about her past, he refused to disclose one single, minuscule fact, except of course that she was in limbo, and by mistake at that!

"We should join the line so that you can register with the Logger," K.T. suggested. "Unless, of course, you'd prefer to replenish yourself first."

By replenish, K.T. meant sustain herself with food and liquid, which he never required. The rations he'd brought along to supply the necessary human nourishment were the same variety issued to military personnel back on Earth: tins of dried or powdered provisions. Hardly gourmet meals.

"A sip from the canteen will suffice," she told him. "Then let's get on with it. The sooner I get processed, the sooner we can get under way." She cast a wary glance at her surroundings as she brought the canteen to her lips. "Between you and me, I find this refugee camp eerie. It gives me the willies. I'll be glad to leave it behind." She stopped complaining long enough to take a swig of water. "You're sure about which way we should go? I don't mean to be critical, but you did take the long way around to the depot."

"A miscalculation on my part. We went due north when we should have traveled north by northwest. I apologize once more."

"I know. It's all right. It could happen to anyone." She wiped her mouth with the back of her hand and passed the canteen to K.T. "I don't suppose they furnish the newcomers with maps," she ventured.

"What would be the purpose when each newcomer is provided with a guide?" K.T. took no offense; he simply thought her suggestion was impractical.

"Back home, we aren't so logical. Maps, as well as guides, are included with any tour." Desirée brushed back her disarrayed hair from her eyes and offered her companion a nervous smile.

"Your choice of words is incorrect. You are not a tourist in the hereafter, Desirée. By definition that would mean you travel the Cosmos for pleasure as a visitor. It is not so, for your status has yet to be determined," K.T. was earnest in wishing for her to understand her position better.

"I get the point, K.T. You've made it abundantly clear that this may be a one-way trip for me," Desirée said tiredly. A look of worry crossed her lovely face. "I don't mean to keep harping on this, but I have to find a way of convincing whoever I must that I have to return to my life on Earth. Though I don't remember the reasons, I just sense it's where I truly belong. The timing's all wrong for me to be here. It doesn't feel right. I can't adjust to it."

"It is natural to feel so. It is all new to you," the entity told her.

"No, you don't understand what I'm telling you. I'm not like the others. My passing over was a mistake. You said so yourself. This journey may be *their* destiny—" she gestured in the general direction of her fellow travelers "—but it's not mine. Not yet, anyway," she stubbornly insisted.

The blue aura answered her as he had every time she'd broached the subject. "The power to restore you to your former life rests with the Higher Force. I can do nothing but guide you to the Sphere of Light, where all questions are answered and all pleas are heard. You must continue with the process to reach the place I speak of. So, please, let us join the others."

Desirée was annoyed beyond words. She forgot that K.T. could read her every thought.

"Yes. It is true that I'm heartless. My species has no need of the muscle you humans require for survival. The term 'airhead,' however, is unfamiliar to me. Would you care to explain it to me?"

"Not now, K.T." She struck out toward the depot.

K.T. floated after her. "Inside, they will teach you how to communicate in thought. As I said, our ways are more advanced. Telepathy is a superior method of communication. A meaning is not lost in interpretation."

"I'll just be glad to learn how to keep you from poking into my private thoughts. It's really grating on my nerves." Desirée plopped herself down on a bench, swung one leg over the other and crisscrossed her arms over her chest.

K.T. was equally adept in body language. Hers told him not to hover too close. "You wish to be alone," K.T. stated without anger.

"That would be a refreshing change." Upset and afraid, she took out her frustration on K.T. She was immediately sorry for her bad behavior, but she wasn't inclined to make amends with her guide. Her aloof mood served to cloak her anxiety. Besides, she'd meant what she'd said. She did want the gentle but klutzy alien to butt out of her subconscious for a while.

Of course, K.T. knew how she felt—the entity could read her mind. The apprentice decided it would be good therapy for her to deal with the orientation on her own. Her outlook would be different later. "I'll wait for you outside the main exit. Do not worry. All will be fine," K.T. reassured her.

She turned her head and pretended not to hear.

Do not worry. All will be fine. Easy for him to say!

The line of travelers was beginning to move inside the depot. Desirée stayed put. She didn't want to follow the others. She wasn't in the same circumstance as them.

The line advanced at a quick and steady pace. Much, much too fast to suit her. She wasn't ready. K.T. had been right. Things seemed to work a lot more efficiently here. She watched with interest and trepidation, her fingers drumming on the armrest of the bench.

What were her options? She could either go through the process or stay parked on a damn bench throughout all of eternity. Some choice! K.T. had said the only one who could correct the situation was a long journey away. The only way to get there was by passing through the depot. So what was she accomplishing by lagging behind? It wasn't as if she could just turn around and go home. *Home.* Wonderfully green Earth where your thoughts were your own and people had a heart. But where on Earth did she come from? Did anybody mourn her passing over? What sort of life did she leave behind?

Damn! She had to know the answers, had to remember what preceded her coming here. She looked toward the entrance to the depot. Only a few souls remained to be admitted.

With a resolute lift of her chin, Desirée got up off the bench and proceeded along the platform toward the doorway. Her legs were a bit unsteady and her heart pumped in double time. It was scary to think of voluntarily giving up control and flowing along with inevitability or fate or whatever one wanted to call it.

At the entryway she paused to glance back in the direction from which she'd come. She felt helpless. She was stuck between an endless limbo and an unknown future. Her only chance was to seek understanding and assistance from a power greater than herself.

"Desirée Warren Malone," a voice from inside beckoned. "We welcome you."

Desirée Warren Malone! It was the first time since the mishap that she knew her full name. It sounded right. Yes, she definitely remembered being addressed by that name.

She smiled to herself. It was a beginning. At least she now knew exactly who she was. She supposed it would be all right for the Logger to count Desirée Warren Malone's soul in with his daily tally. What could it hurt? Surely the records weren't written in stone. K.T. had told her her fate had yet to be decided.

Suddenly her dilemma didn't seem quite so overwhelming. It was merely a matter of reaching the proper authority—a question of connecting up with the being who possessed the power to rectify this tedious mistake and restore her to her former self—the one K.T. called the Higher Force. Perhaps the hereafter wasn't really so very different from Earth. A certain degree of mismanagement and red tape existed here, as well. Okay, so they had a slightly different system. How did the saying go? When in Rome, do as the Romans do.

She sucked in a deep breath and crossed the threshold.

Desirée Malone had officially passed over into the beyond.

CHAPTER SIX

TWO DOZEN SCARLET and snow white roses were arranged in a vase on a table next to Desirée's hospital bed. Valentine's Day marked no change in her condition.

Jacob stood at the window of her room, mindlessly watching the activity on the street below. His thoughts traveled back to bygone Valentine's Days, when his wife was full of life and love. Being a traditional sort of guy, Jake had always observed the special date by bringing her a bouquet of roses. Though roses were her favorite flower, she had often remarked on the brevity of their sweetness, the shortness of their time. It bothered her that something so beautiful withered away so quickly.

Jacob turned to look at his wife, so still beneath the hospital sheets. His gaze took in the red roses on the table beside her. Unwittingly his subconscious compared the two; both were sweet, fragile and beautiful—simultaneously budding and withering away.

He hated the image his mind conjured up. Repelled by the negative thoughts he was experiencing of late, he spun away and once more contemplated something less threatening—like exactly how many cars would make it through the intersection before the signal light reversed the flow. It was a crazy diversion, but then he hadn't exactly been rational since her accident. He spent most of his time counting minutes, hours, days. Why not cars? Anything to pass the time. Anything not to have to think about the present or the future. Dwelling on the past wasn't helping, either. It only magnified his frustration at being unable to do a damn thing about Desirée's condition or, for that matter, his own. She was imprisoned in her subconscious, and he was trapped in a painful reality.

How much longer could it go on? He kept waiting, hoping, praying that any second Desirée would open her eyes and ask for him. But she didn't. Though her eyelids fluttered occasionally, there was never any other sign of life. The physical therapists worked with her inert body, toning the muscles, keeping her fit in the event she might emerge from the coma.

She was fed intravenously. The nurses tended to her physical and personal needs, bathing and dressing her in a fresh gown each day. Jacob had even made arrangements to have her hair and nails done twice weekly. But the extent of Desirée's response to the fine care she received was no more than breathing in and breathing out. And the more time that went by without any sign of improvement or a single encouraging report from the doctors, the harder it became for Jake to fend off his own doubts about a positive outcome. Yet a part of him still believed that his wife would return to him.

She had to.

Jake's shoulders slumped. He squeezed his eyes shut and pressed his forehead against the window's cool glass. He tried to blank everything from his mind. The roses cast a hauntingly sweet smell throughout the room. The aroma filled his senses. Memories of Desirée started to swirl in his head. He felt as though he were suffocating.

"Jake?"

His eyes flew open, his heart lurching in his chest as he pivoted in the direction of the female voice. For a split second he thought it was Desirée calling to him.

Seeing that she had startled him, the woman standing a few feet away offered him an apologetic smile. "Sorry. The door was open, so I just walked in."

"No, uh, it's okay," he said weakly. "It's good to see you, Addie." He wasn't just being polite. It really was good to see a friendly face. Especially Adeline Van Cleve's.

His former partner crossed the distance to where he stood and hugged his neck. "You, too," she murmured against his cheek. It was her first visit to the hospital, and she felt awkward—more than awkward, actually. Wholly embarrassed would have been a more apt description.

She retreated a step, her gaze traveling to Desirée's still form. Jake's wife had never been her favorite person. It wasn't that Addie disliked her; she had just never thought of her as being right for Jake. In fact, her first and permanent impression of Desirée had been

that she was a strange little number. Even so, over the
past couple of years, Addie had developed a certain
grudging respect for the woman. She'd come to realize
that the two of them shared something in common—
they both wanted Jake's happiness. And there was no
denying that Desirée made him extremely happy. Why
it was so, Addie never understood, but she accepted it.
Jake finally seemed content.

While looking at Desirée, Addie had to wonder why
things happened as they did. She'd only been back in
the country a day when a business associate informed
her of the grim news. She'd gotten up from the late-
afternoon meeting and come straightaway to the hospital, dashing into the gift shop downstairs to pick up
a small token of her concern.

As she stood fingering the slick-glossed wrappings of
the gift she'd purchased, she felt self-conscious. What
had ever possessed her to select a box of chocolates?
She'd grabbed the first thing that had caught her eye;
namely, the shiny mauve paper. If that wasn't bad
enough, though the sole purpose in her coming here
had been to comfort Jake, now that she was actually
with him, she couldn't think of a thing to say. She was
just standing there gawking, tongue-tied and bearing a
gift of chocolates his wife couldn't eat. Starting to feel
panicky, she searched for a fitting opening remark.

"I feel terrible about not coming sooner, Jake. I
didn't know. I took my folks to Switzerland for
Christmas and only got back yesterday. You should've

had someone get in touch with me." Her pale blue eyes returned to him.

"It's okay, Addie. There was nothing you could do."

"Be with you. Be your friend," she said sincerely. "It's tough going through something like this." She realized how silly that sounded. How the hell would she know?

He slanted her a look that echoed her own thoughts.

She shook her head and grinned. "I'm a real comfort, huh?"

For the first time, he broke into a full-fledged smile. "Just seeing you has cheered me up. You look swell. Globe-trotting agrees with you."

She got rid of the box of chocolates, setting them on the table by the roses. Maybe he hadn't noticed.

"And you look awful. Worse than that day you showed up in the courtroom before my big solo cause." By his blank expression she could tell he didn't recall the incident. "I was representing the nighttime talk-show host. His ex-mistress was suing him for breach of promise, remember?"

Recollection dawned in his eyes. It also conjured up a memory. The reason he'd shown up in Boston looking like hell and feeling worse was that he'd checked out of Desirée's boardinghouse—and out of her life. Or so he'd believed at the time. He remembered telling Addie that he couldn't handle the relationship with Desirée anymore. He had thought he could, but her Wicca ways had proven to be too much for him. Yet in less than an hour's drive, he was miserable without her.

Addie had known he'd eventually go back to Desirée. She was in his blood. It had taken him a little longer to reach the same conclusion. He had returned to Marblehead to defend his landlady's honor and, in the end, had proposed to her. It seemed so long ago.

Addie realized his attention had drifted. He'd missed her point entirely.

He reached over and ran his fingertips along Desirée's arm. Touching her made his bottom lip quiver.

"When's the last time you ate, Jake?"

He didn't answer. It was as if he'd sunk into the same oblivious state as his wife.

Addie's concern escalated. He was in a bad way. It was no wonder, being stuck in such a depressing environment for weeks on end. She decided to rescue him for a few hours by taking him to dinner. Knowing him as well as she did, she figured she'd have to be firm in order to get him to cooperate. Wordlessly she took his hand and tugged him back from the bed. "You're on the verge of a collapse, Jake. I won't stand by and watch you grieve yourself into a mental ward. Come with me. A hot meal and a stiff drink will do you a world of good."

His gaze traveled indecisively between Addie and his wife.

"She'll be all right without you for an hour or so. Where's your coat?" Addie wasn't taking no for an answer.

"I don't need one. There's a cafeteria downstairs," he said automatically.

"We're not going to the cafeteria. I'm taking you someplace away from here. You need a break." Her gaze swept the room. She spied his coat slung over a chair in a corner of the room. Determinedly she retrieved it and tossed it at him.

He didn't protest any further. He was too exhausted to put up a fight.

She nudged him toward the door, talking fast before he changed his mind. "We can have a long talk while I get some food into you."

Outside in the hall, he balked a bit. "I don't need a mother or a lecture, Addie."

"On one point we agree. I'm not the mother type," she shot back. Linking her arm through his, she pulled him along toward the elevators. "I'll tell you about my European adventure. You'll never guess who I ran into on the Alps."

"Charles and Diana," he replied as they stepped inside the lift.

"Cute, Jake. Do you want to hear the gossip or not?"

He figured he didn't have a choice. From their days of practicing law together, he'd known she could be willful on occasion. Back then, she was also slightly neurotic—a worrier deluxe. She seemed to have outgrown the tendency since being on her own. She'd also matured. There was an air of assurance about her. Addie had never lacked spirit, but now it was more focused and contained. She'd acquired a certain aplomb, and on her it was becoming. Yet in some respects, she was the same old Addie—somewhat hyper, sometimes snooty, always opinionated. She could make small talk all she wanted. He knew there was a lecture in store for him sometime between the before-dinner wine and the after-dinner coffee. He could count on it.

THE MEAL WAS DELICIOUS. It was nice not to eat alone. Jacob was grateful to Addie for insisting on dining away from the hospital. The change of atmosphere had a positive effect on him. He could feel his tension melting away.

"Let's have another brandy with our coffee," she suggested, wanting to prolong his return to Desirée's bedside as long as possible.

"Sure," he agreed, settling back against the booth's rich tapestry.

Addie grew pensive. He sensed a turn in the conversation from light to serious.

"What do the doctors tell you, Jake, about Desirée's chances of recovery?" There, she'd finally asked the sixty-four-thousand-dollar question.

He didn't answer her immediately. Instead, he swirled the last of the brandy about in the snifter, then took a hefty swig. "They don't say much, except that the tests reflect no change. The longer she stays under, the slimmer her chances." His eyes were trained on the flickering candle centerpiece.

Basically a straightforward person, Addie articulated what he tried not to think about. "What are you going to do if..."

Jake cut her off. "I honestly don't know. I take it a day at a time."

She studied him as the waiter brought two more brandies, refilled their coffee cups, cleared away the empty snifters. "I'm going to say something you're not going to like, but somebody needs to speak candidly, even at the risk of seeming heartless."

"Don't bad-mouth her, Addie." Abruptly his eyes and tone took on a steely quality.

"Ease up, Jake. I'm sick about what happened. I'd do anything, give all I had, if it'd bring Desirée around. We're not the best of friends, I admit, but we're certainly not the worst of enemies."

Jake's features and manner softened. "I shouldn't jump down your throat that way. I'm touchy these days."

She reached across the table and squeezed his hand. "You have a right," she commiserated. "Your life's a mess at the moment, and you feel like striking back at someone. I would, too."

Though Addie was a dear friend, her touch made him ill at ease. There was nothing intimate in the gesture, but, crazy as it seemed, he was too keenly aware of the contact. Somewhere in the recesses of his mind if felt like a betrayal. He removed his hand on the pretext of taking a sip of brandy.

"I meant it when I said you look awful, Jake. Your eyes are sunk back in your head, you've lost weight and you need a haircut."

"Thanks for noticing." He grinned good-naturedly.

"You want tact or the truth?" She pulled out a silver case from her purse, extracted a cigarette and lit up.

"Where did you pick up that delightful habit? In Europe?"

"A lot you know. I've been smoking for quite some time. It's cheaper than an analyst. We haven't exactly kept in close touch over the past year. The last time we saw each other was at Sam Abbott's retirement bash."

"Oh," he answered. He'd been so wrapped up with his homelife and heavy caseload at the ACLU offices that he hadn't realized.

She exhaled a whiff of smoke and tucked the drape of blond hair that had spilled across one side of her face behind her ear. "You're deliberately trying to sidetrack me. We were discussing the shape you're in." Addie never allowed herself to be derailed from a point she wanted to make. "You're becoming obsessed with Desirée's condition, Jake."

"Well, it's a little hard to ignore," he snapped back.

"I'm not suggesting you pretend you haven't a wife in a coma or problems out the kazoo. I'm only saying that you have to be realistic. What good is it doing for you to keep a vigil at Desirée's bedside from dawn to dusk, day in and day out? Whatever is to be, will be, Jake. Your presence in her hospital room won't change anything."

Logically, she was right, but Jacob wasn't in a logical mood. "I want to be there for her. It's that simple." He averted his gaze, afraid she'd see the anger simmering inside. It wasn't exclusively directed at Addie. It was more as if he was angry at the world.

"I understand how you must feel, but . . ."

"You understand," he said wryly. "No, I don't think you do. In fact, I don't think you have an inkling of what I'm going through. It's like my life just stopped when Desirée went under the ice. I function, but that's about the extent of it. The only thing I can think about is her. The only time I experience any joy or peace is during the few hours I spend with Megan. It's because I see a part of Desirée in my daughter." He paused, then smiled.

Addie thought his smile curious. There was a trace of irony in it.

"Well, that's not exactly true," he corrected himself. "On those nights when I can sleep and escape into dreams, I cope better. Afterward I feel nearly whole again, not quite, but almost," he qualified.

Something about the casual way he spoke of escaping into dreams worried Addie. She didn't mind Jake venting his frustration on her. She took it as a good sign that he was talking out his innermost feelings. It wasn't even his mention of the dreams; it was the odd, almost transported expression on his face that gave her pause. "Why do your dreams bring you peace, Jake?" she prompted.

"I probably shouldn't try to explain. You'll think I've flipped." He debated whether it was wise to confide in her.

"Try me." She lit up another cigarette. Her entire nervous system went on red alert.

"My dreams aren't really like dreams. They are but they aren't," he attempted to explain. "I know it's a dream, but I'm also outside of the dream, analyzing it, trying to separate the fantasy from what's real."

"Uh-huh," she said, taking another puff.

"Desirée comes to me in dreams. We're together again. Sure, there's a surrealistic quality about it all, but there's also something tangible, actual...uh, physical in it." The difficulty was in finding a proper term for the phenomenon. "Hell! I don't know how to put it." He leaned forward, slanting a beseeching look across the table at her. He wanted her to try to relate on some level to what he described. "There isn't a word for it. All I can tell you is that I know that I'm touching her, talking to her, that I'm really, really with her, just like I'm here with you."

His confidence *really, really* unhinged Addie. She did her best not to show how much and chose her words carefully. "Maybe you only believe it's so because you want it so much?"

"Yeah, that's the same reasoning I used on myself at first." He'd had enough brandy to be frank. "Believe me, I know how insane this sounds. In the beginning I thought it was a result of the stress, but after several such experiences I knew I wasn't just manufacturing the dream dates. On some level, in some dimension, they're real. It's wild, Addie. Wild and wonderful. It's gotten so I can't wait to fall asleep so I can be with her again. The strange part is, it doesn't happen every night. Sometimes I can't sleep, no matter how hard I try. Sometimes she just doesn't show up.''

Addie stubbed out her cigarette and took a gulp of brandy. *The strange part! He had to be kidding! Everything he had told her was bizarre.* Addie squirmed in her seat and offered him a shaky smile. ''I'm no psychiatrist, Jake. I'm sure you *believe* these sleep experiences are partially based on some kind of reality. You haven't told anyone else about them, have you?''

''Don't worry.'' Jake's green eyes shone with amusement. ''I'm not completely nuts. I don't want people thinking I'm a candidate for the funny farm.''

''Good.'' She breathed a small sigh of relief. ''Listen, Jake, after what you've just told me, I'm more convinced than ever that you've got to start pulling back a little from the situation. You're losing yourself in it. Are you working at all?''

He smirked and sat back again. It was obvious to him that Addie was rattled by what he'd related and didn't wish to delve into it further. ''No. My frame of mind hasn't lent itself to pleading other people's causes. Right now I'm engrossed in my own.''

''You need a distraction. Something other than Desirée to focus on. I'm not saying you should return to a full-time caseload. I'm suggesting something less involved, like acting as consulting counsel.''

He glanced at the watch on his wrist, noting that they'd been at dinner for more than two hours. He was anxious to get back and spend a little time with Desirée before the nurses ran him off.

"You're not listening, Jake."

Addie's voice recaptured his attention. "Sure, I am, but could we finish this conversation in the car? It's getting late and visiting hours will be over soon."

"Sure, if that's what you want," she agreed reluctantly. As he started to reach inside his pocket for his wallet, Addie held up a hand. "Since I suggested dinner, I'll pick up the check. I don't want any macho arguments to the contrary."

He knew she could well afford the price of the dinner. He and Addie had built a very lucrative law practice together. It was all hers now. Besides, the Adeline Van Cleve who sat across from him now was a more confident and assertive woman than the partner he'd left behind. The woman who now sat across from him was obviously accustomed to winning most of the arguments she engaged in—legal or otherwise.

"Whatever you say, Miss Addie." He indulged and teased her at the same time—something he'd done quite frequently in the old days.

Addie found the devilish gleam in his eyes encouraging. "I love it when you're humble." She signaled the waiter and took care of the check.

As they got into her car, Jake realized it had slipped his notice that it was brand-new—a sleek, midnight blue Lotus. "Nice wheels," he commented.

"I treated myself after winning the Hughes case." She turned the key in the ignition and pulled out onto the boulevard.

They drove along in silence for a few blocks. As she stopped for a red light, Addie ventured a question in spite of her resolve to avoid the topic. "How's Megan handling it?"

"Okay. Some days she misses her mother more than others. It sort of comes and goes with her. She thinks Desirée is taking a long nap."

The light turned green. Addie shifted and accelerated. "Do you think it's wise to let her believe her mother's condition is only a temporary thing?"

"Apparently *you* don't think so," he shot back.

She decided to let the matter slide. "So, is she staying with your parents?" She pushed in the car lighter, preparing to smoke another cigarette.

"Mostly she's with me, but Marilyn Estes spells me occasionally. She's a good friend of Desirée's and has a daughter just a few months older than Megan. They're big pals. Even so, I don't like to impose." His eyes burned from the cigarette smoke. He opened the window a crack.

"No one could possibly think of Megan as an imposition." Addie almost missed the turnoff for the hospital. She hung a sharp left, and Jacob clung to the armrest.

"Sorry. The car's got a lot of pep. I haven't quite gotten used to it." She cast a sideways look at him, noticing he was checking his damn watch again. She also couldn't help but notice his handsome profile. Would she ever *not* notice? she wondered. Just as quickly, she mentally chastised herself for the thought. *Straighten up, Addie!* What sort of person was she to be admiring another woman's husband, especially when the woman was lying unconscious in an intensive care unit? *Good grief!*

"My folks are planning an extended trip to Florida," Jake was saying. "My mother has relations down there, and she's finally succeeded in talking my father into making the trip. They suggested taking Megan with them. It's an opportunity to show off their granddaughter and a legitimate excuse for a couple of overgrown kids to visit Disney World."

"It sounds like a fine idea."

"I don't know," he said. "I'm not sure I can stand being separated from Megan for so long. They're planning to stay two months. Besides, I keep thinking it would be a shame if Desirée came out of the coma while Megan's away. She'd want to see her and hold her, and Megan would be off sight-seeing in Florida."

"For pete's sake, Jake. She'll only be a two-hour plane ride away. It isn't fair to deny Megan a wonderful childhood experience because you want to keep her on standby." Addie failed to see a speed bump as she entered the hospital parking lot. The Lotus bounced over it. "Sorry. I guess I wasn't paying close enough attention."

Jacob merely shook his head as she zipped the sports car into a visitor-parking spot and lurched to a stop.

She geared into neutral but left the motor idling. After switching off the headlights, she turned about in the contoured leather seat and faced him. "About Megan..."

Jake marveled at how she had managed to keep her train of thought after the wild ride through the parking lot.

"You need to let her lead as normal a life as possible, Jake. Kids thrive on fun stuff like Disney World. I know you would miss her, but, practically speaking, it would be a help to you not to be concerned about Megan's welfare for a while. You have plenty to contend with at the moment. Your parents adore her. You needn't have any concerns about her care, and she'll have the time of her life. Now, what's so bad about that?"

Listening to her slant on things, his parents' offer took on a whole new perspective. "Yeah, maybe you're right. It'd be good for Megan."

"And you," Addie slipped in.

He found her single-mindedness amusing. "And me," he grudgingly admitted.

She smiled, but the worry lines between her brows deepened as she scrutinized him by the instrument panel's dim light. He looked so haggard. "You can't keep this up forever, Jake." Her arm stretched across the center console, her fingertips gently tracing the dark circles beneath his eyes.

"Luckily I'm in better shape than I look."

Her hand dropped to her lap. "If you're so damn determined to be here every waking minute, you could at least make it easier on yourself by subleasing an apartment in town. You'd save yourself a lot of wear and tear, especially while Megan's away."

He hadn't thought that far ahead. It wasn't a half-bad idea. "You're just full of suggestions," he said in a kidding tone.

"How about I check around and see what's available?" she offered. "I have a friend who's an agent. I can have her look into it. I'll screen the apartments for you, and when I've narrowed your choices down to two or three, I'll get in touch."

"You're a busy lady. I can't ask . . ."

"You didn't. Shut up and let a friend be useful."

"Okay," he relented.

Their gazes locked. For a moment he thought he detected pity in her eyes. She looked down and fumbled around for the cigarette lighter. He became aware of hot blasts of air from the heater vents. It was getting uncomfortable inside the Lotus.

"Thanks for everything, Addie. I'm glad you came by. You were right—taking a break helped. I feel better."

With a toss of her bobbed blond hair, she rearranged herself in the seat. "It was great seeing you again. Take care, Jake."

He got out of the car and slammed the door. The cold night air was a relief after being cooped up inside the hot sports car.

Addie tooted her horn and sped off.

Jacob stood in the parking lot, his eyes following the Lotus until its taillights disappeared. His gaze shifted and he looked up at the black, starlit sky. He remembered Desirée's speaking of a thing called starlight vision—the ability to see beyond a material reality into a spiritual dimension. He'd wondered why everyone wasn't capable of seeing things in this manner.

"It isn't that some are blessed with the gift and others are not," she had answered. "All have eyes, but what we visualize is not the same. Even when we look at a work of art, we each see something different in it. Some see with imagination, some see the flaws, some are struck by the colors and others by the design. There are those who see nothing of value at all—only a canvas and paint," she'd tried to explain.

"What do those with the starlight gift get a glimpse of when they see beyond a material barrier? Can they see the future? Or maybe the meaning of life?"

"I don't know for sure, Jacob. Starlight vision is not something I've experienced personally," Desirée had answered.

"Then how do you know it exists?" he'd persisted.

"I don't know for certain, but I like to believe it's possible. Surely it must be a more wondrous and broader view of what we are all about."

Jacob blinked. The stars came back into focus, and Desirée's voice disappeared.

A part of him wished to experience that starlight vision she'd spoken of; a part of him was terrified at the prospect of what might be revealed. What if he glimpsed his future and Desirée wasn't in it?

A chill ran through him. He shoved his hands into his coat pockets and walked at a brisk clip across the parking lot.

Let the stars keep their secrets. He'd keep hope alive through blind faith. He didn't care about a more wondrous and broader view of life; he only cared about one thing—his wife—well and safe in his arms once again.

CHAPTER SEVEN

FAR ABOVE the earthy plane, Desirée Malone had just undergone an experience beyond her husband's, or any mortal's, comprehension. It was not something that could be explained to another. The experience was too profound, too moving, too personal to be put into words. Besides, no one would have believed it possible to review every moment, no matter how insignificant, of one's lifetime. Yet, in a region known as the Remembering Realm at a site appropriately named the Revelation Rotunda, such a phenomenon had occurred. Desirée had witnessed her past from the instant of her birth to the moment she slipped beneath the icy waters of Redd's Pond.

UPON HER ARRIVAL, she was ushered inside an enormous domed structure. The inner chamber was empty, except for two cinema-type seats in the very center of the rotunda. She was grateful that K.T. accompanied her. The place was eerily quiet. Only the echo of her own and the usher's footsteps reverberated throughout the big hollow shell. K.T. moved in silence, since he floated wherever he went. She wanted to ask a million questions, but it seemed somehow inappropriate.

The only thing K.T. had told her was that it was part of the process. How sick she was of hearing that phrase. As far as she was concerned, going through the process was akin to cutting one's way through an endless maze of waist-deep sludge. She decided to go along with the silly formality without protest in the hope of hurrying things up, though she hadn't a clue as to what to expect. When the usher indicated that she should sit in one of the two theater seats, she did as he bid. K.T. lighted in the other.

"Okay, now what?" she whispered.

"Be patient," K.T. answered telepathically.

She fidgeted in her seat, accidently discovering that the chair reclined. Lying back, she surveyed the white domed ceiling. The toes of her sandals tapped together impatiently as she studied the concave surface. Upon closer inspection, it dawned on her that she was staring up into a giant screen. There were faint seams, like the sort she'd noticed when she and Jacob had visited the brand-new IMAX theater a year or so ago at the Museum of Natural Science in Boston. Was it possible that after all the days and miles of journeying, all the wondering and worrying, her quest for answers had led her to this—an afternoon matinee someplace in the middle of a time-warp zone? What would be the point?

"The comparison is correct but your conclusion is wrong," K.T. informed her.

She slid the chair to an upright position and stared at him disbelievingly. "Are you telling me that we traveled all over God's creation to see a movie?"

"We have found that most mortals are visual learners. The communication medium humans refer to as slides seems to serve as a most powerful device. It is used to make new arrivals aware of the positive and negative effects of their former presence on the worldly plane. You will understand shortly," the blue aura explained.

"Unbelievable," she muttered, slamming herself and the seat backward again.

"Why are you upset?" K.T. ventured.

"There's no popcorn."

Her sarcastic intent was lost on K.T. The earthly treat was unfamiliar to him.

Without warning, the sunlight within the Revelation Rotunda disappeared. Gradually the inner chamber grew darker and darker until the interior was pitch-black. As the overhead screen began to fill with images, Desirée shrank deeper into the chair. The hint K.T. had dropped about her being featured in the upcoming presentation was rather unsettling. Though returning to her former life was her sole desire, there was something innately disturbing about looking back on what once was.

The concept reminded her of a long-ago television show that her grandmother tuned into faithfully called "This Is Your Life." The show's host would announce some unsuspecting person's name and then, for thirty long and excruciating minutes, his or her life was chronicled for the whole world to scrutinize. Being a shy person, Desirée had always found the concept repugnant. The poor people on display didn't even win a decent prize.

Why was this necessary? She knew all she needed to—that she was stuck here by virtue of a terrible mistake and something inside of her wouldn't accept the fact of her premature demise. Though she remembered very little about her former self, of one thing she was certain—Desirée Warren Malone's destiny had been cut short on Earth. Something or someone kept tugging her back; an inner voice kept saying this transition wasn't meant to be. Perhaps the reason would be forthcoming.

Suddenly she was very frightened of what might be revealed. Who was she really? What if she had been a horrible person in her previous life? Was this the moment of judgment referred to in Scripture? Was it now that one's ultimate fate was decided—the good separated from the bad? When the churning was done, where would she be—at the top or the bottom of the barrel? She had no way of knowing if she'd been a believer. After what she'd encountered since passing over, it was easy to accept the idea of a higher power at work. But was it too late? What if one wasn't given any second chances? A no-return policy? Or what if she were told that there was only one shot at getting in—take it or leave it—no rain checks in Heaven?

These doubts and worries raced through her head so fast that K.T. had difficulty reading her mind. There was no opportunity to break into her thoughts.

But as the slide show depicting her life began and the stereophonic sound system told the story of Desirée Warren Malone, another presence—a loving and powerful beam of light—spoke to her concerns. Only she could hear the gentle voice. It was a personal communication between a troubled soul and the All-Knowing Spirit. *Be at peace. See through the eyes of love. Observe and learn.*

There was no judgment of her, no criticism of her acts. Under the guidance of the Loving Presence, she came to view her life objectively. The funny part was that the moments that she would have previously thought to be significant were not. It was the small acts of charity and love that mattered most—the little day-to-day kindnesses. These moments pleased the All-Knowing Spirit. As for those times when she harbored ill feelings or thoughts or behaved in an unkind manner toward her fellow man, the Loving Presence did not censure her. Instead, the slide was frozen for a second to focus her attention on the needless frustration such deeds wrought. There was only a gentle suggestion that there was another choice, a better way to have handled the situation. When seen through the eyes of love, the acts of anger and spite, jealousy and bitterness seemed so petty, so unnecessary.

And as the portion of her life unfolded that included Jacob and then Megan, she knew the reason why she was unable to let go of her former self and make the crossover. They were what tugged at her heart. She could not release them, nor they her. Even now, surrounded by such peace and realizing what wonders awaited her by becoming part of the whole, Desirée was still reluctant to accept her place in the hereafter.

As she witnessed her near drowning and K.T.'s merciful but hasty intervention, her thoughts were the same as they had been on that fateful day. They centered on her love and concern for Jacob and Megan, rather than the certainty of an awful death.

And as the screen went blank, she once again experienced sorrow for those she'd left behind and the heartache they must have endured. Her mind was filled with questions. How were they coping with the loss? What was happening in their lives? Was Megan being taken care of? Had Jake recovered from the shock?

"Please, I have to know more," she begged of the Loving Presence.

Because her reasons were unselfish, the request was granted. The screen grew bright once more, and a few final slides were presented to her.

She saw a much thinner version of herself lying in what appeared to be a hospital bed. Jacob was by her side, looking weary and miserable. Though he was speaking softly to her, she could clearly hear his voice. Every fiber of her being responded to him as she watched the scene unfolding. Yet the spiritless figure on whom he showered so much attention was totally unresponsive. Her eyes remained closed, and she lay motionless.

"I've decided to give in and let Megan go with my folks to Florida," he was telling her. "She'll have a blast. I just wish she weren't going to be gone so long. It's a tough proposition having to be without both my girls." He smoothed back the hair from her forehead. "Mew-Sinh's more finicky than ever. I've resorted to buying canned chicken to see if that will whet her appetite." He expelled a heavy sigh. "I'm considering closing up the house and leasing an apartment in town. It was Addie's suggestion. She's lining up some prospects for me to look at. I suppose it is a more practical arrangement. Addie means well, but sometimes I wish she wouldn't push so hard. I need a little time to warm up to the idea, but you know how persistent she can be."

He picked up her hand, mindlessly fingering her wedding band. "It's so hard, Desirée," he murmured. "Every day I hope, but..." His voice cracked. He closed his eyes for a second. Clearing his throat, he gently put her hand down and tried to smile. "I'll bet you're sick of hearing me ramble on day after day, huh? Well, I'll give you a break tonight, since I need to wash and pack Megan's things for the trip. Last time I washed the colored clothes with the whites. I won't make that mistake again." He smiled.

"Oh, I almost forgot to tell you that Mrs. Doblinkov stopped by the house the other evening to tell me that she's finally decided to move to one of those retirement villages she's always talking about. She never fails to inquire about you. I think the poor old soul still feels partially responsible for what happened. She's convinced that if she hadn't distracted you that day at Redd's Pond . . .''

He did not go on. What was the use of speaking, as Mrs. Doblinkov was wont to do, in terms of hindsight? He glanced at his wristwatch. "I guess I'd better go. Otherwise, I won't get back to Marblehead until well after midnight." He stared at her for a long moment. There was such sadness in his dark eyes. "Love you, babe," he told her as he leaned and pressed his lips to hers. "See you tomorrow, sweetheart."

Collecting his jacket, he walked out of the room. Desirée had hoped he would pause and turn around at the doorway so she could gaze on his handsome face a last time, but he did not. Her own eyes filled with tears. She wiped them away with the back of her hand as the images faded and sunlight slowly filtered back into the rotunda.

This phase of the processing was over. She had had the first contact with the Higher Force and been given a glimpse of the wonders in store for her in the hereafter. She had also been supplied with the facts of her past and present state on the worldly plane.

As always, K.T. was attuned to her mood and thoughts. "You are still troubled," he stated.

"Only because *he* is so troubled." For the first time she used the telepathic capabilities she'd been taught in orientation. It seemed natural. "Will I be allowed to glimpse him again?"

"If the Higher Force thinks it is important that you do, then you will."

"At least I know that Megan is being looked after. Jake's parents are wonderful people. It's him I'm concerned about. The change he's contemplating bothers me," she confessed to her guide.

"It is his mention of this person called Addie that disturbs you."

There was no use denying what K.T. already knew to be the truth.

She nodded. "I have mixed feelings. I don't want him to endure so much pain. Maybe it was selfish of me to drag this thing out. I was so sure it was a stupid mistake that could be fixed in short order. Now I'm questioning my motivation. Am I holding out for the right reasons? Could it be that I'm a possessive woman who would put her husband through sheer hell because I can't adjust to the idea of his finding happiness with someone else? I hope not, K.T. I want what's best for everyone."

Her guide knew she would reach the point where her nagging doubts would be replaced by clear perception. In the time it took to cover the last length of the journey, she would reach a decision. She might not realize it was so, but so it would be. The final answer awaited her in the Sphere of Light, where the Higher Force dwelled. There, crystal clarity and total love abounded. There, she would receive compassionate counsel.

There, her future would be settled and his assignment would be done.

"Trust in the Higher Force, Desirée. It is not a random journey we undertake. It has a purpose. It is the way to true understanding," K.T. told her.

"The beam of light with the gentle voice—was that the Higher Force you constantly speak of?"

"You ask what you already know" was the reply.

"I've never before experienced such a feeling. I felt accepted and protected. The light radiated love. I had the weirdest sensation while it was present. It was as though all the divisive factors within myself disappeared, as though a tremendous weight I never realized I carried suddenly lifted. I felt as if my spirit was free to climb higher and higher until I was enfolded into and became one with the light, if only for an instant. It was so strange, yet so perfect."

"The word you have chosen to describe your experience is not accidental. *Perfect*. Does it not mean complete in every detail, lacking in no respect, having no blemish or defect, faultless, of supreme moral excellence, in a state proper and pure?"

"I don't have a dictionary handy just this minute, but I suppose it must mean something like that."

"I do have access to a dictionary. On my planet, such information is programmed into our memory banks in our second year of life. I also can give you synonyms, such as absolute, ideal, consummate..."

"I get the point," she surrendered.

"I think not yet, for it would require meditation. Perhaps you will consider these meanings as we continue our journey," K.T. suggested.

"I'll try to give it some thought. Right now all I have on my mind is Jacob."

K.T. decided it was not the moment to impress upon her the importance of the suggestion. Her preoccupation with her husband's welfare was obvious. "Come, there is another place I would like you to visit before leaving the Remembering Realm."

She stayed anchored to the chair. "I'm pooped, K.T. We've been on the move ever since I arrived. It's so quiet here. Couldn't we just stretch out and take a nice long nap?"

"No, no. Come," the guide insisted, hovering in a holding pattern. "Where I wish to take you is much more restful."

"Okay, okay," Desirée relented. The blue aura glowed so brightly at the prospect of showing her this special place, she didn't have the heart to refuse. "This had better be good, K.T."

When K.T. became excited, navigating was a problem. The apprentice took off in the wrong direction once more. The special place her guide wished to share with her was located in the far west quadrant of the Remembering Realm. Were they traveling on Earth—a planet that rotates around a sun—K.T. would have soon realized his mistake. Unfortunately things were different in the Cosmos. Although there was sunlight, dusk and darkness, as on Earth, these conditions were not directly attributed to a source of energy. Like the always-temperate climate, these conditions were a matter of predesignated control patterns.

Of course, by now Desirée had come to expect K.T.'s navigational blunders. Once or twice she had considered trying to replace her guide, but she hadn't the faintest idea of how to go about finding another. It wasn't as if she could pick one out of the Want Ads or the Yellow Pages. Besides, K.T. meant well and, even though the alien was a queer little aura, she'd grown rather fond of him.

So they were off again—headed in the wrong direction, but there was a plus side to the wild-goose chase. It gave Desirée plenty of time in which to think. Once, she actually did try to meditate on the meaning of her Cosmic experience, but mostly her head was filled with thoughts of Jacob and Megan. Selfish as it might be, she wanted to be reunited with them at almost any cost. She was glad K.T. could not see into her heart the way he could read her mind. For then her guide would know that even at the risk of eternal damnation, she wished to be with her husband and child. A month, a day, a couple of hours, it didn't matter. Nothing mattered except a second chance to be near them, touch them, kiss them just once more.

K.T. did not know what was in her heart as they made their way through the Remembering Realm, but there was one who did. The Higher Force possessed the power to peer into her very soul.

CHAPTER EIGHT

AN INVISIBLE and miserable Alistair Mackey sat sulking in the front room as Addie gave Jake a tour of the last of several apartment prospects.

"This one's my personal favorite. Don't you just love the color scheme?" Her voice trailed off as she led Jake down a hallway to show him the master suite.

The guardian angel rubbed his smarting tailbone as he got to his feet. Being cramped inside a two-seater sports car most of the morning while the Van Cleve woman hauled them from one end of Boston to the other to view apartments had aggravated Mackey's back condition. In fact, the woman aggravated him, period. Alistair didn't care for her much. He glanced about, deciding he didn't care for the apartment much, either. Too modern for his tastes—the place was all angles, beams and smoked glass. There wasn't a curtain anywhere. He didn't understand why she was so taken with the color scheme. Everything was done in black and white, except for a daub of red here and there. It looked like a giant checkerboard with red gashes.

Mackey twisted his trunk, trying to work the kinks out of his spine. He popped and crackled more than the bowl of breakfast cereal he'd been forced to abandon because *she* wanted to get an early start. As he limped to the window to take a look-see, he thought about how much he wanted to return to Heaven. He needed an adjustment, and it wasn't just his back that was out of kilter; it was his attitude, as well.

"Stuck down here and doing not a bit of good. It's a bloody bore," he complained aloud.

The angel's gaze panned the row of boats moored along the channel of the Charles River below. He was thinking about how to convince the Fisherman that he'd be more help to Malone in Heaven than he was on Earth. He'd already made one unscheduled trip back to the Cosmos to discuss that very thing with his superior. The Fisherman had been displeased by his impromptu return. Mackey hadn't been very respectful, especially upon learning that Desirée's soul, though officially counted, was now listed as missing in the vast reaches of the Remembering Realm.

"It's ridiculous for me to stay on Earth twiddling me thumbs when I could be tracking the little lidy down," he'd argued. "Send another to look after Malone. A trainee will do. All he does is mope about. It's a waste of me time and talents."

The Fisherman had not been swayed. "Your concerns are misplaced, Angel Mackey. It would seem that they are more for yourself than for your charge. Rest assured that we are looking into the matter of Desirée Malone's missing soul. I'm sure she'll be accounted for shortly. You have forgotten the most important teaching of all—to consider and act for the good of the whole. Though there may be rare instances when independent initiative is called for, such a moment is not at hand. Return to Earth and your assignment. We will expect you to remain until we decide the situation no longer warrants your presence. Do as I ask of you, Alistair. Do it in good faith and without misgivings,'' his superior had ordered.

"But I do have misgivings, Fisherman. How can I not? I watch me boy grieve for his lost lidy and I know it could all be set straight in a blink if you'd give a nod and let me strike out for the Remembering Realm. K.T. has botched the assignment. A floating jug-head, it is. Send me instead, Your Eminence. I promise you, I can deliver her to the Higher Force,'' he'd boasted.

The Fisherman had reprimanded him with a look.

His pleading was in vain. "There's no changing your mind, then?'' he'd ventured with decreasing optimism.

The Fisherman had shaken his head, and that was the end of it.

Alistair was dispatched back to Earth to keep watch over Malone. Instead of doing his best on high, he was stuck in a checkerboard high rise with little else to do but watch the boats bob on the river. It was a sorry state of affairs. Mackey's pride smarted from the Fisherman's lack of regard for his ability. All the real action was taking place in Heaven, and he was missing out. One of the finest trackers in the bush reduced to a nursemaid. It was a slap in the halo, it was, Mackey fumed to himself.

"The owner is anxious to lease it out," Addie was explaining as she and Jake wandered back within hearing range. "He's away in South America and, according to my friend the rental agent, the place is a steal at twenty-five hundred a month."

The rental fee sounded more like highway robbery to Mackey. How could Malone even consider it? As the two came into the living room and ventured closer to the window, Alistair sidestepped the pair and situated himself on the couch.

"I thought you'd appreciate the view of the Charles," Addie pointed out.

Jake merely nodded.

His apathy deflated Addie's upbeat mood. "Damn, but you're a hard sell."

He knew she expected him to be more enthusiastic, but he had more on his mind than ample closet space, sunken bathtubs and a Jacuzzi. "I like it fine, Addie," he told her in an attempt at graciousness.

"Enough to lease it?" she pressed.

"Yeah, I guess." He deserted his spot at the window, starting to sit in a chair, then changed his mind and settled on the couch instead. Mackey had to scoot over quickly so Malone wouldn't land on his lap.

Addie joined him on the couch, forcing Alistair to scoot in the opposite direction. He found himself sandwiched between the pair.

"Listen, Jake, I didn't expect you to be bubbling over with excitement, but you could act a teeny bit interested." Addie had expended a lot of effort. A reaction of some sort would have made it worthwhile, but Jake wasn't cooperating. She could have shown him the Taj Mahal or a prison cell and gotten the same response.

For her sake, he forced a smile. "It's exactly what I had in mind. Maybe you should give up the law and hustle real estate instead," he kidded. "Tell your friend to draw up a leasing agreement, and I'll sign it."

Her mouth curved in a pleased grin. "Okay. I'll take care of it this afternoon. I'll need a thousand-dollar deposit and the first month's rent in advance. There's just one hitch . . ."

He pulled out a checkbook and pen from his inside coat pocket and started filling in the amounts. "What's that?"

"No pets allowed. You'll have to make arrangements for Desirée's cat. Maybe you can put it in a kennel or something," she suggested.

At the mention of the puss being farmed out, Mackey scowled. Mew-Sinh was a bother at times, but at least the cat provided a bit of diversion. Now *she* wanted to send the animal packing and have her looked after by strangers. The woman seemed to enjoy shuffling bodies around from place to place. First Malone and now Mew-Sinh.

Jake paused midstroke. He, too, had concerns about Mew-Sinh being boarded with strangers. "I can't do that," he said flatly. "Mew-Sinh is not your run-of-the-mill cat. Burmans are very sensitive animals." Spooky creatures was what he really meant. "She'll do better in her own habitat. I'll see if maybe Archie or Marilyn could take her in for a while."

Alistair's gaze swept about the checkerboard room, comparing it to the cozy quarters he shared with Mew-Sinh in Marblehead. He hated the idea of a stint in Boston. He briefly entertained the traitorous notion of deserting his charge when he moved into the city. Marilyn or Archie would never know they'd taken in a homeless angel as well as an orphaned cat.

"However you want to handle it." Addie wisely dropped the subject.

Jake finished filling out the two checks. Alistair sucked in his paunch as Malone stretched an arm across him. "I didn't know who to make them payable to," he remarked when making the transfer.

"I'll take care of it." Addie picked up her handbag and tucked the checks inside.

Jake stared into space.

Alistair grew more peevish.

Addie sat for a moment longer, admiring the striking decor. She felt good about having convinced Jake to take this step. It was a positive thing. A healthy change.

Jake was not so sure.

Alistair sensed it was a bad move. The last thing Jacob needed was yet another major upheaval in his life. Though the reason to temporarily relocate was to be nearer to Desirée, the angel feared it could have just the opposite effect. It wasn't the physical contact that mattered so much. It was the emotional ties that bound the two of them. Mackey's instincts told him that Desirée's influence over Jacob was stronger in Marblehead. It was Adeline Van Cleve's influence at work in Boston. Maybe the Fisherman had made a sound judgment call in refusing his request to return, Mackey mused. Was it possible his services were needed more on the earthly plane than in the beyond?

He took stock of Ms. Van Cleve from the top of her golden head to the tip of her stylish pumps. As he studied her, she turned to gaze long and thoughtfully at Malone. Jake was preoccupied with second thoughts and unaware that he was the focus of her attention.

It was then that the hair on the back of Alistair's neck prickled. Within those suspended few seconds, he witnessed something that disturbed him very deeply. What he perceived in her eyes was unmistakable. There was loving concern in the way she regarded her ex-partner, which was understandable since they'd been close friends for many years, but there was something more. Something she struggled to keep contained and hidden from view. Something she only revealed when she thought no one could see it—an unspoken and inappropriate desire for a married man.

As though she sensed his silent observance, Addie quickly averted her gaze and flicked back her hair. "Goodness! Look at the time. I have a one o'clock with a client." She bounced up and grabbed her handbag from the coffee table. "I have an idea. Why don't you sit in on the meeting? I haven't definitely decided to take the case. I'm not sure I'm ready to tackle as complex an issue as the rights of an Alzheimer's victim. I'd be delving into untested waters and, to tell you the truth, I'm apprehensive. I could really use a second opinion."

Jake didn't want to seem ungrateful, but he had an appointment of his own to keep—a two o'clock meeting with Dr. Granger at Boston General.

"I wish I could, but I have to..."

"Get back to the hospital," she said with a sigh.

He decided not to elaborate. "Yeah," he answered as he got to his feet and squared his coat on his shoulders. "Thanks for all you've done, Addie. I'll return the favor one day. You're going to be late. Go on ahead. I'll catch a cab."

"Are you sure?"

"I think I can handle it." He grinned and motioned her on.

"Okay, but call me later. Better yet, come by the office after you're finished. You remember Liz Butler— the receptionist we hired to fill Dodie's spot shortly before you left the practice?"

He recalled the name but not the face. "Vaguely."

"Well, she's getting married next week, and I'm throwing a small get-together for her after-hours. Just a few people, some wine, cheese and laughs. You wouldn't have to stay. Just drop in and wish her well," Addie coaxed.

"Yeah, I might," he lied.

"Make an effort, okay? Liz is very fond of you, and it'd be a nice surprise." She flashed him a smile and dashed out the door.

Once she was gone, both Malone and Mackey shook their heads. Malone was relieved; Mackey was troubled.

JAKE HELPED HIMSELF to a cup of coffee while he waited for Eric Granger in the doctors' lounge. By the time the doctor arrived, there was only a swallow left.

"Sorry. I got tied up with a patient. It never fails. You want a refill?" Granger asked, lifting the pot.

"No, thanks." Jake's hands were already unsteady. He was concerned about the reason Dr. Granger had requested a private meeting with him.

For weeks Eric Granger had postponed this discussion with Jacob. He had no good news to convey, and he wished to God someone else could have performed the unpleasant task. But he knew it was his responsibility to apprise Desirée's husband of the hard facts. Jacob trusted his judgment and would be more likely to accept the alternative care he was about to suggest if the recommendation came from his lips.

Granger's professionalism was marred by one shortcoming. He had a tendency to become too involved with his patients and their families. It affected his objectivity. He tried to remain detached, but there were certain patients and circumstances that got to him. Desirée Malone's situation was perhaps the most mov-

ing of any case he'd encountered in his years of practice. Though he'd known from the beginning that her
chances of recovery were slight at best, he had hoped
he'd be proven wrong. Unfortunately that wasn't the
case, and now the review committee was pressuring him
to recommend a transfer to a more suitable facility.

He sprinkled the powdered crème into his coffee and
broached the touchy subject he could no longer avoid.
"I won't beat around the bush, Jake," he began. "As
you know, we ran another series of tests on Desirée
earlier this week." Granger adopted a somber tone as
he arranged himself in a leather chair across from Jake.

"Nobody told me the results." Jacob's demeanor
was guarded.

"They were the same as before," was the disheart-
ening reply.

"I see." Jake had no choice but to take the news in
stride.

There came an awkward pause. Usually after Dr.
Granger delivered a negative report on Desirée's progress, he followed it up with a positive comment. But
not this time.

Jake met his eyes. It was obvious that the man had
something more to add but didn't quite know how to
phrase it.

"Sometimes I wish I had become a concert pianist
like my mother always wanted." Granger exhaled
slowly.

Jacob almost felt sorry for him, but he needed to
hear whatever it was the man couldn't quite bring

himself to say. "What's going on? You said the tests were the same. That means she isn't getting any worse, doesn't it?"

Granger met his questioning gaze levelly. "It means there is no improvement. It's been more than two months since Desirée was admitted."

The doctor's grave features spoke volumes. He looked like a judge about to pronounce a death sentence. Jacob had an urge to flee the lounge. He felt queasy and feared he was dangerously near to throwing up all over the plush carpeting and the doctor's white shoes. "It isn't going to matter how you tell it to me. Just be straight, Doc."

"We have a thing called a review committee here at the hospital. It's their job to evaluate the treatment and progress of patients and then make recommendations. They've deemed that in your wife's case, the damage is irreversible and she should be transferred to an extended-care facility. I did my best to dissuade them, but they remained firm in their decision. I'm sorry, Jacob. I wish I could have done more. I've grown very fond of both Desirée and you."

Jake hadn't heard anything he'd said beyond *irreversible damage . . . transfer her.* "You're telling me to store her away in some cellar of a place like a decayed vegetable," he boomed back at Granger.

"No, no, that's not the type of facility we're recommending," Dr. Granger told him hastily. "St. Anthony's is a rehabilitation center with an excellent staff and the most up-to-date medical services. I took the liberty of talking to one of the staff physicians about Desirée. Dr. Dixon's a fine doctor and most willing to oversee her care.''

''I don't want another doctor.'' Jake was barely in control of himself. It was all he could do not to grab Granger by his green smock and bounce him off the walls. Even though the man was a dedicated physician and a good person, Jake forgot all that for the moment. The only thing that registered with him was that Granger was giving up on his wife, transferring the problem to someone else. Desirée was more than a complex medical history, a chart, a subject of a consultation: she was a flesh-and-blood human being who deserved to be treated with dignity.

''Please, Jacob. Do you think I want to relinquish care of Desirée?''

The paging system blared out an urgent summons for Dr. Granger's presence in the emergency room. He rose from the chair and tossed his cup into the trash can. ''It wasn't my choice. I have to abide by the review committee's decision. I'll continue to act in a consulting capacity, and anytime you need to talk, I'll be available to you.'' Caught between two ongoing crises, he seemed stymied. ''I'm truly sorry,'' he uttered lamely.

Jacob's more rational self prevailed. Deep down he knew the man had done everything humanly possible to help his wife. ''It's okay, Doc,'' he said in resignation. ''Save the ones you can.'' He spared him any further discomfort by walking out of the lounge first.

Mackey tagged along behind. It was a dark, dark day for his boy. The guardian angel intended to stay very close and do what he could to help the poor bloke through the ordeal of Desirée's transfer. Like Dr. Granger, he sometimes wished to be something other than he was—in his case, a renegade angel trying to cope with an assignment he deplored.

SOMEHOW JAKE SAW to Desirée's transfer to St. Anthony's. He wasn't aware of how he'd accomplished the distasteful task. In fact, as he prepared for bed that night, he could only recall a few foggy details of what had occurred after the traumatic meeting with Dr. Granger. He remembered going into the men's room and vomiting, then going to Desirée's room and packing up her personal belongings. He had no memory of following the ambulance over to St. Anthony's, of signing her in or of staying with her until long after dark. The return trip to Marblehead was a blank.

Jacob rinsed the toothpaste from his mouth, switched off the bathroom light and collapsed across the unmade bed. Perhaps the gaps in his memory were a blessing. It was too hard to think of his wife in the terms Dr. Granger had used—irreversibly damaged. It couldn't be so. They were wrong—the doctors, the review board, the friends who visited less and less often and regarded him with increasing pity in their eyes. Let them believe what they wanted. It didn't matter, for he knew differently. One day it would all be normal again and these awful months would be no more than a blip in his memory.

He draped an arm over his eyes and tried to visualize what normal used to be. Normal once was Desirée cuddled up in bed beside him. Normal was feeling her warm breath fanning his neck; a soft thigh resting on top of his; the pleasing smell of her perfume; a sexy sigh; the touch of cool silk; contentment; peace.

He was drawn deeper and deeper into a myriad of sensations. His arm slid to the pillow. All traces of stress and sorrow left his face. Jacob found relief in his dreams.

SHE WAITED FOR HIM beyond the black edge of gravity and reality. The space between them narrowed, yet he knew he moved not under his own power but rather was being propelled by an outside force. He traveled through a shower of stars. The nearer he came to his wife, the more dense and consolidated the stars became, until they formed a prism of light behind her.

She beckoned him forward. At first the brightness was mesmerizing, like staring into a multikarat diamond and becoming absorbed in the flashing facets of pastel colors. As he drew nearer to her, the brilliance magnified. His eyes stung from the glare that now blotted out Desirée's silhouette completely. It was as though a hundred flashbulbs had gone off simultaneously before his eyes. He reached out a hand, shouting her name.

Her fingers locked around his, and she pulled him into the light. He gathered her to him and held on for dear life. "I can't see you. I can't see you," he cried out in panic.

"I'm right here, sweetheart," she assured him, pressing her lips to his.

He groaned with relief and pleasure, kissing her again and again. It had been such a long, aching lapse between dreams. He'd missed her so much. Greedily he tried to make up for weeks of deprivation in a moment.

"I've been crazy without you," he murmured between feverish kisses. His hands roamed her body—stroking, squeezing, savoring the soft contours beneath the thin muslin sarong she wore. "These weeks have been a living hell." He buried his face in her hair, inhaled the sweet scent and exhaled a deep sigh. He'd yet to open his eyes. He was afraid—afraid to find out that he was only holding on to a fragile illusion, not his beloved wife.

"I love you, Jake." Her voice was as caressing as her touch. She disentangled herself from his embrace, took his large hand in her small one and urged him to follow her.

Startled, he opened his eyes. Standing before him was a vision who would look beautiful in any light—the most beautiful woman he'd ever known. She looked even lovelier in his dreams than she did in reality. Oh, yeah, it was Desirée, all right. The anxiety melted from his face, and he smiled back at his wife.

"Where are we going?" he asked.

She did not answer him. Her fingertips slid free of his, and she walked ahead, venturing farther into the bright light.

Jacob's eyes were extremely sensitive to the glare, although she seemed immune to it. He didn't dare give in to his impulse to blink. He didn't want to risk losing sight of her. Some inner voice warned him that if he lost track of her now, it might be for forever. She'd gained ground on him as it was. He hurried to catch up.

She did not break stride or glance his way. Her gaze remained fixed straight ahead, and still she did not speak. He wanted an explanation. Even more, he wanted to hold her, to make love to his wife. A midnight hike in the outer limits was not at all what he had in mind.

He looked around, trying to make some sense of his surroundings. The panorama kept changing color. Waves of pale yellow, then pink, green and blue washed over him. It was like walking through a shimmering rainbow. The colors grew more vivid, then started swirling, creating a funnel around them.

Suddenly he had the oddest feeling of sliding downhill. Something made him want to put on the brakes— to forestall slipping through the small opening at the end of the funnel. "What's happening here, Desirée?" His voice took on a nervous edge. "I don't mind telling you that I'm getting a *lit-tle* bit uneasy."

"Everything's fine, Jake. Relax and enjoy it," she told him.

"Terrific. We're strolling through the aurora borealis, and she tells me to relax and enjoy it," he muttered.

She grinned but kept advancing.

"Let's stop. I don't want to go any farther." He grabbed her by the shoulders and held her in place.

The swirling motion ceased. The atmosphere grew cool. The collage of colors gave way to an iridescent hue of golden purple. Finally he could see his wife with crystal clarity. He cupped her face between his hands and searched her eyes. "Something's different about you . . . I don't understand, but it isn't the same as the other times we've been together."

"No, it is not the same," she agreed.

"I can't handle any more shocks, babe." His face contorted with worry. He slipped his hands up into her hair and brought his mouth down upon hers. His tongue parted her lips and delved deeper in search of the passion he yearned to quench. "I ache for you," he groaned, folding her in his arms and pulling her fast against his aroused body.

"And I for you," she murmured. "It upsets me that you are in distress. I want to ease your mind."

His hands slid to her hips, gathering the sarong and hiking it up. "Ease my desire," he rasped. "We'll worry about my mind later." As soon as his fingers made contact with the creamy flesh of her thigh, he shuddered with urgency.

The last thing he expected was for her to draw back from him. A mixture of bewilderment and hurt registered on his face. "You don't want me to make love to you?"

She smiled. "Of course I do, but there is a better, more fulfilling way for us to join than sharing a physical act."

"A better way," he repeated numbly. His shoulders sagged. "God Almighty! Desirée, I don't want to experiment with new techniques. I miss you, dammit! I need to be with you. Have you forgotten what it was like between us?"

"It was wonderful," she answered.

"Then what's the problem?" he exploded.

She came closer and pressed a finger to his lips. "Trust me, Jacob. You need more than physical gratification. I know things you do not. I know that the days to come will be the most trying of all. I want to sustain you, to make a gift of a memory you will not fully understand but which will nourish you when I am unable to do so. The memory is knowing, Jacob. It will only remain with you for as long as you want or require it."

Her expression was serious. He could see she would have it no other way. "Okay," he sighed. "What do I do?"

Her eyes lit up at his acceptance of her gift. "There are only two conditions necessary. First, that you truly love the giver, second, that you be receptive."

"That's it!" he scoffed.

She was ever so patient. "Yes, but it will not work if either condition is not fulfilled."

"How exactly does it work? Should I close my eyes or take off my clothes?"

She tried not to laugh. "No, my love. Just stand near and be still. I'll do the rest." That said, she placed the fingertips of her left hand at his temple and her other hand on his heart. "Are you ready to receive my gift?"

Something made him hesitate. "I do love you, Desirée," he vowed. "With all my heart and soul."

She leaned forward and lightly brushed her lips over his. Then her face grew very calm and her eyes seemed to penetrate his very soul as she softly spoke the words.

"From my mind to your mind. From my heart to your heart."

For a fraction of a second Jacob wondered if that was all there was to it. Pretty simple stuff. A moment later a stunning vibration hit him. It felt as though a thousand volts of electricity were passing through his body. It knocked the breath from him. Though he was left shaken, he also felt wonderfully exhilarated. His physical urges had vanished. It was as if he'd just experienced the most intense climax of his life.

The only description Jacob could apply to the phenomenon he'd undergone was a sensation of total renewal—utter rapture. "Wow," he gasped. "Where on earth did you learn how to do that?"

When he regained his senses and opened his eyes, he found himself stranded in the dazzling light. The golden purple hue was gone, and so was his wife. He squinted, searching the brilliance for Desirée's form. The white radiance was overpowering. He was forced to turn his head away and shield his eyes. Then, without warning, the momentum that had brought him into the outer limits took control once more, this time carrying him backward through the star cluster at an ever-increasing pace.

He didn't want to return. Not yet. He fought against the tug of gravity and reality, but it was useless. Second by second he sped farther and farther away from the light and his wife.

"Nooooo. It's too soon." His screams were swallowed up by the whoosh of the wind as he tumbled through black space.

"Desirée, help me, help me, help me!"

ALISTAIR AND MEW-SINH were both jarred awake by the sound of Jacob's hollering. Alarmed, the two scurried down the hall to the master bedroom. When Mackey opened the door to take a peek, Mew-Sinh scampered inside.

Hampered by the dark, the angel ventured a step or two farther into the room himself. He couldn't see much, just the shadowy figure of Malone in the bed. He was sitting upright amid the rumpled covers, his big shoulders slouched, his head bowed, breathing hard. Mackey had no way of knowing that he was also covered in a film of sweat, but it was obvious to him that Malone had suffered an unsettling dream.

After a minute or so, Jacob's breathing grew more even. Mackey's attention was diverted as his eyes locked with a pair of glowing sockets peering at him from under the dust ruffle of the bed. The rascal puss had decided to camp out with Malone, and there was no budging her.

In one swift motion, Jacob swung his legs onto the floor and snapped on the lamp, giving Alistair a good look at him. Malone's face was ashen, his eyes hollow and glazed. His hands trembled noticeably as he grabbed up the phone receiver and began dialing.

Who could he be calling at this hour? Mackey wondered.

In a second or two, the angel had his answer.

"Hey, Addie. Sorry to wake you." Malone's voice was unsteady. "No, nothing's wrong. I just wasn't having any luck sleeping and, uh, well, I've been thinking about that case you mentioned earlier."

He glanced at the clock beside the phone and smirked. "Yeah, I suppose it is a hell of a time to bring it up. I just wondered if you still wanted a second opinion, is all. Mmm, so you didn't meet with your client yet," he repeated, propping a pillow against the headboard and settling back. "Tomorrow, huh? What time?"

He rubbed his eyes while listening to his ex-partner. "I decided maybe you were right. I can't go on the way I am. No, nothing in particular happened to change my mind," he lied. "Okay, so maybe it did," he was forced to admit. "I've been dreaming again, only this time it was scary as hell. Maybe I am losing it, Addie. I don't know what's real and what's not anymore. I had to

transfer Desirée today. They call it a rehabilitation facility, but to me it's more like a cold-storage place."

As he talked and listened, the despair on his face and
in his voice lessened a smidgeon. "Yeah, I guess it's
natural," he agreed. "I'm sure your analyst is terrific,
but…mmm…uh-huh," he humored her. "Yeah, well,
I'm not quite ready to get prone on some stranger's
couch and relate the intimate details of my dreams." A
glimmer of a smile touched his lips. "It's different for
you. Your dreams are probably dull."

Mackey didn't agree. In fact, he'd bet Ms. Van
Cleve's dreams bordered on erotic. What's more, it
would probably shock Jacob to find out that he was the
object of her fantasizing. The angel wished Malone
would sever the connection with her—in more ways
than one.

"Sure, I can be at the office by two. No, I won't
stand you up," he promised. "Just for the record, I'm
only sitting in on the consultation. In no way is this a
commitment to sit second-chair. Mmm, right, uh-
huh," he hummed. "Quit blowing smoke. You're not
going to coerce me with flattery. Go back to sleep, Addie. I'll see you tomorrow."

He dropped the receiver onto the cradle and stared
into space for a moment. Unconsciously his hand
stretched to the barren space where Desirée normally
lay and smoothed the sheet.

He was thinking of her—unwittingly remembering
bits and pieces of the dream. She'd looked so beautiful—radiant, actually. He'd told her she seemed dif-

ferent to him, and she hadn't disputed the fact. Her
words came back to him.

*I want to sustain you, to make a gift of a memory
you will not fully understand but which will nourish
you when I am unable to do so. The memory is knowing, Jacob. It will only remain with you for as long as
you want or require it.*

Jacob shook his head, trying to clear his mind. He
had to get some rest—had to quit reading more into
these dreams than he should. They were only subconscious manifestations of his conscious longings,
meaningless abstracts born out of his frustration, not
some kind of spiritual link between himself and his
comatose wife.

He turned off the light and pulled the covers up to
his chin. Under the bed, Mew-Sinh curled up and forgot about the interruption. Alistair wished he could
dismiss the happenstance as easily. Malone's calling out
for his wife in his sleep and then ringing up the Van
Cleve woman for comfort bothered him immensely.
How much more complicated could things get? Desirée only half-alive, Malone half-crazy with grief. And
Adeline Van Cleve still half in love with an old friend.
Things were getting sticky.

The guardian angel tiptoed out of the room and went
back to his own quarters in the attic to try to catch a
few winks. He needed to be operating at full throttle
tomorrow when Jacob kept the appointment with the
blond sheila. Mackey had no objections to Malone's
decision to work. What worried the guardian angel was

the possibility of his becoming personally obligated to his former partner in the process. Considering Malone's fragile state of mind, Alistair believed he could very easily become confused about the nature of that obligation.

CHAPTER NINE

IN THE MUG AND Muffin Shoppe a pensive threesome sat gathered around a window table. They were n't a talkative group. Their energies were mostly concentrated on chewing Danishes and monitoring the activity taking place across the street at the Magic Herb Hut.

"So, what's your guess?" Patsy finally broke the awkward silence. "Do you think he'll be back?" She referred to Jacob, who was preoccupied with arranging a set of luggage and cardboard boxes in the trunk of his car.

Marilyn responded with some irritation. "What a dumb question. He's not leaving home for good, Patsy."

"It looks pretty final to me," Patsy rebutted between slurps of coffee. "Personally I think he's doing the best thing. I wish I'd had the good sense to start anew some place after Steven, er, well, you know." She couldn't articulate the word, not even after so many years.

"Split, took off, left you?" Marilyn suggested. She was sick of constantly having to tiptoe around the issue. "How can you possibly compare the two situations? Desirée hasn't deserted Jacob."

Patsy lowered her mug and her voice. "In a manner of speaking, she has. I mean, I know it's not her fault and it's a sad situation, but let's be realistic about it, shall we?" She leaned in, adopting an even more exaggerated hush-hush tone. "It's been months, and she isn't coming around. It's got to be a strain on the marriage. A man needs a woman to be there for him. If she isn't..." She settled back in her chair with a listless sigh. "Well, life goes on and none of us are naive enough to think he'll wait around forever."

"Some of us are," Marilyn snapped back.

Archie merely shook his head in disgust.

Patsy shrugged off their disapproval. "No one could blame him. I marvel at his patience and devotion, but I suppose there comes a time when even the most loving man has to accept the obvious. He's young and there's Megan to consider. A child her age needs a stable home life. Hard as it may be, Jacob will have to put the past behind him for both their sakes."

"It's a lot easier said than done, Patsy," Archie put in.

"I didn't say it'd be easy," she corrected him. "Am I the only one who sees the big picture? He's packing up, folks. Moving to Boston. Sure, he claims he'll be coming back, and maybe he fully intends to, but unless a miracle happens, Desirée's permanent address is going to be in a sanatorium and Jacob will eventually get on with his life. What reason would he have to return to Marblehead? This was Desirée's hometown, not his."

She brushed flakes of the Danish off her lap and donned a patronizing attitude. "Think what you want. It'd be swell if life were like the storybooks and everything turned out as it should in the end. But it isn't, my friends. Desirée won't be awakened from a deep sleep by a kiss on the lips. Prince Charmings do lose heart. Take a good look, because you're probably seeing the last of Jacob Malone in Marblehead. Mark my words, the Magic Herb Hut will be up for sale very soon," she said matter-of-factly.

Marilyn and Archie exchanged anxious glances. Was it possible? Though neither one wanted to admit it, Patsy had succeeded in planting a doubt in their minds.

"You're always so cockeyed sure of everything," Marilyn said. "You..."

"Why are you jumping down my throat? I'm entitled to my opinion." Patsy immediately grew defensive.

"Because it's a thing with you. You seem to take some kind of perverse satisfaction in being negative. Just once I'd like to hear you express a positive opinion or, at the very least, keep your mouth shut." Marilyn was beyond caring about offending Patsy's sensibilities. For years she'd been butting into other people's affairs and making her snide remarks. It was time she was put in her place.

Finding himself caught between two riled-up women, Archie wisely elected to keep his opinions to himself.

Patsy's momentary shock at being reprimanded by the likes of Marilyn Estes lasted all of about ten seconds before she recovered herself sufficiently to find her tongue. "Rest assured that you'll not hear another word from me, Marilyn Estes. It'll be a cold day in Hades when I speak to you again," she huffed, springing up out her chair and fumbling for her out-of-date coat with the imitation fur collar.

"That suits me just fine," Marilyn popped off as Patsy hustled past. "Oh, and by the way, I happen to know for a fact that Jacob Malone *will* be returning to Marblehead," she added confidently. "He brought their cat over early this morning for me to keep for him."

"Congratulations on the new addition to your family," Patsy shot back as she stormed out.

After Patsy's dramatic exit, Archie gave Marilyn a puzzled look over the rim of his bifocals.

"I don't know why I did it," she said in answer to his unspoken question. "She struck a nerve this time," she admitted.

"Maybe because you're worried about the outcome of it all yourself," he surmised.

"Maybe."

"Me, too. Patsy was right about one thing. What's to be, is to be," he said, patting her hand.

"Don't tell me you think it's hopeless, too?" She searched his kind old face for a trace of moral support.

"Maybe I am what Patsy accused me of—naive. Or it could be I'm just plain mule-headed." He winked at her. "But I still believe in storybook endings. It happens now and then."

Their gazes traveled across the street again. They watched as Jacob tacked a sign to the front door of the Magic Herb Hut. The task done, he placed the hammer in the trunk and slammed the lid shut. His hand rested on the back fender for a moment as he contemplated the dark red frame Georgian structure with the slate blue trim. Whatever he was thinking, he didn't reflect on it long. With a resolute lift of his chin, he stepped around to the side of the car, climbed in and started it up.

The twosome in the Mug and Muffin Shoppe returned his curt wave as he drove out of town. Archie had trouble making out the sign's black-and-white lettering. "What's it say?" he asked.

"Temporarily closed for business," Marilyn told him.

They fell silent again. Each was absorbed in private thoughts.

Was he just a foolish old man who put too much faith in the power of love? Archie wondered.

Maybe it had been wrong of her to criticize Patsy for voicing a possibility that she herself had considered a time or two—a possibility with implications too disturbing to allow, Marilyn ruminated.

"I hope he doesn't forget about Mew-Sinh," she said, unaware that she had spoken aloud.

Archie knew what she meant. He knew she hoped Jake wouldn't forsake his wife and the life he'd discovered in Marblehead. He gave her hand another comforting pat.

CHAPTER TEN

JACOB WAS PUNCTUAL for the two o'clock meeting at the law firm. The prospective client had yet to arrive, and Addie was tied up on a long-distance conference call. Jacob took advantage of the extra few minutes. It gave him a chance to refamiliarize himself with the territory.

His old office was still vacant. Addie had chosen to remain in the smaller, less showy one down the hall. He found it peculiar, but then Addie had never cared as much about appearances or material comforts as he. The Jake Malone of old had champagne tastes—fine furnishings, custom-made suits, Rolexes, fast cars and classy women. Those days were over.

Jake really hadn't missed the high life very much, but as he stepped within the space he used to occupy, he experienced a twinge of nostalgia. He immediately noticed the fresh vacuum stripes in the plush Hunter green carpet, to which he added his size-ten shoe prints. The extensive law library that covered two walls from ceiling to floor caught his attention next. Some of the leather-bound volumes lining the shelves were originals—invaluable collectors' items he'd acquired over the years. The black cherrywood bookcases and sliding ladder were in themselves a work of art—custom-built. Throughout the room were displayed watercolors and sculpture he'd bought at auction in Europe. The matching cherrywood desk had once belonged to a nineteenth-century lord barrister who'd reportedly chummed with the likes of Rudyard Kipling and was a favorite guest of Victoria and Albert. The Tiffany lamps were a gift from a grateful client of wealthy means and less than sterling character whom he'd represented shortly after entering private practice. The corporate raider's trial had made all the papers and newscasts and ultimately had made Jake's reputation. It had also precipitated an era in which he'd defended scores of rich, influential and, usually, guilty-as-sin clients.

Jake smirked to himself as he smoothed his fingertips over the polished desktop. Sure, he'd gone into private practice with the intention of getting a bigger share of the pie, but he hadn't meant to become cynical in the process. Maybe if he'd lost a few of those spectacular cases, especially the ones he'd won on technicalities and theatrical summations, he might have been able to justify his part in the legal game.

Things hadn't worked out that way, though. He kept securing ''not guilty'' verdicts; his fame and practice doubled and tripled. Eventually he'd reached a point where he could no longer stomach his elite but tainted clientele. The scales of justice tipped in favor of the wealthy and connected and, unlike the blinded figure that held them, Jake finally couldn't ignore the lopsidedness of the judicial system any longer. What did the finer things matter when a man lost his self-respect?

Yet, in all honesty Jake had to admit that a secret part of him did miss the grandness of the past. It had been exciting—the media attention, the best table at the best restaurants, the awe he commanded in a courtroom. It wasn't the same, fighting small skirmishes for the little people. There wasn't any glory in it. There was more satisfaction, yes, but no pizzazz, and certainly no big bucks.

Luckily he hadn't blown all his earnings on rare antiques and good times. He'd invested a sizable portion in municipal bonds and money-market certificates. He was financially secure and hadn't once suffered any second thoughts about his decision to leave private practice. His life had been too full, the future too bright to consider the possibility that he might have made a bad career move. What mattered most was the time he spent with his wife and child.

Everything was different now. Megan was with his folks sight-seeing in Florida, and Desirée was...not the same. Where were her thoughts? Did she have any? Or was her world nothing but blankness?

"Reminiscing?" Addie caught him by surprise.

"Yeah, just rehashing the good old days." He quickly collected himself and came from behind the desk. Removing his coat, he draped it over one of the coat tree's ivory knobs. "So...what's the background on this guy?" He referred to the tardy client.

"I've only had two phone conversations with the man. I really don't know any particulars, except that his wife suffers from Alzheimer's disease, and there seems to be some sort of disagreement with the children about the method of treatment she should receive," Addie replied.

Jacob purposely selected one of the overstuffed visitors' chairs to sit in. "That's tough," he empathized. He was thinking of the similarity to Desirée's condition. It would seem he shared something in common with the gentleman in question. They both were having to contend with a wife in an altered state of consciousness and the devastating aftermath.

Addie noticed the faraway look that had crept into his eyes. "I'm glad you decided to sit in. I've read an article or two and watched a TV segment on Alzheimer's, but I certainly don't pretend to be knowledgeable on the subject." Feigning ignorance was a ploy on her part—an attempt to involve her ex-partner in the case. It was her intention to drag him, if necessary, back into the mainstream of life. She'd done her homework and knew the facts of the disease. Jake was the only question mark.

A caustic laugh erupted from him. "Oh, and you thought I had some practical experience in the area and could lend support. Poor Jake's sort of in the same boat—invite him over and see if he can shed some light on the subject."

Addie flicked back the hair from her eyes and braced her hips against the desk. "Don't be so sensitive. I wasn't thinking anything of the kind. I could use some backup, and you were available. That's all there is to it. Is it okay with you if we meet in here? I'm in the midst of researching another case, and my office is a mess.''

He thought it odd that she'd ask him such a question. Though the lettering on the firm's door still read Malone & Van Cleve, it was only because Addie had neglected to change the logo. He no longer owned an interest. The practice—liabilities and assets and head-aches—belonged to Addie now, including his former office. ''Fine with me'' was all he said.

A soft knock on the door, which had been left ajar, alerted them to another's presence.

Addie stood away from the desk and straightened her suit jacket. ''Mr. Helms, I presume.'' She crossed the room and extended a hand to the dapperly dressed gentleman standing in the doorway.

Jacob stifled a grin. She sounded as if she were greeting Dr. Livingstone.

''Yes. Sorry about being late. Rozalyn gets upset whenever I leave her with somebody else,'' the fellow explained.

He presented a tall, slim figure. Jacob guessed him to be fiftyish. When he removed his hat, Jake's attention immediately homed in on the bare spot on the top of the man's head. Though the neatly trimmed salt-and-pepper beard added a sort of scholarly quality, it was the contrast between his hairless crown and the facial brush that was most striking.

"That's quite all right." Addie gestured for him to step inside. "I'd like to introduce you to Mr. Jacob Malone, my former partner. I invited him to sit in on our meeting. I hope you don't mind," she chatted.

"Sure. It's all right with me." Helms cast Jake a lame smile and gestured for him to remain seated. He skimmed out of his coat, arranging it over his arm before placing himself in the chair next to Jake's. "Nice office you have here," he remarked, trying to appear at ease when, in fact, he seemed terribly uncomfortable.

"Thank you. Can I take your coat for you?" Addie offered.

"It's okay." He acted as though he wanted to be prepared in case he decided to make a dash for the door.

Addie pretended not to take any special notice of his apparent nervousness. "Actually this was Mr. Malone's office when he was still with the firm," she continued, stationing herself in the wing-backed chair behind the desk.

"Nice office," he repeated, this time addressing himself to Jake.

"I liked it." Jake was growing a little uncomfortable himself. Helms seemed wary. Though he was polite, he behaved like someone who'd been summoned to appear rather than the person who'd requested an appointment. Something wasn't kosher. Jacob suspected that Helms faced a more serious legal problem than a mere difference of opinion about the type of

care his wife should receive. The man was a bundle of
nerves. He couldn't sit still. His leg kept bouncing beneath the coat.

"Why don't we talk about the reason you're here,
Mr. Helms?" Jake suggested.

"I don't know where to begin," Helms answered,
casting a helpless glance in Addie's direction.

"Since your dilemma centers around your wife's
condition, let's discuss it," Addie guided him gently.
"She suffers from Alzheimer's disease, is that correct?"

He nodded.

"When was she first diagnosed?"

"Nearly six years ago. At first it wasn't so bad, but
it's gradually gotten worse." Helms's gaze dropped to
his lap. "My wife was a lovely, active woman before the
disease. She's still lovely, of course," he quickly added.
"My point is that in those days Rozalyn was full of vim
and vigor. She always took care of everybody else.
That's what makes it so hard on her now. I don't mind
taking care of her needs. It's her who's bothered by the
way things are now."

Jacob wondered if his claim was totally true. He was
disturbed by something. If not the fact of his wife's
helplessness, then what? He injected himself into the
discussion. "And exactly how are things now, Mr.
Helms? Is your wife solely dependent on you to meet
her basic needs at the present time?"

Helms raised his gaze and met Jacob's levelly. "I
care for her twenty-four hours a day, seven days a

week, Mr. Malone. I dress her, feed her, bathe her, see that she gets her medication, take her to the bathroom, talk to her, read to her, hold her and cry with her. The only thing I don't do is sing to her, and that's because I can't carry a tune. Rozalyn used to kid me about it," he told him with a small smile.

Jacob smiled back. "I don't mean to pry into private matters. It's necessary for us to try and gain an understanding of the situation in order to advise you properly. If my questions seem unfeeling, please let me assure you that I empathize with the difficulties you face."

Helms nodded. "I appreciate the sympathy, but no one can know what it's like unless they've dealt with the problem themselves. I'm not complaining," he said hurriedly, "but I'm human. Sometimes I get tired and discouraged. I feel it's so unfair. You find yourself wondering, why us? Why not somebody else? It's not something I'm proud to admit, but it's a fact."

"That's what we deal in, Mr. Helms—facts," Addie put in. "So be good enough, if you will, to tell us more about the circumstances that brought you in today."

"Okay, well, like I said, Rozalyn first showed symptoms about six years ago. Small things, like forgetting engagements and where she put things. We all thought it was just a matter of overload because Roz always went at such a pace. After a while, though, we realized that she was confused a lot of the time. She just couldn't seem to focus anymore. Her mind wandered. It began to upset her. That's when we saw a doctor. They ran all kinds of tests, then sent her to a specialist who ran even more tests. Finally they told us she suffered from Alzheimer's and that there wasn't a cure.''

Recalling the memory caused Helms to release a heavy sigh. ''I won't ever forget that day. Such a shock...such a shock.'' He lapsed into thoughtfulness.

''I'm sure it was. What was the doctors' recommendation concerning her treatment?'' Addie prompted.

Helms redistributed his weight within the chair. Now his right leg jiggled. ''Back then Alzheimer's was treated like a closet illness. It wasn't openly discussed, as it is now. A disease that lacks public attention also lacks research funding. The best they could offer in the way of treatment was to put Roz on a program of choline enhancers. You see, in Alzheimer's patients, the nerve endings that transmit messages in the brain deteriorate. Choline is the chemical that stimulates the transmitting process. By supplementing the chemical into the system, the debilitating effects can be lessened. The doctors suggested a program of daily doses of a choline enhancer. As her condition worsened, the number of capsules she took in a day increased. That was the only treatment available for quite a while. I gave her increasingly larger doses of choline enhancers, patience and love.''

It was a sad story, but Jacob was convinced there was a lot more to it. "Do these choline enhancers have dangerous side effects, Mr. Helms?"

The client shook his head. "No. You don't even need a prescription to purchase them. Of course, after a couple of years had gone by, Roz required as many as sixteen gel-caps a day. That much can sometimes cause minor problems such as bloating. The doctors kept a close watch on her. If she began to show symptoms, we'd just decrease the amount for a while."

"Then I don't understand why your children should object?" Jake probed deeper.

Helms finally set aside his coat, placing it over the back of the chair. He also seemed to set aside caution. "Well, that's because there's more to it than my giving Roz over-the-counter medication. You see, a few years back I read an article about a doctor in California who was treating a small group of Alzheimer's patients with an experimental drug. The results were encouraging. I contacted him, and he finally consented to let Roz become part of the carefully controlled study group. Like I said, the drug was experimental, but the results were nothing short of a miracle. Roz got better almost right away. She could function on her own. Do things she hadn't been able to do in a very long time. The doctor had received a grant to test the drug, and the program was closely monitored. Eighty percent of the test patients improved. I thought we'd found the answer."

"Did your wife stop responding to the new drug?" Addie interrupted.

"No, ma'am, the FDA put a halt to the program," he responded.

"The FDA deemed the program to be unsafe," Jake guessed.

"There was a side effect to the drug. In some patients, not all, it caused the liver enzymes to rise, and the FDA had concerns about prolonged use. I think it was an excuse. I believe big drug companies put pressure on the FDA to delay production until patents could be secured. We're talking about huge profits, Mr. Malone. I'm convinced the FDA ban is a result of strong pharmaceutical lobbying."

"Perhaps, but there is a legitimate question of risk being raised, sir," Jake put forth.

"Dr. Patterson constantly ran liver-function tests checking for abnormalities in his patients. If toxicity was found, he'd reduce or discontinue the drug. No patient was ever in danger. Besides, the drug's value has been recognized and is available in other countries—Canada, Sweden, England and the Canary Islands."

"The children were opposed to your putting your wife in the experimental program?" Jake still wasn't clear about the issue.

"They really never said much about it," Helms replied.

"Then I'm confused. If they didn't object at the time, what's their complaint now that the treatment is no longer available?"

"It's complicated," Helms conceded. "The FDA halted the California program, that's true. But they didn't ban the import of the drug from other countries. Roz and I agreed about going outside to get it. I conducted the transaction through a pharmacy in the Canary Islands and had the drug flown in. We weren't the only ones doing it. A lot of folks got around the red tape that way. But then the FDA went a step further, saying we couldn't import the drug. I, among others, resorted to smuggling it into the country."

"I'm still unclear as to what your children are opposing?" Addie couldn't get an angle on the crux of the matter, either.

"We—Roz and me—during a time when she was still able to make informed decisions, decided there was more than one way to skin a cat. If Mohammed wouldn't come to the mountain, then the mountain would go to Mohammed. I made plans for us to travel to England for an indefinite stay so Roz could get the medication she needed to live a halfway normal life. We applied for visas about six weeks ago. Roz was already beginning to show signs of slipping back into her confused state. It was when the children learned of our plans that all hell broke loose. They wouldn't even discuss it. They got a lawyer and an injunction to stop us from leaving the country. My wife is getting worse by the day. I need that injunction lifted. I need you to do whatever it takes to allow me to take care of my wife as I see fit."

On the surface it seemed the issue wasn't all that complex. Otto Helms had no qualms about opting for the experimental treatment; his children did. Yet Jacob felt there was more to the story. Helms's body language said he was holding something back.

Stiff from sitting so long, Jake got to his feet and sauntered to the window. He assumed Addie had also recognized the evasiveness in Otto Helms's eyes. It was her client, her firm, her move.

"Is that all we're dealing with, Mr. Helms—an injunction prohibiting you from taking your wife out of the country in order to continue a more radical method of treatment?"

By her phrasing of the question, Jake knew she was on the same wavelength as he.

Helms took his time answering. He drew in a deep breath and let it out slowly. "No," he finally said. "I suppose there's some background information you should know." Helms addressed himself to Addie, since Jacob's back was to him. "The children are Rozalyn's, not mine. I'm Rozalyn's second husband, and her kids have never liked me much."

"I see," Addie said noncommittally.

"No, I don't think you do. Does the name Harcourt strike a bell?"

"*The* Harcourts?" Addie couldn't disguise her astonishment.

"I thought you might have heard of them. Anyone who's spent any time in Boston soon learns the name."

For the first time Otto Helms actually smiled. "I married Henry Harcourt's widow."

Jacob turned to face the man. The Harcourts were old Boston society—almost royalty and worth a mint. Somehow it was hard to imagine Otto Helms filling the shoes of a man like Henry Harcourt. He didn't have "the look." Harcourt had possessed a presence, a power that was legendary. He'd inherited a fortune and turned it into a communications empire. At best, Otto Helms resembled an Ivy League professor, but his conversation would soon put that notion to rest.

"You're wondering why a woman like her would get involved with a man like me," he said flatly, voicing their thoughts.

"Uh, no, not at all," Addie replied tactfully.

"Don't bother to deny it. Believe me, I've encountered the same reaction more times than I care to remember. I'm used to it." He shook his bald head in bemusement. "I can't even offer an explanation. I never traveled in her circles. It was a fluke that we even met. You might say we bumped into each other." He chuckled to himself. "I mean, we quite literally bumped into each other. Her driver ran a stop sign and hit my car."

"Amazing," Addie murmured.

"Damn lucky," Otto stated. "She was wearing a blue dress that day. It matched her eyes. It seems like yesterday," he reminisced. "Her Rolls wasn't damaged very much, but my car took quite a lick. She was so nice about it. It worried her that I might be hurt. I was stunned, all right, not from the collision but from coming into contact with someone as smashing as her.

"To this day I can't recall half of what I said to her. She told me later that I offered to pay her for the honor of being broadsided by her. Probably so," he said, grinning. "Anyway, I'd given her my home and business number and, believe it or not, she phoned me a few days later to make sure I was okay. Maybe she was afraid I'd scream whiplash or a sprained back. We talked for an hour or more. I didn't want to hang up. Somehow I found the nerve to ask her to dinner. I never expected her to accept, but she did. Six months later we were married. I don't think her kids ever got over the shock of it."

Addie found his recounting of their first meeting touching.

Jacob found it intriguing. "As I recall, the Harcourts have two children. There's Henry, Jr., who would be about my age, and a sister a few years younger."

"Marion," Helms told him. "She's thirty, I think."

"Who have they retained to represent them?"

"A firm by the name of Lange and Litton." Helms didn't seem aware of the prestigious stature of his adversaries.

"Lange and Litton," Addie parroted, just in case Jacob hadn't caught it. Her heart beat a little faster at the mere mention of L and L. Louis Lange was the standard, the king of the hill, the legal icon every law student wanted to emulate. She had dreamed of an opportunity like this—a chance to go head-to-head with him. Talk about an honor. Like Helms, she'd gladly pay for the privilege of being involved in such a lucky collision.

"There's something else you should know before you decide whether or not to take my case." Helms's leg started jiggling double-time.

"Now is the time to enlighten me." Addie sat straighter in the wing-backed chair.

"Henry, Jr., and Marion want something more than simply to stop me from taking Roz to England. According to the papers I've been sent, they want guardianship over her. What's more, they've used their connections to get an early court date."

"When and in whose court are you supposed to appear?" Jacob's reservations about taking on Helms's cause mounted by the second.

"In three weeks. I believe the subpoena said it was to take place in the 108th District Civil Court."

Once again Addie and Jake traded glances. The 108th was presided over by Judge James McCallahan. He'd been on the bench forever. Not only was he ultraconservative, but he was also totally intolerant of the sort of theatrical oratory that had made Jake's reputation. The only encouraging aspect Jake could glean from landing in McCallahan's court was that the judge was in his seventies himself. There was a slim possibility he might identify more with the older Helmses than with the younger Harcourts.

"That doesn't leave us much time to prepare," Addie pondered aloud.

"I know I probably should've consulted you right away, but I just couldn't believe the kids would actually go through with it. I tried to reason with them and get them to drop the suit, but they refused. At first I thought they hadn't considered how upsetting a hearing of this nature will be to their mother. Roz is aware enough to know what it means—that her children want her declared incompetent. They might as well be asking the court to pull the plug, because, if they succeed in what they're attempting, Roz will lose the little bit of hope she has left. More than that, she'll lose her dignity. For a woman like her, it amounts to the same as a death sentence."

The man seemed sincere, but Jacob still had a gut feeling Helms hadn't told them the entire story. That alone made him want to pass on the case. In addition, there were other considerations to take into account. Lange and Litton were the best—top-notch trial lawyers with years of experience. Addie was good, but not seasoned enough to go it alone against a firm of their caliber. She'd be in over her head, and he wasn't sure how much help he'd actually be. He hadn't argued a case of this magnitude in several years. He was rusty.

Worst of all, though, Jake had to admit that he wasn't completely in the client's corner. He could foresee that even if they somehow won at the lower court level, the Harcourts had the wherewithal to take the issue to the limits—all the way to the U.S. Supreme Court. A lawyer had to totally believe in the veracity of his client and be convinced of the moral right of an issue in order to endure such a grueling crusade. It could be years before a final decision was reached. Jake was skeptical, tired and doubtful of his own ability—three big strikes that made him want to bow out.

One look at Addie told him she felt just the opposite. Her eyes gleamed with a feverish intensity. She was challenged by the cause and excited by the prospect of facing the Goliaths, Lange and Litton. He cleared his throat, trying to gain her attention so that he could telegraph his reluctance.

Addie either didn't hear him or deliberately chose to override his unspoken objections. "We'll take your case, Mr. Helms. I believe the key to securing a favorable ruling is substantiating the active, full life your wife led prior to her illness, then proving she understood the risks the experimental treatment involved at the time it was undertaken. Once we've established these facts, it becomes a matter of convincing the judge or jury that her best interests are better served by the granting of your continued guardianship and pursuing the treatment arranged according to her wishes. We'll move that the injunction be lifted and that you be allowed to travel to England to obtain the necessary drug."

Addie sure made it sound easy, but it would be a hell of a lot more difficult in actuality. Jake turned back around to the window and kept his thoughts to himself.

"How do we do that?" Helms asked.

"By supplying a thorough history of your wife's physical condition and mental attitude prior and subsequent to her illness. We'll show the court, through an array of witnesses and documentation, that your wife wished to live a life that afforded her a degree of quality and dignity even if it encompassed risk. We'll make it clear that what she didn't want, and feared most, was to be condemned to a vegetating existence because of regulative red tape and restrictive legalities. It's a question of individual rights versus societal constraints, of unheard-of medical complications being addressed by out-of-date laws that must be amended to accommodate new needs and ethics. The testimony of this Dr. Patterson you mentioned will be crucial to our case. Do you anticipate any problem in getting him to agree to testify?"

"No. He's been very cooperative through our ordeal. It's just a matter of his schedule. He'll have to fly in from California."

"We'll work it out," Addie said confidently. "Mr. Malone and I will fine-tune our strategy over the next few days, and then the three of us will consult again. I'll call you and set up a time," she concluded, standing.

Mr. Helms collected his coat and hauled himself to his feet. "I have to tell you that I'm worried, Ms. Van Cleve. Roz's future is at stake. Her children aren't going to budge from their position, not even if it means breaking their mother's heart."

Jacob turned from the window and watched—still analyzing the man's motives and manner. He had misgivings, too, and it wasn't just Rozalyn Harcourt Helms's future that concerned him. He was considering Addie's and his own. Did he really want to get involved in this mess? God knew he had troubles enough. But now that Addie had committed herself, how could he refuse to assist her with the biggest case of her career?

"Please try not to worry, Mr. Helms. We'll present a good argument in your behalf. I'm confident in the outcome," Addie assured the client.

At least one of them was confident, Jacob thought as he walked over to Helms and extended a hand. "We'll be in touch soon," he promised.

"Yes, well, I'd better get back to Roz. It upsets her when I leave her with somebody else." Helms seemed unaware of repeating himself. His opening and exit lines were identical. Giving first Jacob's, then Addie's hand a pump, he practically sprinted out of the room.

Addie felt Jacob's burning gaze before she met it. "What?" she asked, casting him a quizzical look.

"I'm wondering if you're just reckless or plain crazy," he said matter-of-factly.

"It's a challenging case." She plopped back down in the chair and nonchalantly crossed her legs.

"It's a killer case, and Mrs. Helms isn't going to be the only victim when all's said and done." He raked his fingers through the front of his hair, then began to pace off the head of steam that had been building steadily.

"So what are you saying? That we're junior leaguers compared to Lange and Litton?" Addie's chin jutted a fraction.

"To put it bluntly, yes," he answered without hesitation.

Addie's head twisted from side to side as he wore out the carpet in front of the desk.

"We're talking about a pair of sharks here, sweetheart. The theory of your argument might impress Mr. Helms, but it isn't going to mean diddly squat to L and L. They're going to rip you to pieces in that courtroom."

She caught the key word in his rantings. He'd said *you,* not *us.* "And where do you intend to be while the feeding frenzy takes place?"

He stopped pacing. Addie noted that he avoided making direct eye contact with her. "You forget our arrangement. I told you last night that I wasn't signing on to sit second chair—I was only going to give you the benefit of an opinion." He rubbed the back of his neck and expelled a sigh. "If you'd bothered to ask me, I'd have advised you to pass on this case."

She said nothing. The only sound in the room was a crisp swish of silk when she rose from the chair. His gaze followed her as she crossed the room and confiscated his spot at the window. She just stood there with her arms folded across her chest, staring at the Boston skyline.

"Say something." Jake took in the rigid stance.

"I'm disappointed, but I understand," she said frostily.

He felt self-conscious for some reason. "It isn't just that it's a tough issue, Addie, or the fact that you're too green and I'm too rusty. It's this gut feeling I have that Helms isn't being up-front with us. Something tells me there's more to the rift between him and the Harcourt kids."

She spun around and pinned him with a look. "Like what?"

"I don't know exactly. Who do you suppose controls the Harcourt fortune?"

She shrugged. "Is it important?"

"Yeah, I think so. You can bet it'll become significant during the course of the hearing," he warned her.

She mulled over his point for a second, then replied, "You're right. It's an avenue I should've explored before committing." A slow smile spread across her lips. "Look, Jake, I admit that I allowed my ego to cloud my judgment. Maybe I agreed to represent Helms too quickly, but I happen to believe in the right to choose one's fate, so long as a person is capable of making a rational decision.

"Put yourself in Rozalyn Helms's place. Would you want someone else deciding how you should live out the final chapter of your life? Did it ever occur to you that Rozalyn Helms wanted to derive something meaningful out of her tragedy? Her part in the research program might contribute to a breakthrough, or at the very least supply needed information. She made

He didn't answer her straightaway. His heart and his mind were divided about how to respond. His sensible, safe self could think of many reasons not to get involved. There was only one argument to the contrary—loyalty to a friend and colleague. As much as he would have liked to decline, he couldn't. He just couldn't.

"Okay, Addie," he relented.

"You mean it!" she yelped, springing from her perch on the edge of the desk and flinging her arms around his neck. Her momentum almost sent the chair toppling backward. "Thanks, Jake. I knew you'd come through for me." She planted a smacking kiss on his cheek before releasing him. Straightening her jacket and hair, she flashed him a big grin. "It'll be like old times."

"Yeah, almost," he answered as he came to his feet.

"Almost?" Addie didn't understand the remark.

"This time it's you in the driver's seat. I'm only along for the ride," he clarified.

"The switch doesn't bother you, does it, Jake?" She wanted to be sure he was comfortable with the arrangement.

"Hell, no. I can't take the pressure anymore," he kidded.

After all that he had been through lately, and especially considering the strange phone call she'd received from him the night before, Addie wondered if maybe the statement was truer than he realized. She tried to look amused. "Let's grab a bite to eat and hash over strategy. I'll buy."

"You bought last time. It's my turn. Besides, you forgot to quote a figure to Helms. I wouldn't spend that huge retainer fee you plan to stick him with just yet. He might not be able to afford you."

"Give me a break," she scoffed, smiling for real as she walked out of the room first. "We're talking Harcourt money. I think he's good for it."

Jacob wasn't as sure. Exactly who controlled the Harcourt fortune was one of the troublesome facets of the case he intended to investigate further. Collecting his coat, he followed Addie's lead. It felt funny to him—bringing up the rear. Back in the good old days, it had been the other way around.

MACKEY TAGGED ALONG behind the pair. For a change, he wasn't hungry. He was too stressed-out to think about food. The guardian angel had hoped Malone wouldn't get involved with the case for one reason and one reason only. His participation meant that Malone would also become more involved with the blond sheila. That was something Mackey wanted about as much as a toothache or, worse yet, another tour of duty on Earth.

"No good can come of it," he grumbled to himself. The way he saw it, Jake and Addie combining forces meant trouble. He was doing his best to keep things in check, but right about now he could use a little help from his heavenly mates. If they didn't get it together pretty soon up above, things were going to fall apart in a hurry down below.

CHAPTER ELEVEN

TEN DAYS PRIOR to trial time, the bottom fell out in the Helms case. All the many hours of preparation were nullified in the space of time it took to conduct a three-minute long-distance phone call. It was late afternoon when Addie was hit with the devastating news. Her key witness, the doctor who headed up the California test program of which Rozalyn Harcourt Helms had been a part, had been involved in an auto accident. Dr. Patterson was in traction in a San Francisco hospital, and he wasn't allowed bathroom privileges let alone a travel pass. Possibly in a couple of months he could withstand the trip, his wife had said. Definitely not any time soon.

A frantic Addie had pushed for a videotaped deposition. It could be done at bedside, she'd suggested. She'd make all the arrangements and try to minimize the inconvenience. That idea was a no-go, too, since it seemed that in the course of the collision Dr. Patterson's jaw had been shattered. According to his wife, he was literally wired from ear to ear.

Out of options, Addie had but one last card to play—to push for a postponement. After sending Dr. Patterson her best wishes for a speedy recovery, she immediately filed a plea, citing Dr. Patterson's un-availability and requesting a later trial date.

It took several days for Addie to receive a ruling. Her motion for an extension was denied by the court. *Harcourt v. Helms* would remain on the docket. Ready or not, the court would hear arguments on the issue of guardianship six days hence.

Addie had not told Jake about the calamitous development. She'd banked on Judge McCallahan's granting of her motion. She'd presented good cause and felt reasonably certain of getting the necessary extension. Why upset Jake needlessly? she'd rationalized. In truth, she just wanted to avoid having to hear what she knew; he'd be sure to point out what he'd said in the beginning. The case was trouble, and if she had listened to him in the first place, she wouldn't be swallowing antacid tablets by the handful now.

As she sat in her office and stared at the notice of denial, she suffered a return of the stomach spasms that used to plague her before she'd discovered the therapeutic benefits of stress-management tapes. Unthinkingly she reverted to old habits and reached for her trusty roll of antacid tablets. It was definitely a half-a-package-at-once moment. Next, she reached for her pack of cigarettes.

Slinging aside the card in disgust, she picked up the phone and started to dial Jake's apartment number. "He's not there," she muttered, slamming down the receiver. "I'm sure he's wife-sitting." She lit up a smoke.

Flicking back the blond hair that draped over her eyes, she reconsidered how to approach the problem of breaking the bad news to Jake. "In person would be better," she mumbled aloud. "Mustn't just spring it on him. No, handle it right, Addie," she coached herself. "Let him unwind first. Stop by his place later and then drop the bomb." She puffed away.

The mere thought of telling him about the kink in their trial strategy made her wince. What if he backed out on her? He wouldn't, she told herself. He did once before, a voice inside her head reminded her. But that was different, her reasonable self argued. He was in love back then. Desirée had cast her spell over him. Jake had changed after getting involved with her. He'd left Boston a successful, levelheaded, carefree bachelor. Then zap, bam, alakazaam! He started making totally out-of-character decisions—like giving up a partnership in a lucrative law practice and choosing a mousy little shopkeeper for a wife.

Addie's first contact with Desirée had left a lasting impression. Initially she hadn't thought too much about Jake's sabbatical in Marblehead, but when he kept delaying his return to Boston and spouting non-sense about redirecting his purpose and energies, she'd made a weekend trip to the seaside resort town to check it out. Once inside the place where he temporarily re-sided, it took her all of two minutes to form a negative opinion of both his lodgings and his landlady. The woman was in the bell, book and candle business, for chrissake. Weird stuff. She'd tried to warn him—tried to get him to see that he was wading into something way over his head—but Jake was already bewitched by Desirée and refused to come away. He wasn't the type to fall head over heels. Even more baffling was the object of his obsession. Desirée was such a strange little creature. He could have done so much better than wasting his life in a fishing village. And all because of a woman with whom he shared nothing in common. Oh, there was Megan, of course, but what else, actually?

Addie ground out the cigarette in the ashtray and gazed thoughtfully into space. The case wasn't uppermost in her mind any longer. She'd gotten sidetracked. In the middle of a crisis, Adeline Van Cleve was suddenly daydreaming. She couldn't help herself. Her mind skipped over the past couple of years. For a wonderful few minutes, things were as she wanted them to be—as they should have been. It was just her and Jake, just the way it used to be. No Desirée. No marriage. Malone and Van Cleve, picking up where they left off—only with one minor alteration. Her version of the continuing saga of Jake and Addie included plenty of steamy romance. She knew it was foolish, even unseemly, for her to be contemplating the outcome of a tryst rather than a trial, but that was the best part about daydreams—nobody but the daydreamer knew how foolish or unseemly they might be.

JAKE HAD NOT HAD a good day. In fact, as far as bad days went, it ranked second only to the fateful date of

Desirée's accident. First he'd been awakened from a
rare good night's sleep by a predawn phone call from
a colleague at the ACLU offices. The guy had inherited one of Jake's long-pending cases. Interpretation of
a lower court opinion was at stake. ACLU was seeking
a reversal on the grounds that the ruling was discrimi-
natory in nature, and the issue was to be argued before
the State Supreme Court in less than thirty-six hours.
Hodges had been up all night going over the brief and
wanted to confer about every detail while it was fresh
in his mind. It didn't matter to him that it was an inconvenient time or that they could have conferred on
the matter days, weeks or months ago.

Hodges was one of those down-to-the-wire types
who put everything off until the last possible moment.
He actually got a boost from the pressure. Jacob had
known a score of his sort back in law school—the ones
who claimed that cramming before finals psyched them
up for the big test in the same way that pep rallies
psyched up the jocks for a big game. He didn't particularly care for Hodges's methods, but the issue was an
important one and he'd already invested a lot of hard
work in the case. So, for two tedious hours, he talked
him through the ins and outs of the pending hearing.

He'd no sooner gotten rid of Hodges than his mother
called to tell him that they'd decided to stay in the
Florida sunshine a while longer. Jacob missed Megan
terribly and was upset by the change in plans. He suggested that they put Megan on a flight back to Boston,
but his mother wouldn't hear of it.

"She's only two years old, Jacob. I can't believe you would entrust that precious baby into the care of strangers. For that matter, I don't know why you are so insistent about bringing her back. I know it's hard, dear, but it's so much better for Megan this way. She's well looked after and happy as a lark here in Florida with us. But if you just want her with you . . . well, I suppose we can cancel the rest of our plans and head back early. Your father will be disappointed, but he'll get over it. It's Megan who's going to be broken-hearted. We promised to take her to one of those places where the children can play with the dolphins."

His mother had always been so good at laying a guilt trip on him. "Okay, mother. You win. She can stay a while longer. Now, can I at least talk to my daughter?"

"Why, of course, dear. She's right here. Hold on."

By the time he hung up from Megan, he felt like crawling back into bed and pulling the covers over his head. It had been wonderful to hear her sweet voice, but it made him all the more conscious of his almost unbearable loneliness. One day merely stretched into another. He got up alone and went to bed alone. The hours in between, he worried alone. Keeping constant company with himself was monotonous. Each day he felt a bit more isolated, a little less stimulated, increasingly depressed. The only things that gave his life purpose were his daily visits to St. Anthony's or the times when he and Addie got together to brainstorm about the Helms case. Not exactly a charmed life. Not even close. He missed the love and laughter of his yester-days. He missed Megan. Most of all, he missed Desi-rée.

Jacob tried to shake off the blues, but it seemed nothing went right that day. In the middle of his shower, the temperamental hot-water pipes quit work-ing. By the time he had toweled off, purple epithets spewed from his purple lips. Things went from bad to worse—from a frigid shower to a dead car battery. He lost track of the cars that went by before someone stopped to give him a jump.

The garage mechanic said he'd have the new battery installed in a jiffy. A jiffy turned out to be two and half hours later because of a clogged fuel line. Jacob passed the one hundred and fifty-odd minutes in a drafty side room, planted on a miserably uncomfortable plastic chair, cooped up with a harebrained woman and her yipping, hairless chihuahua.

By the time he arrived at St. Anthony's, his nerves were really frayed. When he entered Desirée's room and was confronted by an empty, freshly made bed, his entire body froze. He couldn't move or speak. His eyes stayed fixed on the vacant spot where his wife should be. Even though he had navigated on autopilot, he was positive he had the right room.

In the first split second, he didn't know what to make of it. *No trace of Desirée! All of her personal items had been removed. What the hell was going on?* Then the full implication of her missing person really struck him. *Oh, God, no. It can't be!*

Through sheer willpower, he finally forced his paralyzed legs to move. Backing out the door into the hall, he looked around helplessly. "Nurse! Somebody! Anybody!" The bellow erupted from a hollow cavity deep in his chest.

A stunned aide stuck her frizzy head out of the next room. "What is it, Mr. Malone?"

His head snapped around in the direction of the voice. "My wife isn't in her room. What's wrong? Where is she?"

Alerted by the commotion, the shift supervisor hurriedly made her way down the hall.

The aide stepped from the doorway and attempted to put a calming hand on his arm. "Please, Mr. Malone. You're upsetting the other patients."

He thrust her off with a violent jerk of his arm. "I don't care about them. I want to know about my wife." His shouts boomed through the quiet corridor.

"I'm trying to tell you..." At a tap on her shoulder, the intimidated aide gladly stepped aside and let her supervisor take over.

"It's all right, Mr. Malone," the even-mannered woman told him.

"The hell it is!" he exploded.

The wild look in his eyes caused the supervisor to retreat a step. She bumped into the aide, who in turn bumped into the wall. "Go back to your duties, Miss Olson. I'll handle this."

"You'll handle what?" The last fraction of control Jacob possessed snapped completely. His large hand lashed out and clamped the supervisor's upper arm. He snatched her to him with such force that a section of her pinned-up hair came tumbling down.

Alarmed by his roughness, the aide skittered off to summon security.

The supervisor remained unruffled. "You've jumped to the wrong conclusion, Mr. Malone. We merely changed your wife's room. If you'll take a deep breath and release my arm, I'll take you to her."

It took a second for her words to register, and another for Jacob's fingers to unlock from around her starched sleeve. His stare penetrated like a laser beam. "You switched her room?" he repeated numbly.

"Yes, we transferred her this morning. A private room in the new wing came open and, since that was your preference, we didn't think you'd object. Usually we advise the family of such moves, but your line was busy most of the morning. I was hoping to catch you when you came in. I'm sorry to have upset you. I can imagine what must have gone through your mind."

Jacob melted into the wall behind him. His body felt like a mass of quivering jelly. He tried to respond, but nothing came out. He wanted to tell her that there was no way in hell she could relate to the blood-chilling dread, the sense of utter helplessness or the awful, petrifying feeling that you had to face the days, months and years ahead without the one you loved. It was something everyone said: "I can imagine." It was an asinine cliché.

The supervisor spied the security officer out of the corner of her eye and held up a staying hand. Mr. Malone had been put through quite enough. She wanted to stabilize the situation, not aggravate it. "Why don't you come into the lounge and sit for a moment? A glass of juice might help ward off the shock."

A stiff drink sounded a lot better. "I just want to see my wife," he finally got out.

The supervisor did not press the point. "Certainly. I'll show you the way." Repinning the fallen section of hair, she led him to his wife. It was a shaken, drained, shell of a man that followed the neat, composed supervisor through the new east wing.

JACOB STAYED longer than usual at the rehab center. The routine of his daily visits to his wife had a deceiving effect. The more time that passed without any change, the more normal abnormal became and the less he thought about the good or bad alternatives. But the shock Jacob had been dealt that day drove home the uncertainty that always hovered near. Mostly he'd learned to live with Desirée's comatose state by balancing hope with acceptance. He'd come to think in terms of two possibilities: Desirée's getting better or Desirée's remaining the same. In the process, he'd blocked out a third possibility: Desirée's physically ceasing to exist. Today the third possibility became very real for him. He could hardly bring himself to leave her for the night.

When he finally returned to his apartment and found Addie perched on the second-floor landing, it didn't even faze him. There was nothing in her manner or perky "Hiya" that forewarned him.

"What's up?" he asked as he let the two of them into the apartment.

Addie held up a brown paper bag for his inspection. "They were having a two-for-one special at Changs. In this goody sack are two cartons of Hunan shrimp, two bottles of Sing Tau and a couple of lucky fortunes." She breezed past him, placing the bag on the coffee table and proceeding into the kitchen in search of plates and silverware.

Jacob shut the door and threw his coat over a chair without comment. He couldn't help but compare Addie's appearance to his own when she came back into the room. She looked fresh and relaxed. She wore stone-washed jeans, one of those oversize, hand-painted sweatshirts that cost a mint, matching socks and a pair of hundred-dollar, preppy tennies. Her hair was pulled up on the sides and secured with an ivory hair clip. She was all smiles, and the only darkness around her eyes came from cosmetics, not from lack of sleep.

Jacob didn't need a mirror to know he looked twice her age. His clothes were rumpled, his hair mussed and he was sporting a heavy five-o'clock shadow, as well as several newly formed crinkles at the corners of his eyes. If they had used-car lots for humans, he'd be parked in the section for mile-aged junkers.

"Come dig in." Addie plopped down on the couch and started scooping the shrimp out of the cartons onto the plates. "It smells good, huh?"

Actually the aroma was halfway inviting. He settled on the couch beside her and nodded.

She passed him the bottles of beer. "I can never get these easy-twist-off caps to cooperate. Do the honors."

He managed the feat and handed one back to her. They both took a long swig before tasting the shrimp dish.

"Not bad," she said. As a take-out connoisseur, Addie had definite standards and a rating system all her own.

Jacob hadn't realized how hungry he was. "It's a definite improvement over what I would've been eating if you hadn't come by. I haven't been to the store in weeks," he told her in between bites. "I'm down to a can of chili, half a package of Oreos and a bottle of cream soda."

"You should take better care of yourself, Jake." Addie slanted him a worried look.

He shrugged off her concern. "I'm doing okay," he lied. "I'm just not a shopper. Desirée took care of house things. Before we married, I had a maid."

"Maybe you should consider hiring one again," she suggested.

He nixed the idea with a firm shake of his head. "I'm getting by on my own."

"Whatever." Addie dropped the subject and handed Jacob one of the two fortune cookies. "Let's see what's in store for you and me."

Jacob passed on the fortune cookie. "Have mine, too. I'll just finish my beer."

"Chicken," Addie teased, cracking her cookie open and pulling out the small slip of paper.

"Don't tell me. Let me guess." Jake closed his eyes as he contemplated her fate. "It's an old Chinese proverb. It says, 'Life is a sweet-and-sour tradeoff.'"

"What's that supposed to mean?" Addie gazed at him quizzically.

He polished off the last of the beer and set the bottle down on the table. "It means that while I appreciate the dinner, I suspect there's another reason you came by. What is it, Addie?" He leaned back against the cushions and studied her.

"I hate it when you're smug." She munched on the cookie, wishing she were crunching antacid tablets instead.

"You hate it when I'm right," he corrected her.

"That, too," she grunted, swallowing the fortune cookie and washing it down with a gulp of beer.

"Are you going to tell me what this is all about or am I supposed to guess?" He wondered why he was pushing it. Another crisis to deal with was the last thing he wanted.

"Oh, all right," Addie conceded, sighing. "First I want to explain that I thought I had taken care of the problem myself. That's why I didn't tell you right away."

"Just spit it out," he said impatiently.

"Dr. Patterson can't appear for us. He's in traction in a hospital in San Francisco. He can't even give a deposition because his mouth's wired shut."

The bad news elicited no visible reaction from Jacob. He didn't even blink. He just sat there with a fixed, blank stare. Addie had no way of knowing that hers was but one more in a series of blows he'd taken on the chin today. She was baffled by his passiveness.

"I filed for a reset right away. I got word today that it was denied. What do we do, Jake? I'm all out of ideas."

He didn't answer her. He was wondering how much worse it could get. His next thought was truly scary. There was one area of his life as yet untouched by sorrow or setback—the most vulnerable part of him— Megan.

"Did you hear me? We're up the proverbial creek without a paddle, my friend." Addie was beginning to get peeved in the face of his apparent apathy.

Jake's expression hardened. "I don't have a solution in my back pocket." His eyes locked with hers. They held no hope of a quick fix. "The case was iffy to begin with, Addie. Without Patterson we're shooting blanks. You have to go with what you've got. Run a bluff and pray that Judge McCallahan is sympathetic to Helms." Listlessly he let his head fall back against the cushion. He closed his eyes and rubbed his forehead in a feeble attempt to arrest the awful ache pulsing behind his eyelids.

It was evident to Addie that he was wiped out. Poor Jake, she thought. Everybody demanding a piece of him, including me. "Rough day, huh?"

"Yeah. You could say that." He didn't elaborate or open his eyes.

She eased off the couch and came to stand behind him. "I'll bet you didn't know that I've got magic fingers. Let me have a try." She removed his hands and replaced them with her own.

He discovered that Addie possessed a hidden talent. Exerting just the right amount of pressure, she worked her fingers into his scalp and began massaging his temples with her thumbs.

Her hands were strong and soothing. After a few quiet minutes, Jacob could feel a difference. The ache behind his eyes had subsided a bit. "When did you become such an accomplished masseuse?"

"Shut up and make your mind a blank," she ordered, sliding her hands to the juncture of his neck and shoulders. She rolled the knotted muscle mass between her fingers. Forward and back, backward and forward, like the flow and ebb of the sea over the shore. It felt fantastic. It felt familiar. It felt so damn good to experience a woman's touch.

Jacob sighed and gave himself over to the sensation of small, soft, soothing hands traveling over him. For the most part, he'd complied with Addie's instructions and succeeded in putting everything else from his mind. Not completely, though, for there was a tiny corner of his subconscious where Desirée dwelled. It was Addie who provided the hands-on therapy, but it was Desirée who was his source of comfort. It was his wife's beautiful face that he visualized, her lilting laugh that he heard in his mind, her sensuality that he responded to.

Beneath her fingertips, Addie could feel him relax. He'd become limp and pliable—a substance without form or will—clay in the hands of the potter. She had not meant for that to happen. It was not a deliberate ploy on her part. Yet an opportunity she had longed for—imagined so many times—had literally fallen into her hands.

"Put your head back against the cushions, and I'll rub your forehead again," she offered.

He did as she told him.

As Addie gazed down into his swarthy face, her heart beat faster and faster. In stark contrast, the tips of her fingers moved methodically across his forehead—back and forth, again and again, over and over—smoothing away the deep furrow between his brows. Involuntarily her eyes were drawn to his lips. What would it be like to kiss him? she wondered. Only inches separated her mouth from his. It would be so easy. His body language said he was needy. Only an insensitive fool or a nun could miss the signals. Was this the right moment to make him aware of the strong feelings she held for him, to let him know that his solitude could be amended with just the slightest display of encouragement on his part?

"Better?" Her voice was husky—the result of collective hormones zipping through her system, she was sure.

"Mmm, much." He did not open his eyes or give any indication that he wanted her to stop what she was doing.

Dare she try it? What if he rejected her again? Maybe it would be better to curb her desire and wait it out. Her cautious side urged restraint, but her secret passion proved too strong. In spite of the risk, she decided to test the bounds of their relationship. Her hands stilled as she bent her head to his.

ALISTAIR MACKEY, who had been watching the scene unfold, could no longer stand by and let the situation play out to its carnal conclusion. He had to make an on-the-spot decision. Going against the most cardinal Cosmic rule, he interfered with the natural order of things and injected himself into Malone's subconscious.

"She's not Desirée," he whispered to his charge. Mackey's warning produced the intended effect. Malone's eyes flew open.

A startled Addie, midway in her own intent, instantly straightened. A medley of emotions played across her face—disappointment, embarrassment, guilt and defiance.

Jacob realized immediately what had nearly transpired. He didn't blame Addie for the awkward situation. It was his fault entirely. He was the one who had allowed things to go too far. He'd used Addie as a substitute, a bridge by which to remain connected to his wife. He had not meant for it to happen, yet an opportunity he had longed for—dreamed of so often—fell into place. It didn't matter if the illusion was not the physical truth. It was a selfish indulgence. He felt only one emotion—disgust.

Jacob sat forward, bracing his elbows on his legs, his forehead in his palms and webbing his fingers into his hair. It was one of the most uncomfortable moments of his life.

More than anything, Addie wished she could think of a clever remark—something that would give them each a convenient out. But she knew, just as he knew, that there was little margin left for subtlety. She came around the couch and sat down beside him. "There was a song I used to like a lot back in my Radcliffe youth. I can remember the tune and some of the words, but for the life of me I can't recall the exact title or who sang it."

He did not look up. He was shriveling up inside and she wanted to play Name That Tune. What was the point?

"Anyway," she went on, "the lines of the song said something about not caring about the right or wrong of it or trying to understand what's all behind it."

"Don't, Addie," he begged, still not able to look her in the eye.

She paid no heed. "I wish I remembered exactly, but the essence of it was that the devil can take my soul tomorrow, but tonight I need a friend," she paraphrased.

Jacob raised his head from his hands and looked her straight in the eyes. There was a mixture of sadness and tenderness within his own. "I do need a friend, Addie. Emotional bonding is fine. Anything beyond that is wrong for both of us." He exhaled heavily. "I remember the song, and using you as a crutch isn't the answer. Don't worry. I've made it through a lot of lonely nights. It's just one more. I'll be okay."

"I don't mind being a substitute," she told him frankly.

"I do mind," he said flatly. "Please, Addie. Let's not say any more. Leave things as they are and go home. My life is complicated enough as it is."

For one brief and rash moment, she considered not honoring his request, but the moment passed. He knew where she stood. If they were ever to be anything more to each other than friends and colleagues, he would have to cross the line. Twice now she had done so, which was perhaps one time too many.

She managed a weak smile. "Well, it would seem that your prediction of what was in store for me was a lot more accurate than the drivel tucked inside my fortune cookie. We do make trade-offs in life. I will see you in court Monday, won't I?'' The question was delivered casually, but the implication was very clear.

"Sure. Nine a.m. sharp," he assured her.

"Good. See if you can come up with an angle over the weekend.'' She retrieved her purse and salvaged what was left of her pride. There was nothing else to say or do, except to make as dignified an exit as possible under the circumstances. "Night, Jake.''

"Is everything square between us, Addie?" he asked as she reached the door.

"I don't have a problem with it," she answered honestly. "But you may. I hope not, but I think it's a very real possibility.'' She left him to ponder her meaning.

Jacob sank back on the couch and stared into space. Though he was utterly exhausted, the mere thought of spending another miserable night within the confines of the Boston apartment had an almost suffocating effect on him. He needed a change. Fresh air to clear the cobwebs out of his brain. A few hours of respite from the worry. Suddenly he was picturing Marblehead, his sailboat *The Mariah* scudding over the open water. He was smelling salt air, reminiscing about the town and dear friends. The attack of homesickness was severe enough to rouse him from his stupor.

What was to stop him from packing up and striking out for Marblehead tonight? Nothing, except for missing his visits with Desirée. Surely if he kept in constant touch with the center, she would be all right for a weekend. Desirée would understand. She'd want him to go.

His decision made, Jacob sprang from the couch and into action. In short order, he was on the road.

Malone wasn't the only one suffering pangs of homesickness. Alistair Mackey was delighted by the turn of events. At last a reprieve from the bloody checkerboard cell. Maybe Marblehead wasn't exactly heaven on earth, but the good mates and home-cooked tucker awaiting them at the end of the journey made it seem almost as divine. Mackey intended to look up Mew-Sinh straightaway. Mostly because Marilyn Estes cooked like a dream, but partly because he actually missed the furry heathen.

Alistair was too excited by the prospect of returning to Marblehead to think much about the impropriety of what he had done. Under no circumstances was an angel to superimpose his or her will over that of their charge. By doing so, Mackey could have altered fate, and such an infraction of the rules could cost him his wings upon his return to the Cosmos. Perhaps it was Malone's destiny to share a life with Adeline Van Cleve. Perhaps it was not. Alistair decided that his intervention had altered the course of only one night, and that would be his argument before the tribunal of his peers that would doubtless be convened.

It was a poor defense for a serious offense. "The weight of one small pebble can be a catalyst for a landslide,'' the Fisherman had often pointed out. Nevertheless, the renegade angel knew he would often reflect on, but never sincerely repent of, his actions that particular night.

CHAPTER TWELVE

IT FELT GOOD to be home. Really good. He was in his own element, among friendly faces and surrounded by familiar objects. Best of all, he was ensconced within his own bed once more. Perhaps it was nothing more than the cozy groove he'd worn in the mattress over the years that provided such a peaceful rest. Perhaps it was the symbolism of the antique marital bed that gave him comfort. Whatever the reason, Jacob forgot about his problems for just a few hours and drifted into a deep and dreamless state.

He had intended to set sail on the bay before sunup. Daybreak came and passed and Jacob continued to snore. It was midmorning before his body clock went off. Even then, he was slow to rise. Instead, he lay quietly, basking in the silence and the pleasing warmth of the sun on his face. His eyes roamed about the cheery room, lighting here and pausing there whenever he spied an article that bore Desirée's special touch. A heavy film of dust had collected on the furnishings during his absence. He remembered how meticulous Desirée was about such things. She'd disapprove of the way he'd let things slide. Some polish and elbow grease would fix it. Later today he would hunt up the cleaning supplies and give the place a quick once-over.

Realizing that his mind was running along a danger-ous track, Jacob flung off the cover and rousted him-self from the bed. It wasn't good to think in terms of Desirée's homecoming, as though it might happen any day. It could be months away, or years, or...

Jacob squelched the thought before it completely formed. Marching into the adjoining bath, he turned on the basin spigots and doused his face with water. The cold splash helped revive his senses. He grabbed a towel and dabbed at his face, then examined his re-flection in the mirror. There was a slight improvement in his appearance. Yesterday the only thing he looked fit for was a human scrap heap. At least today he re-sembled something recyclable. He opened up the med-icine cabinet door and took out his razor and a can of shaving cream.

Closing the door, he gazed unseeingly into the mir-ror as he lathered his face. He shaved automatically, but as he tilted back his head to scrape beneath his chin, he noticed a reflected image hanging from a peg on the back of the bathroom door. As his gaze locked on target, his hand halted midstroke. It was one of those sights that blend with the room and into one's subconscious. Nothing extraordinary. Just a plain old chenille bathrobe resting in its usual spot. Yet the sight of it made his heart miss a beat.

He had bought his wife two other robes in the hope that she might pitch her old standby out, but it had been a gesture in futility. She preferred the one she had, claiming that bathrobes, like husbands, took time to break in. "I love my old robe almost as much as I love my husband. You're both irreplaceable to me," she'd told him. The fine robes stayed in the back of the closet with the price tags still attached. The ancient chenille garment retained its favored status and its rightful spot on the back of the bathroom door.

Jacob took a couple more wipes with the razor, then rinsed and towel-dried his face. There was something compelling about the faded robe, something that made him walk over and take it down from the peg.

As his fingers worked the worn material, he could picture Desirée so clearly, looking exactly as she had on countless other mornings—her kinky curls topsy-turvy, no makeup on her face, a darling smile on her lips and wrapped from neck to ankles in faded chenille.

A dreamy expression came over his face as he raised the garment and buried his face within its soft folds. For a crazy but satisfying moment it was as though the robe became Desirée and she was actually there with him—really, really with him again. There was no distinguishing her from the softness against his skin or the scent of her dusting powder filling his senses. He wanted more than a mere whiff of her. He wanted to be caressed by her—to slip her on like another layer of skin.

In the privacy of his home, behind closed doors, Jacob could act out his desperate yearning. Sliding his arms into the fleecy fabric, he cocooned himself within the precious aura of his wife. To an outsider, it might have appeared to be an irrational expression of grief, but to Jacob it was a natural response to an uncontrollable craving.

"It's you who are irreplaceable," he whispered to his absent love.

Now the image in the medicine cabinet mirror was the reflection of a man's inner struggle. At first glance, it was almost a pathetic sight—a burly fellow garbed in a lady's housecoat, his shoulders slumped and his head bowed. But there was another, more positive essence captured in the silvered glass. A glimmer of hope.

ARCHIE HOOPER had been waging an inner struggle of his own. He'd noticed Jacob's car parked outside the Magic Herb Hut when he'd opened up the shop early that morning. For hours he'd been anxiously keeping watch for signs of life across the street. So far there had been none. The lack of activity at the Malone residence worried the older man. He debated about whether or not to fabricate an excuse to drop in on Jacob. He hated to intrude, but it wasn't like Jacob to stay cooped up inside the house all day.

Archie found it odd. What if Desirée's condition had worsened and Jacob was too devastated to deal with anyone else's shock? Then again, maybe nothing was wrong and he was letting his mind run away with him. Jake might just want a little space and peace. Archie decided to bide his time. He gave himself a noon deadline. If Jake wasn't out and about by then, he'd take a chance on making nuisance of himself and visit his neighbor.

At precisely five minutes before twelve, Jake emerged from the two-story house across the street. Archie was in the process of removing his apron when he spied Jake's tall figure sauntering toward the shop. The old gent breathed a sigh of relief and rushed to put on a fresh pot of coffee.

"Good morning, Arch." Jake appeared to be okay—not terrific, but not awful, either. He shot Archie an abbreviated smile and sat down at the counter.

"How are things?" Archie did his best to behave casually.

"About the same" was all Jake answered.

Archie knew he referred to Desirée. He filled a mug and placed it before him. Pulling over a wooden stool he kept behind the counter, he planted himself on it and leveled a look at Jake. "Are you back for good or just staying the weekend?"

"I have to be in Boston Monday morning. I'm help-ing out my ex-partner on a case," he explained.

"Well, I suppose it's good that you're keeping yourself busy. Less time to worry." It was the proper response to make, yet Archie felt uncomfortable. Ja-cob was going through unimaginable hell, and here he was offering him meaningless drivel.

Both men fell silent and sipped from their mugs.

"Would you like something to go with the coffee?" Arch finally asked.

"Sure. Whatever you pick out is fine," Jake responded, knowing it would please the old man.

Archie scooted off the stool and went to the glass case, selecting a couple of blueberry muffins and putting them on a plate. "These are my favorite. I took them out of the oven not fifteen minutes ago." He scooped up several foil-wrapped pats of butter, put them on the plate and plopped it down in front of him. "That's real butter, not that tasteless, low-cholesterol stuff. I wasn't chintzy on the blueberries, neither. Eat them while they're warm," he said, resuming his position on the stool.

"They smell good," Jake complimented.

"Eh, ya, they are." With a flick of his hand, Arch motioned for him to sample his wares.

Jake buttered one of the muffins and took a bite. "Melts in your mouth. You should franchise the family recipes. I can see it now—a national chain of Archie's Muffin Shops."

Archie beamed. "Too darn much trouble. I'm thinking in terms of retiring, not expanding."

Jacob grinned and changed the subject. "Anything important take place while I was away?"

"Things are about the same around here, too," Arch answered. "Nathan Pritchard has the gout and Calvin Sweeney was ticketed for speeding again. The only excitement to speak of happened about a few weeks back when Patsy's boy, Junior, set off the fire alarm at school. It was quite a commotion. Fire trucks whizzing by and folks running down to the school. Of course, at first Junior denied everything, and Patsy raised nine kinds of hell with the principal. It didn't matter to her that another student had seen him set a trash can ablaze in the boys' rest room. And she said it didn't prove a thing that he was carrying a book of matches in his back pocket. But neither she nor Junior could explain away his blistered fingers. You might say he got caught red-handed."

The old man chuckled. "It seems the boy isn't too adept with matches yet. Patsy had to eat crow and Junior had to make a public confession at assembly and repaint the boys' bathroom. It was a humbling experience for them both." Archie's eyes fairly danced with amusement as he told the story.

Jacob grinned. "Pretty scandalous stuff."

"Eh, ya, it was a hot time in the old town," Arch said dryly.

"Is Nathan feeling better?" Jake polished off the last of the muffins.

"He's not a hundred percent yet, but he feels a whole lot better than Calvin Sweeney. That speeding ticket cost him nearly a hundred bucks and, considering how tight Calvin is, he's probably been sick to his stomach ever since he paid the fine."

Both men burst into laughter.

"So," Archie said between swallows of coffee, "How's Megan?"

"I talked to her yesterday morning. She's having a ball and doesn't seem to miss me at all."

"I'm sure she does," Arch told him, his face suddenly sobering. "And she's not the only one," he added.

Jake's head shot up.

"You're missed in Marblehead," Arch explained, noticing the perplexed look in his eyes. "And I'm not just speaking for myself. People ask about you often. 'Course, there's some folks who say you won't ever be back," he said carefully, choosing to stare into his mug rather than hold Jake's gaze.

"And you're wondering if maybe they're right." Jake wiped his mouth with the napkin and shoved the plate aside.

"Eh, ya," the old man admitted.

"I'm not in Boston because I prefer it. You know why I'm staying there for now." His facial muscles grew taut, and his voice thickened with emotion. "I suppose *some folks* also say that it's a lost cause—that Desirée won't ever be herself again. I'm sure there's plenty of speculation about how long it will be before I give up and move on." He shook his head and smirked ruefully. Though he knew such conjecture was only natural, it seemed callous somehow.

"I've hit a sore spot," Arch surmised.

Jake leaned his elbows on the counter and exhaled. "It's me, not you. I tend to overreact these days. Maybe it bothers me because there's a chance they might be right." He cupped his forehead in his palms and webbed his fingers into the front of his hair. "I can't honestly tell you that I haven't considered the possibility that Desirée may not recover. Deep down I have a fear of us never being a family again. It's possible that Megan and I could end up on our own, that Desirée could spend the rest of her life in a sanatorium—or even die.''

Jake shuddered. ''It's a terrifying prospect—one I try not to think about—but sometimes, no matter how hard I try to block it out, the thought crosses my mind. Every time it does, I feel as if I'm betraying Desirée.'' He looked up into a pair of understanding eyes. ''I haven't told anyone what I just told you. I'm afraid to. It's as if saying it out loud gives it the power to come to be. I know it sounds crazy.'' He unlocked his fingers from his hair and sat straighter on the stool. ''But then again, nothing much makes sense anymore,'' he concluded with a shake of his head.

Archie made no comment for a long moment. He mulled over Jake's remarks while pouring them a refill. Finally he ventured an opinion. ''It's rough, what you're going through, Jake. You're bound to wonder, and you wouldn't be human if you weren't afraid. I don't know any more than you what the outcome will be, but I do know that Desirée would be proud of the way you've held up through it all. She may not be able to tell you, but she's aware of the devotion you've shown her these past months.'' He reached across the counter and patted his shoulder.

The comforting gesture caused Jacob's pent-up frustration to erupt. ''Sometimes I just want to shake her—to keep shouting her name until she wakes up. It's as though she's trapped in a deep, dark pit, and I can't pull her up because she won't reach out to me.''

''Maybe she is reaching out, Jake. Contact doesn't always have to be physical.'' It was plain to Archie that Jacob wasn't catching his drift. ''The Warren women have always possessed a special attunement. The grandmother had it, the mother, Chelsey, had it, and so does Desirée. I don't know if you could call it genetic, exactly. I suppose it's sort of like being gifted— only the gift is passed on from generation to generation. At first I was just as skeptical as your expression tells me you are at this moment. I scoffed at the idea that someone could sense what was physically impossible to know, but through the years the Warren women proved me wrong time and again.''

Archie paused reflectively, and then an odd, almost startled look crossed his face. He gazed past Jacob, trying to sort out the memory. ''I don't know why I haven't made the connection before now,'' he muttered to himself. ''It's such an eerie coincidence. How could I have forgotten something as significant as that?''

Jacob hadn't a clue as to what the old man was talking about. ''Does this have something to do with Desirée?''

He nodded. ''It was back when she was small— about ten or so. It was fall, and Chelsey and I were visiting in her shop. Whenever business was slack, I'd drop by her place and pass the time with her.''

Jacob could have done without the incidental background information, but he didn't interrupt.

"The days were growing shorter, and dusk was beginning to set in. Chelsey kept looking out the window. She said that Desirée was later than usual. It wasn't like her. Chelsey decided to close the shop while we looked for her. We checked the most likely places first, but there wasn't a sign of the child. Though I hadn't been overly concerned at first, I began to grow uneasy when it started to get dark. Chelsey wasn't one to let her emotions show—she seemed strangely calm, in fact. Finally she suggested that we swing by Redd's Pond."

Jacob took a deep breath at the mention of the spot where his wife had nearly died.

Archie was so engrossed in telling the story that he failed to notice Jacob's pallor. "I remember it so clearly now. I don't know how it could've escaped me," he rambled on. "We were walking along, nearing Redd's Pond, when suddenly Chelsey drew up. I'd taken a couple of steps before I'd even realized she wasn't with me anymore. Her eyes were locked on the pond straight ahead, and she wasn't moving a muscle. I must've asked her three or four times what was wrong. She never answered me in so many words. She just walked past me and went down the hill to the edge of the pond. I didn't know what to make of it, so I did the only logical thing and followed her."

Arch gulped down a mouthful of coffee and continued. "Well, her behavior grew even more odd once I caught up with her at the pond. She just stood there, staring out over the water so intensely. I could feel it. Her face was like a mask and she was breathing hard. I asked her what was wrong, but she didn't answer me. I told her we needed to move on before we lost all the light. I thought we should get some help.'' Archie set the mug on the counter, looking at Jake, who was hanging on his every word.

Archie paused a moment longer. ''This is the eerie part,'' he told Jake. ''When Chelsey finally dragged her gaze from the water and looked at me, I saw both relief and pain in her eyes. I didn't understand it even after she explained the reason.''

''Which was?'' Jake prompted.

''Chelsey told me that we had been right in coming to the pond to look for her daughter. Desirée had indeed been there. According to Chelsey, Desirée had been daydreaming and lost track of time. She'd left shortly before we arrived. Chelsey related the facts as matter-of-factly as I'm telling you now. She said the danger had past and that Desirée was safe at home. I wasn't comfortable with her decision to call off the search, but I abided by her wishes. I honestly thought she based her conclusion more on hope than on fact, but when we arrived back at the shop, lo and behold, there was Desirée, just like she claimed.''

''How did she know that?'' Jake interrupted.

''I asked her that very same question.'' Archie picked that particular moment to blow his nose.

Jake marked time by tapping his finger on the counter.

Archie stuffed the hanky into his back pocket. "She never really fully explained it. She just said it was something she sensed. I didn't argue the point at the pond because of the odd mood she was in. And I sure as heck didn't later, because it turned out to be true. Desirée confirmed that she had stopped off at Redd's Pond and did, in fact, lose track of the time. She solemnly promised not to do it again. But it was what Chelsey said as I took my leave that night that has come back to haunt me," he confided. "I don't know how in the world I could have forgotten the conversation. I must be getting senile."

Jake wished to goodness that he'd quit getting sidetracked, but he was not insensitive to the old man's concern. Jake trod carefully while trying to guide him through the memory. "Don't let it throw you, Arch. Hell! I'm half your age and sometimes I can't remember what happened yesterday. Details get hazy after so many years. Don't force it. Just picture the moment and place yourself back in it. Were you and Chelsey alone when this conversation took place?"

"Eh, ya, we were. She'd followed me outside onto the sidewalk to thank me for my help," he recalled. "I told her I was glad everything turned out all right. It was then that she said the strangest thing. It's coming back to me clear as a bell. I remember her exact words. 'This time' was what she said... *'this time'*... and I could tell by her voice that she was troubled. I asked if she was concerned about Desirée not keeping her promise. She had the same queer expression in her eyes as the one she'd had at the edge of the pond. It gave me the shivers.

"'Desirée will not break her promise,' she said. 'At least not intentionally. But Redd's Pond holds danger for her. I know it. I saw it clearly when I looked into the water.'"

As Jacob sat listening to Archie's voice quoting Chelsey's words, he experienced a cold sensation in his solar plexus. The numbness spread to his limbs, engulfed his heart and paralyzed his vocal cords.

"I pressed her to tell me what she thought she saw reflected in the water. 'Desirée's destiny,' she told me. I was stunned and shaken, but that was twenty-odd years back, and I guess it sort of wore off. Time passed, Desirée grew up and the memory of that night faded. Even after Desirée's accident, I didn't make the connection. To tell you the truth, I don't know what dredged up the memory now, except for the fact that we were discussing the different dimensions of awareness."

Jake finally found his tongue. "So are you telling me that Chelsey knew her daughter would one day almost drown in Redd's Pond?"

"It would seem so to me," the old man answered. "I know for certain she sensed the danger and, though she didn't share her vision with me, she said she saw it clearly. I believed her then and I believe it now. Chelsey was not prone to discussing her gift. Not with me or anyone. She never denied it—she just didn't refer to it or display it because of the ridicule and grief it might invite. I think she trusted me more than most, but it still wasn't a subject we talked about much.

"There were other occasions, too, when I believed she had foreknowledge of certain events," Archie went on. "Whenever someone related the details, I could tell by her expression that it wasn't unexpected news to her. If we were alone, I'd sometimes make a remark about her gift, but she never elaborated on why some possess it or how it worked. And she never shared any other premonition with me."

Archie paused and grinned. "Once, though, when me and Nathan were supposed to pitch a game of horseshoes to decide who was the grand champion of Marblehead, I went to Chelsey and asked her about the outcome. I pretty well figured she wouldn't predict a winner, but I was hoping maybe I could read her face. True to form, she wouldn't say which of us would claim the title, but she did give me a wink. That one little wink renewed my confidence. I threw nothing but ringers that day and won the match hands down."

"Congratulations," Jake said absently. He was still in a state of shock from the earlier memory Archie had shared.

Archie noticed his preoccupation and returned to the point he'd been attempting to make. "My intention in telling you all this, Jake, is not to stir up the pain, but to ease it. There are sensitivities beyond our understanding. I truly believe that. Chelsey's gift is only one example. I believe it is possible for Desirée to be aware on some level of your constant devotion to her. I believe it gives her the strength to continue her battle to live. It's not in vain, Jake.''

''I pray you're right.''

''Look at it this way. There's no denying that when two people love each other, there's a physical bond involved. But it's so much more, especially when you stop to consider how much of your time is spent apart from one another. If you added up the hours, it'd amaze you. It could account for as much as half your lives. So what replaces a touch, a look, a smile, a voice during those moments when our senses are deprived of the human experience? What keeps us tied to one another? A state of mind, my friend.

''Love isn't just sharing vows, a bed, a mortgage and the good and bad that comes and goes throughout a lifetime. It's a union of your thoughts, dreams, fears, and energy. It's only one old man's opinion, but I think too many of us think in terms of acts of love instead of exploring the emotion itself. I'm speaking of raw emotion, Jake. The kind that comes straight from the heart is true to itself. It's only when it becomes diluted by our insecurities or polluted by outside influences that things go awry.'' Archie lowered his head and peered at Jake over the rim of his half glasses.

It made Jake uncomfortable. He shifted his weight on the stool and fingered the sugar packets. ''You've certainly given this a lot of thought,'' he said lamely.

''Eh, ya, I have. The question is, have you?''

"Of course," he responded a little too defensively.

Archie donned an indulgent expression. "I'm not judging you, son. I know you love her deeply. All I'm trying to tell you is that no matter how complicated it gets, there's a way to cope. What I'm about to suggest sounds easy, but it's hard to do. Whenever you suffer doubt, you close your eyes and open up your heart. Let those things I mentioned flow from you to her. Commune in spirit, Jake. Trust that she's aware and doing the same. Don't confuse what I'm suggesting with Chelsey's gift. Don't expect psychic visions or an instant miracle. If you do, you'll be disappointed, because what I'm describing isn't anything more than simply having a silent heart-to-heart."

Heart-to-heart. Heart-to-heart. The phrase repeated in his head. There was something familiar about it, yet Jake couldn't place it. Sure, he'd heard the expression before, but the words triggered a reaction in him that implied a deeper significance. "Heart-to-heart," he repeated thoughtfully.

Archie misunderstood. "Eh, ya, you've got the general idea," he said.

Jake didn't bother to correct the misconception. "I've missed our talks, Arch," he said sincerely.

"Me, too." Archie started to pick up his mug with the intention of refilling it.

"I've had plenty for now," Jake told him, reaching into his back pocket for his wallet.

"It's on the house," Archie insisted.

"Thanks, but I really have to go." Standing, he extended his hand over the counter and smiled into the kind eyes of the first acquaintance he'd made in Marblehead. "I'll be back, Arch," he assured him. "One day soon, we'll all be back—Desirée, Megan and me."

Archie gripped his hand tightly. His voice broke under the strain of the moment. "I'll keep an eye on the house across the street until you do," he pledged.

"Yeah, you do that." Quickly squeezing the older man's hand, Jake exited the shop. He didn't dare look back, for he knew if he did that he'd find Arch stationed at the window, his eyes watery. There was a miserable weightiness in his own chest. Goodbyes were never easy. It was even harder under a cloud of uncertainty. Would things ever again be as they were? Fixing his gaze on the path that led to the place where *The Mariah* was moored, he walked on.

IN THE LATE AFTERNOON, Jacob sailed the bay. At first the wind was gusty and the waters choppy, but he didn't mind. *The Mariah* was fit and he enjoyed the challenge. He gave her more sail and sped through the white-foamed waves. For an hour or so, he didn't think about anything in particular. He lifted his face into the salt spray and let the wind blow the cobwebs from his mind. As a copper sun dipped lower on the horizon, the gusts died down and the shimmering bay became as smooth as a sheet of glass.

Fascinated by the stillness, Jacob piloted the boat to a serene inlet and dropped anchor. He sat listening to

the rhythmic lapping of water against the hull of the
boat and gazing at the picturesque shoreline. It was
hard to imagine trouble and stress in such a peaceful
setting. By coming to Marblehead he'd distanced himself from the pressures of Boston. But out here he'd
also succeeded in distancing himself from worldly pain.
Out here, there was only a fuchsia sky, fresh air, white
gulls, emerald water and God.

Jacob leaned his head back against the rigging and
breathed deeply. He closed his eyes for a moment and
attuned himself with the buoyant movement of *The
Mariah*. The gentle rocking motion soothed his soul.
He allowed his thoughts to drift. He thought of faces
and places. He thought in fact and in abstract. And
while in that state, somewhere between waking and
sleeping, he realized when he had heard the heart-to-
heart analogy before. It had been in a dream during
one of those subconscious flights into a star-studded
never-never land with Desirée. The dream had disturbed him so much that he'd buried the memory, but
now the details of it flooded his mind.

*... I want to sustain you ... a gift ... the memory is
knowing ... for as long as you want or require it.*

Then she had placed her fingertips at his temple and
her other hand on his heart. *From my mind to your
mind. From my heart to your heart,* she had said.

"From my mind to your mind. From my heart to
your heart," he whispered. "From my mind to your
mind. From my heart to your heart," he repeated,

shutting his eyes even tighter as he concentrated with all his might. "Come on, sweetheart. Do it again."

Nothing happened.

He tried one more time. "Please, Desirée. I think I'm slowly going mad. From my mind to your mind," he willed. "From my heart to . . ."

Just as in the dream, a charge of energy passed through him. Only this time he knew the source. It was the spirit of Desirée's love that coursed through his body like white lightning, leaving him dazed but renewed. The cold spot in his solar plexus was gone. His heart felt light. He no longer hurt inside.

When he'd set sail, the most he'd expected to derive from the outing was a few stolen hours to commune with nature—a chance to collect his thoughts and gather strength. Instead, he underwent the most incredible experience of his entire life.

Trust me, Jacob. Desirée's words echoed in his head. *I know things you do not.*

But what things did she know? If only she could tell him what was in store for them. Her contact had to have been a good sign, but what did it all mean? She'd given him so few clues.

"Dammit, Desirée! Dreams and double-talk." With a deep sigh, he got to his feet and made ready to pilot *The Mariah* in to shore.

On the way back to port, Jacob found himself playing mind games, wishing for another sign, some small indication that the contact really had meant something positive. Just as he reached the slip, he saw it—or at least that was how he chose to interpret the shooting star that blazed across the twilight sky. It was a much heartened man who returned to Boston the following evening.

Chelsey may have believed she saw her daughter's final destiny when gazing into Redd's Pond, but Jacob would never accept that. Perhaps she glimpsed a part, but not the whole. No way was Desirée lost to him forever. *No damn way.*

CHAPTER THIRTEEN

JACOB DID NOT MENTION his experience on the bay to anyone—partly because it was such a personal thing, but also because he didn't want to have to deal with the skepticism such a far-fetched claim would produce. He could imagine the comments: "Poor, Jake. He's finally cracked under the strain. Well, it was bound to happen sooner or later. Maybe with a little rest and a lot of therapy he'll pull out of it. What a shame. Tsk, tsk." He especially did not want to confide in Addie. So far, she'd been humoring him, but if she thought for one second he honestly believed he'd achieved spiritual contact with his wife, she'd draw up commitment papers.

As it turned out, they did not have an opportunity to discuss much of anything before the hearing. He got held up in a major traffic jam and only made it to court a few minutes before the session was due to start.

By the time he arrived, Addie was slurping water from a drinking fountain outside the 108th and attempting to choke down three headache tablets. She was not in a good humor. "Dammit, Jake! I've been worried sick. Where have you been?"

She was undone in more ways than one. Besides having the jitters and being royally miffed, she'd missed fastening the center button on her blouse. It was the first thing he noticed when she lifted her head from the porcelain bowl.

"You know what a stickler McCallahan is about beginning on time," she fussed.

"How does he feel about attorneys exposing themselves in his courtroom?" he teased.

"What?" Her mouth, like her blouse, gaped open.

"Check your blouse, Addie," he suggested. "I know you want to make an impression, but..."

"Not funny, Jake," she snapped back. In one nimble motion, she buttoned up and reclaimed her attaché case from off the bench. "I hope you're half as clever in court. Come on, everyone else is already inside."

Her sarcasm didn't faze him. He was accustomed to it. Addie always got feisty before a trial. He merely smiled to himself and followed her lead through the giant oak doors.

Louis Lange, the opposing counsel, was already seated at one of the two tables at the front of the courtroom. Even from the back, he presented an imposing figure. Though he was nearing sixty, he had the physique of a college linebacker. His black suit coat must have been specially tailored to accommodate the massive spread of his shoulders. As they passed his table, Addie's forward momentum abruptly stopped. Louis Lange was going over his notes and unaware of her presence behind him until she tapped him on the shoulder.

Jacob hoped that, unlike him, Lange did not catch the small gasp that escaped her as he turned about in his chair.

"I'm sure you don't remember me," she managed to say.

"I'm sorry. Should I?" he asked smoothly.

"Uh, no. I'm Adeline Van Cleve. We've never really met, but you once spoke to my law class. You were wonderful. Really inspiring," she gushed.

"Well, thank you. I always thought my lectures were dull, but I did enjoy the lively debates that took place afterward. Unfortunately I haven't had an opportunity to visit a campus in years. You'll pardon me for saying so, but you hardly look old enough to have been present at one of my lectures." He had the ability to appear totally focused on the person who addressed him while, in fact, his sharp eyes were taking in everything around him. Without diverting his gaze from Addie, he noted Jacob—and decided that he was the one to take heed of.

To Jacob, Lange's tone and manner seemed patronizing. He might as well have patted Addie on the head. She, however, seemed oblivious to the subtle babe-in-the-woods implication. She just stood there like some moonstruck teenager.

Jacob felt compelled to speak up. "The lady is more seasoned than she looks."

"I'll take care not to underestimate my colleague throughout the hearing," Lange countered, his eyes flitting over Jacob.

Lange had the intonation of the late actor Richard Burton. He, too, was Welsh, and he was every bit as ruggedly good-looking as his countryman. He had a galvanizing effect on Addie. She knew she was acting like a fool, but she couldn't bring herself to move away.

"I look forward to matching wits with you, Ms. Van Cleve." Lange smiled and extended his hand.

Her name sounded like music when he spoke it. "Yes, uh, it should prove interesting," she managed to respond. Her skin actually tingled at his touch.

"Mr. Malone." With a curt nod of his silver-streaked head, Lange returned to studying his notes.

Jacob felt reasonably sure that the old fox had done his homework and probably knew everything about Addie and him—name, class rank and what cereal they usually ate for breakfast.

Jacob nearly collided with Addie, who was still fixed to the same spot. He claimed her attention with a none-too-gentle nudge. She slanted him an annoyed look and moved on to their own table. Otto Helms was already seated. He had dark circles under his eyes, and his leg jiggled worse than ever.

"Good morning." Jacob looked confident as he set his briefcase on the table and clicked open the catches. "Are you feeling uneasy about this?" he asked casually.

Their client shot him a panic-stricken look. "Queasy would be more like it."

"Good," Jacob said matter-of-factly. He continued to unload his papers and did not bother to offer Helms so much as a sympathetic look.

"You think it's good that I might embarrass myself at any minute? I'm not kidding. I think I might throw up." Helms stared at him in disbelief.

Jacob shoved his briefcase aside and sat down beside his client. "Yes, it's good because it means you realize the importance of what is about to transpire here today. I want you to be nervous, Otto." For the first time, he met his client's eyes. "What I don't want is for you to take anything for granted. If you weren't queasy and full of anxiety, I'd be worried. I'd suspect that maybe you weren't as committed to winning this guardianship suit as I am.

"Make no mistake, Otto, I am committed. I'm going to do everything in my power to see to it that no one's interests but your wife's are served by these proceedings. So don't apologize for being scared and half-sick at the thought of the ordeal ahead. If you need to hit the bathroom, just go on. I'll make your excuses to the court. Now, do you have any questions you want to ask me before court convenes?"

Helms smiled weakly. "Just one. Where might the bathrooms be?"

Jake almost laughed out loud. "Down the hall to your left."

"It's not an emergency. I just need to make a quick trip before it starts."

"Sure. But make it fast. The judge is a stickler for punctuality." Jake had aimed his dig at Addie, but she wasn't paying any attention. Instead, she sat gazing off into space.

As soon as their client was out of earshot, Jake leaned over to have a word with her. "What's with you? You haven't said a word to Helms."

"You were doing fine without me. I think you managed to reassure him and prep him for what's ahead."

Since Jacob had left the firm, Addie had developed her own style. Usually she was much more assertive and took charge of every aspect of a case. But not today. Jacob was baffled. Suddenly she'd reverted to being the silent partner again, allowing him to take control. He didn't want the lead. He'd only signed on to sit second chair. Evidently she needed to be reminded of that fact.

"We need to talk, Addie. You've been acting strangely ever since we walked through those doors. First you behaved like an adoring puppy with Lange, then you . . ."

"I most certainly did not," she hissed beneath her breath.

"Okay, maybe not quite that bad, but . . ."

"I respect him. What's wrong with that?"

"Nothing, except you can't let your admiration, if that's really what it is, get in the way of doing your job."

Her blue eyes blazed with indignation. "What is that crack supposed to mean?"

Jacob wished he had left out the snide remark. Things were deteriorating badly. Instead of combining forces to do battle with Lange, they were hacking away at each other. He decided not to press the point. "Okay, I was out of line. I'm just trying to remind you that he's not your idol in here—he's your adversary."

"I'm well aware of that." Her chin lifted a fraction of an inch.

"Great, then we have nothing to worry about." He cast a sideways look at the opposing counsel's table and was surprised to find the Harcourt children seated across from him.

"When did they slip in?"

Addie leaned forward to sneak a peek at the pair. Henry Harcourt, Jr., looked to be about Jake's age. He, too, cut a dashing figure. Although he wasn't as large a man as Louis Lange, he did have an equally distinguished air about him. His sister, however, was very plain. She wore little makeup and a bland ensemble; her hair was pulled straight back into a clip at the nape of her neck. The only thing striking about her was the amber-tinted glasses she wore. Addie was surprised. She'd expected her to be one of those elegant types whose pictures were plastered on the society page every Sunday.

Addie settled back in her seat. All of a sudden, she was hit by the full impact of what she was up against—the legal mastery of Louis Lange combined with the

Harcourt name and influence. She, on the other hand, had no expert witness and no solid evidence to prove that it was Rozalyn Harcourt Helms's wish that she be allowed to continue the experimental treatment.

"Helms isn't the only one feeling shaky." The half-whispered confidence reclaimed Jake's attention. "Maybe you should give me a pep talk, too. God! What have I gotten us into?" She reached for the silver water pitcher, filled one of the glasses and drank down four ounces of water in two gulps.

He wasn't surprised by her reaction. In fact, as far as he was concerned, Addie was running true to form. In spite of the bravura she'd worked so hard to cultivate, she hadn't really changed. Deep down, Addie was a born pessimist. "Keep drinking the water, and maybe you can float your way through this," he said, staying in character, too. Whenever things got tough, she could count on him to be flip.

"Cute, Jake. Are you going to jump in and bail me out if I blow it?" She wasn't kidding.

"Didn't I always?" He winked at her just before Helms took his seat between them.

Helms had barely made it back when the bailiff barked, "Oh, yea, oh, yea! The 108th Civil Court is now in session. The Honorable Judge McCallahan presiding. All rise."

The assemblage came to their feet as Judge James McCallahan whisked through the door of his private chambers and took his place on the bench. "You may be seated," the bailiff announced.

There was the sound of chairs scuffing across the floor and then dead silence.

"Are both sides prepared to present arguments in the cause of *Harcourt versus Helms?*" the elderly justice asked.

"The petitioner is ready, Your Honor." Louis Lange's distinctive voice rang through the courtroom.

Addie stood and cleared her throat. "As is the respondent, Your Honor." Her voice carried only a row or two back into the gallery.

"I can barely hear you, Ms. Van Cleve. In the future, please make your remarks louder." It was well-known that Judge McCallahan wore a hearing device. It was also well established that he hadn't any patience with attorneys who mumbled in his court.

"Yes, Your Honor," she answered, not only raising her voice but exaggerating her words.

"I'm a little hard of hearing, Ms. Van Cleve, not slow." The judge's remark produced a few snickers from the gallery.

"I was only trying to..."

"No explanation is necessary. Let's proceed," the judge rumbled.

Addie sank into her chair and shot Jake a look of despair. He could almost read her thoughts. In a matter of twenty seconds, she'd managed to offend McCallahan and appear more like a court jester than a member of the bar—and she'd done it in front of Louis Lange.

Sensing that Lange was monitoring them, Jacob kept his expression neutral and said nothing to his partner. He merely scribbled a comment on the pad in front of him, tore off the top sheet, folded it and passed it over to Addie.

Addie opened up the folded sheet and glanced at it. "Move in front of the table, keep your head up and talk straight at him. Don't let the old goat rattle you!" She allowed herself a faint smile and discreetly slipped the note into her skirt pocket.

"All right. As I understand it, the Harcourt children have filed an injunction to prevent their mother from leaving the country in order to seek a form of medical treatment currently banned by the Food and Drug Administration. Further, they are asking this court to decide the matter of guardianship over Rozalyn Harcourt Helms, who, in their opinion, is no longer capable of making informed and rational decisions in her own behalf. I want to make certain that these are the facts at issue and make clear that none other will be introduced without my prior knowledge. Does either counsel have any addenda to make at this time?"

"None," Louis Lange answered.

Addie not only stood up, but spoke up. "Not at this time, Your Honor."

"If it is agreeable to both counsels, I'd prefer to dispense with opening remarks, since the issues are well-known to all parties."

Judge McCallahan conducted court according to his own rules, which did not always adhere to the written rules of civil procedure. Addie and Lange could, of course, insist that they be allowed to present opening remarks, but neither did.

"I have no objections to waiving my opening statement, Your Honor," Louis Lange stated for the record. "My clients' position will be fully examined during the course of their testimony."

"A simple yes or no will suffice, Mr. Lange," Judge McCallahan replied.

Louis Lange acknowledged the judge's verbal wrist-slap with a polite smile and a respectful nod.

Addie did not make the same mistake as her colleague. "As you wish, sir," she said clearly.

Judge McCallahan glanced to the court reporter. "Let the record reflect that both counsels have waived opening statements." He looked back to Louis Lange and then over at Jacob. "We are dealing with a sensitive and untested issue. I must be fully informed in order to render a right and compassionate opinion, so I will therefore allow a certain degree of leeway as you present your arguments. I will not, however, allow any testimony that I feel is irrelevant, nor will I allow this issue to be reduced to a mudslinging circus. We are not here to air family grievances. Stick to the issue, gentlemen. After forty years on the bench, I know every trick in the book, and I tell you here and now, if you try to inject immaterial evidence, you will suffer the consequences of my ire. Is that perfectly clear?"

Addie could not believe the gall of the man. How dare he exclude her from his remarks? She quickly scrambled to her feet. "The court's wishes are so noted," she asserted, making it plain by her manner that she also noted the insult.

Louis Lange cast a glance over at the opposing table before responding. It was evident to him that Ms. Van Cleve was not as seasoned as her partner would have him believe. She had yet to master the art of detachment. Judge McCallahan had struck a nerve and she'd winced. "Your Honor's instructions are most clear," he stated evenly.

Judge McCallahan put a finger to his ear, as if to make sure that the hearing device was tucked snugly in place, and then settled back in his chair. "Good. Mr. Lange, call your first witness."

"I call Mr. Henry Talbot Harcourt, Jr."

Henry, Jr., marched up to the witness chair, raised his right hand and repeated the oath the bailiff recited. A low murmur rippled through the gallery of spectators. For most, it was an occasion to remember. The Harcourts were the closest thing to royalty in the Boston area. Though Henry, Jr., would never be elevated to the kingly position his father held in the hearts and minds of Bostonians, he was, at least, a prince and was accorded all the respect due to his station.

Henry, Jr., was well aware of the awe he commanded. It showed in his confident manner. He appeared quite comfortable sitting on display while his attorney waited for the courtroom to quiet down.

Louis Lange finally stood up and began his examination of the witness. "Please state your name for the court," he led off.

"Henry Talbot Harcourt, Jr.," the golden-haired mogul replied.

"And what is your relationship to Rozalyn Harcourt Helms, who is the subject of this hearing today?"

"She's my mother," Harcourt answered.

"You are how old, Mr. Harcourt?" Lange went on.

"I'll be thirty-eight next month."

"And is it not true that your father, now deceased, over his lifetime acquired and developed many holdings which you now oversee?"

"Yes. My father founded Harcourt Communications and had controlling interests in several other companies. I took over as head of all of his enterprises after his death."

"Did these responsibilities just fall upon your shoulders, or was it your father's wish to see you at the helm of his empire?"

Harcourt smiled at the question.

"Someone in my father's position cannot afford to gamble with a fortune, Mr. Lange. He named me as his successor, but he would not have allowed me to assume such an enormous responsibility if he thought for one second that I couldn't manage the task of protecting all his interests. More than likely, he expected me to double them," he added with a disarming boyish grin.

Jake looked amused, but Addie was not entertained. She knew what facts Louis Lange was establishing with his methodical line of questioning, and she also knew he would accomplish his intent.

In the next breath, Lange fired the first shot of the war. "So, Mr. Harcourt, would you agree that it would be reasonable to assume by your father's actions that he trusted your judgment?"

"Yes, I think his will speaks for itself. He trusted my judgment." Harcourt's matter-of-factness was convincing. Who could doubt such self-assurance?

Lange continued to steadily build his case. He came from behind the table, walked over to the empty jurors' box, then turned back toward his witness. "Please describe for the court your relationship with your parents," he prompted.

Harcourt answered without hesitation. "I respected my father, but he was not an easy man to understand or know. He was away a great deal of the time when we were young. It was my mother who raised us and provided the security we needed. I love her very much," he said simply.

Harcourt had replied honestly. His sincerity could not be doubted or the effect of his answer diminished. He was not a resentful rich kid who resorted to parent-bashing as an adult. Louis Lange had hit his mark once again.

Jacob was still unsure about Harcourt's motives for bringing suit. They might not be as pure as he wanted the court to think. There was the possibility that he had not acted solely out of love and concern for his mother. Otto Helms had never said anything derogatory about his stepson; it was just something Jacob sensed. There was more to this standoff than met the eye. Jake had already considered the underlying male rivalry for Rozalyn's affection. That was a given. But even though he couldn't put his finger on it, Jake knew the mistrust between the two men went deeper. He jotted down a reminder to push Helms harder for an answer at the break.

"And it is out of love that you have come before the court to ask its assistance in staying your mother from pursuing a treatment you fear is detrimental to her?"

In spite of what she'd told Jake, Addie couldn't help but be a little in awe of her adversary. Damn, but he was good! He was so smooth and methodical in the way he established fact upon fact, slowly but surely building a solid case. But with each of his courtroom salvos, she was beginning to feel as if a razor-sharp stiletto had been thrust between her ribs. Such a small, yet so deftly inflicted, puncture. Suddenly she pictured countless scenes in movies when the victim looks down at the knife handle planted in his chest and stares with utter disbelief into the eyes of his killer. Meanwhile, the blood drip-drip-drips.

"Yes, I want to stop her from going any further with this craziness. I want her to return to a conventional form of treatment that doesn't put her at risk," the witness stated.

Addie rose to her feet. "We wish to object to Mr. Harcourt's choice of words. Calling the drug therapy Mrs. Helms wishes to continue craziness is only his personal opinion, not a proven fact. I ask that he be cautioned against expressing unqualified conclusions."

Judge McCallahan brought his chair upright. He studied her for a long moment before saying, "There is no jury to be swayed here, Ms. Van Cleve. I don't think it's necessary to weigh our every word. I promise you I remain open-minded in regard to the treatment in question. The only conclusions that count are the ones I draw. Please, let's not quibble over these small points. Your objection is overruled. Continue, Mr. Lange," he ordered.

Quibble over the small points indeed, Addie thought as she sat down. McCallahan's condescending attitude toward her was really beginning to rub her the wrong way. Perhaps she'd made a mistake by not insisting on a jury trial. There was definitely a personality clash between His Honor and herself. It happened occasionally. But not to her—at least until now.

Jacob didn't even try to catch Addie's eye. This was not the time or place to regroup and rethink their strategy. Otto Helms might get the idea that things were going badly. They were, but that wasn't something an attorney told a client within the first thirty minutes of a hearing. Jacob jotted down a note to himself and another to pass to Addie, which simply read, "Stay cool." Then he returned his attention to Harcourt's testimony.

"Could you please tell the court in your own words about the events that led up to these proceedings? Take your time and give us as accurate a picture as you can of the circumstances as you remember them."

Harcourt rearranged himself in the witness chair and drew a deep breath. "Certainly. My mother did not display any symptoms of the disease while my father was alive. She was diagnosed with Alzheimer's disease six years ago, but I believe she suffered the beginnings of it long before she actually went for help. In fact, I recall my mother behaving strangely shortly after re-marrying."

"That's not true," Otto Helms whispered to Jacob. "He knows better. Rozalyn was fine up until a few years ago."

Jacob nodded and made another notation.

"Can you be more specific, Mr. Harcourt?" his attorney asked.

"Yes. My mother was what you would call a quiet person. She liked reading, working in her garden, an occasional concert—that type of thing. Of course, she'd go to certain social affairs, but she didn't gad about town or travel much. After she married Otto, everything changed. Suddenly my mother was taking rumba lessons and hot-air ballooning and taking cruises to anywhere and everywhere. At first I tried to rationalize the change by telling myself that it was natural in light of her new marriage. But after a while I began to notice a total turnaround in her disposition, as well. She no longer could deal with more than one detail at a time. She lost patience easily and had difficulty keeping her emotions in check.''

"What is he talking about?" Helms's leg began to jiggle violently under the table. "Rozalyn was never a shy violet like he's making out. There wasn't any sudden change in her disposition back then. It was a gradual decline," he insisted to Addie.

"It's okay, Otto. Let's see where he's going with it," she counseled him.

"Was your mother normally erratic or short fused?" Lange asked.

"No, just the opposite. It occurred to me that maybe she and Otto were having problems and that was the reason for her strange behaviour. I asked her about it, but she only became more agitated. She said it was none of my affair and told me to mind the Harcourt shop and keep out of her business. I did as she asked, but that didn't appease her, either. She'd call me up and cry and carry on about how cold I was to her. She'd accuse me of deliberately trying to upset her. None of these outbursts were at all like my mother.

"For that matter, neither was the habit she developed of spending money like water. It was hers to spend on what she wished, but it became absurd. She accumulated more debt during that period than during the entire time she was married to my father. She spent thousands upon thousands of dollars on shopping sprees, gambling tables and jaunts to the far corners of the earth.

"It wasn't the money," he insisted, turning and addressing his remarks to Judge McCallahan. "It was the change in her—the up-down mood swings—that caused me concern. I knew something was very wrong with her, but I didn't know exactly what or how to deal with it. Once I did suggest that she see a professional, but it only made matters worse."

"Did you discuss your concerns with her present husband, Otto Helms?" Louis Lange asked.

"I tried to broach the subject with him several times, but he either minimized my concerns or implied that I was merely manufacturing problems. I gave up after a while," he stated with a deep sigh.

"When was it that Mr. Helms realized that you were, in fact, not manufacturing problems and that your mother did indeed have a serious problem?" Louis Lange left his post at the jurors' box and approached the witness.

"Not until a few years ago when my mother's behavior became so confused that he had no choice but to consult a doctor," Harcourt answered. "By then the disease had progressed to the point where she forgot the simplest of things—turning off the stove, letting the water out of the tub, telling time, where she was expected and the why and with whom of the meeting. She knew herself that she was in a bad way. Unlike before, she wanted help."

Louis Lange's forward momentum stopped when he reached the edge of the witness box. He stood at the side, directing his gaze at Helms, not his client. "At that time were you included in the decision process concerning your mother's treatment?"

"At that time, yes," Harcourt responded. "The treatment was pretty standard. Primarily it consisted of periodic testing and daily doses of a natural soya lecithin that can be purchased at any health food store."

"But your mother ultimately sought another form of treatment, did she not?"

"Yes, but I had no knowledge of her consulting another doctor in California and participating in an experimental program until after the fact."

"Did you object when you *did* learn of it?" The distinguished lawyer let his gaze wander over the occupants of the courtroom.

"No, I did not," Henry, Jr., admitted. "I really didn't know very much about the program, except for what my mother and Otto deigned to tell me. I probably should've investigated it more thoroughly, but I was very busy with other matters at the time and I accepted their account of it."

Otto Helms shoved back his chair and folded his arms across his chest. His eyes never strayed from the face of his wealthy and influential stepson. He was confused and angered by Henry, Jr.'s, testimony, but he refrained from making any further comments to his attorneys.

"I want to be clear about who was taking responsibility and making the decisions about your mother's care at this particular time. Please, think before you answer," Louis Lange told his client.

"When they first went to California and opted to participate in the program, I'm sure it was a joint decision, but..."

"By joint decision you refer to your mother and her current husband, Otto Helms," Lange clarified.

"Yes, but I want to finish my explanation if I may." Henry, Jr., was obviously used to being in charge.

"Excuse my interruption," Lange said smoothly. He'd obviously dealt with Henry, Jr., during witness preparation and knew how to handle him when he became difficult.

"I was about to say that because of my mother's condition, she was easily influenced. She listened to Otto, trusted him and wanted to please him. Looking back on it, I now realize that she probably just went along with whatever Otto decided. You have to understand, she is incapable of independent action. Her mind is fuzzy most of the time. She relies on others to guide her through these horrible days."

Otto could no longer contain himself. He jumped to his feet and banged the flat of his hands on the table. "That's totally untrue, H.T., and you damn well know it! Your mother knew what she was doing. She wanted to try the program. She wanted to try anything that offered her a chance."

"Mr. Helms, sit down immediately," Judge Mc-Callahan ordered. "I expect you to conduct yourself properly or I will cite you, sir."

"But, Your Honor, he's not telling you the way it was. Rozalyn and I *did* discuss it. She knew exactly what the treatment entailed and agreed that it was her best option," Helms tried to explain in frustration.

"I said to sit down and be quiet," the judge declared with a bang of his gavel.

Jacob grabbed the back of Helms's coat and yanked him to a seated position. Addie put her hand on his arm. She didn't say what she really felt—that she reveled in his spunk. He'd done what she ached to do—talk back to the judge. She merely reminded him of what was at stake.

"I realize that the issue is an emotional one, Mr. Helms, but I will not tolerate outbursts of that nature in my courtroom. You will have your say, sir, but it will be done in the proper manner and order."

Helms nodded and straightened his suit coat.

"Continue, Mr. Harcourt." Judge McCallahan settled back and dropped his gaze as before. It was hard to tell from the position he assumed whether he was listening thoughtfully or merely catnapping.

"Since that time, I have investigated the program and the drug my mother took and am of the opinion that it is much too experimental to warrant continued use. Otto Helms and I disagree about the benefits versus the risk. I am not willing to put my mother's life in jeopardy in order to gain a few extra months of improved memory skills. What's more, I am beginning to question more than his judgment.''

''What exactly do you mean by that statement, Mr. Harcourt?'' Louis Lange pushed ahead.

''I mean that I also now wonder about his motives,'' Harcourt responded.

Addie could feel Helms's muscles tense underneath her staying hands.

''If my mother was impaired from the days shortly after her marriage to Otto Helms, as I've always suspected was the case, then his unwillingness to acknowledge my concern makes sense only if his intentions were to hide the fact of her illness.'' Harcourt squared his chin and avoided looking at Helms.

Jacob risked a glance at Addie. She was reaching for the water glass again.

''What would he gain by doing that?'' Lange provided the opening Harcourt had wanted all along.

''Access to and control of my mother's money,'' Harcourt accused. ''He's made a hobby out of marrying wealthy women.''

Helms could not sit by and let the accusation go unanswered. Before Jacob or Addie could prevent it, he was shouting back at Henry Harcourt. ''You're twisting everything. You want me out of the picture so you can stick her away. All you've ever cared about was the money, you greedy bastard.''

An excited buzzing stirred through the gallery. Judge McCallahan called again for order in the courtroom and threatened to have it cleared.

Jacob felt that he had to say something in Helms's defense. Addie had her hands full trying to contain their client. He got to his feet and shouted over the bangs of the gavel and the noise from the rear. "With all due respect, Your Honor, my client was provoked by the witness's speculative and inflammatory remarks."

"I am very close to citing this entire courtroom with contempt." The judge's reply caused a hush to fall over the room. "I am going to overlook this incident, but it had better not happen again. These are serious allegations you have made, Mr. Harcourt. You had better be able to substantiate your belief to my satisfaction, or else, sir, you will find yourself answering to me, and I won't be lenient. Do you wish to retract anything you have said?"

"No, Your Honor." Harcourt didn't flinch.

Judge McCallahan could not disguise his irritation. He glared at Louis Lange. "I am going to recess court so that you may have an opportunity to advise your client fully about this line of testimony, Mr. Lange. Court will reconvene at 1 p.m."

The bailiff barely had time to say "All rise" before the black-robed McCallahan disappeared into his private chambers and slammed the door.

Jacob happened to be looking straight at Henry Harcourt, Jr., while everyone else was focused on the judge. He was the only one who caught the satisfied smirk that flickered over his face.

CHAPTER FOURTEEN

ADDIE, JAKE AND OTTO spent the recess in an empty office across the hall from the courtroom. They arranged to have sandwiches and soft drinks sent in, but the food sat untouched in a paper sack. None of them had any appetite.

Addie paced back and forth while Jake and Otto conversed. She was content to let Jacob handle the curve they'd been thrown at the end of the session while she thrashed out her own problem.

"Okay, Otto." Jake tilted back the chair on its hind legs and leveled a look at him. "Let's start by you filling in the blank spaces for me."

Helms drew a deep breath and fiddled with the soft-drink can he held in his hands. "I didn't mention my previous marriage because I didn't think it mattered."

"Obviously it does," Jake pointed out.

Helms concurred with a weary nod. "It's true what he said. I do seem to marry women who are better off than me. But it's not intentional. It just worked out that way," he insisted, glancing nervously at his attorney to see if he was buying his side of the story.

"I need more than your word for it. Give me details, Otto."

"My first wife's name was Lila Richards. We met while I was stationed in Texas. Her family was in ranching and had money, but I only found that out after we'd been dating awhile. From the beginning Lila and I were not right for each other. There were big differences between us. She had a manner that was cute at first, but it got under my skin after a bit. But you know how it goes. I was young and sexually attracted to her. We started sleeping together, and one thing led to another. Before I realized it, we were making wedding plans. Her family was against the match, but Lila threatened to elope if they didn't consent. I wanted to back out but I didn't know how to do it gracefully. We were married in 1959."

Otto took a drink from the can and then continued. "We didn't have a bad marriage—it just wasn't a good one. Lila was a strong-willed woman. The only thing she ever really compromised on was moving to the northeast. I told her I felt I could establish myself better in an area I was comfortable in. So we moved to Boston. I did all right. I got a job at the hardware store where I'd worked before I went into the army and made manager in a few years.

"Lila did better in Boston than me, though. She was bored, and she started giving makeup lessons to the ladies in the neighborhood. The makeup lessons blossomed into a small cosmetic business, and before too long, there were Lila Cosmetic parties all over Boston. Lila knew what it took to look good. She'd had a lot of practice at it, since she'd spent most of her life primping before a mirror. It was a natural talent, you might say. And she made the most of it. She'd found something she was good at, and it gave her a sense of self-worth she'd never had before.

"I was glad for her success, but after a while it only put more strain on our marriage. Lila was never home. Her whole life was that business. She had aspirations of it becoming a multimillion-dollar operation. The funny part is, Lila would try to ease her guilty conscience by sharing the profits. She constantly bought me things—cars, clothes, a membership in an exclusive country club. It was crazy. I didn't play golf, but she didn't even bother to check. I wanted a wife, not a cosmetic queen. I finally told her so, and she told me the quiet life in the suburbs didn't work for her. We just didn't want the same things out of life. So, we ended it while we could still be friends at least."

"A lot of men would have been happy to trade places with you," Jacob remarked.

"I suppose." Otto smiled and shrugged. "Lila is one of a kind. She even bought the damn hardware store and gave it to me as a sort of consolation gift for being so cooperative about the divorce. I guess she secretly feared I might try to ask for part of her business or something. The thought never crossed my mind. I only wanted to correct a mistake we'd made in our youth and do it without creating any hard feelings.

"Rozalyn knew everything about my first marriage, but I'm almost positive she wouldn't have discussed it with H.T. I have a hunch he had me checked out once he realized his mother intended to remarry. I'd like to give him the benefit of the doubt and believe that maybe he truly thinks I'm some sort of gigolo. I could live with the fact that he simply drew the wrong conclusion, but I don't think that's the case.''

"Why do you think he's bringing this up now?" Jacob pressed.

Helms exhaled a deep sigh. "I wish to God his reason was to protect his mother. It would break her heart to know that her son misconstrued my past in order to gain complete control of the Harcourt fortune."

"I really don't understand why he would go to the trouble. According to my information, Junior already controls the bulk of Harcourt holdings. The old man's will set aside sizable endowments for Rozalyn and Marion, but together their trusts only represent a small portion of the total estate."

For the first time Otto Helms was aware that his attorney had researched more than the medical aspects of the case. He was surprised. "H.T. is impatient, Mr. Malone. What's more, he doesn't want to have to cope with his mother's problem. He'd prefer to ignore it by stashing her away in some home for the aging. Neither Marion nor H.T. has even offered to help me out with Rozalyn for a weekend. I don't know if it's that they can't face reality or that they're just spoiled, ungrateful children. In any case, I don't feel they have earned the right to say much of anything about their mother's care."

"It wouldn't seem so," Jacob agreed.

Helms polished off the soft drink and pitched the can into the wastebasket. "I want to make something clear to you, Jacob."

It was the first time Helms had called him by his first name. Jake eased the chair upright. Whatever Helms had on his mind, it must be important.

"I love my wife dearly and I want what is best for her. I was very angry at God when Rozalyn's condition was confirmed. I felt I'd been cheated. My first marriage was hardly fulfilling, and it was years before I met Rozalyn. She was like an answer to a prayer—everything I've ever dreamed of in a wife. We were so happy together.

"H.T. is trying to make it look as if it was my influence that suddenly caused Rozalyn to become adventurous. It's simply not true. Rozalyn had always yearned to do those things, but she'd never had a husband who wanted to share new experiences and be a playmate, as well as a provider. As Rozalyn put it, Henry, Sr., was always too obsessed with making more money to enjoy what he had. He never took time out to savor the pleasures of his labors. Roz regretted the lost years. She wanted to pack as much fun as she could into the time she had left. And, boy, we did do that," he said with a puckish smile.

Jacob glanced at Addie. She'd perched herself on a low, wide windowsill. Her high heels were on the floor beside her, and she sat stretching her stockinged toes, quietly listening.

"Rozalyn was almost ten years older than me, but she was younger at heart than any twenty-year-old. I'm glad we had those moments together. When I got over the shock of her illness and stopped to consider our life together as a whole, not just from that awful moment when the doctor said her condition was incurable, I realized that God hadn't cheated me at all—he'd blessed me. Before Rozalyn, I was a middle-aged, divorced man without joy or purpose. I never thought I'd know the happiness I received from her.

"Yes, when I think about the future, it pains me. But I tell you, Jacob, when I think about the past, I know I'd do it all again in an instant. She means everything to me. That's why I'm fighting so hard to keep my promise to her. But no matter what happens in court, I won't let her be put away in a home, lost and alone. They don't have to worry about me making a claim on their inheritance. If necessary, I'll sign any damn paper they draw up to that effect. What I won't do is let them or anyone strip her of all hope and dignity. I swear I'll do something drastic before I let that happen."

Jacob no longer had any doubt about his client's character or motives. There was no question that the man was devoted to his wife. Otto Helms had no way of knowing, but by his example he'd bolstered Jacob's own spirits. He'd shown him that loyalty and love, if it is unselfish, cannot be dimmed by circumstance or time.

"Don't worry, Otto. We're going to win this suit. You and Rozalyn are going to England just as you planned, if I have to row you across the Atlantic myself."

Otto Helms felt somewhat encouraged, but even Jacob's unqualified support didn't dispel all his concerns. "How do we repair the damage done by H.T.'s testimony?" he asked.

"You let Addie and me worry about that. You have to trust our judgment implicitly, Otto. When I put you on the stand, I want you to relate your side of the story to the judge in the same way you told it to me. Don't try to force it, just be yourself.

"Lange will try to rattle you when he cross-examines. He'll bait you and turn your responses into a noose that will tighten around your neck if you make the mistake of engaging in a verbal contest with him. Just answer his questions. If he rephrases them, respond exactly the same way as you did before—no additions, no retractions. Look at me when he asks the question. Look at him when you answer. If I think it's a trap, I'll rub my brow, like so."

Jake demonstrated the signal.

"Got it," Helms assured him.

"I intend to subpoena your ex-wife as a witness, if that's okay with you. Her testimony will knock the props out from under Junior's gigolo claim."

"I hate dragging Lila into this. We don't communicate often. She travels a lot. I'm not even sure you could trace her in time."

"I'll find her," Jacob said confidently. He turned to Addie. "We'll need to apprise Lange and McCallahan that we intend to call two unscheduled witnesses."

"Two?" Addie and Otto exclaimed simultaneously.

"Who's the other witness, Jake?" Addie slipped her shoes back on and hauled herself to her feet.

"Have you ever heard of a Phillip Kensington?" he asked.

"No," she answered, even more baffled than a moment ago.

"Neither had I until this past weekend when I happened to be reading an old issue of *Newsweek*." He didn't bother to tell her that he'd found the magazine while tidying up the house in Marblehead and only browsed through it as an excuse to delay having to clean the bathroom. "I came across an article about this guy, and it caught my attention."

"So?" Addie prompted.

"So it seems that Phillip Kensington won the Nobel Prize in the field of physics some years back."

Addie knew there had to be a connection, but she was having difficulty making it.

"He's from England," Jake threw in.

He'd stretched her patience to the limit. "Will you get to the point." She jabbed her fingers through her hair and tapped the toe of her leather pump.

"It seems that he, too, has Alzheimer's disease and that he underwent the same drug therapy as Rozalyn. The article told about the marked improvement he'd shown since the treatment and went on to say that though there is a measure of risk involved, the drug is the first real breakthrough researchers have discovered so far.''

"Jake, that's wonderful news. Why didn't you tell me before now?" Addie's spirits soared.

"I didn't want to get your hopes up. When I got in touch with Kensington, he wasn't real keen on the idea of testifying. He's an egghead and doesn't like notoriety of any sort. I finally got him to agree by telling him I would only call upon him as a last resort.''

"So when is he arriving?" Addie wanted to know.

"For pete's sake, Addie. We're only three hours into the hearing. I was saving Kensington as an ace in the hole.''

"With Lange on the other side, you should have told Kensington we were already in a desperate position." Addie threw up her arms and let them drop with a slap against her thighs.

"I suppose we *could* use the added insurance of his testimony," he said casually.

"You suppose right," she answered in a huff. "Get on the phone right now, Jacob Malone. Tell him we'll pay for his flight, his hotel, his meals, his every whim. Ace in the hole, indeed," she muttered beneath her breath. "Maybe you like flying by the seat of your pants, but I definitely do not."

"Okay, okay," he agreed. "I'll call him before court reconvenes. If he catches a plane out today, he can be here for tomorrow's session."

"*If* he doesn't change his mind. *If* he can get a reservation. *If* the plane doesn't crash over the Atlantic," she fretted.

Jacob loved it when she got crazy. It took the edge off. He'd forgotten how much he enjoyed trial work. The challenge of a courtroom never failed to get his adrenaline flowing. It was exciting work to him; unfortunately it represented something entirely different to Otto Helms. He looked across the table at the drained man seated opposite him. He hated having to bring up the next step in his strategy. "There's something else we must do, Otto," he told him gently. "I'd hoped to avoid it, but I'm afraid it's necessary."

"What?" Helms had no inkling of what was to come.

"Rozalyn needs to be present in court tomorrow, too."

His client immediately rejected the notion with a firm shake of his head.

"I know you wanted to spare her, but I really believe her presence might make the difference," Jacob explained. "In the absence of Dr. Patterson's expert testimony, we have to make adjustments. The only thing that will be as convincing as technical testimony is a demonstration of the amazing results. If the judge has an opportunity to hear a victim of the disease describe the treatment, its side effects and benefits, I'm positive it'll make an impression, especially when the witness has Kensington's credentials.

"I'm gambling that it'll swing McCallahan over to our side completely if he can see the difference the drug can make for himself. I'm not putting Rozalyn on display, Otto. I'm only trying to ensure that she gets the same opportunity to improve her life that Kensington got. I wouldn't ask if it weren't important for the judge to make the comparison between Rozalyn and Kensington. It may be the only way he'll ever really understand what his ruling will mean in human terms."

Otto Helms considered his logic for a long moment. "All right," he agreed at last. "I'll bring Rozalyn with me to court tomorrow. I only pray I'm doing the right thing."

"You are, Otto," Jacob assured him. Glancing to the clock on the wall, he realized he needed to get under way if he intended to ring up Kensington before the afternoon session. "If you want to make another trip to the men's room, you'd better hurry," he told Helms.

"I don't feel queasy anymore, but I *would* like to catch a bit of fresh air before we have to go back in there." Helms left them to talk privately.

Believing they'd about covered everything, Jake pulled out his wallet and started searching for his credit card in order to place the overseas call.

"There is one more thing we need to discuss." Addie's tone was subdued and serious.

"Yeah, what's that?" He was only half listening.

"I want you to take over in the hearing."

His head snapped up. She now had his complete attention. By her expression, he knew she wasn't putting him on. "Why? You're doing okay," he said, not very convincingly.

"You know better." Her eyes locked on his. "Among his other idiosyncrasies, McCallahan obviously does not like women lawyers in his court. He deliberately tried to embarrass me, and then he intentionally excluded me. We have to be realistic here, Jake. His prejudice against me does nothing for our case. I can object all day long, and that old bastard is going to rule against me every time."

"Maybe not." He didn't really believe it, but he felt he should say it.

"We can't chance it. It's not fair to Rozalyn or Otto. You have to be the one."

They stood only a few short feet away from each other. He knew how hard this was for her. It was never easy to swallow someone else's guff in addition to your own pride. He wanted to make it easier somehow, but there was no way to do it. Not after what had happened at his apartment. It would only complicate things. More than space stood between them. He knew it and she knew it.

"Okay," he said.

"Okay," she seconded. It took a moment before she broke eye contact and walked out of the room. In that brief moment, they both knew that more had been settled than who would go the last mile in McCallahan's court. Addie gave up on two men that day—a chauvinist judge and a secret flame. She had no more illusions about Jake. He belonged to Desirée forever.

THE AFTERNOON SESSION brought no surprises. During the course of Henry Harcourt, Jr.'s, continuing testimony, the circumstances of Otto Helms first marriage were brought out. Harcourt's version, of course, was slanted and painted Otto in a most unflattering light. Lange asked all the right questions, and Harcourt's answers stopped just short of out-and-out blackening Otto's character. Instead, Henry, Jr., insinuated that his stepfather was more a "shady gray" sort of guy—an opportunist who preyed upon rich, lonely women. The implication of his responses was clear—it was Rozalyn Harcourt Helms's second husband, not her son, who took advantage of her disoriented state, and it was the loyal son who had her best interests at heart.

Jacob didn't press him very hard during cross-examination. He decided to let Lila Richards's testimony take care of discrediting Harcourt. Jacob did, however, grill Henry, Jr., about the financial arrangements of his father's will. He wanted to make sure that Judge McCallahan understood that the bulk of the family fortune remained in the Harcourts' control. He ended his cross-examination by firing a rapid succession of questions at Henry, Jr.

"Tell me, Mr. Harcourt, at the present time is your mother able to care for herself?"

"Not really," he answered.

"She must be assisted with even the basic things—eating, bathing, dressing, receiving her medication and trips to the bathroom—is that correct?"

"Yes."

"Who does these things for her, Mr. Harcourt?"

For the first time, Henry, Jr.'s, composure slipped. He appeared slightly off balance. "I have tried many times to provide a private nurse," he said defensively.

"You haven't answered the question, Mr. Harcourt. I asked who actually, physically takes care of her?"

"Otto. But as I said, I've offered over and over again to hire professional help or to place mother in a facility where she can be cared for properly. Every time I bring up the subject, he refuses even to consider it. That's part of the reason I initiated this suit. I feel my mother is suffering because of his stubbornness."

"And how long would you say your mother has been in this dependent stage of her illness?"

"Off and on, over two years," Harcourt said stiffly.

"In those two years, how many times have you lent a helping hand, Mr. Harcourt?"

"Excuse me?"

Jacob approached the witness box. "I'd like you to tell the court about the instances when you either fed, bathed, dressed, medicated or assisted your mother to the bathroom."

Henry, Jr., had the decency to redden. "My mother is an extremely proud and modest person. She wouldn't want me to see her in that state. The relationship between mother and son is not the same as that between a husband and wife. I'm sure you can appreciate the difference."

"I don't see how spooning a little soup into her mouth or dropping a pill into her hand could be indelicate, Mr. Harcourt. But even so, then at least you must have made trips to the house just to sit with your mother for a bit while Otto Helms ran an errand," Jake continued.

The flesh about Harcourt's mouth grew tight. "I visit my mother when I can. Running a conglomerate like Harcourt Communications takes a great deal of time. I can't just spell him on a moment's notice. Money is no object. We can well afford to hire whatever assistance he needs. I've told him so on numerous occasions."

"Could you estimate for the court approximately how many visits you have paid your mother since her condition has limited her so severely?"

"I can't recall offhand," Harcourt hedged. The wooden seat creaked as he resituated himself in the chair.

"Weekly, monthly, yearly?" Jacob pressed.

"Maybe a dozen times," Harcourt admitted in a barely audible voice.

"I didn't catch your answer, Mr. Harcourt. Would you repeat it?" Judge McCallahan broke in.

"A dozen or so times," Harcourt was forced to say once more.

"Obviously a son's relationship is *very* different from a husband's. Thank you, Mr. Harcourt. I have no further questions at this time." It gave Jacob some small measure of satisfaction to see the disapproval in the many sets of eyes that gazed back at Harcourt from the gallery. People now knew him for what he was—a far cry from a prince of a fellow.

Louis Lange seemed not at all disturbed by his client's admission. Either he had anticipated the setback or he was one hell of a bluffer. Jacob thought it significant that Lange went fairly quickly through Marion Harcourt's testimony. He did not seem inclined to keep her on the stand long. She added very little and mostly confirmed what her brother had attested to.

When it was Jacob's turn to ask the questions, he concentrated on a single point. "I'm interested to know—as is the court, I'm sure—what sort of relationship you maintain with your mother, Ms. Harcourt."

"I'm not sure I understand what you're asking," the young woman replied.

"I'll rephrase myself and be very clear, Ms. Harcourt. Do you, unlike your brother, assist Mr. Helms in caring for your mother's needs?"

There was a long pause as Marion Harcourt considered her answer. It surprised Jacob how coolly she reacted. Where Henry, Jr., had seemed embarrassed by having to admit publicly the lack of attention he'd shown toward his mother, his sister seemed less concerned about appearances. Jacob had the distinct impression she only hesitated in order to formulate her reply. "No, Mr. Malone, I am not involved in the physical aspects of my mother's care. Maybe to some that seems unfeeling, but I assure you I do love my mother in my own way. She would be the first to tell you that I did not inherit her nurturing ways. I suppose I am more like my father in that respect. I know my shortcomings, which is why I never married, never wished to have children and have no desire even to own a pet. I visit my mother once a week without fail. The extent of my caring is limited to brushing her hair, reading to her from her favorite book and bringing her flowers or a new outfit to cheer her up.''

Jacob had to work hard at disguising his personal dislike. Baby sister had the disposition of a chunk of ice. "I'm sure you do, as you say, love your mother in your own peculiar way," he couldn't resist rebutting.

Louis Lange rose and objected. "Mr. Malone's remarks are unnecessary and abrasive. I ask that the court caution him about badgering the witness."

"I hardly think Mr. Malone's observation constitutes badgering the witness, Mr. Lange. Your objection is overruled. Proceed, Mr. Malone." Judge McCallahan gestured with a flick of his wrist for Jacob to get on with it.

"I have but one final point to make, Your Honor." Jacob's gaze returned to the witness. "Ms. Harcourt, may I presume that you also *love* your brother?"

"Of course," she stated flatly.

"And do you trust his judgment?"

"I never had any reason not to," she replied coldly.

"And you were present in the courtroom through-out the entire time your brother offered testimony in this case?" Jake continued.

Marion Harcourt expelled an impatient sigh. "I was sitting right there," she told him, pointing a finger to the empty chair beside her brother.

"Please, bear with me," Jacob entreated. "I merely wished to have you substantiate a part of what I be-lieve your brother said in regard to the treatment in question." Jacob read over his notes before continu-ing. "Did he not state that he was unconvinced your mother fully understood the experimental program or the risks involved? That her decision to participate, in fact, was not a joint one, as my client claims, but more a matter of being influenced because she loved her husband and trusted his judgment?"

Marion Harcourt glanced over at her brother and then at their attorney. She knew Malone had twisted her brother's meaning and trapped her. By her expres-sion it was obvious she preferred not to answer the question.

Louis Lange vacated his chair once again and ad-dressed the bench. "Your Honor, I don't see any pur-pose in going over testimony previously presented," he said in annoyance, trying to head off a potentially damaging rebuttal.

"Have you a specific purpose, Mr. Malone?" the judge wanted to know.

"I do, Your Honor."

"Then answer the question put to you, Ms. Harcourt," Judge McCallahan ruled.

"He said something to that effect," she was forced to admit.

"You are a joint petitioner in this suit, is that correct, Ms. Harcourt?"

"I believe that's established, Mr. Malone," she shot back.

"Are you here today because you were in some way coerced or influenced by your brother to participate in this action?" Jacob's tone was deceptively gentle.

"I most certainly was not," she answered emphatically.

"So would you agree, then, Ms. Harcourt, that loving a person and trusting in that person's judgment does not necessarily imply the loss of free will or an inability to make independent decisions?"

"It depends," she hedged. "I can only speak of my personal situation. I was not in any way influenced," she repeated.

"You've witnessed the way your mother conducted herself through the years. Generally speaking, would you say that she was prone to acting out of a need to please and appease her husbands?" Jacob kept coming at her.

"Well, uh, no, I guess not," she stumbled.

"So why would we conclude that the experimental drug she opted to take was a result of her being unduly influenced by your stepfather? Isn't it more reasonable to assume that her participation in the program came about because of a *joint* decision reached by her and Otto Helms?''

Marion Harcourt turned and addressed Judge McCallahan. ''How can I answer that?'' she protested. ''I don't know. I wasn't in California with them.''

''Perhaps you should have been,'' the judge responded.

Louis Lange could not believe the liberties both Malone and the judge were taking. ''I really have to object to this line of questioning. It calls for a conclusion by the witness.''

Jacob decided there was no need to continue with his cross-examination of Marion Harcourt. He'd accomplished his intent. ''I withdraw the question. It wasn't my intention to upset the witness. I merely wanted to clarify the differentiation Ms. Harcourt makes between the joint decisions reached in the two separate instances which, in effect, are the basis of this suit. Thank you, Ms. Harcourt. You've been most cooperative.'' He offered her a curt nod and a confident smile, then retook his seat.

''You may step down,'' Judge McCallahan instructed Marion Harcourt. ''Have you any further witnesses to call, Mr. Lange?''

''Yes, Your Honor. We wish to call Mrs. Harcourt's personal physician, Dr. Stuart Bernard, to the stand,'' Lange informed him. Louis Lange did not realize his blunder.

''It's Mrs. Helms,'' Jacob reminded the court.

"Helms or Harcourt, I know who we are discussing, Mr. Malone." The judge slanted him a perturbed look. "As for you, Mr. Lange—" his gaze moved to the opposing table "—I want it understood that we are not going to get bogged down in technical mumbo jumbo. I do not want to spend hours debating medical issues even the experts cannot agree upon. Keep it simple, and preferably short."

Louis Lange complied. Dr. Bernard, however, went to great lengths to explain his twenty-year association with Rozalyn, as well as his position in support of a more conventional form of treatment. Next, he outlined in tedious detail the dangers he foresaw if his former patient were to continue in the experimental program. He took great pains to describe the fine and compassionate care she would receive if Rozalyn Harcourt Helms was placed in one of the many outstanding facilities designed to meet the special needs of Alzheimer's patients. Lange rested his case on Dr. Bernard's very qualified but long-winded opinion.

It was only when Addie and Jacob asked for a side conference in the judge's chambers that Lange learned of the two unscheduled witnesses they wished to call. Though he argued persuasively against the granting of such a request, he was forced to accept the unanticipated setback. Though the last-minute addition did not sit well with Judge McCallahan, he kept his word and allowed a certain degree of leeway in the proceedings.

Lange was visibly upset. Addie and Jake were secretly relieved. Judge McCallahan was late to a Celtics game. He ended the session as soon as the four of them emerged from his chambers.

Tomorrow would be Rozalyn and Otto's day in court. There would, however, be one less spectator observing from the gallery the following day. Satisfied that his charge was in a better frame of mind of late, Alistair Mackey decided to skip the courtroom show-down and take the midnight shuttle to the Cosmos. The judicial drama being played out on Earth was nothing compared to the high drama about to take place up above. On the astral plane, time was marked by a dif-ferent standard, and Mackey knew that Desirée's transitional period was about over. If she didn't make it to the Sphere of Light very soon, her fate could never be reversed. He was determined to find her lost soul and deliver her to the Higher Force in the nick of time. If the Fisherman chose to clip his wings for shirking his assignment, then so be it. He couldn't just stand by and do nothing to prevent the permanent separation of two souls who were meant to be together.

Alistair paused at the courtroom doors and turned back to take one last look at his boy. His chest swelled with pride. Malone was fine, mate, for a fact. He'd miss the close contact with him, but he took heart in knowing that he'd always be able to monitor his pro-gress from beyond.

"I'll keep in touch," he promised him silently. "And I'll send your lady back to you, if I can."

The guardian angel sniffed and wiped a sleeve across his misty eyes, then struck out for home.

CHAPTER FIFTEEN

THE HALLWAY OUTSIDE the courtroom was packed with reporters and television cameras. Jacob requested the constables to clear a path before he attempted to usher the Helmses into the courtroom. Otto and Jake did their best to shield Rozalyn from the flashbulbs and microphones. Still, it was a terrifying experience for her. She clung to Otto until they managed to reach the sanctuary of the 108th.

Even after they were seated at the table, Otto behaved like a samurai protecting his shogun. It amazed Jacob how fiercely he guarded his wife and how tenderly he treated her. Every two seconds, he was either patting her hand, smoothing her hair, straightening her collar or kissing her cheek. Rozalyn Helms was not what Jacob expected. He'd pictured her differently— wan and wasting away. Though she was frail looking, she was still a very attractive woman. She had lovely blue eyes, high cheekbones and a pretty smile. Her black hair was streaked with silver, cut short and smartly styled. She looked like a fragile doll. Jacob understood perfectly why Otto adored her.

"Are you all right, sweetheart? Can I get you anything?" Otto fussed over his wife.

Rozalyn merely stared off into space. She no longer seemed aware of the hubbub about her. No sign of recognition registered on her face when her children came into the courtroom and sat down at the table across from them.

It seemed odd to Jacob that a mother no longer knew her children. It seemed even stranger to him that Henry, Jr., and Marion could come into a room and not even acknowledge their mother. Occasionally they cast a glance in Rozalyn's direction, but they made no move to cross the distance between the two tables and offer even a small display of affection.

"Did you ever locate Lila?" Otto's inquiry recaptured Jake's attention.

"She'll take the stand first. Then Kensington. You'll be last," he informed him.

"Where's Ms. Van Cleve?" Helms wondered.

"Picking up Kensington at his hotel. Don't worry. They'll be here in plenty of time." Jake glanced at his watch. Actually Addie should have arrived long ago. What was holding her up? If Kensington didn't appear, a major portion of their rebuttal would run aground.

At the "all rise" instruction from the bailiff, Jacob stood up and squared his tie.

Judge McCallahan took his place on the bench and convened the session with a whack of the gavel. "I will hear evidence from the respondent. Call your first witness, Mr. Malone."

"We call Lila Richards," Jacob announced.

The summons was answered by a woman in her early fifties. She wore a wine-colored dress, matching turban-style headpiece and heavy gold jewelry. Her tinted contacts made her eyes a vibrant shade of turquoise. After repeating the oath, she took a seat in the witness box.

"Would you please tell the court your name and relationship to my client?" Jacob began.

"Lila Richards Helms. I was once married to Otto," she answered, drawing out her words Texas-style.

"You are here today to testify in behalf of your ex-husband, is that correct?"

"I sure am, sugar." She smiled broadly at Otto.

Laughter rippled through the gallery. Even Judge McCallahan could not keep a straight face.

Jacob smiled and continued. "Would you mind providing the court with a little background on your marriage to the man who is now in a fight to retain guardianship over his present wife?"

"I'd be happy to," she said brightly. "First, let me make it clear that I think the world and all of my former husband." Lila reached up and adjusted her turban, then reached down and pulled the hem of her dress an inch or so higher over her crossed legs.

Judge McCallahan scooted up in his chair and inspected the witness.

"I would've stayed married to Otto forever if it had been left up to me. He was the one who thought we should split up. He was probably right. We weren't exactly well matched. Rozalyn is much more his type.

Even though my daddy was a rancher, I'm more of a wildcatter at heart." She turned to explain herself to the judge.

"I like to go for broke and break new ground, only my business is cosmetics, not crude," she went on. "It was when my cosmetic business started doing well that Otto and I drifted apart. And I don't want anybody blaming him for it, ya hear!" She shook her finger at the Harcourt kids.

"I was the one who didn't come home at night and didn't bother to call. Now that I've matured some and have a bit more sense, I'm sorry about how badly I behaved back then. I truly am, honey," she drawled, directing her apology to her ex-husband.

Otto's grin let her know that all had been forgiven long ago. He slipped an arm around Rozalyn in the hope that she might realize that she alone was the true love of his life.

"Mrs. Helms?" Jacob regained the cosmetic queen's attention.

"I go by Miss Richards, because of the business," she clarified.

"I'll try to remember," he replied. "I would particularly like for you, Miss Richards, to tell us if you in any way feel that your ex-husband took advantage of you. In previous testimony presented in this courtroom, it has been implied that Mr. Helms is not interested so much in his present wife's welfare as he is in her money. He has been characterized as an opportunist at best and a gigolo at worst. I want you to be as straightforward as possible and tell us in your own words whether or not you believe these allegations are true." Because Lila was so natural, Jacob decided it was better to let her express herself at will.

"Well, let me set the records straight," she said hotly. "I was married to that man for more than ten years, and I can tell you for sure that he doesn't have a greedy bone in his body. Whoever claimed such a thing is an out-and-out liar." Her turquoise eyes shot daggers at the Harcourts. "Otto Helms never asked me for a dime. I bought him gifts, sure, but that was only to ease my guilty conscience for the miserable way I treated him. A lot of men would have been jealous of a wife who'd made a success of herself, but not Otto. He was genuinely happy for me. I'm not telling you that he didn't ever get upset with me. Lord knows I tested his patience. I will, however, claim until my dying breath that he never mistreated me or took advantage of me in any way, shape or form."

"You bought him a business of his own, Miss Richards. Are you telling me that the idea was solely yours?" Jacob decided to play the devil's advocate before his opponent got the chance.

"I damn sure am," she shot back. "To tell you the truth, I did it on the advice of my divorce lawyer. He had this silly notion that Otto might try to make a claim on my cosmetic business as part of the settlement. I knew better, but I purchased the store for him anyway, not because I felt obliged but because I felt so guilty for doing such a good man wrong."

Once more, she turned and directed her remarks toward Judge McCallahan. "You appear to be a fair man to me," she told him with a bat of her mascaraed lashes. "Back in Texas, we don't hold with people spreading lies. I've told you the gospel truth, Judge, and I hope you see fit to rule in Otto's favor. He's seen some hard times lately and he could sure use a break."

Louis Lange had had enough of her outrageousness. "Your Honor, could you please instruct the witness to confine her remarks to the issue at hand. Miss Richards seems to suffer from the impression that this is some kind of informal gathering. She acts as though this is some down-home Texas barbecue rather than a serious hearing."

Judge McCallahan's eyes narrowed at Lange's overbearance. "Need I remind you, sir, that I preside over this hearing and it is I who decide whether or not a witness is out of order. I will instruct the witness as I, not you, see fit. Now, do you wish to exercise your right to cross-examine the witness?"

"I do not," Lange said sharply.

"Then sit down and do not presume to tell me how to run my court again."

Lange glared back at McCallahan, but the judge's superior authority caused him to relent. With a yank of his chair, he lowered himself to his seat, dropping his point as well as his gaze.

Jacob stifled a smirk. "That's all for the present, Miss Richards. We thank you for the enlightenment you've provided us today."

"You're sure enough welcome." Bestowing one last bright smile on Judge McCallahan, she popped up out of the witness box and swished through the swing gate.

Otto leaned across his wife to make a comment to Jake. "You see what I mean about her? Lila can be overwhelming at times."

"Yeah," Jake agreed, his expression amused. "I think your ex-wife has an admirer in Judge McCallahan. He found her delightful." He cast a glance over his shoulder and scanned the rear of the courtroom. He'd hoped that Addie and Kensington had snuck in during Lila's testimony and taken a place in the back so as not to disturb the proceedings. No such luck. They weren't in court.

"Addie and Kensington are late, so we'll have to change the game plan," he told Otto. "You'll have to go next."

"I can't," he contended, casting a worried glance at his wife.

"What's the problem?" Jacob hadn't the foggiest notion what had prompted his sudden reluctance.

"Rozalyn," Helms answered in a word. "I'll be up there testifying, and you'll be busy asking me questions. Who's going to look after Rozalyn?"

"Jesus! You're only going to be ten feet from her. I'll be even closer. It's not like she could wander off without us realizing." Jacob really couldn't relate to his anxiety.

"I'm not worried about that," Helms argued. "You don't understand how it is with her or any Alzheimer's patient. In a way, they're like the children you see clinging to their parents in a crowd. They need the reassurance of having someone physically close to them. All this commotion is upsetting enough for her. I'm not going to leave her side without somebody taking my place. That's it, Jacob. Stall, ask for a recess, I don't care how you do it. Just get a delay until Ms. Van Cleve can relieve me.''

Jacob knew by the stubborn jut of Otto's bearded chin that he was not going to budge on the matter. He also knew that McCallahan was not going to go for an early recess. His mind raced to find a compromise. ''Okay, how about if I promise to stay close to Rozalyn the whole time you're on the stand. I'll stand behind her and keep my hands on her shoulders. Will that work?''

Otto thought it over. He didn't like the idea much.

Jacob pushed him. ''Look, Otto, we have some momentum going here. If we delay, we may lose it.''

''I don't care if I keel over with a heart attack up there, don't leave her by herself,'' he stipulated.

''Not even if you drop dead,'' Jake promised with a wry grin.

''Okay, put me on next,'' Otto relented. He'd been holding Rozalyn's hand, and he raised it to his lips. ''Mr. Malone is going to be right beside you, sweetheart. Everything is going to be just fine.'' He gazed into his wife's eyes. His own were full of concern and undisguised love.

"Is there a problem, Mr. Malone?" Judge Mc-Callahan inquired.

"No, Your Honor. Mr. Helms will be the next witness to take the stand."

Otto lowered his wife's hand and reluctantly got up and walked to the front of the courtroom.

"Do you swear that the testimony you are about to give is the truth, the whole truth and nothing but the truth, so help you God?" the bailiff recited.

"I do," Helms swore before taking the witness chair.

Jacob kept his pledge to his client. The entire time he questioned Otto, Jacob stood behind Rozalyn, his hands gently fastened on her shoulders. Addie arrived with Phillip Kensington in the middle of Otto's testimony. Without creating a disturbance, she slipped through the gate and into her seat, giving Rozalyn's hand a reassuring squeeze.

Otto followed Jake's instructions to the letter. He told his side of the story in the same plainspoken manner that he had related it to Jacob. Otto heeded Jacob's advice when answering Lange's challenges—he said what was necessary, nothing more. The strategy was working. Jake could see it in the eyes of the judge and the faces in the gallery. The Harcourts squirmed under the weight of his sincerity, and Louis Lange failed to make a dent in Otto's chivalrous attitude.

When Jacob called Phillip Kensington to the stand, every person in the courtroom wondered what role the man played in the drama being enacted before their eyes. His mission soon became clear.

"Please tell us a little about yourself, Mr. Kensington," Jacob began.

"I reside in London. By occupation, I am a physicist but I am no longer active in that endeavor," the thin-faced Kensington told the court.

"Why do you no longer work in the field of physics?" Jacob asked.

"I suffer from Alzheimer's disease, Mr. Malone."

A hushed murmur arose from the gallery.

"And when were you diagnosed with the illness?"

"More than five years ago," Kensington answered.

"Before that time, did you not win the Nobel Prize for your contributions to the field?"

"I did. If my memory serves me correctly, it was in 1982." Kensington's announcement caused even Judge McCallahan to sit up and take notice.

"And is it not a fact, sir, that you have participated in a program similar to the one Mrs. Helms wishes to continue, the risks and benefits of which are under debate in this courtroom today?"

"It is a fact," Kensington stated. "I underwent the experimental drug therapy at approximately the same point in time as your client."

"Of course, the experimental drug is a legal form of treatment and an accepted practice in your country, is it not?" Jake continued.

"Yes. There is no ban on the drug in England, and anyone who chooses can avail themselves of the treatment," answered Kensington.

"Would you please describe for us your condition before and after the drug therapy?" Jacob positioned himself at the jurors' empty box, giving Kensington center stage.

"The difference in me was striking. Before, I was unable to focus my mind. I had difficulty performing the simplest of tasks. The best analogy I can give you is that it is like functioning in a perpetual fog. I've been told I no longer recognized members of my family or old acquaintances. It was a most frustrating time for both myself and my family, especially my dear wife.

"At the risk of sounding melodramatic, I must tell you that the results of the drug therapy are miraculous. I am not the man I was—I have no illusions about that. I am, however, aware and able to do quite a bit on my own now. No, I cannot calculate formulas or make the contributions to society I once did. But I'm not a burden on it, either. You brought me here today to serve as an example, Mr. Malone. You had hoped that by making a comparison between myself and Mrs. Helms, His Lordship might see the positive rather than the negative side of the issue."

Judge McCallahan overlooked Kensington's error in calling him "His Lordship." He sort of liked the title. Jacob didn't bother to correct the Englishman, either.

"If I may, I'd like to inject a personal comment," Kensington requested.

"Certainly," Jacob acquiesced.

"I better than anyone here understand the living hell Mrs. Helms is going through. I tell you straight out, I am very thankful that my wife sought out the treatment and had the fortitude to stand by her convictions. I am advised that it was claimed that Mrs. Helms did not understand the risks involved. I tell you, it makes no difference. Anyone in her place would submit themselves to any form of treatment, no matter how radical, no matter the dangers, so long as it afforded a chance of partial recovery. There are no alternatives when all that the future holds for one is to become a veritable vegetable."

"I know Mrs. Helms appreciates your candor, Mr. Kensington. Your presence here today may very well mean the chance at life you have been given, the same one Mrs. Helms hopes to be granted. Thank you. I have no further questions for the witness, Your Honor. We rest our case."

"Do you wish to cross-examine, Mr. Lange," asked the judge.

Louis Lange saw no advantage to keeping the Englishman on the witness stand. "No, Your Honor."

"You may step down, Mr. Kensington." Judge McCallahan looked thoughtful.

When Jacob returned to the table, Otto gave him a slap on the back. "You were brilliant, Jacob," he whispered.

"Kensington was brilliant," he said distractedly, gazing over at Addie. "What a lucky break it was that I stumbled across that article. It's a close one, but I think we pulled it off."

Addie sent him a thumbs-up sign. "How soon do you think McCallahan will rule?" she asked.

"Your guess is as good as mine."

The Harcourts and Louis Lange were already gathering up their belongings, along with their pride, and preparing to make a quick exit from the courtroom.

Judge McCallahan struck the bench with his gavel and regained everyone's attention. "Usually I would take a matter of this magnitude under advisement for several days before rendering a decision, but it will not be necessary in this instance. I see no need in prolonging what has already been an excruciating experience for everyone involved."

Addie and Jake could not believe the swiftness of his ruling. They, as well as Louis Lange, were caught off balance by the suddenness of the justice about to be dispensed.

"If I believed that the Harcourt children had proven by the preponderance of the evidence that their mother's best interests would be better served by appointing them guardianship over their mother, I would rule accordingly. However, such is not the case. Instead, I believe they used this courtroom as a forum to slander and castigate a man they do not like and, further, attempted to use their mother's illness as an excuse to seize total control over the family estate. The petitioners should consider themselves fortunate that I am not inclined to make an example of them. I will let society judge their actions.

"As to the matter of Mrs. Rozalyn Harcourt Helms's illness and the treatment thereof, I feel that at the time of her entry into the program, the decision to participate was a joint one and that it was then, and is now, her wish to continue with the drug therapy. Her decision will be upheld by this court. Her husband, Otto Helms, will be allowed to act in her behalf, and guardianship over her interests will hereby be legally awarded to him." Judge McCallahan's eyes softened as they fell upon the Helmses. "My prayers go with you both. Court is dismissed."

Without any further ado, the judge gathered his black robe about him and swept from the room before anyone had a chance to stand.

"I don't believe it," Addie breathed.

"It's over!" Otto exclaimed, turning and clamping his wife's face between his hands and planting a smacking kiss on her lips. "We're going to England, Roz! You're going to get the drug to make you better."

Rozalyn Harcourt Helms flashed him a pretty smile. Whether or not she understood was anybody's guess. Jacob chose to believe that she did.

He got up and walked to the back of the court to thank Phillip Kensington for appearing. He was standing by the door when Otto and Rozalyn made their way out of the courtroom.

"How do I thank you?" Helms asked.

"By taking good care of your wife," Jake said with a warm smile.

"I always have and always will." Helms clamped his arms about him in an awkward but meaningful embrace.

"You might drop me a postcard from England. I'd like to know how Rozalyn's doing."

Otto nodded. "I'll be sure to get your address before we leave."

"Yeah, you do that. Now, go on and get out of here. You've got a lot to take care of in the next few days."

With a last pat of Jake's shoulder, Otto guided his wife out the door and down the hall. Relieved and vindicated, Helms handled the mob of reporters just fine on his own.

Henry Jr. and Marion walked past Jacob without a word or a glance. They were more intent on ducking their heads and dodging the press. Louis Lange paused and offered his hand.

"I'm impressed," he congratulated him.

"Don't be. I got lucky, is all."

There was no one left in the courtroom but Addie when he returned to the table to collect his briefcase.

"You were great, as usual," she told him with a perky smile.

"You deserve a lot of the credit." His briefcase in hand, he motioned with a gallant sweep of his arm for her to proceed him out the doors.

She took a few steps and turned back to him. "Thanks for bailing me out, Jake. I was in over my head."

"No, you weren't. You're a fine lawyer, Addie. I predict that you'll sit on the bench one day."

She beamed at his confidence. "I only hope I get appointed to fill McCallahan's seat when he vacates it. Wouldn't that be poetic justice?"

He laughed at the idea.

"I'd invite you to dinner, but I think we should just go our separate ways." Her eyes met his, and he read the unspoken message. *Let's not drag this out.*

"Yeah, I need to go by and check on Desirée." He was uncomfortable, and it showed.

"I hope you get your wish, too, Jake. Take care," she bid him, pivoting on her heels and walking out without a backward glance.

Oddly reluctant to leave, Jacob sat down in the front pew of the gallery and absorbed the silence. It had been a surprising day.

The last thing he anticipated was another emotional jolt.

CHAPTER SIXTEEN

MACKEY WAS RELENTLESS in his pursuit of K.T. and Desirée. Starting at the edge of the Sphere of Light, he worked his way backward, crisscrossing the border area of the Remembering Realm. He was looking for tracks—small, size-five footprints—that might give him a lead as to the direction in which to search. K.T. should have been traveling due east, but knowing the apprentice's penchant for choosing a totally opposite direction, Mackey elected to do the same. He made the right decision. After hours of scouting out the western quadrant of the Remembering Realm, the ex-croc poacher located the pair camped near a stream in a peaceful glade.

Desirée was the first to comment on the approach of the stocky figure dressed in khaki attire. "We have company, K.T.," she alerted her guide.

The blue aura was already aware of Mackey's presence. K.T. had sensed Mackey's arrival moments before he materialized out of the vastness. "I know," K.T. replied. "It is Alistair Mackey who comes our way."

"Who is he?" she asked.

"A presence who has touched your life in the past," K.T. explained.

Desirée did not understand, but by now she'd grown accustomed to her guide's manner of responding without really addressing her curiosity. She waited for Mackey's identity and purpose to become clear to her.

"G'day, little lidy," the ruddy-faced stranger greeted her.

"Hello," she returned pleasantly.

"Lost again, eh, K.T.?" Mackey scowled at the blue aura. "A hopeless case, if ever there was one. You'd never have made it in the bush, mate. The crocs would be licking their chops and sunning themselves whilst they digested the blue boob they'd ate for supper."

His scolding caused the aura to dim with shame. "I did make a few miscalculations, but we are not camped here by error. I wished for Desirée to know the peace of this spot before we pushed on."

Desirée wanted to defend her guide, but Mackey gave her no opening.

"Are you daft? This wasn't a pleasure trip, K.T.! You were supposed to deliver the little lidy straight-away. Because of your blunder, she might not make it before…" He stopped himself short of blurting out the dismal facts of her desperate straits.

"Before what?" she asked anxiously.

"Nothing to worry yourself about," Mackey assured her with a weak smile. "Not now that I'm here to keep you on course."

"Who are you?" Desirée demanded to know.

"Alistair Mackey, guardian angel, at your service." He introduced himself with a deep bow.

He was a funny fellow, Desirée decided. She instantly liked him and just as instantly drew the wrong conclusion. "It's nice to meet you at last, Alistair. I only wish you hadn't been busy on the day of my accident. I don't mean to sound ungrateful about the years you dedicated to watching over me, but . . ."

"Oh, I'm not *your* guardian angel, missy," he hastened to tell her. "That would be Gilda, and a fine angel she is, too."

"Gilda?" she repeated, more confused than ever.

"You would prefer Gilda to Alistair," K.T. put in. "Her disposition is much sweeter."

Mackey thumbed his nose at the blue aura.

Desirée found him amusing. "Well, if you are not responsible for me, then why have you searched me out?"

"It's a long story, little lidy, and time is growing short." He motioned for her to come along with him. "We can chat while we do a walkabout." His eyes lighted on the hovering apprentice. "You can tag along so long as you don't stray off. And none of that deep double-talk of yours, or I'll leave your blue butt to find its own way back," he threatened.

K.T. did not argue. Mackey could be impossible when he was full of himself. The apprentice was careful to stay in the rear of the procession.

Desirée felt obliged to speak up in his behalf. "K.T. has been very good to me. I don't know why you're being so hard on him. We are very close to the end of the line, aren't we?''

Alistair curbed an impulse to tell her precisely how close to the end of the line she was. "K.T.'s awright, I suppose," he allowed. "But you and I have more in common." Alistair picked up the pace.

Desirée had to hustle to keep abreast of him. "Like what?" she pressed.

"Like your husband."

At the thought of Jacob, Desirée stumbled. Only Mackey's quick reflexes saved her from a nasty spill. The ex-croc poacher didn't miss a step.

"How are you connected with Jacob?" she wondered aloud. No sooner had she voiced the question than she knew the answer. She gazed at the stocky tracker through wide but comprehending eyes. "You're *his* guardian angel. You watch over Jacob!" she exclaimed.

"That's me job," Mackey confirmed, pushing ahead.

She cast a look back at K.T. "That's what you meant when you referred to him as a presence who had touched my life in the past."

"Yes. Alistair Mackey played a part in bringing you and Jacob Malone together. He sometimes tampers with fate—a fault he has been reprimanded for and one which he obviously intends to repeat," the guide asserted.

"Keep your thoughts to yourself, Kappa Theta 99." The black look Mackey shot K.T. over his shoulder had the desired effect.

Desirée was doubly confused. "Is it true what K.T. says? Did you have a hand in Jacob's and my relationship?" Her legs were starting to become cramped from the strenuous march.

Mackey showed no signs of tiring or slacking off the pace. "I was sent down to have a look-see because me boy was experiencing discontent. I found him boarding at your place. I watched the two of you together and could plainly see that you were in love with him. His feelings toward you weren't as easy to distinguish at first," he told her.

She remembered it the same way. And then she recalled something else—her dabbling in love potions and attempting to bind Jacob by magic spells. "Oh, my!" she gasped. "You saw it all, then. You know the lengths I went to in order to get him to notice me."

Alistair grinned. "I know what you thought you accomplished with a sprinkle of herbs and a chant or two. You sold yourself short, missy. It wasn't the magic ways of your mother, or even the bit o' tampering I did to the carburetor wires of his car, that kept him close to you. No," he said with a bemused shake of his head. "I know me boy better than anyone. He can be headstrong and sometimes foolish, like the time he left you behind and returned to Boston just when you needed him most. I wanted to wring his neck for that stunt."

"But he came back," she said in Jacob's defense.

"He did, for a fact. What's more, he did it on his own. He realized how much you meant to him and how bloody empty his life was without you. I had no power over him. The magic had no power over him. Only the power of love was at work."

"You must think me a silly person for resorting to such drastic means." Desirée was embarrassed. She had thought no one knew of her secret desperation to find and hold a lover in those bygone days.

"You're anything but silly," he told her. "I always thought you were very special, Desirée. Me boy is a lucky bloke. If I were younger and not in this angel state, I'd consider giving him a run for your affections." Mackey gave her a cheeky wink.

His kidding made her laugh. "I think it's Jacob who's the lucky one. You're pretty special yourself, Alistair."

"Why, thank you. I don't mind telling you that he's been a handful at times, especially in his bachelor days. The stories I could tell you."

K.T. sent a high-pitched directive to the talkative angel. Mackey knew better than to divulge private facts about his charge. It was privileged information and expressly prohibited by the Angel Code of Ethics.

"I wasn't going to give away any details," Mackey grumbled, rubbing his smarting ear.

It wasn't hard for Desirée to figure out what had gone on between the angel and the alien. "I'm sure he was a rascal," she said dismissively. "But I love him nonetheless."

They traveled in silence for a while. Mackey estimated that they were a half hour's distance from the Sphere of Light; they'd made good time. He glanced over at Desirée to see how she was holding up. She was visibly weary, breathing hard and lagging a little behind. Alistair weighed her exhausted condition against the time element and decided they could pause to rest for a few short minutes.

Desirée was glad when he stopped. She sank to the ground and tried to catch her breath. K.T. hovered in a holding pattern. Mackey seemed unaffected by their arduous journey. She supposed that angels and aliens didn't work up a sweat. "Kappa Theta 99," she mused aloud. "Is that your full title, K.T.?"

"Yes. But I much prefer to be called K.T. or K.T.-99," the blue aura told her. "In my culture, beings are named for the planet on which they live. I come from Kappa Theta. The number sequence signifies the house of your birth and your place in the generational cycle. So, I am of the ninth generation of the ninth house of Kappa Theta," her guide explained.

"I'm sure it is an extremely efficient practice, but it sounds terribly impersonal," she ventured.

"I have come to realize it is so, and that is why I prefer to be known as K.T."

"I like the nickname—it suits you."

"Thank you. I like and think your name suits you, as well."

Mackey felt excluded. The two of them seemed to have developed a special rapport during the journey.

He felt a twinge of jealousy—not a very angellike trait and one he had truly tried to overcome.

Desirée grew quiet and thoughtful, thinking of Jacob. "I presume you've been with him, Alistair," she said softly.

The guardian angel knew immediately to whom she referred. "I only left him a few hours ago," he told her, squatting at her side.

"How is he?"

"Aside from missing you terribly, me boy is awright," he assured her. "It was hard for him at first, but he's adjusting."

"I want so much to see him." Her voice quavered with emotion. "Sometimes when K.T. thinks I'm meditating, I'm not really. I close my eyes and concentrate on sending Jacob and Megan my love. I have no way of knowing if it helps them, but I pray it does. I try not to question what has happened. K.T. claims there is a purpose, but it's difficult for me to accept," she confessed.

"I know," he consoled her, patting her hand. "I've been in your position, only my exit from the bush was a one-way-only proposition. Maybe it's not so in your case. That's why I've come back ahead of schedule. Time hasn't run out yet. If I can get you to the Higher Force before it does, there's a chance you might be granted a return trip to Earth. We have to hurry, though. In a few more hours, it'll be too late. If a spirit is separated too long from the physical shell, it becomes impossible to merge the body and soul again."

Alistair got to his feet and gave her a hand up. "Are you strong enough to make it the rest of the way, little lidy?" he asked in a worried tone.

She lifted her head. Determination glowed in her lavender-blue eyes. "I'd walk across hot coals and crawl through broken glass to be with Jacob."

Mackey looked amused. "It's not going to be as bad as all that."

THE THREESOME REACHED the Sphere of Light in what they hoped was plenty of time. The second they crossed over from the Remembering Realm, Desirée realized she had reached the end of her journey. Unlike the other places she had traveled through, there was no definite terrain—no vegetation or buildings to distinguish her destination. Nothing but soft, swirling, vaporous white light. It was the same as the ray of light she had encountered in the Revelation Rotunda—only intensified a thousand times. It penetrated to the center of her soul—filling her with peace. Matter and form evaporated. There was but a single life force and an indescribable feeling of being cradled in the very womb of love.

She was no longer aware of Alistair or K.T. They, like her, were not separate entities anymore but part of the white light, part of one another, part of the whole of mankind. It should have been a strange sensation to her, yet it was familiar. She had known this place, this feeling, this womb before. Or so it seemed to her as she stood in the midst of the Sphere of Light.

"Desirée," called a voice—the same voice that had arrested her fears at the Revelation Rotunda.

"Yes," she answered.

"Are you ready, my child?" the loving voice asked.

She was torn. It was such a wonderful feeling to be part of the whole, just as K.T. had told her. But to remain here would mean she must leave Jacob and Megan behind. Her spirit wavered. "Not yet," she heard herself respond. "Not if there is a chance I might be able to return to my husband and child. *Please* allow me to return."

The voice did not respond. Instead, the white vapors parted to form a circle. When Desirée peered into the center, she could see herself and Jacob in the hospital room once again. "I have already seen my fate at present. I want to see into the future," she begged the Higher Force. "Can you show me more?"

"That is the future," the voice replied. "Until you cross over, only the shell that housed the soul of Desirée Malone will continue to exist on the Earth plane."

Desirée hung her head. Alistair must have misjudged the time left to her. They were too late. The sadness she felt was for her husband.

"Jacob's heart will mend, but only if you are willing to allow him to go on without you," the voice informed her, reading her innermost thoughts.

"Then for his sake, let me cross over," she decided swiftly. "I don't want to make him suffer a minute longer. I want him to be happy again. But there is one request I beg you to grant. If I can't return, please allow me to communicate to him how much I have loved him. It's important that he know I leave this life with no regrets. It will make it easier for him to release me."

The loving voice did not answer right away. By rescinding one request and making another, Desirée had caused the Higher Force to ponder her fate further. An event that could only be explained as miraculous on Earth was but a minor adjustment in the Cosmos—a matter of modifying the divine timetable in order to serve a great purpose. The question was, did Desirée Malone's future contributions on the Earth plane merit reversing her fate? Her decision had been loving and unselfish, and the Creator of all planets and beings in the vast universe and beyond took heed. She could prove to be the mortal example of everything the Higher Force hoped to see demonstrated on Earth.

But the Creator needed further assurance. "If I grant you your heart's desire, Desirée, there are two commissions you must fulfill—love and accept others, as I do you, and always seek knowledge."

"I'll try to do that always," she promised.

The radiant while light embraced her and filled her heart with joy. "Share the love. I am with you always...always...always...'

CHAPTER SEVENTEEN

BY THE TIME JACOB arrived at St. Anthony's, the skeleton staff was already on duty, the halls were quiet and the patients had been tucked in for the night.

He proceeded into his wife's room and closed the door. On the ride over, he'd made up his mind to carry out a desperate plan of action—something he'd been contemplating for quite some time. He would never have a better opportunity. It would probably be a good hour or so before anyone came by to check on Desirée.

After removing his suit coat and loosening his tie, Jacob sat on the edge of her bed.

Usually he spoke to her, even though he knew she would not respond. He would tell her of his day or what cute new thing his parents had reported that Megan had said or done. Not tonight. Tonight Jacob was in a strange frame of mind. He most definitely was not in a mood to conduct a one-sided conversation about trivia.

Usually he was content to touch her cheek or brush back her hair. Not tonight. Tonight Jacob had no wish to expend any more energy on small, one-sided gestures, either.

Usually Jacob could accept the way things were between them—Desirée lying flat on her back, motionless; him perched on her bedside, his thoughts and emotions vacillating between daydreams and despair. But not tonight!

Determination marked his face as he stood up and threw back the sheet. In one swift movement he scooped Desirée up off the bed and into his arms.

It had been such a long, long time since he'd been this close to his wife. It felt natural and oh, so wonderful to hold her in his arms again, to feel her head nestled against his shoulder as he buried his face in her hair. Cradling her like a baby, he walked to a chair in the corner and eased their intertwined forms down upon the leather cushion. He settled back, closed his eyes and cuddled her closer, against his pounding heart.

"You have no idea how good this feels, babe," he whispered to her. "Day after day of empty arms can drive a man crazy." His fingers glided through her curly hair, and he pressed his lips to her forehead. "From my mind to your mind. From my heart to your heart," he repeated.

He felt an ever-so-slight movement—the subtlest of stirrings—against his body. His heart stood still. He didn't open his eyes. He'd imagined it, he told himself. He had wanted it to happen so much that his mind had played tricks on him.

He heard a soft moan—barely a breath of a sound, but it brought his eyes abruptly open. "Desirée?" he choked, tipping her chin and tilting back her head. "My God! Desirée, can you hear me?"

"Mmm," she responded groggily.

"Sweet Jesus!" he gasped, his arms clutching her tighter. "Please, baby, please, open your eyes. It's Jacob, darling." He began to shower her face with short, frantic kisses.

Desirée's lids slowly parted.

He stared down into the open eyes of his wife—the spellbinding, soul-binding, lavender-blue eyes. "I can't believe it's true. I have you back." He half laughed, half cried. Tears streamed down his face and dropped onto her gown. "I love you, babe. Do you hear me, Desirée? I love you so much."

"Me, too," was her faint answer. "I had the strangest dream, Jacob."

"Shh, don't talk. Save your strength," he cautioned. He was crazy with joy. Unwilling to release her for an instant, even to summon a nurse, he scrambled to his feet and scurried into the hallway to call for help.

"Come quick!" he shouted at the top of his lungs. "My wife is awake! She's responding! Where *are* you people? I need help!" He glanced down to make sure she was still responsive. "Don't close your eyes. Stay with me, babe. For God's sake, stay with me."

"Such a fuss, Jacob," she murmured, her head and tongue still thick from her long sleep. "You'll wake the dead."

A hearty laugh rumbled up from somewhere deep inside him and rolled from his lips. "Oh, Desirée, if you only knew. If you only knew..."

EPILOGUE

ALISTAIR MACKEY and the Fisherman sat discussing the matter of his disobedience.

"You left your duties, Alistair. It was a reckless act and I truly do not know how to deal with your lack of regard for the rules."

"Begging your pardon, Your Eminence, but if it hadn't been for my lack of regard, the little lidy might have not made it to the Higher Force in time." He scratched his head. "I'm still a bit confused though, mate. When she asked to go back, she was shown a bleak future. It was then that she changed her mind and consented to cross over."

"Ah, but why was she willing to let go of her worldly ties, Alistair?"

"She did it for his sake," Mackey put forth.

"Exactly. It was an unselfish act. A sacrifice of love. The Higher Force recognized her goodness and was convinced that her purpose would be better served on Earth than in the Beyond, at least for the present."

Mackey was still confused. "But she only asked to be allowed to convey her love and say her goodbyes to me boy."

"She made two requests, as I recall. First to return permanently, and then to communicate her love to her husband."

"You're right. She did. In all the excitement I'd forgotten that."

The Fisherman smiled. Obviously Mackey was not as infallible as he thought. "The Almighty chose to grant her *first* request, and in so doing He also granted the second. There is nothing that cannot be altered, not even the future, if the reason is just and good. The Malones have much love to share. She will teach him what she came to know—to see through the eyes of love. On Earth there are so many in need—the homeless, the troubled, the sick, the abused and the forgotten. Good souls are in great demand. Desirée Malone will have a rewarding life. And when it is done, her purpose fulfilled, she will have no more reservations. She will know the time has come to willingly cross over. In a sense she is a very fortunate woman. Few mortals ever know the why of their existence or understand that they are part of something bigger than themselves. We are all sisters and brothers, Angel Mackey."

Mackey cast him a dubious look. "Even meself and the blue boob?"

The fisherman shook his head in frustration. "What are we to do with you?"

"I suppose another loverly furlough on Cloud Nine is out of the question," he ventured.

"It was not even a consideration, Alistair." With a wave of his hand and a deep sigh, the Fisherman ended the audience.

Harlequin
Superromance®

CHILDREN OF THE HEART
by Sally Garrett

Available this month

Romance readers the world over have wept and
rejoiced over Sally Garrett's heartwarming stories of
love, caring and commitment. In her new novel,
Children of the Heart, Sally once again weaves a story
that will touch your most tender emotions.

You'll be moved to tears of joy

Nearly two hundred children have passed through
Trenance McKay's foster home. But after her husband
leaves her, Trenance knows she'll always have to
struggle alone. No man could have enough room in his
heart both for Trenance and for so many needy
children. Max Tulley, news anchor for KSPO TV is
willing to try, but how long can his love last?

"Sally Garrett does some of the best character studies
in the genre and will not disappoint her fans."
Romantic Times

**Look for *Children of the Heart* wherever
Harlequin Romance novels are sold.** SCH

Harlequin
Superromance®

**Available in Superromance this month
#462—STARLIT PROMISE**

STARLIT PROMISE is a deeply moving story of a
woman coming to terms with her grief and gradually
opening her heart to life and love.

Author Petra Holland sets the scene beautifully, never
allowing her heroine to become mired in self-pity. It
is a story that will touch your heart and leave you
celebrating the strength of the human spirit.

**Available wherever Harlequin books
are sold.**

MILLION DOLLAR JACKPOT
SWEEPSTAKES RULES & REGULATIONS
NO PURCHASE NECESSARY TO ENTER OR RECEIVE A PRIZE

1. Alternate means of entry: Print your name and address on a 3″ ×5″ piece of plain paper and send to the appropriate address below.

In the U.S.	In Canada
MILLION DOLLAR JACKPOT	MILLION DOLLAR JACKPOT
P.O. Box 1867	P.O. Box 609
3010 Walden Avenue	Fort Erie, Ontario
Buffalo, NY 14269-1867	L2A 5X3

2. To enter the Sweepstakes and join the Reader Service, check off the "YES" box on your Sweepstakes Entry Form and return. If you do not wish to join the Reader Service but wish to enter the Sweepstakes only, check off the "NO" box on your Sweepstakes Entry Form. To qualify for the Extra Bonus prize, scratch off the silver on your Lucky Keys. If the registration numbers match, you are eligible for the Extra Bonus Prize offering. Incomplete entries are ineligible. Torstar Corp. and its affiliates are not responsible for mutilated or unreadable entries or inadvertent printing errors. Mechanically reproduced entries are null and void.

3. Whether you take advantage of this offer or not, on or about April 30, 1992, at the offices of D.L. Blair, Inc., Blair, NE, your sweepstakes numbers will be compared against the list of winning numbers generated at random by the computer. However, prizes will only be awarded to individuals who have entered the Sweepstakes. In the event that all prizes are not claimed, a random drawing will be held from all qualified entries received from March 30, 1990 to March 31, 1992, to award all unclaimed prizes. All cash prizes (Grand to Sixth) will be mailed to winners and are payable by check in U.S. funds. Seventh Prize will be shipped to winners via third-class mail. These prizes are in addition to any free, surprise or mystery gifts that might be offered. Versions of this Sweepstakes with different prizes of approximate equal value may appear at retail outlets or in other mailings by Torstar Corp. and its affiliates.

4. PRIZES: (1) *Grand Prize $1,000,000.00 Annuity; (1) First Prize $25,000.00; (1) Second Prize $10,000.00; (5) Third Prize $5,000.00; (10) Fourth Prize $1,000.00; (100) Fifth Prize $250.00; (2,500) Sixth Prize $10.00; (6,000) **Seventh Prize $12.95 ARV.

   *This presentation offers a Grand Prize of a $1,000,000.00 annuity. Winner will receive $33,333.33 a year for 30 years without interest totalling $1,000,000.00.

   **Seventh Prize: A fully illustrated hardcover book, published by Torstar Corp. Approximate Retail Value of the book is $12.95.

   Entrants may cancel the Reader Service at any time without cost or obligation (see details in Center Insert Card).

5. Extra Bonus! This presentation offers an Extra Bonus Prize valued at $33,000.00 to be awarded in a random drawing from all qualified entries received by March 31, 1992. No purchase necessary to enter or receive a prize. To qualify, see instructions in Center Insert Card. Winner will have the choice of any of the merchandise offered or a $33,000.00 check payable in U.S. funds. All other published rules and regulations apply.

6. This Sweepstakes is being conducted under the supervision of D.L. Blair, Inc. By entering the Sweepstakes, each entrant accepts and agrees to be bound by these rules and the decisions of the judges, which shall be final and binding. Odds of winning the random drawing are dependent upon the number of entries received. Taxes, if any, are the sole responsibility of the winners. Prizes are nontransferable. All entries must be received at the address on the detachable Business Reply Card and must be postmarked no later than 12:00 MIDNIGHT on March 31, 1992. The drawing for all unclaimed Sweepstakes prizes and for the Extra Bonus Prize will take place on May 30, 1992, at 12:00 NOON at the offices of D.L. Blair, Inc., Blair, NE.

7. This offer is open to residents of the U.S., United Kingdom, France and Canada, 18 years or older, except employees and immediate family members of Torstar Corp., its affiliates, subsidiaries and all other agencies, entities and persons connected with the use, marketing or conduct of this Sweepstakes. All Federal, State, Provincial, Municipal and local laws apply. Void wherever prohibited or restricted by law. Any litigation within the Province of Quebec respecting the conduct and awarding of a prize in this publicity contest must be submitted to the Régie des Loteries et Courses du Québec.

8. Winners will be notified by mail and may be required to execute an affidavit of eligibility and release, which must be returned within 14 days after notification or an alternate winner may be selected. Canadian winners will be required to correctly answer an arithmetical, skill-testing question administered by mail, which must be returned within a limited time. Winners consent to the use of their name, photograph and/or likeness for advertising and publicity in conjunction with this and similar promotions without additional compensation.

9. For a list of our major prize winners, send a stamped, self-addressed envelope to: MILLION DOLLAR WINNERS LIST, P.O. Box 4510, Blair, NE 68009. Winners Lists will be supplied after the May 30, 1992 drawing date.

Offer limited to one per household.

LTY-H891

Coming Soon

Fashion A Whole New You
in classic romantic style
with a trip for two to Paris
via American Airlines®, a
brand-new Mercury Sable
LS and a $2,000 Fashion
Allowance.

Plus, romantic free gifts* are yours to
Fashion A Whole New You.

From September through November, you can take part in
this exciting opportunity from Harlequin.

Watch for details in September.

* with proofs-of-purchase, plus postage and handling

 *Harlequin Books*®

"There is [...] in the compound"

Alex Nanos shrank against the outside wall when the glass doors swung onto the open arcade. His breathing was virtually imperceptible. The long white curtains flickered back and forth in the moving air. Two men stood in the doorway. Nanos prayed that they would not come farther. They spoke. In English. The Greek felt an eerie chill rise up the back of his neck. He knew the voice!

Pounding and harsh shouts came from inside as soldiers stormed the room. Voices argued and demanded in rapid Arabic. The prisoner stepped onto the arcade and took a deep breath of fresh night air.

Alex Nanos gasped in spite of himself. He shook his head, insisting that what he saw with his own eyes could not be. The man he saw was dead, blown to bits in a fiery explosion on a bridge high over the shark-infested waters of Tampa Bay. There had been no remains.

The man was Geoff Bishop.

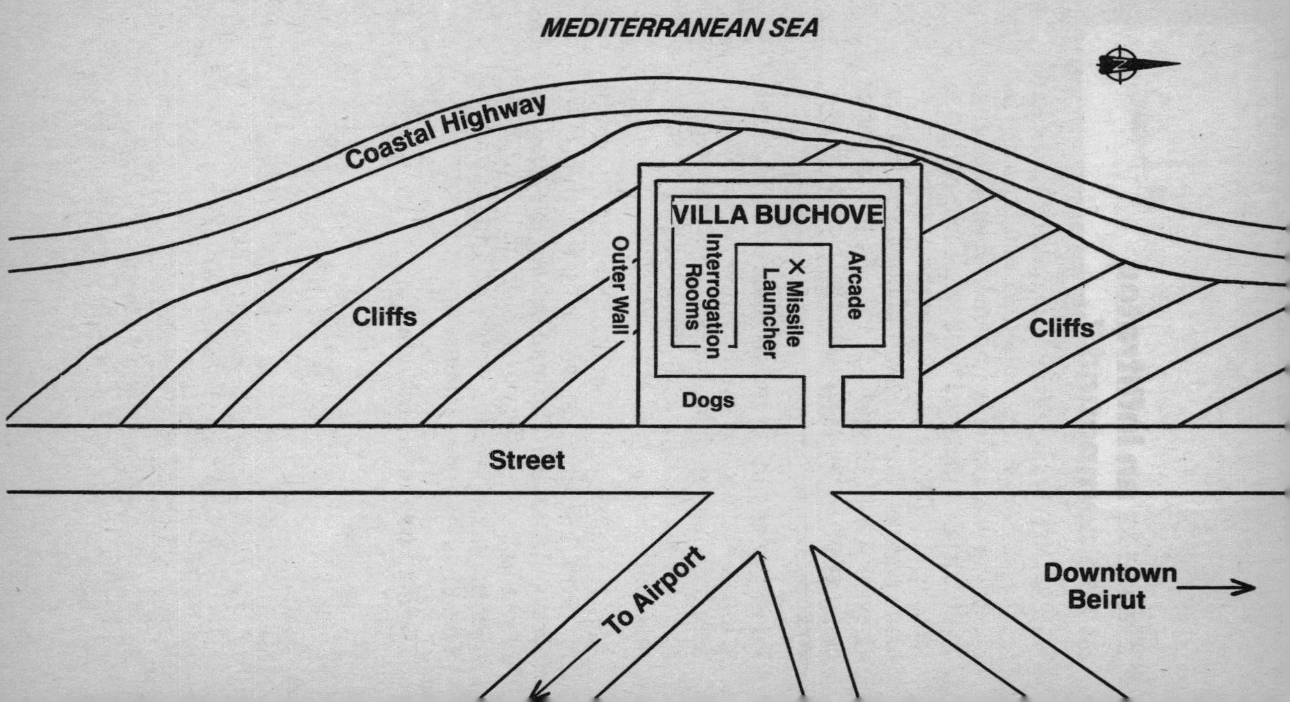
MEDITERRANEAN SEA
N
Coastal Highway
VILLA BUCHOVE
Arcade
× Missile Launcher
Interrogation Rooms
Outer Wall
Dogs
Cliffs
Cliffs
Street
To Airport
Downtown Beirut

SOBs
SOLDIERS OF BARRABAS

SKYJACK

JACK HILD

A GOLD EAGLE BOOK FROM
WORLDWIDE

TORONTO • NEW YORK • LONDON • PARIS
AMSTERDAM • STOCKHOLM • HAMBURG
ATHENS • MILAN • TOKYO • SYDNEY

First edition July 1987

ISBN 0-373-61619-8

Special thanks and acknowledgment to
Robin Hardy for his contribution to this work.

Printed in Canada

1

The cavernous bulk of the 727 squatted over the darkened runway. Hidden by the low forest a thousand feet away, Nate Beck sighted the big Star Tron camera over the wing. Flexitube snaked into the open emergency exit from a portable air conditioner on the tarmac. He adjusted the focus.

The pattern in the tiny screen set inside the scope shifted slightly. The outline of a man, his face covered with a black mask, was clear and distinct against the background of the airplane's fuselage.

"Hijacker partially concealed in doorway. Clear for head shot."

"Hmph," William Starfoot II, or Billy Two as his friends called him, grunted, moving the butt of the British L4A1 sniper rifle along his shoulder. The two crack commandos were into their second hour of surveillance, and their need to remain motionless was taking its toll.

"Can you make the shot?" Beck, a diminutive Jew from New York, asked the grizzly-sized full-blooded Kansas Osage.

"I can make the shot." Billy Two's modified Enfield was equipped with an infrared night scope—primitive compared to Nate's hi-tech optical device.

The muscles around his left eye were painfully cramped from two hours of constant squinting. Through his right eye, he saw the terrorist's heat image outlined against the residual heat radiating from the airplane's aluminum fuselage. The infrared scope ignored the niceties of outlines, barely distinguishing male from female.

"Finger is itchy. Ve-ry itchy." The Osage's voice was low and threatening. He was a word away from squeezing the trigger the last half millimeter.

"Ve-ry soon." Beck dragged it out. "Because . everyone's . . . in place."

He held up a tiny portable computer monitor slightly larger than the palm of his hand. An electronics wizard, Beck had converted an ordinary Japanese pocket television. Its two and a half inch high-resolution screen glowed with a computer map of the runway, marking the exact location of the airplane.

Each of the other mercs surrounding the airplane was equipped with a small modular radio transmission unit—basically a car telephone, minus the receiver. The little hi-tech box at his side picked up the signals, translating them into red dots no bigger than the head of a pin that appeared on the screen of the tiny monitor.

The voice from the command post rumbled through Nate Beck's two-way communication plug. "It's a go, Eagle. One minute. Bad Dog out."

Beck looked up from the tiny screen. Five bulky figures in black trotted quickly across the tarmac, shadows approaching the airplane from behind. A moment later a ladder was pushed up against the undercarriage of the fuselage at the rear exit. Two of the figures started to climb. The other three continued forward, carrying a second ladder between them. They propped it against the wing and began to climb.

Nate sighted with the image-intensification scope again. There were two figures at the door of the airplane. The masked terrorist stood behind the second person—a hostage with a gun pressed against his head.

Suddenly orange muzzle flash popped in the open door, with the report of a single shot. A body flopped onto the wing, rolled like a stuffed doll and fell onto the runway.

A shout through Beck's earplugs stung his ears.

"Take him out, Eagle!"

"Now, Billy!"

The Osage fired once, the L4A1 bucking slightly.

The terrorist disappeared from the Star Tron screen when the bullet flipped him back into the airplane.

"He's down."

Billy Two heard Nate through the echo of the blast from the L4A1. The red heat shapes of three commandos scudded across his scope as they rushed the hijacked airliner. He swung the rifle smoothly to the left in tandem with Beck and the Star Tron system, sighting carefully on the windows of the cockpit.

NILE BARRABAS LEAPED onto the wing as the impact slammed the terrorist back into the airway. Liam O'Toole and Alex Nanos crowded up the ladder behind him. Another man dashed past the open entrance, the muzzle of his handgun flashing brightly in the interior darkness. The merc leader felt a lead fist against the bulletproof padding on his chest.

Barrabas swung his arm forward and pumped the trigger of the Walther P-38. The man tumbled forward, the upper half of his body protruding from the door. His gun clattered to the tarmac. Barrabas stomped across the body.

At the rear of the airplane, Claude Hayes shouldered the exit door, ripping it from its hinges, then using it as a shield as he made a blind rush up the aisle. Close behind him, Lee Hatton pulled the pin on a flash grenade, counted and tossed it over her shoulder. A deafening explosion thundered through the airplane, and then the interior was lit by a brilliant flash that illuminated three armed hijackers in black masks.

One pivoted, aiming his handgun. Hayes crashed into him, bowling him over with the door, and kept going. Hatton hesitated over the supine body long enough to fire her Beretta twice. Crimson flowers blossomed across his chest and head.

At the wing, Barrabas, O'Toole and Nanos fanned through the door almost on top of one another, garnering a quick view of the interior in the brief illumination from the flash-bang. The second terrorist stood in the entrance to the first-class section. Barrabas fired twice.

The first shot hit the masked hijacker high in the chest with a big red splat, punching the center of his body back and his head forward. The second bullet smacked clear into the center of his forehead. The black mask exploded into a fury of bleeding red, and he went down.

Liam O'Toole pushed past his commander, rushing the forward cabin. Alex Nanos threw a second stun grenade. He spun around in time to see Claude Hayes bear down on the third hijacker with the airplane's rear door. Nanos tracked and fired. Lee Hatton opened up over Hayes's head. Bullets pounded simultaneously into the man's head and chest. Red splashed across the fuselage, splattering the white fabric-covered door as Hayes pushed the dead man out of the way.

At the front of the airplane, O'Toole bulldozed the door to the cockpit at full speed. The fiberglass partition ripped off its hinges with the full impact of the big Irish American's weight and drove into the cabin, knocking over a hijacker on its way. O'Toole dropped, pinning the man to the floor and stabbing the barrel of his pistol against his head.

"Freeze! No one move!" Nile Barrabas filled the door, instantly surveying the dark cockpit. The crew of three sat at their controls, their hands in the air. Two were enemy. He fired. The first took the hit in the neck. The impact of the bullet flung him over the control panel. He clawed at his neck with sticky reddened hands, searching for a way to breathe. Barrabas pulled back into the first-class section for cover. A muzzle flashed to his right, and two bullets chunked into the doorframe.

The merc leader threw himself around the corner, holding the trigger down and pumping rounds in the direction of the muzzle flash. For an instant there was a high-pitched whistle at the open window beside the pilot. An ugly red wound suddenly opened across the far side of the last hijacker's face, throwing him back against the wall.

An abrupt silence fell over the airplane.

A man groaned.

The lights went on.

The last hijacker down picked himself up slowly from the floor. He ripped the black mask from his face and smiled at the two mercs.

"Those paint bullets pack a wallop," he said, smoothing his hand over the red goo that ran down his clothing. "Even with these padded monkey suits."

"You ain't kidding," the second man said, pulling his mask off. He put his hand to his neck, coughing to clear his throat.

"Six point three seconds from entry to total elimination!" The man in the pilot's seat held up a digital stopwatch. "Congratulations, Colonel Barrabas. Your team holds the record for an assault on a hijacked jetliner."

"Practice assault," Barrabas corrected the FBI agent. "But that was a good twist, putting a couple of extra of you in here. We expected the main force to be in the fuselage."

The man underneath the door moaned and put his hand to his back as O'Toole helped him up.

"Where in hell did that last bullet come from?" the FBI agent "terrorist" asked. "I thought I had you!"

Barrabas peered out the cockpit window and saw the great bear-sized shape of Billy Two lumbering across the tarmac toward the airplane. Beside him ran the diminutive electronics expert for the commando team, Nate Beck.

"I told you I had the best sharpshooter this side of the Iron Curtain." Barrabas laughed.

For a week, the "unofficial" team of professional warriors, known as the Soldiers of Barrabas, had been on anti-terrorist group maneuvers with a comparable number of seasoned FBI agents at a secret training sight in Kentucky. They'd practised a variety of exercises jointly, going through motions dozens of times, until everyone had it right. Then they squared off in a final "game," using harmless paint bullets.

The two groups had been tied at the end of the embassy hostage simulation. But for the hijacked airliner, the SOBs had come out ahead of the FBI team's time. The good-natured competition continued.

"Hey! Who won!" Alex Nanos, "The Greek," shouted from the cabin. Barrabas and the other men poured from the cockpit into the first-class section as the other mercs congregated with unmasked "terrorists" and compared strokes.

"Six point three for the good guys!" Barrabas yelled, a smile creasing his face. The SOBs cheered and crowded around their tall white-haired leader. Billy Two added a bloodcurdling war whoop of his own to the fray. The FBI agents clapped, slapping the mercs on the back.

"The one thing—" Barrabas shouted over the noise, then waved his hand to silence them. "The one thing that wasn't here was the passengers. Remember that. For next time. Sorry to end on a sober note."

"Well, we'll just have to see what we might do about that," O'Toole crowed. "Training is now officially over, and if I recall, there's a bottle of whiskey or two at the refreshment stand in our local FBI resort hotel.''

Another cheer went up from the anti-terrorist fighters. This time, Lee Hatton's voice rose above the fray.

"Hey! Hey, guys! I just wanna ask this one question.'' The woman was small and slender, but when she belted it out, she could be heard. The men cleared a space around her, and she confronted Barrabas and their FBI instructor.

"When I came in the back of the airplane, I found myself automatically tracking and killing anything that was standing in front of me. That's what I've been trained to do in an assault situation. In a hijack situation, any assault is going to be a surprise, so what happens if a lot of the passengers are on their feet? They're also easy targets for a terrorist slaughter. So why don't we shout as we come through, you know, 'get down!'—stuff like that.''

A murmur went through the crowd of men. They nodded and looked to the instructor.

"Good question. The kind of small detail that can be overlooked in an intensive training session, but not the kind that has been overlooked by the people who study these things. And they've done studies—in hostage simulations and from debriefings in real hijack-hostage incidents. At Entebbe, the Israeli commandos went in shouting 'Get down!' and shot anything standing—including two passengers. By the standards of anti-terrorist warfare, that assault was a success. But that approach doesn't work with Americans. For some reason, Americans are naturally inquisitive, curious people. To our credit, I guess. But every goddamned time it's been tried, no one gets down, they all just turn around and crane their necks to see what's happening.''

The man shrugged and looked at Barrabas.

''Sounds like a judgment call to me,'' Barrabas commented. ''Who's on board, how well trained the assault team is...''

''And whether the terrorists are armed with BB guns or grenades,'' the FBI instructor finished with a nod. ''Let's hit the hotel,'' he said, referring to the less than glamorous accommodations they shared in the barracks that made up the secret training site. ''We can talk about it over a few beers!''

A chorus of assent was sounded, then the men and women warriors descended from the airplane and straggled in smaller groups across the tarmac.

Alex Nanos walked beside Barrabas and Lee Hatton.

''Colonel, I wanted to ask about José Sanchez,'' Nanos said quietly, naming the man they'd worked with on a recent mission. ''He wants to know when he's coming back. He's out of the hospital now. He's real sorry he's missed this training session but says the surgeons made his legs better than new.''

Barrabas had needed a trained pilot to replace Geoff Bishop, the ace Canadian airman who had been killed on an anti-terrorist assignment in Florida. José Sanchez, a trained former military pilot, had made friends with Nanos and Hayes on an extended deep-sea fishing trip, and initially he had seemed to fit in well with the mercs. But now it was time for the hard news—the part of the job Barrabas hated most.

"We owe him a lot for saving Lee's life when she was looking down the twin barrels of 60 mm howitzers," the former Special Forces Airborne colonel began. "But the mission was for us to get a videotape of highly classified information on the KGB out of the Soviet Union."

"He should have let me die." Lee Hatton's tone was perfectly matter-of-fact.

Barrabas glanced at her, his icy blue eyes taking in her assurance. All his soldiers knew the occupational hazards of professional soldiering and accepted them. That's why they'd been chosen. He nodded.

"Lee, you had a lucky break. But Sanchez got his legs shot out from under him when he made that save. Consequently he was unable to fly us out. When it comes down to one of us or the task we've accepted, there's only one choice. That's what we're paid for. That's one of the major rules. In saving one life, Sanchez jeopardized all our lives and, more importantly, the entire mission. He should have let Lee go. There are no second chances. He didn't make the team."

There was silence as the mercs approached the compound of small one-story buildings that housed the FBI trainees who regularly used the facility. The colonel was boss, and his word was final. Their respect for Barrabas as a leader came from trust. He was right. They knew it. It didn't lessen Nanos's disappointment. But at least, they could accept his judgment call with a good conscience.

"Any more questions?"

The Greek—Nanos had carried the nickname from the days just after his dismissal from the U.S. Coast Guard, when he had whored his way up and down Miami Beach as a well-paid gigolo—shook his head.

"Don't you get the feeling sometimes that Geoff Bishop is going to walk around the corner and say 'Hey, I gotta chopper out back, let's take a ride!'?"

"I hear you." Lee Hatton sighed, momentarily casting her eyes down and smiling with resignation. Alex put his arm around her shoulders in a gesture of comradeship.

All the SOBs had been chosen for the variety of battle skills they possessed. Hatton was a medical doctor and intelligence expert, as well as skilled in the martial arts. It was common knowledge among the mercs that she and Bishop had been lovers.

"Colonel!" Nate Beck ran up from behind and fell into step beside them. "What are the chances we're going to be called out for this kind of airline hostage work?"

"Not too bloody high, I'd say," Liam O'Toole commented, pulling up beside Barrabas. "It's always high-profile work, you know, hundreds of press and photographers covering it as an international incident. We're more the 'go in and knock 'em out before anyone knows any better' kind of team."

"Especially with all the competition," Nanos added. "In the U.S. alone there's Delta Force, the FBI squads, and local SWAT teams."

"Not to mention the special teams in other countries where these kinds of situations are most likely to occur," Lee joined in. "Let's face it. Much as we hate to hear about it happening, when it does, everyone who's spent weeks or months training for it wants a piece of the action."

Barrabas laughed. "Including us."

The mercs stopped for a minute outside the door to Shangri-la—the facility's affectionately named recreation building. Inside the open doors, the FBI trainees were opening up the bar. Billy Two and Claude Hayes, the two brawniest members of the SOBs, were already taking bets on arm-wrestling contests.

"You're all so hot to trot, you forgot one thing," Barrabas told his people. "The reason we exist is because sometimes there are jobs that can't be done by the official special-action teams. That's why we're covert. But the short answer to your question, Nate, is—" the colonel gave an exaggerated shrug "—who knows?"

"Hey!" one of the FBI trainees inside shouted to the mercs. "Training is over, and seriousness is now against the rules!"

Liam O'Toole sniffed at the air. "I believe I smell some fine whiskey in close proximity. If I'm not back by tomorrow morning, send out a search party." He hit the steps.

"Well, what the hell," Nate concluded as Nanos followed the red-haired Irishman. "We're so secret, even if they do call us in, no one will know the difference, and someone else will get the credit."

"Rules of the game," said Lee. "Not even these FBI guys really know who we are or why we're here."

"And have better sense than to ask." Barrabas motioned Hatton and Beck ahead of him into Shangri-la. "Let's enjoy."

He watched his soldiers for a moment before joining them, reflecting on Nate's question. It was unlikely, he admitted. But two decades as a soldier had taught him to expect the unlikely. At the unlikeliest of times.

2

The Orly terminal of Planet Airways was frantic with midmorning traffic. Thousands of transatlantic passengers clogged the main lobby. Long lineups snaked through the melee from ticket and baggage counters, while red caps barged through the herds with luggage-laden carts.

Mike Mitchell winced at the sight of the people to whom he would shortly be serving coffee and lunch and anything else they demanded on whim. Five glorious days in Paris were over, and it was back to work. He clutched his flight bag close and slipped around the side of the crowd until he reached the unmarked door that led to the flight attendants' lounge.

A few minutes later he was in full purser's uniform, rummaging through the galley of the 727 and making final preparations for the flight to Athens. There were five flight attendants. Two, Christine and Valerie, were women whom he'd worked with on the flight from New York. He also knew two of the three guys, Tom and Ron, from several previous rotations. The fourth flight attendant, who introduced himself as Al, had just graduated from Planet Air's St. Louis training center.

"They don't train them like they used to," the New York native muttered to Christine from the side of his mouth. "The new guy's standing around with his finger up his ass."

"I didn't think they put new attendants on international flights," the pretty young woman answered absentmindedly, too busy to look up. She rapidly counted tiny two-ounce bottles of liquor and made a notation on an inventory sheet. "You're supposed to sign this."

Mike scribbled his initials at the bottom of the list and leaned into the aisle. "Hey, you!"

The new man was standing midway down the economy-class section. He was tall, his hair dark and his skin either tanned or naturally olive toned. He was quite young, barely out of his teens. Mike Mitchell doubted that he was old enough to shave.

"Yeah, you!" the purser shouted when the new attendant turned. "You check the toilets yet to make sure all the dispensers are full? And guess what. You're doing the emergency procedures announcement. So get a move on."

The attendant moved quickly toward the tail of the airplane where the toilets were located. As Mitchell ducked back into the tiny galley, he kicked a flight bag sticking from the bottom shelf below the microwave unit. Valerie and Ron were ripping the foil covers off the precooked lunches.

No matter how much time they gave themselves for setup, it ended in a frenzied, frantic attempt to finish before the passengers boarded. Sticking him with a neophyte attendant on a fully booked flight was typical of airline management.

"Goddamn it, whose is this?" Mitchell cried, tugging the flight bag from its resting place. Al's name was written on the tag. "Jeez, don't they even teach them where to stow their fuckin' stuff? Christine! Can you stick this in the crew compartment." He motioned to the flight bag as Ron handed him another inventory list to initial.

The woman grabbed the flight bag and dragged it from the cubbyhole. "What's he got in here, anyway?" she asked rhetorically, opening the door to the crew's storage compartment.

Mike Mitchell looked around, halfway through counting out float money for the other attendants. The bag was obviously heavy. Something clunked inside. He should check it, he thought.

Christine dropped the bag in the compartment and closed the door. "Liquor or one of those three-hundred-ounce bottles of cologne from duty free," she said, shrugging.

"Or a teddy bear and personal nursing bottles," Ron joked as he shoved dinners into the microwave heating slots.

"Nursing bottles." Mitchell snapped his fingers, his memory jogged. There were always a thousand and one details for a purser to remember. He grabbed the clipboard with the passenger list. "We have two newborn babies on this trip, people. Two. Be warned and get the bottle warmer out. Okay, let's give the seats one last check before they board."

"Who's in charge of the animals?" a boisterous voice called into the galley. It was followed by a rotund bald man with a blond mustache. He extended his hand to the purser, his merry blue eyes sorting out the gender of the attendants as they filed out. "David Ratcliffe, the pilot of this ancient bird. I think we worked that Paris–New York run for a few weeks a year or so ago." He lowered his voice and leaned toward the purser. "Only two of the female variety?" He gestured with a nod of his head toward the attendants and mocked a look of skeptical disappointment.

Mitchell laughed and shook hands. "You think Planet Air is in the business of expanding your personal stable of lovely young things?"

"Uh, no. But do four out of six have to be guys?"

"And I got more news. We're all straight. Three of us, anyway. You can check out the new guy. I don't know what he is—except useless." The intercom receiver buzzed, and Mitchell reached for it.

"I'll pass." Ratcliffe slapped him on the back.

"Man the battle stations, Captain, sir." The purser hung up the intercom receiver. "The animals are boarding."

The friendly pilot headed back to the cockpit.

Mike Mitchell looked about in anticipation of the arrival of the passengers. There was something else he was going to check, something important, and then he had been distracted. Damned if he could think of what it was. Impatient footsteps sounded on the boarding ramp. A million little details. Two or three things were always forgotten. The first passenger stepped into the airplane. Mike straightened his tie and smiled.

THE 727 FLEW among popcorn-shaped clouds, thirty thousand feet above the rolling green farmlands of France. The pilot steered the airplane south, circling the distant Alps and heading toward the sparkling Mediterranean. The flight attendants had just made their first trip up and down the aisle, and a hundred and forty-three contented passengers sipped their drinks.

Matt Chicago, a San Francisco native, stuck his blond head above the back of the seats and surveyed his fellow travelers. They were a docile bunch—tourists, businessmen and Greek Americans visiting their extended families in the home country. The rowdiest was a collection of loud-talking frat boys from Wisconsin, on their way to a week of sun and women on a small Greek island.

Having missed breakfast in the rush to get to Orly for the midmorning flight, he was hungry and impatient for lunch. The flight attendants had disappeared after serving drinks. They were nowhere in sight.

Chicago deserved this trip. A friend of his had just been through the far side of a long terminal illness. He had been there, helping him to die. The personal toll was something he hadn't reckoned on. After eight months of home care, and later, daily hospital visits, he was exhausted. With a few thousand dollars from the small inheritance, he'd fled. All his life he'd wanted to tour the ruins of antiquity. At long last, saddened by the recent tragedy but relieved that his old friend had found peace, he was finally on his way.

Chicago groped for the button in the armrest and leaned his seat back, stretching his long legs forward until they could go no farther.

"Cramped." The man beside him looked up from a magazine to make the one-word statement. He had the same problem. Long legs. He was roughly the same age as Matt Chicago, in his mid-twenties, neatly dressed in conservative slacks and a white polo shirt. His blond hair was clipped short at the sides.

"You army?" The man was looking at Chicago's baggy camouflage pants and his olive green tank top.

The San Francisco native laughed. "Are you kidding? This is called *style*."

The man grinned and nodded. "John Lorch." He stuck out his hand. "U.S. Marines. That's why I asked."

"Matt Chicago." The two men shook hands, and the Marine concentrated again on the pages of his magazine.

On Chicago's other side, an elderly man sat quietly, staring out the window as the airplane left the French coast below and headed across the Mediterranean toward Italy. His legs were squeezed into the narrow space left by a large leather-bound case tucked into the narrow space on the floor in front of him.

"Got a hat in there?" The San Franciscan smiled, distracting the older man from his thoughts.

"What? Oh, that. No, not a hat," he said. "The last five years of my life. I'm a scientist. It's a research project."

The young Marine lowered his magazine and looked at the elderly man.

"Aren't you Dr. Samuel Wheatley from the Aeronautics Research Institute?"

The scientist nodded, his blue eyes twinkling with amusement. "Why, yes, how did you know?"

"I'm in the Marine Corps. You were a visiting lecturer at the academy!"

Chicago nodded with interest. "Are you going to a conference or something in Athens?"

"Oh, no, just a stopover to change planes. I'm off to..." He smiled at the young man and put up his hand. "Here I am blathering away, and my boss told me it was a secret."

David laughed. "Sorry for asking."

"Not at all. And where are you off to, young man?"

"Greece. Then Egypt. I've always wanted to see the ruins of the classical world. Name's Matt. Matt Chicago."

"Lieutenant John Lorch."

"Well, I'll tell you," Chicago said, "if they don't get some food down here real soon, all they'll find is skeletal remains."

"It shouldn't be long now," the elderly gentlemen said with a smile. He turned back to gaze in silence out the window.

Matt Chicago craned his neck over the headrests of the seat in front once again to see if there was any sign of lunch. One of the flight attendants tied back the curtain between first and second class. Several stern-looking men, dark-haired and young, congregated in the aisle and blocked the view. The smell of microwaved cuisine wafted down the aisle from the first-class section. He salivated.

Across the aisle, a baby in the lap of a plump woman with a beehive hairdo began to fuss. She lifted the infant, clucking and cooing, and handed it to an older woman in a black dress who sat beside her. Immediately the baby let out a plaintive cry, strong enough to be the first of many. Matt Chicago sighed and sunk low in his seat, more aware of his stomach than ever. He had a feeling it was going to be a long, long flight.

In the galley, Christine and Ron stacked steaming hot trays of food on the dolly. The thin, desperate cry of a very young baby stretched into the galley.

"Fe-e-e-e-e-d m-e-e-e-e-e!" Ron mimicked in a little-shop-of-horrors voice, breathing heavily in Christine's ear. She pushed him away with an elbow, carefully balancing one tray of food on her forearm and clutching two more between assorted fingers.

"Goddamn kid. Now watch, the other one will go off like an alarm clock set in tandem."

Mike Mitchell burst into the galley, his lips tight with anger. "First class is done. Where in hell's that new guy! I'm gonna bust his ass when I file the evaluation report."

Christine and Ron began wheeling the dolly into the aisle.

Ron jerked his head at the door of the toilet next to the cockpit. "In the john."

"He asked for his flight bag a minute ago. Freaked out when he noticed it had been moved," Christine added. ''Did you tie the curtain back?'' Carefully walking backward, she edged the dolly into the first-class section. She glanced quickly over her shoulder and saw the dark-haired men who had congregated at the door to the economy class.

The pretty young flight attendant resisted the temptation to roll her eyes and sigh in frustration. Passengers insisted on being in the most inconvenient places at the worst times.

''There are more rest rooms at the rear of the plane, gentlemen. If you'll just move back so we can get this through...''

In the galley, Mike Mitchell raised his voice angrily.

''Find the new guy and tell him to move his ass in here.'' One of the other flight attendants was bearing the brunt of the purser's frustrations.

The door of the toilet next to the cockpit entrance swung open just as Mike Mitchell stepped into the first-class aisle. He turned, fully prepared to blast the new flight attendant, then he caught sight of something clutched in the man's hands. The words lodged in his throat, cut off by a gasp. It was a gun.

''Hijack! No one move!'' The man in the flight attendant uniform screamed the order, the tendons of his neck clearly visible. He held a 9 mm pistol with both hands and waved it at the passengers from the front of the plane.

At the other end of the first-class cabin, the man in front of Christine grabbed her blouse at the neck.

''Hey, what...!''

Her protest was short. She felt herself being lifted, and she landed across the passengers in the seat next to her. The men pushed into the first-class section, knocking the food trolley askew. A thermos of coffee tumbled, spilling its scalding contents into the lap of a female passenger.

"Hafez!" the young man with the gun shouted, holding the flight bag up with one hand.

"Alli! Here!" The first man into the cabin reached out his arms to receive it.

The scalded woman shrieked, rising in her seat to grab at her dress and blocking the aisle. Hafez cuffed her, his fist smashing into the back of her head. She gasped in shock and fell into the lap of the man next to her, pulling hysterically at her steaming clothing.

"Omigod," a passenger exclaimed in a weak, querulous voice. A murmur of fear swept the passengers of the first-class section like an icy wind.

Alli heaved his heavy flight bag past the flight attendants. Hafez caught it. The two men behind him rushed the attendants. Mike Mitchell was pushed face first against the compartment wall. Hafez ripped the flight bag open and withdrew two guns.

"Nabil! Ahmed!" he called to the men who had the flight attendants against the wall, and threw them the guns. His hand went back into the flight bag. It came out clutching grenades.

The scalded woman was crying hysterically, her moans growing with the mounting agony of her serious burns.

"Shut up!" Hafez yelled savagely. He struck her across the side of the face with his gun, and her last sob stuck in her throat for a second of stillness. Blood spurted from the open wound on her forehead, sluicing down her face and spraying across the passengers in the row of seats. Her eyes rolled upward, and she passed out.

In economy class, Matt Chicago was still on the lookout for lunch, craning over the headrests of the seat in front when the painful scream reverberated back. The men who had gathered at the front of the cabin disappeared into first class, leaving the curtain swinging closed in the door behind them. Passengers rose, peering into the aisle in search of the source of the commotion. The Marine beside Chicago looked up from his magazine with an expression of concern.

"What's happening?"

Chicago shrugged.

Two of the flight attendants marched quickly up the aisle toward the front of the plane. They were almost there when Nabil and Ahmed moved in.

"Holy fuck," the Marine muttered.

"Hijack! You are our prisoners! No one move! Put your faces down! Everyone now! Or we kill you!" Ahmed screamed and pointed his gun around the cabin.

Near the rear of the 727, a dark-haired woman stepped into the aisle from her seat and ran forward. Ahmed pulled another gun from his belt and threw it to her. She caught it expertly, bringing it down to point at the two flight attendants. They froze in fear, throwing their arms into the air as the terrorists closed in on them from both sides.

Nabil grabbed Tom, spinning him around and pushing him into Valerie. The woman ran at Valerie, grabbing the jacket of her uniform and roughly pushing her into a vacant seat.

"Sit!" she screamed, pointing her gun around the cabin. "Everyone put your heads down now! Heads down! To your knees! No one move or we shoot!"

The three terrorists took positions up and down the length of the cabin, moving quickly from seat to seat to ensure that their captives complied.

"Now!" Ahmed shouted, towering over a reluctant and angry businessman in an aisle seat. His gun came down, cracking the man across the top of his head. The American grunted, dropping low in his seat, cowering from the hijacker's upraised arm. Ahmed whipped around and moved on.

"This is a hijacking!" the woman screamed from the center of the plane, inches away from Matt Chicago. "In the name of the Islamic Jihad, we have made you prisoners of war! You are our hostages!"

IN THE COCKPIT, Captain Ratcliffe had just eased the 727 into its final cruising altitude at thirty thousand feet.

"Weather's good. Minimum of stratospheric turbulence," the flight engineer reported, reading the data from his instruments.

"Just a matter of sitting back for an hour or so and waiting for the coast of Greece to come into view," the copilot said. "Then two wonderful days to enjoy the women of Athens."

"If you can find one without a mustache," Ratcliffe snorted cynically, recalling a frustrating weekend in Athens a few weeks earlier.

The cockpit door crashed open. The crew turned.

"Freeze! You will not move!" The terrorist named Alli moved in. He held his gun with both hands, tracking from side to side to cover the three-man crew. "Your airplane has been seized by the Revolutionary Army of God. You are hostages. *Allah akbar!* God is great!"

"Jesus fuckin' Christ." Captain Ratcliffe wasn't aware of the curse escaping his lips. He thought—vainly, in defiance of the evidence in front of him—that it was a joke. A surprise training drill. They were making a movie. It couldn't be real.

The man's voice was stretched as thin as a razor, his brown eyes bulging, the whites large from the rush of adrenaline. The gun trembled in his hands. He was scared as hell and extremely dangerous. He moved the gun slowly and trained it at Ratcliffe's head.

"We have guns! We have explosives! You will follow instructions exactly!"

The terrorist paused and examined the faces of his prisoners. It was obvious they understood. He couldn't resist smiling. The hijacking had been accomplished.

"This is a suicide mission." He reached inside the open collar of his shirt and withdrew a grenade. He bounced it in his hand like a tennis ball. "If there is trouble, we will destroy the plane with everyone aboard."

3

With a gun inches from his head, Captain Ratcliffe was ordered to radio the air traffic controllers in Rome when the 727's flight path took it over the city. Almost instantly, the world knew of the imperiled airliner. The front pages of the dailies exploded with black headlines two inches high, and television news anchormen interrupted regularly scheduled programming to broadcast the story to millions of viewers, inflecting their speech with tones of hallowed urgency.

Planet Air's toll-free switchboards in Denver, Colorado, were overwhelmed by hundreds of callers who feared for friends and relatives traveling in Europe. At Athens airport, a forty-four-year-old woman died instantly of a massive coronary when she learned her son and husband were being held hostage at thirty thousand feet somewhere over the Mediterranean.

In Washington the press and the curious congregated like noisy wolf packs outside the houses and offices of the mighty, baying for statements.

In the posh residential area in nearby Georgetown, a silver stretch limousine turned onto a narrow cobblestone street and slid past high red brick walls. Wrought-iron gates and giant shade trees afforded brief glimpses of great mansions the size of barns. The

limousine slowed as it neared the end of the street. A
gaggle of reporters and photographers had converged
in front of the last gate. Security men maintained a
cordon, waving the reporters behind police barricades on either side of the drive. The reporters looked
angry.

In the back of the limo, an enormous man lowered
his plump index finger onto a button in the armrest.
The window between the back and front seat hummed
and lowered.

"Ah guess we'll jes' keep on drahvin'," Walker
Jessup drawled in the heaviest accent of his native
Texas that he could muster. He was able to turn it on
or off at will, depending on his mood or the circumstances.

A few minutes earlier he had been walking across
the lobby of his Washington hotel before heading back
to his New York office. An out-of-breath desk clerk
had caught up to him just as he went through the automatic door. There was a message from the senator.
It was terse. It read, "Urgently require export arrangement. Come now."

So here he was. The television in the back of the
limo gave him the first clue as to why. A Planet Air
727 had been hijacked over Italy. The reporters mob-
bing the front gates of the old politician's mansion
underlined the urgency.

"Ain't nothing more dangerous than a reporter
sniffing the scent of a story on the wind. Drives 'em
crazier 'n a bull in a ruttin' pen," he told his driver.
"Turns 'em career simple."

If he dared to go in the front gate under their noses, they'd mob the car and photograph it. Some eager beaver would check out the license number, grease a palm down at the chauffeur service and find out that one Walker Jessup, a.k.a. "the Fixer," had paid a visit to the powerful senator on the first morning of the crisis.

For twenty years, Jessup had maintained the secrecy of his role as a CIA operative. He'd earned his nickname, "the Fixer," the hard way in his years with the Company. For the past ten, he had surreptitiously operated in the private sphere.

His agency's name, Walker Jessup, International Consultants, was vague enough to conceal high-priced global skulduggery, covert operations for the highest bidder in the gray area between the rule of law and the demons of nihilism. A sufficient number of powerful people found his services vitally important.

As long as his profile remained virtually non-existent, the powers that be allowed him to operate in peace. He wasn't going to blow it now by driving up to the front door of the senator's house on the morning of a grave international hostage crisis.

Jessup pressed his face close to the tinted glass as the limousine approached. Most of the journalists here were second-string, keeners desperate to work their way up. The main men from the wire services, the networks and major dailies would be congregating outside the White House, waiting for the President to make a statement. Some of them turned at the sight of the approaching limo. They began moving in a predatory run toward the car, ready to pounce.

Just in time, the luxury limo picked up speed and continued past the gates. The reporters quickly lost interest and turned back to their confrontation with the senator's security people. That's why they're second-string, the Fixer reflected. They gave up too easily.

"Turn down the first side street and pull over," he instructed his driver. "I'll get out there, and you can wait."

He gazed back at the mob receding in the rear window. To his surprise, he recognized the pointed vulpine features of Calhoun Bellow in the crowd. The Washington columnist for the big New York daily stared after the disappearing car.

What in hell's name was Bellow doing with this bunch? Jessup asked himself. Why wasn't he at the White House? The answer was obvious. Cal Bellow was in the major league for good reason. He knew where power was really wielded and the shields that covered it from the public eye.

The senator was sometimes used as an outlet to the press for informal statements of Administration policy on foreign affairs. What the world didn't know about—and never would—was that the old man headed a secret House Committee. Bellow had been around, probably long enough to hear rumors.

Jessup left the car. He walked down the tree-lined side street and around the corner of the senator's estate. There was a small service entrance next to the gate house. He approached the noisy rabble of reporters stealthily from behind and caught the eye of the security guard at the narrow gate. He slipped his hand inside his suit jacket and withdrew a laminated identity card. Flashing it, he moved directly toward the entrance. The security man flicked his eyes quickly over the card and gave a curt, silent nod. He signaled to the second guard inside and pushed the gate open. Jessup slipped through into the cool, shaded tranquility of the lush estate.

"Senator's expecting you immediately," the security man said, lowering a hand-held radio from his ear. He fell into step beside the fat Texan, directing him onto a stone path. It led across sloping lawns and through carefully manicured gardens to the enormous Colonial house.

Miss Roseline, the senator's secretary, greeted him at the door. Jessup bowed slightly. A Texan was also a gentleman, but Jessup did it from respect. The attractive woman had once been of enormous help in a difficult situation when his own neck had been in the noose. He trusted her every bit as much as he distrusted the wheezy manipulations of the crafty old senator.

"You're lucky," Miss Roseline told him, leading the way across the wide hallway. "He's in a good mood today."

"With an airplane hijacking on his hands?"

"It's all relative. He thrives on crisis." She held the heavy paneled door open for him.

Two gentlemen waiting with the senator rose from their padded leather chairs when Walker Jessup entered. One, a short man with a bulldog face, wore the medal-bespangled uniform of an Air Force general.

The second was civilian, a tall white-haired man in an expensive dark suit.

"Walker Jessup." The senator spoke sharply in a voice strained thin by age. "General Wally Simmons from the Pentagon, and Dr. Horace Greely, a scientist from the Aeronautics Research Institute at Astute University in Maryland."

The politician remained in his wheelchair, a blanket wrapped tightly around his immobilized legs, while the others shook hands. He was an embittered man, with dark connections to mysterious and wealthy patrons. The many years since he had crossed the portals of power had corroded his ethics with ambition.

Since the injury that had left him paralyzed from the waist down, he was obsessed by revenge. The man whom he blamed was another of the Fixer's clients. The most important client. A man named Nile Barrabas. But Miss Roseline was right about it all being relative. Today, the senator looked positively cheery.

"Sit!" he commanded Jessup. "Let's get right to the point."

"I presume it's something to do with the airline hijacking." Jessup lowered his immense bulk carefully onto the leather couch that faced the senator's desk.

"Among other things, Walker." The senator waved his arm behind him at his polished mahogany desk. "It's also about this!"

For the first time, Jessup noticed a large round object of polished blackened metal. It bore a vague resemblance to a head, although it was large enough to fit a giant. The surface was etched with microcircuitry. Tiny colored wires led to a square protrusion where the eyes should have been. Below that was a breathing apparatus.

"The LX Virtual Cockpit." Horace Greely spoke first. "Our laboratory has spent the past ten years developing it. You're looking at the future of military aviation. And there's only one in the entire world."

The Air Force general cleared his throat. "For some years now, the Air Force has recognized that as our fighter jets become increasingly complex, so do the controls that compete for the fighter pilot's attention. In combat, this could be fatal. The F-15 alone has over three hundred different gauges, dials and controls."

Greely picked up the story on cue. "That's right. Simply put, our fighter technology has advanced beyond human capabilities to manage it. Using the latest developments in computer technology, we've created the LX. Everything the pilot needs to control his airplane, destroy targets and down attackers, is here. On the inside."

"You mean—" Jessup pointed at the device somewhat incredulously "—he wears that over his head?"

The scientist nodded. "You've caught on very quickly, Mr. Jessup. The pilot places it over his head and is connected to the computer. In front of him, he sees a panoramic three-dimensional replication of his total environment, one that includes the earth below him and the enemy fighters in the sky around him. At the edge of the display he sees his own weapons systems, and can call up any engine status instruments or systems indicators he wants."

"Call up?"

"It operates on voice command," the Air Force general answered. "You say 'Zoom,' and the computer immediately zooms in on whatever is in the field of vision."

"Say 'God's eye,'" Horace Greely said, taking over from the military man again, "and instantly the pilot is high above the airplane, looking down on the entire theater of battle. He says 'lock on' and then 'fire,' and a missile is deployed, and the enemy is destroyed. His hands don't have to leave the controls of the airplane."

"It's like fighting a battle on the inside of a video game!" Jessup still found the advances of modern technology totally astonishing.

General Simmons smiled. "That's exactly what it's like. Which gives us a big advantage in training pilots, too. Ground simulations become indistinguishable from the real thing. The airplane cockpit as we know it is obsolete. And the beauty of it is . . ."

The general was unable to resist rising from his chair and walking to the senator's desk. He placed his hand on top of the helmet and patted it like a favorite pet. "This baby comes in at about a tenth the cost of using actual aircraft for training missions. Congress will love it."

"If Congress ever gets a chance to see it," the Senator said with dark relish.

"What's the problem?" Jessup looked among the three men in the reluctant silence that followed.

"There's only one prototype in existence." General Simmons took his hand away from the virtual cock-

pit and returned to his chair as if he had been overcome by sudden weariness.

"This one." Jessup pointed to the desk.

Greely and Simmons shook their heads in unison.

"This is a mock-up. The circuits are fake."

"So where's the prototype?"

"At this moment, as near as anyone can figure, in
a hijacked airplane somewhere over the Mediterranean."

The matter-of-fact way in which the senator answered betrayed an inner excitement. Miss Roseline
was right again. The old pol thrived on crisis.

"Along with Dr. Samuel Wheatley, the developer of
the virtual cockpit," the Astute University scientist
added with obvious concern.

"What in hell was he doing with the single
proto—" Jessup stopped when he saw the Air Force
general wince.

"Our Saudi Arabian allies were interested in viewing our advances in this area since they have a hundred
new fighter jets on order for the mid 1990s—when the
virtual cockpit becomes available."

"You mean the Saudis were going to see it before
Congress . . ."

The senator interrupted with a cough. "That's not
important," he said quickly.

Jessup nodded. Now he understood. Someone's ass
was in a sling for allowing the unauthorized disclo-
sure of defence technology to a foreign power, and
now things were screwed up good by a few fanatics in
an airplane. As he recalled, the senator was one of the

main supporters of the billion-dollar arms sale to the Saudis.

"At this time, we haven't got a clue as to where they're going with that airplane or what their demands are. I needn't elaborate on the threat to America's security if that helmet falls into Syrian hands."

"Right. The Syrians are a client government of the Soviet Union."

"Exactly. And furthermore, there is the matter of the designer of the virtual cockpit, Dr. Wheatley."

"Dr. Wheatley is brilliant," Greely interjected. "He's built this thing from scratch almost single-handedly. If we lose Sam, as well as the prototype, it will set back research and development by several years—perhaps put us right back at square one."

"Of course, there will be negotiations for the hostages," General Simmons added, his hands stretched out in a compliant gesture. "But it occurred to us that it might be necessary to send someone in for preemptive action. Covertly, of course."

"I mentioned to General Simmons and Mr. Greely—" the senator licked his lips and spoke slowly, his oily tones clouding the truth below the surface of his statement "—you had some people who might be interested in an assignment like this."

"Let's get this straight," Jessup said, leveling his eyes first at the senator and then moving them to each of the other two men in turn.

"Sometime in the next few hours, whenever and wherever this hijacked airliner lands, you're going to have it sitting on a runway with a couple of hundred civilian hostages, including women and children on

board, the center of international press attention.
You're going to have, in whatever country it ends up
in, local police, domestic military, crack special commando squads, and depending on which superpower
that country is allied with, assorted advisers, trainers,
negotiators and hardware experts of either the Russian or the American persuasion. And if necessary,
you want to send in a fifth column under all those
noses to free Dr. Wheatley and bring out the prototype virtual cockpit.''

The Fixer's three-man audience nodded in unison.
He had an odd thought. If these men had their urine
tested, what kind of drugs would the laboratory find?
They did not exist in the same world as most living,
breathing people. In a word, they were nuts.

On the other hand—and while he was thinking
about nut cases—it was just the kind of impossible
assignment that Nile Barrabas would find intriguing.
And, there was also the matter of his own percentage.
It tempted him further.

"Of course it will cost . . ." he began tentatively.

"The usual," the senator cut in. He jabbed a button on the arm of his wheelchair. The little battery-
powered motor under his seat whirred. The para-
plegic politician whirled around and slid across the
room to his desk.

"Half a million per man . . . er, person. If they have
to go in. I want them on board and ready for any contingency, understand, Walker? We are still hoping that
this hijacking will be resolved quickly and neatly. But
we are not prepared to take chances on it.''

"No. You want my guy to take the chance instead. I'll talk to him. Let's say he accepts but isn't needed, after all. He and his people will have to be paid, even if the assignment is called. A kill fee, as it's called in the free-lance industry. Fifty percent of the going price."

"Preposterous!" the senator snorted angrily and pushed papers away from the center of his desk. "A quarter of a million each for doing practically nothing. Impossible!"

Jessup nodded. He buried his chin in the crook between his thumb and index finger and rubbed his cheeks slowly, a gesture his Texan father had used when he was considering a bid on long-horned breeding stock.

"So let's lower the kill fee. Say, a hundred thou a man if they don't go in. That'll take care of setup expenses, inconvenience—that's fifty percent of the job, anyway. But if they do have to go in—eight hundred thousand dollars a man."

The senator froze, ready to reject the offer out of hand until he saw General Simmons and Dr. Greely casting tiny urgent nods in his direction. He hit the trigger on the arm of the wheelchair. The motor whirred. He rolled back from the desk, pursing his cracked lips smugly.

"If they're successful. Eight hundred."

Jessup hesitated, running the figure through his cerebral computer. He didn't like the qualification about being successful. On the other hand...

"And if they're not successful, fifty percent. Four hundred thou. Payable to their estates."

Jessup saw his mistake too late. The senator broke into a broad, thin-lipped smile.

"To their estates? Why certainly, Walker. That sounds reasonable. If they are not successful." The politician's milky eyes glistened with reptilian joy. Jessup knew exactly what he was thinking. At that price, the total annihilation of Nile Barrabas was a bargain.

The Fixer stood, drawing the meeting to its conclusion.

"I'll talk to him," he said. "Gentlemen." He gave a curt bow of his head and began moving his vast bulk toward the big oak door.

"We must have that prototype back." General Simmons stood as he spoke, unable to conceal his eager desperation. "At any cost!"

Jessup stopped, halfway through the door. His hand rested on the brass doorknob. He turned and looked at them.

"Including the cost of a suicide mission?"

An awkward silence hovered as he closed the door behind him.

4

Greece's fabled coast rose from the cerulean waters, and the land climbed to the mountainous interior. In the cockpit of the hijacked airliner, the crew worked feverishly. The tension was palpable.

Captain Ratcliffe looked sideways at the terrorist standing by the door. The handgun never wavered, maintaining its aim directly at his back. It gave him the creeps. He noticed that the terrorist was sweating heavily. He glanced down at his own uniform. Large dark patches spread out from the armpits. His hands were clammy. The cockpit was beginning to smell like a locker room. And despite his fervent hopes to the contrary, Ratcliffe had a heavy feeling that they were in it for the long haul.

He flicked his eyes across his instrument panel, an unconscious impulse born of thousands of hours of flying time. In a second's glance he ascertained that all systems were operating normally. Except the main one—the rule of law. He had recognized the terrorist immediately as the man who had come aboard as the new flight attendant. But his recognition of the truth had been slower. This happens to other people, people on TV, people in the newspapers, not to me, he'd thought, the incredulous voice at the back of his mind objecting, dismissing, until it had been silenced. It happens now, he thought. It is happening. To me.

He forced his voice and facial expression to be as calm and reassuring as possible. "Where we going, anyway?"

Alli ignored him.

The woman came to the cockpit door and conferred with him in a foreign tongue.

"What is your fuel?" the terrorist suddenly demanded.

"Enough to get to Athens," was the captain's terse reply.

The two hijackers talked again.

"How far can you go?" Alli demanded.

Ratcliffe glanced at the fuel gauge. He could stay in the air at least two more hours. The Greek capital was half an hour away. It was a hell of a lot safer to be in a booby-trapped airplane on the ground than at thirty thousand feet.

"Not far," he told the hijacker. "It's a hot day. That means we're flying through less dense air, which increases flight time but makes landing trickier. What we're saving on the way there we'll need on our descent."

It was bullshit, but who cared. He felt the small cold circle of the gun pressed against the back of his head. An ugly shiver snaked up his spinal cord.

"We go to Tehran."

"There's no way. We don't have enough fuel."

Ratcliffe felt the metallic click of a cocked gun. He swallowed. His heart pounded in his chest, and his ears began to ring. The barrel of the gun bored into the back of his head. He tried to imagine what the bullet was going to do, and realized it would be over so fast he'd never know if he was right. Like a fuse blowing, plunging him suddenly into a void of darkness. "I can't do it," he heard himself speak, his voice barely a hoarse whisper. He waited for the lights to go out. The pressure of the gun barrel against his head remained constant. There was a moment of silence.

Abruptly, Alli grabbed the copilot by his collar and pushed him over the instrument panel.

"How much fuel?" he demanded, pressing the trigger of his gun to the man's temple.

The copilot swallowed and shook his head. "Not enough to get us to Tehran."

The terrorist pushed him back into his seat. Waving the gun in the general direction of the flight crew, he turned and spoke rapidly with the woman at the door. Hafez joined them. They began to argue. Alli shouted an order. The other two shut up. The woman nodded. Hafez glowered. Their leader turned around and stood over Ratcliffe, pressing the barrel harder against his head.

"Beirut."

Ratcliffe and his copilot exchanged glances. "Flight engineer, give me estimated distance to Beirut from current position. Flight time and fuel capacity."

The flight engineer punched data into his computer, and examined the changing numbers on the digital readouts.

"We can get there," he sighed. "If we want to measure our fuel reserve in teaspoons after arrival."

Ratcliffe looked up at the terrorist. "Beirut it is." He reached for the intercom microphone. "Shall I inform the passengers?"

WITH HIS HEAD DOWN in his seat at the head of the first-class section, Mike Mitchell watched two of the terrorists emerge from the cockpit. Flight 707's purser felt a tug on his uniform. He looked up.

The barrel of a gun stared him in the face.

He looked higher. The woman terrorist stared down at him.

"I am Nalima. Get up!"

He stood warily, his eyes flicking from the woman's face to the gun in her hand. With long black hair falling over her shoulders and dark eyes, she was strikingly beautiful, or would have been had her face not been hardened and distorted by her deadly purpose. Her lips were thin, pulled down at each side. She looked coldly efficient.

"You will collect all the passports from the passengers," she ordered him. "Take one more of your people to do it. Then bring them all to me."

Mitchell nodded at Ron, who had taken one of the seats in the first-class section.

"You start here. I'll start in economy."

"And quickly," the woman terrorist ordered. She added ominously, "We will make a selection for special treatment."

There was brief static in the overhead speakers, and the captain's announcement went through the cabin. Estimated arrival time in Beirut was an hour and a half. A low murmur swept through the hostages.

"Silence! No noise or we kill you!" Ahmed screamed between gritted teeth. His eyes were ringed with sweat, and the veins of his neck showed red against his skin.

The murmur stopped as quickly as it had started.

As did the other passengers, Matt Chicago had his face buried against his knees. His back ached. The initial shock of the hijacking had worn off after several minutes, leaving him aware once again that he had missed breakfast. His stomach rumbled frequently to remind him. He didn't dare lift his head. The hijackers patrolled the aisle constantly, their legs passing in his peripheral vision.

In his cramped and blind position, Chicago made an inventory of the strange sounds emitted by a hundred and forty-three hostage victims. Periodically stifled weeping and sniffling became audible. At other times, the sounds resembled the pathetic whimpering of an injured dog. Somewhere toward the back of the airliner a baby squabbled. Mercifully, the one across the aisle slept. Most of the time silence was leaden except for the soft padding of boots as the hijackers paced the aisle.

"Passports, please," Mike Mitchell announced quietly from the front of the cabin. "I have to collect your passports." Under the careful eye of the hijackers, he made his way slowly through the plane, murmuring words of encouragement to the passengers.

The baby at the end of the plane wailed. Ahmed shouted angrily at Nabil in their native tongue. For a moment they argued, until Nabil turned away. The

young terrorist spoke in gentle tones to the mother.
allowing her to coddle the infant.

Suddenly Ahmed screamed at a man in the seat on
his right. His arm whipped out, striking him across the
side of his face with his gun. The man yelped in pain
and cowered in his seat, using his hands to protect his
head. Ahmed angrily walked on, his dark eyes filled
with fire as he scanned the rows of terrified passengers. Again he lashed out, striking a young woman.
She slumped in her seat to avoid the blows.

"Stop! For God's sake!" Mitchell faced the volatile hijacker. His heart pounded in his chest. The risk
he was taking could well be his last. "Why are you
hitting them?" he shouted. "They're doing want you
want."

Ahmed's eyes widened. He stopped striking the
woman and regarded the purser with surprise. His eyes
narrowed in anger as he pointed the gun at Mitchell's
stomach.

"Ahmed!" Nalima stood in the door to the first-
class section. The terrorist turned and faced the
woman. She spoke sharply to him again. He argued.

"Please, stop it," Mitchell cried, breaking into the
angry exchange. "They've all been doing as they are
told. There's no need to hit them." Nalima scowled at
Ahmed and shot out an order. Reluctantly he lowered
the gun. He looked at Mike Mitchell, and his lips
parted in a sneer. The purser had just made a serious
enemy. Ron emerged from the first-class section and
relieved the purser of an armload of passports. He
took them to the woman, and she retreated to the first-
class section.

Mitchell bent over the row of seats where Lorch, Chicago and Dr. Wheatley sat.

"Nice going," Chicago whispered, handing over his passport.

"Thanks. Everything okay here?"

"Great," John Lorch muttered. "I'm a Marine. If you wanna get these fuckers, let me know when."

"Shhh." Mitchell looked sideways quickly, ensuring the hijackers were not in hearing distance. "I'll let you know if we figure something out."

"You!"

Hafez and Ahmed stood together at the front of the cabin, sharing a whispered conversation and dark expressions. Hafez scowled and repeated himself, looking straight at the purser.

"You! What you talk about?" He moved forward, suspicion beaming from his nervous eyes like a deadly laser.

Mitchell straightened, taking pains to innocently ignore the terrorist. He pointed to the big round case squeezed into the space between the seats in front of Dr. Wheatley.

"Can I move that for you, sir?" he said, deliberately loudly. "It will give you more room to stretch out."

Hafez approached, looking down at the three seated men and aiming his 9 mm pistol in a line across their chests.

The elderly man looked up, terrified.

"No! No, I'm fine! Please." He handed the purser his passport. With his other hand he gripped the handle on the case, as if he were afraid it might be taken from him.

"Let me know if you change your mind." Mitchell smiled. He turned to Hafez, still smiling. "Just trying to make the passengers comfortable."

Hafez grunted, still suspicious. Mitchell took passports from the two women with the baby across the aisle. The hijacker pointed to the passengers one row in front of them.

"Move these people!" he ordered.

The purser nodded.

"Val!" he called to the other flight attendant, sitting near the rear of the cabin. Together they cleared the row, seating an elderly couple in the tail and a frightened middle-aged businessman in the empty seat next to the two women with the baby.

Hafez motioned Ahmed forward with his gun. The high-strung hijacker hefted Alli's flight bag up the aisle and dumped the contents into the empty seats. Half a dozen small square packets and a roll of wire fell out.

"Jesus Christ," the Marine beside Matt Chicago whispered, so low his words were barely audible. "Fuckin' explosives."

IN THE COCKPIT, CAPTAIN RATCLIFFE looked down at the sand bluffs that lined the beaches along the northern coast of Lebanon, thirty thousand feet below.

The copilot pulled the radio earphones off and threw them onto his instrument panel.

"Beirut airport still won't confirm landing."

Ratcliffe shrugged. "Do they have a choice?"

The copilot thrust the earphones at him. "Wanna ask?"

Ratcliffe thought for a moment and shook his head. "If they're going to play games on the ground, they'll do it with a 727 buzzing the tower."

He glanced quickly behind him. The terrorists named Nalima and Alli were in the galley going through the passports. The purser was with them.

"Hey, Mike!" Ratcliffe shouted. "How 'bout a round of coffee up here!"

Alli stuck his head into the cockpit, his brow furrowed.

"Is that all right? A coffee?" Ratcliffe looked up at him. The hijacker grunted his assent. He waved his pistol in further warning and returned to the galley. A moment later the purser appeared with steaming cups of coffee.

"What in hell's going on out there," the pilot asked quickly, keeping his voice down.

"They want me to identify Jews from their surnames." Mitchell leaned over the instrument panel to set the cup of coffee down, breathing his words quietly into Ratcliffe's ear. "They've picked out, I dunno, a couple of the American passports with diplomatic or military stamps, or something. I'm doing my best to fuck them up, but . . ."

Alli appeared at the door. Ratcliffe nodded, and the purser backed off.

The flight engineer looked up from the navigational controls.

"We should begin our descent," he said. "Beirut's half an hour away."

"How's it look on the way down?"

"Smooth except for some possible turbulence in a thermal layer at around fifteen thousand feet. We'll be fine once we pass through it."

"Prepare for descent," Ratcliffe ordered. The fated jetliner began the long, gradual decline toward terra firma.

MATT CHICAGO FELT A SLIGHT SHIFT in the airplane's horizontal axis as Flight 707 began her descent. Every moment closer to the earth was somehow reassuring, although there was absolutely no reason to be comforted. An uncontrolled drop onto solid ground, even from a few feet, would turn the 727 into a fireball of exploding metal. Or, if the hijacker's bombs went off sooner, hot metal, blood and gore would rain down to the earth.

Free-fall. It would take a couple of minutes. He wondered how much consciousness he would maintain. Knowing that he faced instant death at the moment of impact, would he have the presence of mind to enjoy flight, to swoop and glide among the air currents and wisps of moisture or, like Icarus, feel the beating warmth of the burning sun? Or would he plummet like a stone, the air icy cold and unrelenting, whooshing past him as he fell through it? Considering the hijackers' munitions, it was more likely he would be blown to bits before he could discover the joys of human flight.

Working in the empty seats a row ahead across the aisle, Ahmed pressed detonators into the plastic explosives. He uncoiled the long wire and strung the little packets along it like Christmas lights. Hafez took one end to the front of the cabin and pulled the wire down the length of the aisle.

The businessman who had been moved into the seat across from Chicago and the Marine, sat up and motioned to Ahmed. He had something in his lap. The hijacker looked at him, his dark eyes thundering with hostility. The man waved him to come closer and whispered something. Ahmed bent to listen.

He stood, legs akimbo and his hands on his hips, towering over the businessman. A strange look of amusement came over his face. He reached into the frightened man's lap and came up with a handful of American currency.

"Hafez!" he shouted to the front of the airplane. "He says he will pay well if we let him go." He sprinkled the money onto the floor like sand. Suddenly he went berserk. "Come here, little man!" he screamed, grabbing the businessman by his collar and dragging him from his seat.

"No," the passenger sobbed. He turned red and trembled with fear.

A moment later, Ahmed had strung wire around his neck like a noose. He yanked on the end, and the thin copper line bit deeply into the plump flesh of the businessman's neck. Tears streamed down his face, and he begged to be let alone.

Chicago heard the Marine cursing softly under his breath.

"We kill you all!" Ahmed shouted. "Like this!"

A square of plastique the size of a chocolate bar dangled from the man's neck. Ahmed held it up with one hand. In the other hand he held the black box. A wire led to a detonator imbedded in the plastic explosive. A strange smile opened across his face, and his eyes were filled with insane delight. He was a cat playing with his victim for sport.

He laughed, a reedy, non-human sound, jerking on the wire. The hostage sputtered and coughed, pulling at the noose slicing into the flesh of his neck. At the tail of the airplane, Nabil shouted to Ahmed, telling him to stop. The crazed expression on Ahmed's face changed to uncontrolled fury. He growled savagely and shouted back. Hafez entered from the first-class cabin and shouted at Ahmed, who turned. The hijackers argued furiously.

The businessman began to tremble violently, his knees sinking underneath him. Ahmed jerked him up. The man was crying uncontrollably now, soft whining sounds escaping between hoarse gasps as he fought to breathe against the pressure of the noose.

Chicago closed his eyes, unable to bear it.

"Jeezuz," the Marine beside him muttered again, fidgeting uncomfortably.

From both ends of the airplane, Nabil and Hafez moved slowly toward the center, their hands out to Ahmed, their voices beseeching, calm. Their language was unintelligible to the Americans, but one thing was clear. Ahmed was out of control. Nabil and Hafez had a problem.

IN THE COCKPIT, the flight engineer watched his instruments.

"Approaching fifteen thousand feet, Captain."

Ratcliffe could see Beirut sprawled along the contours of the earth in the distance. He gripped his controls firmly, aware of a new vibration underneath the feel of the jet engines.

"We have strong turbulence—"

The flight engineer's warning was cut short as the airplane slammed into an air mass like a hand slapping against a table. Ratcliffe grabbed the microphone to warn the passengers.

It was too late.

The airplane bounced sharply up and down, leaving the seated passengers with elevator stomachs. Nabil and Hafez grabbed at the handles of the overhead compartments to maintain their balance. Ahmed fell, knocking his sobbing victim across the empty seats. Involuntarily he clutched the black box.

The plastique detonated. The explosion rocked the airplane like a sonic boom. Decompression was instant. The winds of high-altitude hell screamed through the cabin.

5

Walker Jessup took the elevator to the sixth floor of the Plaza Hotel and walked miles of wide corridors, looking for the room number. The elegant old hotel had once been the grand dame of New York, built across from Central Park almost a hundred years earlier. It was still kept up, but with the passing decades it had frayed around the edges. He'd had a stroke of extraordinary luck. Two hours after the meeting with the senator, he'd located Nile Barrabas on his way from Wyoming to someplace else.

The mercenary greeted him halfway through the first knock. The tall white-haired warrior towered over him, shrinking the room despite the suite's twelve-foot ceilings. He had several days' growth of dark whiskers, and his face was tanned from the western sun. He wore a plaid shirt and blue jeans.

Rarely did Barrabas go back to the family ranch in Wyoming. It was a lonely place, all but abandoned. Other ranchers grazed their cattle on his land, and a neighbor cared for the old house. He spent almost all his time there outdoors, riding for days to inspect the fences along the boundaries of his thousand-acre spread, oddly secure in the clear open spaces of prairie landscape.

"Nile, somehow I never picture you sitting here in the middle of all this kind of elegance."

"It's a grand old hotel gone to pot," Barrabas replied, "like the world."

He had always enjoyed the better things in life, and he could afford them. But in fact, the Plaza was Erika Dykstra's favorite spot. She always liked the hotel's European charm when she was in New York. He hadn't thought about it until now. Old habits die hard. He stuck a small cigarillo in his mouth and lit it. He allowed himself one a day when he was not on assignment.

"How are you and Erika these days?" Walker Jessup asked, reading his mind with uncanny precision.

"We're good friends." Barrabas's tone of voice left no doubt that it was none of Jessup's business. "I'd offer you a drink, but the maid must have taken me for a lush. She took the key to the liquor cabinet with her."

He rubbed his hand over his unshaven cheeks. "Why don't we go downstairs to the Oyster Bar? Say, you on a diet?"

Jessup grinned and threw his arms wide open. He looked like a pear wearing a grape's skin. "You noticed!"

Barrabas's white teeth gleamed in an indulgent smile. "In that case, lunch is on me."

The Oyster Bar was a timeless place, where milky light poured through elaborately frosted glass windows facing Fifty-seventh Street, flowing like liquid over the polished walnut surfaces of paneled walls and the coffered ceiling. The air was filled with smoke and the chatter of uptown businessmen cutting deals over two-martini lunches.

The two men ordered whiskey straight up. Barrabas opened his mouth to speak just as the waiter appeared with their drinks. He laid the shot glasses on the table and discreetly vanished.

"So what've you got for me this time, Walker?"

"What? No such thing as a friendly visit, Nile?"

"Jessup, you do this to me every time, and the answer is always no. You're an omen."

The Fixer reached for his glass, sipped the fiery amber liquid and set it down. He narrowed his eyes and leaned as far as he could toward Barrabas. His stomach got in the way before the edge of the table did. He jabbed the table with the fingers of his right hand in sequence with each terse sentence.

"Flight 707. Hijacked and on its way to Beirut. Military secrets are on the plane now along with a certain valuable scientist. Question: Will Syria get them and by proxy..."

"The Russians."

"Ivan himself, waiting in the wings for a character to flub his lines. And get this. Our 'they' want you to make sure the other 'they' don't."

"There are going to be hostages, hijackers, police, the army—and in Lebanon there are about thirteen of those."

When Barrabas was at his most cynical, he threw his words together and spoke without pacing them. He opened his hands in a gesture of supplication. "What are we suppose to do, Jessup? Go in there right under their noses and just spirit this guy away?"

"As soon as the situation appears hopeless. If there's no other way for the authorities to handle it. I dunno, Nile. Anything could happen. They might decide to turn everything over to the Syrians if Syria becomes a broker in the hostage negotiations. Or a Syria-backed army might attack in an attempt to destroy a rival organization. After the hijackers announce they're going to kill their hostages, but before the local commandos get there—you'd have, oh, I dunno, maybe thirty seconds."

Jessup snickered, and his hand did a throwaway. "Of course, nothing might happen at all. Everyone might just go home, safe and sound, not a drop of sweat spilled in vain. And listen to what they're paying. If you go in and you pull it off, eight hundred thou. Then there's the kill fee."

Jessup swallowed. He heard the words after he'd said them.

"Kill fee, Walker?"

"Uh, a hundred thousand free money—if you don't have to go in, after all. It's, uh, a term used in freelance work, if something's commissioned but, uh, not used."

Barrabas winced. Walker Jessup's choice of words left a lot to be desired.

"Wahl, yer right," the Fixer drawled, reverting to his Texan accent. He rubbed the pad of his index finger slowly around the rim of his whiskey glass, his eyes lost in space. "Good way to git killed. Ah spotted it for a suicide mission, but Ah thought, since when has that been a barrier in the past? 'Course Ah knows a man's got to have a limit—why, back in Fort Worth when Ah was a kid and the Texas Rangers rode in…''

Jessup babbled on in long, sleepy words. He pretended not to notice the distant look in Barrabas's icy blue eyes like the shadow of a cloud passing across the sun. He pretended he didn't notice that Barrabas wasn't listening.

His last words dangled midsentence. The light shining through the frosted glass windows reflected on the dark walnut. He looked at Barrabas's face for a moment.

A thin, almost invisible vertical line creased the merc's left cheek, delicately outlined by the colorless light. And along his left temple, disappearing finally into the hairline, was another scar, shiny and white, thick as a finger.

The bullet at Kap Long had done that, pierced his helmet and stopped millimeters from a necessary part of his brain. The man had seen hell then, gone there and come back. No one knew the whole story. Jessup wondered sometimes if Barrabas did.

Afterward, when the warrior had awakened in a Saigon hospital, his black hair was almost completely white. This was the man who wouldn't say die, the soldier who had grabbed the skid of the last helicopter lifting off the roof of the American embassy while Hanoi's legions crowded the gates outside the compound. The last man out of Vietnam.

The Fixer lifted his glass, made a silent toast to the unacknowledged hero and drained his whiskey. He watched an imperceptible change come over Barrabas.

"It can be done."

The gaze between the two men held steady.

Barrabas broke it by reaching for his whiskey. He threw it back. He flicked his eyes up to meet Jessup's. "With expenses."

Jessup leaned back in his chair, scarcely able to resist the smile gathering at his lips.

"The eight hundred thousand is clear," Barrabas reiterated.

"I can talk the senator into that."

"Translation. Or else the old goat can stick it up his wheelchair exhaust pipe."

"I'll relay the sentiment." The fat man inspected his fingernails. "What specific expenses do you have in mind."

He thought he saw the glimmer of a smile crease the warrior's face.

"A private Lear jet. If we're gonna get started in Beirut, we gotta get started now."

ONE MINUTE THEY WERE THERE. The next they were gone. The two women across the aisle, and the businessman disappeared in a swirling wind, swallowed by the mouth of sky that opened in the side of the ill-fated 727. The terrorist held on to the headrest of a seat, his body tugged back by the suction of decompression. His legs ended at the knees. Two entire rows of seats were gone.

Oxygen masks dropped amid the screams of passengers and the wind. Insulation from the gaping wound in the airplane's aluminum skin swarmed through the air, a pestilence of fiberglass that reduced visibility almost to nil.

The wind tugged at Matt Chicago, little fingers prodding him inexorably toward the awesome hole of fatal sky a few feet away. The arm of John Lorch's seat had been blown away, and the Marine had been pulled into the aisle. He twisted back toward the window, fighting against the persistent suction.

The oxygen masks were pulled into the windstream. They coiled and twisted, snaking around the passengers' heads and arms. Chicago felt Lorch's weight pressing against him. He reached around the old man and the seat and held on. The Marine grabbed a handle over the window with both hands. The three of them were braced against the howling wind in a tangle of rubber tubes and masks.

Sheltered from the swirling fiberglass particles by Lorch and the seat, Chicago opened his eyes. Everything was covered in blood. There was a chunk of crimson flesh lying on the carpet below his head. This is what it's like, he thought. Survival was something you measured in seconds.

IN THE COCKPIT Captain Ratcliffe reacted immediately, compensating for the drag on the right side of the airplane caused by the sudden decompression.

"Beirut, we have a failure of pressurization, repeat, failure of pressurization, request emergency landing immediately. Beirut, do you read?" When he signed off, he realized he was shouting.

The airplane quickly approached the capital of Lebanon. Rising from the brown sandy beaches along the Mediterranean were the scorched white towers of Beirut—the Holiday Inn gutted by fire, the condominiums of the wealthy little more than crumbled slabs of concrete. Black smoke rose from several points on the distant horizon, where eastern suburbs and refugee camps sprawled endlessly to the far hills. There was a bright orange flash to the north, and a missile sailed in a majestic arc, a golden rainbow that exploded abruptly several neighborhoods away.

Somewhere in the background Ratcliffe was aware that the woman hijacker and the leader were screaming at each other and possibly at him, as well. He ignored them.

The first time he'd asked for landing permission, he'd expected a routine but prompt reply. Instead, traffic control had told him permission was denied.

No? he thought. With one hundred and forty-three hysterical hostages, five even more hysterical hijackers and eight frazzled crew members on his hands for two hours at thirty thousand feet, they had said no?

It had made him feel better. Now he knew this had to be a bad dream, no matter how real it felt. He was smiling ridiculously when the 727 was rocked by the explosion.

Beirut traffic control replied, "Flight 707, we are considering your request. Stand by."

For the first time, Captain Ratcliffe noticed the tubes from the oxygen mask dangling in front of him.

"Don't need oxygen, Captain," the copilot shouted. "We're down to seven thousand feet. There's the airport. Looks like they don't want us."

The airport control towers appeared beyond the teeming Palestinian refugee camps on the southern fringe of the city. The crisscrossing runways had been cleared of all air traffic. Instead, dozens of buses and trucks had been driven onto the tarmac. It was impossible to land.

Captain Ratcliffe shouted into the radio mouthpiece again.

"Beirut, we are very low on fuel. We cannot hold. Can't you understand that, you bastards. This is a Mayday, Beirut."

Suddenly he felt the barrel of the pistol shoved into the back of his head again. Nalima leaned next to him, screaming into the mouthpiece.

"Five minutes! Then we start killing people. We are suicide terrorists! We will crash plane into the control tower and kill everyone! Five minutes!"

The radio was silent. Then, the traffic controller's voice came back. "Land quietly, Flight 707, land quietly."

Below, tiny stick figures ran toward the buses and trucks. Quickly the vehicles were moved to the side, and a runway was clear. The landing was strangely routine. The pilot and crew heaved a united sigh when they felt the vibration of the wheels rolling along the reassuring tarmac.

"Stop at the end of the runway, where the sand dunes begin," air traffic control instructed the pilot.

Alli suddenly grabbed the microphone. "The airplane is booby-trapped," he screamed into it. "No one approaches! We get fuel, nothing else! Or we destroy everything!"

They were down. And the drama had just begun.

THE FRIGHTENED PASSENGERS buried their faces and clutched at their seats although the danger from the aircraft's wound was long past. A few of the brave ones returned to normal positions, casting worried and incredulous glances at the picture window in the side of the plane. The floor had been ripped open where the missing seats had been torn away, and the dark baggage compartment was visible below.

Ahmed moaned. Shock had anesthetized him to the pain but not to the horror of legs severed at the knees. Another man, the passenger in the seat in front of the Marine, sagged over the armrest, held by his seat belt. The floor below him was awash with blood.

Nalima appeared at the door to first-class, shouting orders at Hafez. Nabil ran from the rear of the airplane and knelt beside Ahmed.

"Leave him," she screamed. "Take this one." She pointed to the dead man in the aisle seat. "Throw him out."

She stood over Ahmed, looking at him with both pity and contempt. He was a fool, but now he was in terrible pain. Hafez and Nabil unbuckled the corpse and kicked the body through the gaping hole. It dropped onto the runway with a thud. Nalima drew her gun and aimed at the whimpering idiot at her feet.

Ahmed came out of shock long enough to realize that his ordeal was over. The bullet hit him between the eyes before he was able to open his mouth. The front of his cranium popped off, and blood showered into the aisle.

"Get rid of him, but not outside." She jerked her head toward the toilet at the tail of the plane. "Put him in there. We don't want them to know that one of us has already become a martyr to Allah."

"May he feast and make love in the heavenly garden that is surely his reward," Nabil murmured in prayer. He dragged the body down the aisle by its arms.

"Everyone sit with their heads up!" Nalima ordered. She took a handful of American passports from her belt and opened them to the photographs. Slowly pacing the aisle, she scrutinized her prisoners' faces, her eyes flicking down the passport pictures. She stopped by a middle-aged man and studied him for a moment.

"American diplomat?"

The man swallowed nervously, but kept his chin up.

Nalima nodded to Hafez. The hijacker pulled the man from his seat and led him at gunpoint to the first-class section. Nalima walked on. She ordered two more men to be taken forward. There was one passport left in her hands. She walked on. Her dark eyes scanned the faces.

Her eyes fell on the old man by the window, then on Matt Chicago's face. His heart stopped. Her gaze was penetrating, like a beam of black light searing through his secrets. He felt guilty. He didn't know what he had done to be her enemy, but he was sure she would find something in his thoughts to convict him.

Like a tracking device programmed for a target, her eyes scanned farther, stopping at John Lorch. She flicked her eyes to the passport photo, then back to the

Marine's face. A strange smile tugged at the corners of her mouth. She tucked the passport in her belt with the others and pointed her gun at him. Hafez came to her side.

"This one is an agent of the great Satan, too. He is in Satan's army. We will make an example of him."

Lorch carefully avoided Chicago's eyes when he stood. He walked toward the first-class section, prodded roughly by the barrel of Hafez's gun.

"There's nothing you can do!" the elderly man on Chicago's left hissed with fear.

"I can't . . . I can't . . ." Matt Chicago wanted to say that he could not just sit there helplessly and do nothing, but he stopped. Nabil took up position near the gaping hole, panning his gun back and forth at the hostages. The cold metal sheen of the hijacker's weapon spoke of death, the dark hole at the end of the barrel staring, a baleful eye lusting to levy a sentence of death with a single casual blink.

A long blood-curdling scream from the first-class cabin tore through the airplane, slashing through Matt Chicago's nerves. Yet the hijacker stood guard, searching among the prisoners for the least sign of resistance. The scream stopped, mercifully, and was followed almost immediately by a worse one that went on and on.

Stop it! Stop it! Chicago chanted in his head over and over, trying to block out the poor Marine's terrible pain. The scream ended in a choked and sobbing plea for help. Almost immediately his terrible cry began again.

"Stop it! Stop it now!" Matt Chicago stood at attention at his seat, screaming himself now. Far, far away, a small part of his consciousness watched. It was amazed at his gall. It called him a fool.

The sudden outburst froze Nabil. He turned in the American's direction, stunned by the unexpected behavior. The two men looked at each other. The hijacker decided to shoot.

"No!" Nalima appeared beside him, pushing his gun down with her own. She looked at Chicago, her chest heaving as if she were short of breath. Her lips curled. "We have a hero here. He can be our second example. You! Step forward!"

She pushed Chicago ahead of her into the first-class section, jabbing him savagely with the barrel of her gun. John Lorch was sitting on the floor, the upper half of his body propped against the wall next to the galley. He was covered with blood, and his head lolled dizzily from side to side.

Chicago caught a flash of the Marine's blue eyes in the red mask of torture. He was alive. Hafez's arms were bloody to the elbows. So were his boots. The hijacker seemed to enjoy his work.

In the cockpit, Alli stood over the pilot and screamed into the microphone. "We have killed one! See the body we threw out for you! Now we kill one every five minutes if our demands are not met. We mean business. Every five minutes!"

Nalima pushed Chicago forward. He fell against a wall, spinning around with his hands up. He was determined to meet her eyes, and he did.

"Listen to me!" he told her. "This is the wrong thing to do. If you want to tell the whole world about your cause, this is not the way. They'll never listen to you. If you start killing people now, you'll use up everything you have to bargain with!"

Hafez moved forward, throwing his fists up. A thin growl escaped his sneering lips.

"No!" Nalima shouted, putting her hand up to stop him. For a moment she looked at the American appraisingly, seeming to consider his words.

"Wait," she told Hafez, then turned to Chicago. "What do you mean, the world will listen?"

"You must have demands. Things you want. A cause you're fighting for," Chicago said urgently, pressing his point. "The media—especially the American media—can help you communicate. But only if you present yourself as people with legitimate grievances!"

Hafez cursed and began to push past the woman.

She shoved him in the stomach with the side of her gun and told him to stay back.

"There might be something to this. We can bargain better if the hostages are alive." She turned away from Hafez.

"Only if there's no more killing. No more beatings." Chicago held his breath. He had committed himself. Now he had to be persistent. The only retreat was the short way out—via the barrel of a gun.

Nalima regarded him for a moment, almost with curiosity, then looked at the battered Marine. Without speaking, she pointed the way back to their seats.

6

In Washington, D.C., a working group had established itself in the antiterrorism suite next to the secretary of state's office at the State Department by the evening of the first day. Immediately the group opened communication lines to foreign governments, monitored events via satellite from Beirut, dissected intelligence reports, gave reassurances to families of the hostages and developed action scenarios for an American response.

Two fifty-man units from Delta Force, the army's crack antiterrorist commando group, were dispatched from West Germany and Fort Bragg, North Carolina, to the Mediterranean Sixth Fleet. In a concisely written statement, the terrorists released their demands—five hundred Shiite prisoners held in Israel were to be released, or the hostages would die. At midnight, the lights in the Oval Office at the White House were still burning.

In Beirut, the first glimmer of dawn appeared as a thin white line over the hilly ridges of the Bekaa Valley, forty miles to the east of the Middle Eastern city. The running lights of a Lear jet blinked rhythmically as the airplane descended to a runway on a mountain plateau north of the city.

Workers rushed to wheel the steps to the side of the plane. The door opened, and Barrabas stepped onto the platform. Dressed entirely in black with only his head uncovered, his white hair shone in the diminishing night. The sky to the east had turned purple, fringed at the edge with blue, and then the first pinkish shades of the rising sun. The breezes of the Lebanese hills brushed against his nostrils, a trace of warmth lingering with the scent of cedars despite the brisk coolness of early morning.

Once, this mysterious land had been paradise. The sweetness of the wind vanished, replaced by the acrid vapors of exhaust from the Lear jet. Now it was a war zone.

He felt the presence of his soldiers gathering in the entrance behind him. The small blue signal lights up and down the landing strip went out, and several Jeeps sped across the darkened runway.

"The exciting life of a mercenary," Nanos said, stretching his arms and back in anticipation of deplaning. "Travel to interesting and exotic lands, meet unusual people..."

"And kill them," Nate Beck drearily concluded the tasteless cliché.

"Ba-a-a-d joke," Claude Hayes issued the gentle reprimand.

"Are you kidding? Memorizing dumb bumper stickers is a major literary endeavor for the Greek," Lee joked, using Nanos's nickname.

Barrabas descended slowly, examining the shadowy figures of the men who stood at attention beside the idling Jeeps. They wore green uniforms and maroon berets, their rigid posture indicating the discipline of intense military training. They were heavily armed with the Third World's favorite weapon—Soviet-made AK-47 assault rifles.

"Welcome to Mifehtish. I am Luke."

The man in front of Barrabas might have been thirty. He was olive-skinned, with dark hair, and wore the markings of the private militia that controlled the valley. There were many such armies in the war-torn country, some little more than the armed security forces of powerful landowning families. The big armies—the Druze, the Shiites, the Christians, the government forces, such as they were—each had major domains where their word was law. Beyond that, the country existed precariously on the brink of anarchy.

"You have transportation to the coast?"

The young militia man nodded. "We must hurry. You will be there within the hour."

The American mercs climbed into Jeeps and were driven up the side of the valley, until, at the top of the hills, the Mediterranean was visible, its roiling sea-blue waters catching the flames of pink from the rising sun. The smooth-paved road became broken and crater-pocked. The vehicles bounced along at a bone-grinding speed, their drivers not slackening pace until they braked abruptly at the end of the a long pier in a heavily-guarded fishing village.

A moment later, the SOBs sat in the cramped space below the deck of a smelly old tugboat with twin diesel engines. The bow of the boat rose in the water. They skimmed across the calm waters toward the northern beaches of Beirut.

The city was built on a triangular point of land that jutted into the Mediterranean. Her fabled white towers straddled the shore like an army of marble giants. In the thick bluish light of the new day, they looked peaceful enough. Only closer scrutiny from a knowledgeable eye disclosed the empty, gutted windows, the scorched and blackened sides of high-rise condominiums, hotels and office towers.

The young soldier named Luke stood at Barrabas's side.

"The Israeli bombardment," he said quietly, following Barrabas's gaze. Sorrow and pride were both present in his voice. "The Israelis, the Palestinians, the Shiites, the Maronites—so many different religions and tribes and families reached for a handful of Lebanon, and then they fought until my country was torn to pieces. But someday we will rebuild, and Beirut will be the Paris of the Middle East once again."

He pointed to a cluster of red brick buildings rising up from the beaches where the shoreline turned to the south.

"That is the American University. We will dock to the left of it. The Green Line ends there, another mile to the east."

The Green Line was a no-man's-land that cleaved the city into east and west, Christian and Moslem. To cross the heavily armed line was an act of suicide.

"West Beirut is under Moslem control. Doesn't that make it dangerous for you and your people?"

Luke laughed ruefully. "Druze, Amal, Hizballah. Take your pick. They are all there, and usually they fight so much among themselves it is easy for us to slip through the middle when it is necessary. Besides, from dawn until noon there is an unofficial ceasefire every day. It allows the children to go to school and the mothers to go to the markets. The shooting does not begin until after lunch.''

''War,'' Barrabas sighed, an edge of incredulity to his voice.

Luke gave him a quizzical look.

''I saw it in Nam,'' he explained. ''Even under the worst circumstances, ordinary life goes on. It's a testimony to how adaptable people are. Sad, in a way.''

The young Lebanese shrugged. ''We do what we must.''

''How does my friend survive in the middle of all this?'' Barrabas asked. Ron Mutz, an old army contact from Barrabas's days with Military Assistance Command in Saigon, had arranged for the mercs' surreptitious entry to Lebanon.

''Ah. He is a smuggler. This boat is loaded normally with Scotch whiskey, or Sony stereo equipment. We charge him duty for his use of the piers in our jurisdiction. And in Beirut he pays duty to Druze militia. The duties in both cases are substantially less than the official government tariffs. The Druze are our enemies, of course, but everyone makes money, and everyone is happy—except the government. It has no power to collect taxes anymore. Instead, the private armies buy guns.''

The tug approached a collection of rundown wooden warehouses standing on pylons in the water. High wire fences topped with rolls of razor-sharp barbed wire bordered the shore. Shipping containers and wooden crates were stacked in the enclosed compounds. Armed guards patrolled the perimeters of the warehouse yards and the piers. Workmen threw thick coils of rope to the crew as the tug drew alongside.

The sun floated above the eastern horizon like a glowing lozenge. The sky was still white with the thin early light. Already the Mediterranean temperature was climbing. In Beirut, almost every day was a scorcher. Barrabas climbed a rotting wooden ladder to the pier, his soldiers following quietly. On the pier, a stocky man with a fringe of close-cropped honey-colored hair approached Barrabas with a welcoming smile.

"You old son of a gun, Nile. Last time I saw you was on an aircraft carrier off the coast of Vietnam. We had our shoulders against a chopper, trying to push it over the side."

Barrabas nodded, shaking hands and slapping his old friend on the shoulder. "The day we lost Saigon."

The other mercs crowded onto the pier, and Barrabas made rapid introductions.

Mutz pointed to a door in the main warehouse at the end of the pier and directed the mercs to it.

"You have fifteen minutes before the convoy to South Beirut pulls out. Figured you'd be looking for some breakfast. Grub's on in there, men. And women." He nodded graciously in Dr. Hatton's direction. "I must say, I do believe in equal opportunity for the Army when I see a chance to fight with beautiful women like you, ma'am."

The mercs began walking up the pier. "Good-looking team," Mutz said to Barrabas, casting an appreciative eye over the SOBs. His inspection lingered on Lee Hatton. A female warrior was a mild surprise to the veteran, although they were common in Lebanon. "Look like real fighters. Course, you always commanded respect from the best, Nile. Even back when you were Colonel Barrabas, First Cavalry Division Airmobile, Special Forces."

"Another lifetime, Ron," Barrabas stopped him, then changed the subject. "Tell me about your operation here. You seemed to have struck a separate peace with the powers that be."

"Sure have. Some people call it smuggling. In polite circles we refer to it as transshipment. Whiskey and perfume for the good life in Beirut. Electronic goods, oil-field equipment, spare parts for Iraqi armies, carpets from Afghanistan, uncut jewels from Pakistan, televisions from Japan, fancy soaps from England, illegal caviar from the Caspian Sea. You name it, I deal it."

Mutz stopped walking and faced the mercenary leader. "Nam changed me."

"Changed all of us."

"Yeah, well, some for better, some for worse," Mutz said, nodding. "I still don't know where I fit in. All I remember during that horror called Vietnamization—we called it retreat...the war no one wanted to fight or wanted to win—is all those carpetbaggers and hustlers who left Saigon with millions of dollars in Bahamian bank accounts."

"It's a part of war. The ones who make a buck off it."

Mutz nodded. "Fucking bunch of parasites, while the good old boys like us were out fighting and dying. Well, I learned the business. I'm one of them now. I was working in a training camp for one of the militia in the Bekaa Valley, instructing them in small-arms handling. When this country blew to pieces with the Israeli invasion, I knew an opportunity when I saw one staring me in the face."

"You paid your dues ten years ago, Ron. Strikes me you're providing a useful service, helping people maintain a semblance of normalcy in bizarre circumstances." Barrabas smiled, sensing a strain of guilt in his old friend's words. "You sure were in the right place at the right time, as far as I and my people were concerned."

"Glad I can help out." Mutz slapped the colonel on the shoulder, and they continued walking toward the warehouse. "Tell me—your presence here have anything to do with a certain hijacked airplane on the runway at the Beirut airport?"

Mutz saw the look on the merc's face. He laughed.

"Okay, I shouldn't have asked. But anything you need while you're here, you let me know. If it's available in this part of the world—and just about everything short of nuclear weaponry is—I can get it. Maybe even that, too, come to think of it. There's a guy in Tel Aviv..."

He opened the door of the warehouse. The familiar smell of coffee, bacon and eggs emanated from within. Barrabas took a deep breath of the delicious aromas. For the first time since his meeting with Jessup in New York, he became aware of his hunger. Mutz looked at his watch.

"It's the only genuine American restaurant in town. All you can eat. You got ten minutes to wolf it down. Then I turn you over to a buddy named Sharif for the grand tour."

SHARIF MAR HASAFF was a high-ranking officer from the Ministry of Defense, one of the main liaisons between the Lebanese government and the civilian authorities in control at the airport.

He arrived with his convoy at the smuggler's headquarters in a green Mercedes. Eight security guards rode in two vehicles, one in front, the other following. They were equipped with submachine guns, pistols and concussion grenades. The Mercedes gleamed, its shiny chrome and polished paint unmarred except for a row of six bullet holes along the front fender.

Sharif was a short man, with a neat round paunch under his immaculate white shirt and silk tie. His oiled black hair was squared at the sides and back. He had a brisk, pleasant manner and spoke Oxford English with a slight French accent. He was savvy enough not to ask questions, but his dark eyes glinted with intelligence.

"Kidnapping attempt. Or assassination," Sharif explained, brushing his finger along the tiny bullet punctures in the fender of his Mercedes. "Ill-planned. They got two of my guards. We killed eight of them. Now they tell me it will take two years to find a fender like this in France and bring it to Lebanon."

His last sentence ended in a sigh.

Ron Mutz gave the fender a shrewd look, which the Lebanese noted. "Yes, I thought you might do something for me, since I'm showing your friend our facilities at the airport. Your timing is interesting, by the way, Mr. Barrabas."

"Give me two months to work on it," Mutz said. This was the way his business worked. Who owed who was irrelevant. The relationship was ongoing and mutually beneficial. The high-ranking army official turned to Barrabas.

"War, at best, is a terrible inconvenience. At worst—well, Mr. Barrabas, I think you know the worst moments only too well."

The American mercenary nodded appreciatively. Sharif was not just an indulged bureaucrat, the kind who thrived in governments everywhere. He had the sharp eyes and considered speech of a cunning fighter. He also took risks. Riding around in Beirut in a shiny green Mercedes was like painting a bull's-eye on your forehead.

"If I am to be a member of the government, I refuse to skulk around the streets of the capital," he told the mercenary later, when the luxury car lumbered onto the road that led into the city. "Someone has to remind the militias that the rule of law still exists, even if it is a little . . . out of fashion."

Reconnaissance of the Beirut airport was a job Barrabas had to do himself. To get there, it was necessary to traverse the entire length of Beirut from north to south. Ron Mutz's piers and warehouses were located near the Green Line in an area of East Beirut controlled by the Christians. Fortunately, the portion of West Beirut on the other side of the line was occupied by the Lebanese army. According to Sharif, relations between the two were cordial at the moment.

The car approached an opening set in the long makeshift barricade. Slabs of concrete from bombed-out apartment buildings had been bulldozed into heaps, and their steel reinforcement rods projected from the sides. The charred skeletons of gutted automobiles were piled between the mounds, topped with coils of barbed wire. A green line was literally painted onto the crater-pocked asphalt. They passed easily through the two roadblocks with a wave of Sharif's badge.

A few minutes later the car was forced to slow to a crawl in busy traffic along a wide shopping boulevard. The signs of war were not immediately evident. Cars and delivery vehicles were double-parked bumper to bumper on both sides of the street, and the stores were crowded with women weighed down with heavy wicker shopping bags.

"Druze militia." Sharif pointed out the window at the upper levels of some of the buildings. Many of the higher floors had been bombed or gutted, and the facades of almost all the buildings bore the signs of bullet holes or mortar explosions. On corner balconies and rooftops, uniformed men wearing the familiar black-and-white checkered *kefireh*s of the Arab world patrolled with automatic rifles.

"Soon we pass into an area controlled by the Amal. Both Moslem groups, but dire enemies. West Beirut is ruled by dozens of rival groups who belong to two factions—the Shiites or the Sunni.''

"The Shiites are fundamentalist, aren't they? The ones who took over in Iran—as well as Flight 707.''

"Exactly. The Ayatollah's medieval dictatorship in Iran has given the Shiites a taste of power. Now they wish to swallow Lebanon whole. I am a Sunni Moslem. We are a little more modern. The Sunni and the Shiite factions hate each other, but both hate the Palestinian refugees, who are considered destructive foreigners in our country, only slightly less hateful than the Israeli invaders whom they brought upon us.''

"Confusing, to say the least. There must be constant fighting.''

"The boundaries between neighborhoods shift daily.''

"But life goes on.'' Barrabas motioned to the street life as the car went by.

"One makes accommodations. The electricity goes off anywhere from six to eighteen hours a day, and water can sometimes be shut off for weeks. Still, out of necessity human beings adapt and bring order out of chaos. That is why the unofficial ceasefire holds until noon every day to allow people to do their shopping.''

Suddenly the sound of gunfire reverberated through the Mercedes's thick glass windows. Instinctively, Barrabas reached inside his windbreaker for his Browning automatic. He felt Sharif's hand close gently over his arm to dissuade him.

"It's not necessary.''

Pedestrians fled to the curb, and drivers made a mad grab for space at the side of the street, reacting much as American drivers did when they heard the insistent scream of an ambulance siren. The driver of the Mercedes was no exception.

An old Jeep burst around the corner so fast that the wheels on one side left the ground. Three men stood in their seats, firing assault rifles into the air. A battered old taxi was boxed in by a four-foot crater in the road. The driver tried frantically to get around it. Brakes screamed momentarily as the Jeep swerved to one side.

One of the militiamen lowered his rifle and fired off a single round. The taxi driver screamed with panic. Sweat streamed down his face. The front end of his car began to sink on one side as the tire disgorged air. He jerked his steering wheel around and hit the gas.

His car jumped the crater, its front end landing on the sidewalk. Shoppers leapt for safety, their abandoned purchases flying in all directions. The militiaman fired off another round as the Jeep accelerated and ripped past. The other front tire collapsed. The front of the car sank completely, marooned half-way across the curb, the rear end dangling over the crater.

"You learn in Beirut, as in any other great city, the meaning and rhythms of sounds and movement," Sharif explained. He added calmly, in the tone of a man who acknowledged his destiny, "Someday they will come for me. There will be no warning shots."

The Mercedes merged back into the stream of traffic.

7

By the time they reached the Beirut airport, the shelling had started. Faint golden tracers arched over the skyline, the mortars whistling a long shrill tune before momentary silence anticipated impact and explosion. Clouds of black smoke billowed over the roofs of the city, almost immediately followed by the report of a second launcher. An answering missile streamed upward between houses and apartment buildings, playing tit for tat.

For a few minutes the sky over West Beirut was alive with vengeful fireworks. The exchange ended as quickly and as abruptly as it had begun. There was a brief lull until sirens began, their long thin wails snaking across the tormented city. Columns of dark smoke spiraled on a lazy trip to heaven.

The airport was located on the southern outskirts of Beirut, beyond the ruined Palestinian camps. In the settlements of Sabra, Shatila and Burj Al Barajneh, impoverished refugees stared silently from squalor at the passing car. The perimeter of the huge international airport was fortified with sandbags and razor wire and manned by the Lebanese army.

While almost everything else in Beirut had been damaged or destroyed by the civil war, the airport survived. Almost by mutual acknowledgment among opposing sides, this was the last connection to the outside world, a reminder that peace and sanity, although extinguished in Beirut, might yet exist elsewhere.

The hijacked 727 stood alone on one of the long runways, a great metal bird with a black-edged open wound halfway down one side. Its image rippled slowly through a field of heat waves rising from the sunbaked asphalt of the runway. Eagle Teams were hidden in the sand dunes on the other side of the runway, and on the roof of the terminal. A fuel truck was parked to one side. The hijackers had demanded power for air-conditioning and light. Told that the portable refrigeration units were broken, they had been offered a generator. They'd bought it, opening the emergency door over the wing for the long tubes to reach inside.

The workmen who had wheeled out the giant unit were police agents, watching, listening, remembering. They had attached the long tube to the airplane, snaking it over the wing and into the waiting arms of one of the hijackers.

Several men had started up the unit. One had crept away, keeping out of the terrorists' line of sight by staying underneath the belly of the plane. He had duck-walked toward the front, carefully slapping sensitive microphones to the metal underbelly. With a pair of pliers he had removed a cotter pin from the nose-wheel assembly.

Just as he was about to go back to the wing, the policeman had noticed a tiny ball of paper on the ground several feet away. Another little ball fell from the plane, from the cockpit window. Quickly and carefully, he had crept forward and snatched them into his palm.

"THEY HAVE DEMANDED three things," Sharif explained as heavily armed soldiers waved the Mercedes through a gate at the side of the main terminal. "The release of five hundred Shiite prisoners held in Israeli prison camps, refueling for the 727, and another airplane, also fully fueled. We picked up a conversation inside the airplane with our hidden microphones. They plan to transfer the hostages to the new airplane tonight under cover of dark."

"Does anyone know who they are yet?" Barrabas asked.

"Let us go into the command center and see what my people have to say."

The terminal lobby swarmed with media. Press reporters jockeyed with TV cameramen who were elbowing the photographers out of their way. Sharif pulled Barrabas through a service door and up a fire escape. A dignitaries' lounge on the second floor of the terminal had been hastily transformed into headquarters for the team of negotiators and liaisons with foreign governments. The broad plate-glass windows that faced the runways were covered with sheets of plywood, and fluorescent lights were strung haphazardly from the ceiling. The elegant lounge was now a maze of tables and desks, a madhouse of perfectly calm men and women who efficiently answered telephones, leaned over telex machines or stared at computer monitors. In one corner, near a coffee machine, several men paced anxiously, and chain-smoked cigarettes.

"The negotiating team," Sharif explained, nodding curtly to several of his officers as he passed. Workers noticed that an important ministry official had entered the room and they made deferential gestures. Some gave the tall mercenary quick, curious stares. "They are not allowed to see the airplane, of course, as it would tend to distract them. They must make decisions based on what they are hearing, what they know. There can be no emotion. They must not be swayed by the sight of a hostage shot in the head and dumped from the airplane, for example."

The high-ranking officer motioned Barrabas through another door. He put his finger to his lips.

"Let us listen in for a while."

The room was white, and almost silent save for the insect hum of a fluorescent light. It had been a storage area. Now it housed the main negotiator. Police strategists and psychologists slouched over desks, listening intently. There were loudspeakers in each corner.

Then a voice burst into the silence of the room. A man who sounded desperate, who sweated to breathe.

"We need food. Sandwiches. Enough for everyone. Food!" The voice demanded, complained.

"Got it, Alli," a burly man at the center desk broke the silence in a bright salesmanlike voice. He had a pencil poised over a notepad and spoke into the microphone on the desk. "Sandwiches, I can do that for you, Alli." He looked up and winked at Sharif. "And

I want to do it right, too, Alli, so I have to know. We have different kinds of sandwiches. You can have cheese sandwiches or tuna sandwiches. So, how many do you want of each? And how many with mayonnaise and how many without?''

The hijacker's voice returned.

"You got two minutes! Two minutes or we kill someone! Two minutes!''

"Hey, Alli! I'm sorry man, I'm really sorry. I just want to do the best job for you, y'know!''

"You're pushing us! I know you're pushing us. Listen to this, American dogs!''

There was a clatter, and a different man was breathing into the airplane's microphone. His voice was slow and weary, hovering between resignation and anger.

"He's not kidding," Captain Ratcliffe stated flatly. "He has a gun pressed against my copilot's forehead.''

The negotiations room came alive. A policeman ran to the door, opened it and snapped his fingers at the backup team of negotiators. A morose-looking man with the grayish skin of a heavy smoker strode into the room, a cigarette dangling from his lips.

"What's happening?'' The cigarette moved up and down as he spoke.

Another voice came through the speakers. "Okay, Alli, you got your food. We're sending it out right away, but we're going to need a couple more minutes, okay? Is that all right?''

"The decisions man in the traffic-control tower,'' Sharif whispered to Barrabas. Both men stood well back, watching the activity. Tension seemed visible in the air. "He monitors the negotiators. Like Russian chess players, they work on the principle of overload. Wear the hijackers down with too much information. When they are at the end of their tether and relations with the negotiator break down, we bring in another one who must start at the beginning."

"The guy downstairs screwed up on you." The decisions man's voice continued through the loudspeakers. "I'm real sorry about that, Alli. I'm going to get another one in there right away. I'm working on getting those guys out of Israel for you. Can you cool it for a couple more minutes?"

The negotiator had left his seat, and the man with the cigarette clenched between his lips took over. An aide put an ashtray at his elbow. Another aide placed a package of cigarettes and a lighter beside it. The new negotiator butted his cigarette and reached for another.

For a few seconds the occupants of the room endured a tense silence. Then the voice of the hijacker came again, amid exhausted breaths.

"Five more minutes. No more."

"That's great, Alli," the new negotiator spoke carefully. "I'm taking over from the other guy. He screwed up on you. I'm not going to screw up on you. We have some sandwiches on their way. I promise."

A man entered the room quietly and met the negotiator's eyes with a nod.

"They're on their way out now. Can you see them?"

Again there was a silence before the hijacker's reluctant reply. "I see them. No tricks."

"No tricks, Alli, I promise. Now, do you want them
to leave the boxes of food at the foot of the ladder or
bring them up to you. We don't mind having them
brought right up—it's okay."

"They carry them up. One at a time. No more."

"Okay, I got it, Alli. That's what they'll do. Now
listen, Alli, let's make a swap, to show good faith. My
boss is going nuts, you know. He wants me to show
him something. Now, I'm getting the food you
wanted, so give me some hostages in return, okay?
Isn't that fair?"

Communication broke off. Everyone in the room
froze, waiting, their blood pounding, men eyeing one
another then looking at the negotiator. He took the
cigarette from his mouth and leaned toward the
transmitter.

"The women and children," he whispered. "Let us
take the women and children off the plane!"

Suddenly Nalima broke in, angrily barking at the
negotiator. "No hostage! We want food now! We
want our compatriots in Israel released now! Or we'll
give you a dead hostage! We'll give all of them to you
dead!"

A man entered with a long roll of telex paper in
hand. He put it in front of the negotiator.

"Give me one, just one, one hostage, to show your
good faith. You're not going to kill these people. You
don't want to kill them, and we can work it all out."

He puffed furiously on the cigarette, then stabbed
it into the ashtray. Immediately he reached for an-

other one and stuck it in his mouth. He held the telex up, reading as he spoke.

"You have a woman on board with a kidney problem. She needs medication or she's going to start getting sick. Give her to us in exchange for the food. How about it? Just this one sick woman. So I can show my boss that you mean what you say."

Again there was a desperate pause.

"One hostage!" the female hijacker snarled. "And no tricks. Or she dies."

Faces around the room lit up in silent delight. It was a victory to win back just one life.

Sharif led Barrabas from the negotiations room. The door closed behind them, sealing the palpable tension of the smoke-filled room behind them.

"It worked," he said, smiling proudly. "The American State Department has been contacting the families of every passenger, looking for this kind of information. Just to get one person off. We can then obtain a great deal of intelligence information in the debriefing. Come to the tower. We can watch as the exchange is made."

On the top floor of the air-traffic-control tower, the elevator door slid open. Barrabas and the Lebanese official stepped out. Sharif was immediately snatched away by a man who led him to a working group poring over mug shots of suspected and confirmed Middle Eastern terrorists.

High plate-glass windows gave a panoramic view of the smoking towers of Beirut to the north and the Mediterranean in the west. A dozen men stood at the windows or sat at the instrument panels that were normally occupied by air-traffic controllers. Some watched intently through binoculars. Others shuffled through photographs and consulted notes. Four sat along a wall of radio receivers and tape recorders, totally absorbed by their earphones. They heard every rattle and cough that took place on board the plane.

While the atmosphere downstairs had been one of frenzied activity, or high tension, here it was relaxed, the only sound the murmur of earnest consultation. A short man wearing an immaculate light gray suit leaned over the decisions man, who had his desk front and center. When he saw the white-haired merc enter, he nodded a greeting and sauntered over.

"Ken Bridgewater. I'm with the Company," he murmured, extending a hand to Barrabas. There was only one Company. CIA. "Friend of Jessup's. Well, let's just say I owe him."

"He told you to expect me?"

"He told me to answer questions for you and not to ask any."

The merc leader considered the offer for a moment and nodded.

"Guess that's why they call him the Fixer."

"Tell me about it. He did me a favor a few years back, and I got a promotion out of it. Kind of forgot about it until yesterday. He phoned from New York."

"Anyone figured out who these guys are yet?"

"Islamic Jihad claimed responsibility. Basically an empty front for a whole range of pro-Iranian fundamentalist Shiite groups. The most powerful is the Amal, who claim to know nothing about the hijackers—even though they demanded to speak with Amal representatives. We're working on a theory that they're independents, possibly relatives of the hostages in Israel whose freedom they're demanding."

" 'Hostages' in Israel?"

Bridgewater grimaced, sucking his lips against his teeth and tucking his head. "Seems when the Israelis pulled out of southern Lebanon they rounded up a lot of prominent Shiites and interned them in Israel—all of them civilians. Basically it was a measure to ensure that the ones left at home behaved themselves. Kind of against the Geneva Conventions of 1949."

Barrabas was stunned. "And that's why at least one hundred and forty-three people are prisoners out there on the runway?"

The CIA man laughed ruefully. "Not as many as there were originally. We finally dragged the body off the runway. It's sitting in the morgue at the American University hospital in West Beirut. The ambassador can't even get to it to make an identification because the embassy is on the other side of the Green Line, and it's currently no go. A shepherd in the hills north of here found the other bodies. They got sucked out of the hole after the explosion. A mother, her daughter, her daughter's infant and a few pieces of two others. Death was on impact. For three of them. They've been beating up passengers in there, too."

"How many hijackers?"

"Four or five. One may have been wounded in the explosion. One is female. All of them around the age of twenty. The situation is highly volatile. The pilot dropped notes from the window. We sent a guy out to pull the pulley pin from the nose wheel. He found them.''

"Does that mean the aircraft is permanently grounded?''

Bridgewater equivocated. "There's no steering control on the ground if they start down the runway. The pilot can explain it as a malfunction. We can either hold them up to fix it, or fix it real quick if we want them out of here.''

Sharif returned from his consultation in a dark mood. "The hijackers have refused to speak to anyone but the Amal leadership. There is talk of a deal between governments. To curry favor, Syria has told the United States it will lean on the Amal for a settlement. For Hafoud Namoud, the Amal leader, it is a great opportunity to play both sides against the middle. He has been given charge of the negotiations. The hijackers say they will issue a political statement tonight. My authority has been taken away.''

Barrabas looked past the worried official. There was movement at the hijacked airplane's door. He strode to the window. A terrorist in a black executioner's mask stepped from the airplane. In one hand he held a grenade, in the other a 9 mm pistol. He prodded a small white-haired woman by jabbing her with his gun. The woman with the medical condition. A grandmother.

Reptilian eyes glinted from the holes cut in the black head stocking. Barrabas stared. The eyes scanned the tower. For a moment, they seemed to stop at him. The grandmother stepped nervously on the first step, while servicemen reached toward her at the bottom. The terrorist darted back inside the airplane.

It was the chance of a lifetime. Barrabas had wanted a crack at an airplane hijacking since as far back as he could remember. As far back as Nam. These were the ones he'd really learned to hate, the parasites who thought they were so goddamned high and mighty they had the right to decide who lived and who died. That prerogative belonged to no one. In taking it they put themselves far outside the realm of civilized behavior, to a world of jungle law and rough justice. Barrabas's world. And when he could, he pursued them through the dark recesses of vengeance, stalking them through the labyrinths of their guilt.

His world. His terms.

It had been that way, since his foot left the roof of the Saigon embassy, the last man out. His sense of desertion then was so violent, so acute that he had vowed to fight forever, but only for the money, for the highest bidder, the one who made him richest. Then Jessup got his hooks in by doing him a favor.

He didn't resent the Fixer for it. He didn't want anyone else doing the kind of jobs for Uncle Sam that Jessup threw his way. And the soldiers he had, his team, they were the best, and they were wild, too.

The fastest way to get the scientist and the virtual cockpit back was to free everyone at the same time. The SOBs knew it as soon as Barrabas laid out the scenario. The terrorists were about to face the best resources that money and connections could provide. And something else—a team of warriors determined to live.

Barrabas had seen it too often—the world forced to stand helplessly by while ordinary men and women got beaten, battered, terrorized and killed. Not this time. The SOBs would see that the little guy had his chance.

On the Beirut runway, the grandmother reached the bottom of the steps, and men took her, lifting her gently to a wheelchair, placing a blanket around her. One at a time, servicemen carried boxes of food up the stairs. The terrorist emerged from the aircraft for the second time and gazed for a moment at the tower.

There was commotion at the control tower. An exit door opened suddenly, and the crowded stairwell beyond it was flooded by television lights. Officers in tan uniforms entered, accompanied by Arab men in tailored suits. Below them on the stairs, reporters shouted questions, and flashbulbs popped.

A short middle-aged man walked into the control tower at the head of the party. His black hair was slicked back, and he sported a tiny mustache over his small plump lips.

"Hafoud Namoud, the political leader of the Amal," Sharif stepped beside Barrabas and whispered. "He is suspected of planning many terrorist activities with a mysterious military leader named 'the Fox.' I do not know why you are here, but I am willing to help you now, in any way I can."

"Why would you want to help me, Sharif?"

"Because now I, the representative of the rightful Lebanese government and armed forces, am powerless. And the mice have been given to the cats."

8

"No, no, no, for the thousandth time, no!" Walker Jessup banged his fat fists on his desk, sputtering at the short paunchy Hispanic across from him.

José Sanchez's eyes had a desperate beseeching quality, and his hands implored. He hunched forward on the edge of his chair.

"Don't do it!" Jessup warned. He vowed that if Sanchez got down on his knees and started begging, he would plant his foot firmly on the man's butt and boot him through the plate-glass window. The New York sidewalk was sixty-four floors below. Good riddance. Sanchez read the look on Jessup's face, and his own began to crumple.

"Oh, God," Jessup muttered in exasperation. He felt sorry for the guy. If it was in his power—really and truly within his power—he would do something. But it wasn't. And he couldn't.

José Sanchez had been hanging around some of the mercs, waiting and hoping to join the team. On a recent mission Barrabas had needed a pilot to fly them out of a Russian island. Sanchez had had his chance. And had blown it.

It was a hard thing to tell a guy—especially when he had taken twin hits in each leg from Russian 9 mm bullets and saved the life of another merc. But the judgment call had been a bad one, and the entire mission had been seriously jeopardized. The Soldiers of Barrabas had spunk—it was a prerequisite for the job. But Sanchez was all gung ho, completely unable to discern fine lines drawn between delicate situations. It was a sad story. An old soldier who craved the camaraderie, who lusted for the thrust and parry of battle. But liquor, ladies and easy living had taken the edge off, and fantasies of heroism made him outright dangerous.

"I'm sorry. There's nothing I can do. Nile Barrabas decides who works for him and who doesn't."

The Fixer felt his conscience prodding him. It wasn't quite true. He knew the right buttons to press, and he had access to them via an unacknowledged intimacy between him and Barrabas that he used sparingly. When the team was being formed, he'd tricked the white-haired warrior into accepting a woman, Dr. Hatton, onto the team. But that was at the beginning, and Lee had had special medical skills to offer.

"I'll do anything," Sanchez pleaded. "I don't care. I'll clean guns. I'll wash Jeeps. I just want to... want..."

Tears welled up at the corner of the man's eyes. It was getting pathetic. The Fixer sure as hell hated feeling sorry for people, but he said it, anyway.

"I'm sorry."

Jessup pushed himself up and stretched his arm toward the door, then accompanied Sanchez to the outer office. His secretary was out. Sanchez ground his eyes with clenched fists and grabbed his jacket, the sorrow replaced by anger and self-pity.

"I'll find my own way out." Sanchez reached for the handle just as the door opened inward, slamming him in the face and knocking him backward.

Calhoun Bellow filled the entrance to Jessup's office, looking strangely from the Fixer to the washed-up warrior. The journalist wore a dapper old-fashioned suit with baggy pants and sported a fedora, tilted jauntily to one side.

"I beg your pardon," he addressed Sanchez, blinking oddly.

Wordlessly the grim-faced soldier threw his jacket over his shoulder and exited.

Bellow took off his hat and scrutinized the Fixer.

"Gained a little weight, Walker? You must be doing well. Are congratulations in order for hard work, or is your agency just another triumph of private enterprise?"

"What do you want, Calhoun? Or are you here to suck on success?" The Texan turned his back on the reporter and walked to his office. Bellow followed. Without waiting to be asked he seated himself in the chair recently vacated by Sanchez, leaning back and crossing his legs.

"Funny," he began, looking at his nails. "I was outside the senator's house in Georgetown yesterday. Could've sworn I saw you slipping in the side gate." His eyes flicked up and met Jessup's across the desk. The Fixer watched him shrewdly. He realized with alarm that his desk was littered with telexes, maps and other data on the Beirut hijacking. He didn't dare draw Calhoun's attention to it.

"Must've been mistaken, Cal." Casually he pushed two sheaves of paper together, closed a file and set it on top of some other papers.

"You're a hard target to miss," the journalist reminded him. He leaned forward, his eyes scanning the surface of the desk, like a hawk searching for prey. He found it. "Maps of Beirut? The airport? Background reading on current events, Walker?"

Jessup picked up the rest of the papers and stacked them in front of him.

"Just looking for angles, Cal. You know how it is. An international crisis, and there are always bloodsuckers like me ready to skim profits off human misery."

"Oh, come on. With your background? A do-gooder like you. Tell me, Jessup. What's the angle? I know who you're working for. So give me the inside dope. I'll do you a favor sometime."

Jessup stood and walked around the desk. He grabbed the collar of Bellow's expensive suit jacket and pulled. The prying journalist rose from the chair.

"No deals," Jessup reiterated. "No favors. I don't know what you're talking about."

Bellow twisted away and turned on him, all semblance of civility gone. He hissed, snakelike, "You're onto something, Jessup! And I'll find out what!"

Suddenly he made a dash for the Fixer's desk and grabbed the top file. Jessup's thick hand closed around his wrist and tightened like the jaws of a vise.

He shook the journalist's arm. Loose sheets of paper flew from the file folder and rained about the room.

"You smug, vicious bastard!" Jessup roared. He took hold of the journalist by his collar and the seat of his pants. Using his weight as impetus, he stampeded Bellow into the outer office and threw him out bodily. He noticed the reporter's hat on the carpet, opened the door and tossed it like a Frisbee. Bellow picked himself up and brushed at his clothing. He narrowed his eyes.

"You underestimate the powers of the fourth estate."

Jessup pointed his finger. "Underestimate me, and you're dead meat."

"Big tough guy," Bellow snarled, setting the fedora at the right angle on his head and walking to the elevator.

On the long ride down, Calhoun Bellow realized that he had overplayed his hand, had been too quick to anger. But like a bloodhound, he had the scent. Something was up, and he wanted his byline under the big black headlines. It meant money in the bank, it meant more editors after him for work, and it meant TV talk shows, guest spots, radio interviews. It meant even more fame—some called it notoriety—than he already had. To Calhoun Bellow, semantics were for little men. As he crossed the skyscraper's marble lobby, his mind raced through the possibilities.

He stopped at the revolving doors. The paunchy middle-aged Hispanic who had come out of Jessup's office was standing beside the big modern sculpture of stainless-steel blobs on the front plaza. He had his hands in his pockets, and he looked like hell.

The perfect victim for an information vampire. At least it was worth a try. Calhoun Bellow sharpened his teeth and pushed through the glass doors.

"Hello there," he greeted Sanchez cheerily. "Saw you coming out of Walker's office."

Sanchez looked at him with moist, dejected eyes, too bitter to utter a word.

Bellow jerked his head in the direction of the sky-scraper. "Fuckin' ogre today, ain't he?" He tested the waters, and saw a brief glimmer in the poor man's eyes.

Sanchez snickered and nodded, still suspicious of the stranger. But Calhoun Bellow had not become an internationally famous snoop without learning how to fine-tune human emotions.

"I guess it's the Beirut thing. Drive anyone bonkers. Crazy stuff."

Sanchez's head rose, and the light in his eyes flashed on again. "Yeah, I guess," he said morosely.

Bellow threw out his hands in a carefree gesture. "Well, Jessup knows what he's doing. It's a good thing they called him in."

Sanchez started to say something but stopped. I have him now, Bellow thought.

"He'll take care the hijacking bastards, won't he?" The hook dangled.

Sanchez snickered again. And then he bit.

"Man, the hijackers will be taken care of all right, but not by that fuckup Jessup."

"Oh, right, you mean . . ." Calhoun nodded knowingly.

"Damn right. Finest bunch of mercenaries on the planet. They really know how to kick ass. Terrorists will never know what hit 'em, man."

"I believe you," Calhoun said earnestly. "After all, you'd know."

"Damn right I know," Sanchez said proudly, puffing his chest. "I've been there. With 'em. Side by side. Man, you ain't seen nothing till you see them guys fighting."

Calhoun Bellow smiled, real friendly, and glanced at his Rolex.

"It's almost noon and I could use a drink. Join me?" he invited. "I'm buying."

BY THE SECOND AFTERNOON of the hijacking, sleep came easier to the exhausted passengers of Flight 707. Sometimes someone woke from turbulent dreams with half-realized shrieks or loud frightened whimpers. They were quickly hushed by their neighbors, less out of fear of the hijackers than resentment at having what little peace they could find, disturbed.

The hijackers were tiring. Hafez and Nabil stood idle in the middle of the economy section, eyeing their prisoners, then drifting into unimaginable daydreams.

Nabil, the gentle one, a young man of barely twenty, was the more vigilant of the two. He began to talk to passengers. He asked a woman if the little girl beside her was her daughter. When she said yes, he burst into tears. He had a daughter the same age, he said. He said he was sorry they had to do this, but it was necessary.

Terror lapsed into boredom. Everyone was thirsty and hungry. The children cried almost constantly, and some of the adults had drifted off into states bordering on shock.

A plastic tarpaulin had been thrown over the blast hole in the side of the aircraft, conserving some of the cool, conditioned air from the baking Middle Eastern sun outside, but only barely. The temperature inside rose slowly but steadily.

The hijackers, unaccustomed to Western toilets, had fouled the rest rooms, and the airplane stank. The body of the dead one had been thrown into the toilet cubicle near the tail. Soon it would begin to stink, too.

That afternoon, when the airport workers brought the food, the hijackers had taken out an old lady. At first she protested, becoming almost hysterical, certain they were going to execute her. But the passengers on one side of the plane had seen her being turned over to the servicemen outside. It gave people hope. Negotiations were ongoing. Something had happened finally!

The hijackers had taken to lecturing their prisoners, for hours at a time. America, the "great Satan," was blamed for all the evils of the world. The Islamic world was rising up in a jihad, a holy war to smite Satan from the earth and institute Islamic rule everywhere. Allah would save a place in heaven for those who died.

It was a mishmash of fundamentalist superstition and political paranoia, but it replaced the beatings for the time being.

There was a heated argument between Nalima and Alli, joined periodically by Hafez or Nabil, who wandered from their positions in the economy cabin.

"We need the Amal," Nalima insisted. "We are almost worn out. Only the Fox will know what to do next. Otherwise we cannot last."

Matt Chicago volunteered to help the purser and the flight attendants distribute food. He moved slowly up and down the aisle, stopping at each row to murmur encouragement to the passengers.

In San Francisco, during his friend's long terminal illness, he had been trained by specialists who helped people to die with dignity. Now, ironically, Chicago found his knowledge and words of comfort useful in helping people to live. He returned to the galley, where Mike Mitchell, the purser, was wearily arguing with Alli. In front of them were two piles of passports.

"No!" Mitchell insisted, jabbing his finger at the vital statistics on an open page. "Bergman is a Scandinavian name. As in Ingrid. Look, he was born in Cincinnati. There are no Jews there. It's full of Swedes and Norwegians."

Alli picked up a dozen or so of the small hardcover documents with the gold American eagle embossed on the dark blue cover. He waved them in the air.

"These are the Jews, then," he said tightly, motioning toward Valerie and Ron, the flight attendants. "Separate these passengers from the rest. They will receive special treatment." The hijacker strode back to the cockpit, where Nalima stood guard over the flight crew.

The purser heaved a heavy sigh and looked at Chicago. He shook his head. "Sure took guts for you to save that guy's life," he said.

Chicago smiled ruefully. "I couldn't stand it. I couldn't stand sitting there listening to someone being tortured like that. Or killed."

Mitchell nodded. "You're doing a great job. You seem to know just what to say to help people calm down."

"I learned how. I'm from San Francisco." He told Mitchell about his training.

"AIDS?" Mitchell asked.

Chicago nodded. "The plague. I've seen too many die. I want to see these people, all of us, live this time around. Terrorism is a plague, too. And no one knows the cure for it, either. Whew! I just hope we all get out of here alive!"

"You worry! I'm the one who had to pick out the Jews."

The San Franciscan lowered his voice. "Bergman from Cincinnati?"

Mitchell carefully stuck his head out of the galley. The terrorists were out of listening distance. "First name Sol. As Jewish as they come. I saved about half of them that way. God help the rest."

"Who's the Fox?" Chicago asked.

Mitchell screwed up his face and shrugged. "Why?"

Chicago shook his head. "I overheard the woman say something about needing his help. It's a person. Maybe one of the Amal. I don't know."

IN THE CONTROL TOWER, there was a glitch. The negotiators finally agreed to turn communications over to the Amal representatives—on the condition that the women and the children were released from the airplane. The hijackers refused. For a few tense moments negotiations came to a standstill. Finally Hafoud Namoud was allowed to speak to the terrorists. They capitulated. The women and children would go free.

Captain Ratcliffe made the announcement just before dusk. For a few seconds the atmosphere aboard the fated flight was joyful, almost jubilant. But for the men, the victory was soon seen to be short-lived.

A woman screamed. "Oh, my God, no, I won't leave you!" She threw her arms around her husband. Cries broke out around the cabin as the realization sank in. For the men, freedom was still a wait away. The hijackers entered and began shouting orders. Farewells were subdued but emotional. Women clutched their children and wept on their way up the aisle. Husbands forced wives to leave with nothing more than brave reassurances and a final kiss.

Night fell in Beirut on the second day of the hijacking. For the hostages left aboard the airliner, darkness was welcome as it veiled them from the hostile attentions of their masters. Light fell into aisles from the galley. The overhead fixtures threw out a dim orange glow. The generators supplied barely enough wattage for the air-conditioning.

Matt Chicago returned to the economy cabin. John Lorch, the Marine, sat alone in a row of seats farther down. He had lapsed into unconsciousness after his brutal beating. At some point, delirium had taken over, lasting most of the night. The flight attendants had pressed dampened cloths to the Marine's swollen, lacerated face and squeezed water into his mouth to prevent dehydration. Now he slept.

Chicago dropped into the seat beside him and shut his eyes. A bone-numbing weariness fell over him. He listened to the soothing hum of the portable generators outside the plane, the hijackers' footsteps pacing in the aisle. Among other things, Matt Chicago had overheard their demands. Despite his words of encouragement to the other passengers, waiting for the Israelis to release over five hundred Shiite prisoners didn't make him optimistic the drama would soon be over.

He felt the Marine stirring in the seat next to him and opened his eyes. Lorch was looking at him.

"Thanks, man. You're a real brave guy."

Self-consciously, Chicago gave him an encouraging smile. "I know what it's like when people gang up on you. I've been on the outside most of my life."

"I owe you my life."

Chicago shook his head emphatically. "You don't owe me anything. You owe it to yourself to get out of here alive."

"Patton," the Marine muttered.

"What?"

"S'what Patton said. No man won a war by dying for his country. You win by making the other guy die for his."

Chicago nodded. "I like that."

The Marine gazed at him silently, thinking but saying nothing.

"Man, you look ugly," Chicago cajoled. It was true. His face was swollen and purple, with deep cuts over his forehead and along his jaw.

"Yeah. Feels like someone rolled a tank over my head."

"So sleep some more. Maybe when tomorrow comes..."

9

Under a dome of light carved from the night, dozens of workers and militiamen swarmed over Beirut airport. The regulars of the Lebanese army had been pushed aside by the ever-growing number of Amal militia. They guarded the perimeter fences and patrolled the edges of the runway as well as controlling the terminal and tower.

In a deserted baggage room at the far end of the terminal's southern wing, Barrabas waited in shadow. He was dressed entirely in black, from the cowl pulled tightly around his head to the soft-soled steel-toed boots. His already massive muscular chest was padded with a Kevlar vest. The belt around his waist carried four concussion grenades and two tear-gas canisters on one side, and his Browning HP automatic pistol on the other. Crisscrossed over his chest were forty-round pencil box mags of 9 mm rounds for the rifle.

The Uzi was only a submachine gun, and normally Barrabas preferred an automatic rifle such as the Armalite for heavy work. But the Uzi was compact and useful for restricted maneuvers—for instance, in the aisle of an airplane—and it was fast and effective. Through the thick dusty glass of a small window, he watched the 727. Beside it sat an empty DC-9, prepared for takeoff.

"I am nervous," Sharif said for the third time from the back of the room. His voice quavered slightly. He held his wrist up to the light flowing in the window and glanced at his watch. Then he paced aimlessly several steps in either direction.

Ken Bridgewater, the CIA agent, crept quietly across the room and stood beside Barrabas.

"It's time?"

The warrior nodded. He held up the tiny portable tracking monitor that Nate Beck, his electronics genius, had perfected.

"My people are in place. The women and children are off the plane. You better go before the fireworks start."

"I don't know who the hell you are and what you're doing, but I guess if Jessup says it's okay..." Bridgewater's words trailed off.

The two civilians looked at each other, each waiting for the other to make a move. Sharif, his face still crossed with doubt, shrugged.

"Whatever you do, it is the Amal problem now. But I too, wish you luck. And I thank you for being of service to my country. Someday, Lebanon will be whole again."

Barrabas remained by the door, his eyes glued to the airplanes and the runways. Suddenly, at the far end of the terminal, headlights beamed from a moving vehicle. A Jeep sped into view, followed by two more. Members of the Amal militia, in tan uniforms and heavily armed, rode in the open vehicles, their checkered *kefireh*s blowing back in the wind. Brakes screeched when they halted abruptly beside the hijacked airplane.

"What the hell..." Barrabas muttered. The hijackers were scheduled to transfer the remaining hostages to the smaller plane at 2100 hours—less than ten minutes away.

The men in the baggage room crowded around the dusty window and watched in silence.

Sharif pulled a walkie-talkie from his belt and spoke into it. He listened to the Arabic reply and snapped it off.

"Custody of the hostages has been transferred to the Amal militia. They are boarding the plane and will ensure the transfer themselves. They continue to demand the release of the prisoners in Israel. Now their release is a matter between your government and the Syrians."

"And the Fox," Bridgewater said ominously. Barrabas looked at him sharply.

"Leader of the military wing of the Amal," Sharif explained rapidly.

"A very dangerous man," Bridgewater added. "Our people believe he and Hafoud Namoud are behind the suicide truck bombing of our embassy and the death of over two hundred Marines. The Israelis are desperate to get hold of him. He's accused of masterminding over a dozen of the worst acts of terrorism against Israel. He kills because he likes it."

"That him?" Barrabas nodded his head at the window where a silent drama unfolded under the high halogen lights. A short broad man ascended the steps to the airplane, followed by soldiers of the Amal militia. On the landing at the top of the steps, a black-masked hijacker greeted him, pistol raised in jubilation. The Amal military leader entered the 727.

"That's him," Sharif confirmed, breathing heavily.

Barrabas checked his watch. "We proceed as planned."

THERE WAS A SUDDEN COMMOTION at the front of the airplane. Hafez left Nabil to guard the hostages and ran toward the cockpit. Loud voices were raised, but in greeting and not in argument.

Chicago leaned across the Marine and looked out the window. An excited hubbub rose from the other passengers.

Armed men wearing Arab headdress climbed the steps outside and entered the airplane.

Suddenly they burst into the economy cabin from the first-class section, almost a dozen of them, in tan military fatigues.

"Silence!" a short middle-aged man who led the armed party shouted into the cabin. He stood for a moment, letting his eyes adjust to the light, and surveyed the hostages. Alli stood behind him.

The new man walked forward. Bandoliers crisscrossed his chest, like the bones on a cannibal's necklace. He wore camouflage fatigues and high black boots. Around his waist, partially obscured by an overhanging paunch, an ammo belt held grenades, two holstered pistols and a sheathed knife. His hand rested on the butt of one of his guns. His hair was covered by a checkered cotton *kefireh*.

Chicago stared. The combined effect of his long, thin mustache, tiny goatee and the small dark eyes that glinted over a narrow protruding nose was unmistakable. This was the Fox. Fear and inexperience made the other hijackers ruthless. Ruthlessness was the Fox's business. It gleamed like the shiny edge of a razor in each eye.

"No, you are not being freed," the Fox shouted, addressing the passengers. "You have been transferred to the jurisdiction of the Amal militia. You are prisoners of war. We are not your rescuers. That will take some time, yet."

His English was flawless, bearing only the slightest trace of an accent. He snapped his fingers twice.

Four armed men pushed in front of him and took positions up and down the aisle. Nabil and Hafez slunk against the wall where the seats had been blown out.

The Fox said something in Arabic to Alli. The hijacker protested. They skirmished verbally, then the Fox silenced Alli with a direct order. The hijacker disappeared. A moment later the sound of the air conditioners vanished, and the bright overhead lights came on.

"Close your windows!" the Fox ordered. Quickly the passengers reached out to slide the plastic shutters across the small round portholes.

The Fox walked slowly forward, his tiny eyes drinking in every detail, scanning every face. He stopped when he came to Chicago's row and stared at the battered Marine. Alli reappeared, and a rapid conversation in Arabic took place. Then Alli went

back to the first-class section. Chicago felt the eyes of
the Fox rest on him, drilling into him. Alli returned
with a handful of passports. The Fox took the Marine's from the pile and scrutinized the injured man
once again. Then he addressed Chicago. "What was
this man to you?"

"A fellow hostage," Chicago replied sullenly.

The man who called himself the Fox nodded. He
reached down and pulled at the San Franciscan's shirt.

"These clothes..." he began. "But you do not have
a military passport."

"It's just...what people wear, back home." Oh, my
God, he thought, army fatigues are standard street
wear in the Castro, and I'm about to be shot for it.

The Fox's eyes narrowed for a moment. He turned
to the soldier at his side.

"Keep a special eye on these two. We may have
further use for them, or reason to question them further."

The Amal militia commander turned to the seat
ahead of them where Dr. Wheatley trembled by the
window. Alli leaned around the massive bulk of the
Fox and pointed to another passport in his hand. The
commander examined it.

"Are you a medical doctor?" he demanded.

Dr. Wheatley shook his head nervously. "No. A...a
scientist. A doctor of physics."

"Ah!" A twinge of satisfaction resounded in the
Arab's voice. "Let me see your wallet, old man."

The scientist gulped and reached inside his jacket.
The Fox opened the wallet and flipped quickly

through his cards. He stopped at one and withdrew it from the plastic folder.

"You are a professor at the Aeronautics Research Institute at Astute University."

Wheatley nodded.

"Then you are an agent of the American government."

"No! No, just a teacher. A professor!"

"Then why do you have a government designated number on your passport!" the Amal leader shouted angrily, waving the document before the scientist's eyes.

Wheatley cowered in his seat.

The Fox stared hard at the old man. His gaze fell and rested on the bulky case squeezed between Wheatley's feet and the seat in front. "And what is this?"

. Matt Chicago watched, surprised at the old man's reaction. As he spoke, his voice cracked, and he began to quake in terror.

"I-it's nothing. Nothing. A hat. It's a hat box."

The Amal put his hand out and motioned for it with his fingers.

"No! You can't have that!" Wheatley protested, his voice shrill with fear. "It's mine! It's . . ."

The Fox casually withdrew his pistol and pointed it. The scientist gasped, then lifted his leather-bound case and offered it up in trembling hands. At a signal from his leader, one of the Amal militiamen took the case and tried the clasps. It was locked. Without waiting for the key, he placed the case on the floor and smashed the locks with the butt of his rifle. Then he kicked the lid open. He reached deep into the case and withdrew the contents.

It looked like a Darth Vader mask, blackened metal crisscrossed with a silver filigree of fine wires, and the geometric contours of chips and transistors. Tubes hung where the nose and mouth ordinarily would be. The Fox lifted it to the light, at once dazzled, mystified and pleased.

"And what is it?" he asked the scientist almost pleasantly.

Wheatley shook his head adamantly. "I . . . I can't say."

The Fox smiled cunningly. He turned to the Amal militiaman beside him. "Our friends the Syrians will be interested. Take this man up front. He is a candidate for very special treatment."

ON THE CRATER-POCKED ROAD that ran between the sea and the airport, the United Kingdom issue SB-301 armored personnel carrier jolted noisily in and out of potholes. Alex Nanos pushed the accelerator down, up a little, down more, coaxing the little ninety-one horsepower Rover engine to pick up speed.

With the help of Sharif Mar Hasaff, the British-made carrier had been temporarily "borrowed" from a cooperative unit of the Lebanese army. Despite a seating capacity of eight, the 301 looked most like an armored version of a suburban commuter's sedan, with a gunner's hatch and a centrally mounted searchlight on top. A number of features made it perfect for civil-war conditions.

The welded armor exterior protected the riders from most high-velocity automatic rifle fire. The hull of the carrier was lined with polyurethane foam, and narrow gutters had been installed over the gunports, the windows and the hood, making it invulnerable to Molotov cocktails—the preferred weapon of home-made revolutionaries from Belfast to Beirut. There were firing ports on each side of the main compartment and one in the rear door. As well, the driver and commander each had side doors with observation hatches.

Nanos drove with the armor plate for the windshield up. They weren't expecting enemy fire.

The Lebanese army controlled the land west of the airport. The official units had been mysteriously pulled out earlier that evening. It had been simple enough for Barrabas to arrange. Sharif and Bridge-water took care of payments to officers and officials in the Ministry of Defense.

The area was deserted, the roadblocks unmanned. In the distance the lights of the runways shimmered. The terminal building was outlined by its glowing plate-glass windows, and halogen lights, high on their pylons, threw a veil of false daylight over the airport. The hijacked 727 waited on the runway, bathed in brilliant light.

Still, Nanos played hard with the four gears in the two-speed gearbox, pushing the heavy vehicle roughly over the cratered road. At times he approached the 301's maximum speed of sixty miles an hour.

In the commander's seat, Claude Hayes gripped the dashboard, an exasperated expression etched across his face. The diffused half-light from the faraway airport shone on his burnished black skin, and a faint clinking sounded from behind him. He'd changed his appearance recently. Part of his black pride, he'd explained to the others. He had always kept his hair closely clipped on top, but now, at the back, it was wound into a half-dozen tight coils strung with tiny beads on each side. "Man, I didn't know we were in a hurry. You check out the suspension on this thing?"

"It sure ain't no Lincoln," Nanos crowed, watching the needle of the speedometer cling to sixty-two. He felt his vertebrae jar as the carrier descended abruptly into a pothole. The indefatigable little vehicle growled and scrambled back onto level road. "Claude, if everything works out, when the job's over we'll just skedaddle away quietly from the scene. But it's always been a good idea to know the limits of the getaway car in case a hasty exit is needed. You know what I mean, baby?"

Hayes nodded as the carrier bounced over another crater.

"Man, you got sense."

In the back, Billy Two sat impassively beside Lee Hatton, undisturbed by the terrible bucking of the carrier. The Osage was planets away from a place called Beirut. Like all the other mercs, he was dressed in black battle fatigues, his face blackened with camouflage paint. But Billy Two had added red-and-green chevrons down both sides of his face. The native Indian had had an enforced vacation in a Spetsnaz psychiatric hospital, and he'd been weird ever since.

Lee Hatton checked him out, watching his face and trying to figure out what was wrong. Her medical training was her special contribution to the team. She fought as well as any of them, but on top of being alert for battle, she kept continual vigil over the other mercs. It was part of the job, and she did it silently, unassumingly, and without them being aware of it.

She figured the Spetsnaz torture—injections of liquid sulfur—had pushed the Osage over the brink into temporary chemically induced schizophrenia. On some missions he was more together than on others. Interestingly, his delusions never seemed to interfere with his performance in battle.

Billy Two had been staring into space since the Lear jet had left American soil, and had barely uttered a word to anyone. Suddenly it dawned on her. She knew what was wrong when she looked at him.

He didn't blink.

He stared, glassy eyed, at something—or someone?—that didn't exist in the back of the armored carrier. As if he had picked up her thoughts, the Osage turned and looked at her. Then he blinked.

"Hawk Spirit has been speaking."

That was what Lee meant about schizophrenia. Hawk Spirit was supposedly an ancestral Osage warrior god. Billy Two and he were apparently on a first-name basis.

"He said 'Trust the unexpected,'" the Osage continued. His face clouded over, and his brow furrowed as if his thoughts had turned to syrup. "But I don't understand the other thing."

"What's that, Billy?"

"Well," the Osage said thoughtfully. Slowly folding his thick arms across his massive chest, he narrowed his eyes and looked straight ahead, as if peering into the distance. "I see a face behind a veil, and I almost know who it is, but just as the name comes it vanishes, and I see—"

He stopped abruptly, his eyes opening, and he looked at Lee again. All trace of craziness was gone. His voice was low and serious.

"A parachute. Someone in a parachute falling through bright blue sky, with nothing above and nothing below. That's all."

Lee Hatton sat back without saying anything. She couldn't help it. Parachutes brought back thoughts of Geoff Bishop and she hated herself for it. For now, she lived only to fight—or at least, that's what she wanted. It was a handy way to forget. Sometimes she felt that she could get rid of the sorrow, excise it from her as if feelings could be cut out with a pair of scissors. But that was a coward's dream.

"What are you thinking?" Billy Two nudged her gently. He gave her a peaceful smile.

"About the stupid kinds of things you think about in the minutes before you go into battle. You know. It's not like, dramatic, remembering all the best people of your life, or the best moments, or the big lesson learned or prayers or vows of good resolutions if you come back alive." She shrugged. "It's just stupid thoughts about . . . things that can't be changed."

Claude Hayes turned around from the front seat and looked at her squarely. "Lee, you are being romantic. Only reason we think about dumb things is because we do this all the time. This is rooo-tine for us, woman. Dull, boring, a job. You bet your ass there's a lot of budding saints on that hijacked airplane right now. If good intentions were crap, you'd be seeing it pouring out the doors and windows. But for us, man, it's just a job."

Lee laughed in spite of herself. "You are one right son of a bitch, Claude."

Hayes brandished his Uzi. "SOB, Lee! Soldier of Barrabas!"

"Amen!" Alex Nanos shouted, and the others joined in. The Greek pulled the armored carrier over. The crumbling ledges of a shale cliff rose beside the road. The mercs jumped out, quickly checking the straps that held their ammo belts and grenades. They pulled black cowls over their heads to cover their hair and necks. Only Billy Two refused to wear one.

Claude Hayes looked over the Indian's warpaint.

"Man, with all that lipstick on, I'd dance with you, then shoot."

Billy Two looked annoyed. "Hawk Spirit is my guide," he replied sullenly.

"Now we get to see how well Nate's little invention works for real," Nanos commented. The dark-skinned Greek clipped a small cellular transmitter to his belt. "Everyone got it on?"

The other mercs nodded. They climbed the cliffs quickly, scrambling lightly over the natural steps formed by the strata of exposed rock. At the top, they found a forest of young cedars, eerie contorted branches twisted by winds blowing off the Mediterranean. Runway lights twinkled through the gnarled branches. They moved through the forest to the grass clearing that began a quarter of a mile from the wire perimeter fence.

Hayes snapped open a compass and took a bearing. "O'Toole's little surprise will be coming from there," he said, pointing north, where the glowing lights of Beirut's southern suburbs and the sprawling refugee camps banished stars from the night sky.

Lee knelt and scanned the airport with infrared night binoculars. The shapes shimmered with their own heat, and while she had trained herself to distinguish between male and female, she could not identify terrorist and hostage. Unfortunately, the passive Star Tron scope was virtually useless, its image intensification-apparatus overwhelmed by the bright airport lights.

"Runway's completely clear," she told the others. "Five minutes until the transfer and counting."

"Counting on who, baby?" Alex murmured smoothly, looking to the north. "Them?"

The headlights had been painted for concealment, but the noise of the engines drew their attention. A convoy of Jeeps and half-ton trucks raced along the perimeter of the airport, then stopped.

"Shit, man," the Greek protested, "they ain't part of the plan!" He tapped nervously on the mag in his Uzi with the palm of his hand.

"Trust the unexpected," Billy Two intoned.

"Now, where have I heard that before?" Lee murmured.

Soldiers, wearing the distinctive checkered headgear of the Amal militia, leapt from the vehicles. A

party of them moved quickly to the fence with wire
cutters. In less than a minute, a large section of the
fence had been cut away and the first Jeep was
through.

Claude Hayes snapped open his compass case and
took another bearing. His arm followed an arc from
the north to the perimeter fence directly behind him.
"Landing there."

He was pointing to the Amal convoy pouring
through the fence barely a quarter of a mile away. He
glanced at his watch and snapped the compass closed.

"Back up, fellas," he told them, retreating with an
easy saunter into the stand of gnarled cedars.
"Whoever they be, they's real soon gonna discover the
wrong place at the right time."

DAVID RATCLIFFE, pilot of the fated airplane, somehow felt defeated by his own inactivity, just sitting in
his cockpit. The long hours of waiting had stretched
to interminable tedium. Finally, things had begun to
happen—the old lady had been released, then the
women and children. The men were going to be transferred to the smaller DC-9 shortly, and he'd wrongly
assumed a new flight crew had been negotiated. Silly
of me, he chided himself.

Alli entered the cockpit and signaled with a furious
jab of his automatic rifle. The little boys had switched
to big toys after the new Amal soldiers had arrived.
The reinforcements had given the original hijackers a
boost, puffing their chests, making them braver than
ever.

Alli was drenched with sweat, and smiling crazily. His eyes gleamed, and his cheeks were rosy from a two-day fix of adrenaline. He poked the barrel of his new rifle at Ratcliffe's copilot. The man woke with a start and almost clawed his way onto the instrument panel in terror, wakening from one nightmare into a worse one.

Alli laughed. "Go! Now!" he shouted. "Out!"

The joke was over. Ratcliffe pried himself from his seat and went to help his copilot.

In the first-class cabin, the Fox tapped his fingers slowly along a headrest and surveyed the occupants of the seats. The scientist. Four Americans with government or military passports. The Jews. Twelve of them. It was time for the selection.

This was the part the Fox liked the most. He loved to watch them squirm and wonder, will it be me? And he would make that decision slowly.

First there were some strategic considerations. Alli pushed the crew into the cabin, where they were surrounded by Amal militiamen. The Fox turned and nodded to the soldier at the door.

"Take the scientist with his magic box," he ordered. "And the pilot and flight crew. Transfer them to the other airplane. I will come, too. Everyone else in this cabin has special treatment. When that is finished, the rest of the hostages are to be transferred to the other aircraft. *Allah Akbar!*"

"*Allah Akbar!* God is Great!" repeated his soldiers, raising their rifles in gestures of triumph.

Captain Ratcliffe and his companions were pushed into single file and led down the steps. It was the evening of a Lebanese summer, and the warm breeze smelled faintly both of the sea and of the Arabian desert. For the first time in thirty-six hours, he breathed clear fresh air, and he realized that the airplane he had left was noxious. His nostrils drank in air until he was dizzy.

The airplane was ringed by Amal soldiers. A half-ton and a Jeep idled nearby, and more vehicles approached from the west. In the distance, lights glowed in the terminal building. The dark runways stretched long and flat on either side, outlined by tiny blue stars set at regular intervals. The DC-9 loomed in the darkness like a great silver bird.

Their guards shouted for them to hurry to the bottom of the stairs. The flight crew and the old man were pushed in the direction of the DC-9. Ratcliffe, in the lead, counted footsteps behind him. Where were the rest? He stole a quick look back when they reached the steps to the DC-9.

The other men—Americans, Jews—were being forced into the back of the half-ton.

"Hey!" a soldier yelled and struck him with the flat of his assault rifle. Ratcliffe staggered against the steps, his chin slamming against metal. Quickly he scrambled to his feet, almost unable to contain the rage that had suddenly exploded within. He gripped the steel railing to steady himself and slowly climbed.

The cockpit was lit only by the dim greenish light from the instrument panel. He made his way to his seat, his trained eye moving over the gauges and dials. Then he noticed something behind the cockpit door. In case of fire.

An extinguisher. And an ax.

IN THE EERIE ELECTRONIC LIGHT inside the control tower, Hafoud Namoud stood by the window, watching the furtive movement between airplanes as the transfer began.

"Sir!" An assistant entered the tower, waving a long sheet of paper furiously. He ran to the Amal political leader and thrust it at him. "You must see this."

Calmly Namoud set his coffee cup down and took the sheet of paper. It was from the wire service. A report from a special edition of a leading New York newspaper. While the American government publicly carried on private negotiations, reliable sources indicated that a team of crack commandos had secretly been sent to Beirut to storm the airplane and free the hostages. His eyes fell on the byline. Calhoun Bellow.

The name was famous, and the story, therefore, credible. He sank back in thought.

"Get me the Fox on the radio," he ordered.

"He has already boarded the second aircraft," the aide murmured, handing Namoud an ear set.

On the DC-9, the leader of the Amal military stepped into the cockpit and took the radio. He listened silently, his breathing becoming noticeably quicker, his face imperceptibly tighter. A muscle in his cheek flexed.

"We will stop the transfer and switch to the contingency plan!" he told Namoud. "The hostages will all be taken to our headquarters for special treatment." The Fox ripped off the ear set and spat orders at his second in command.

"Return to the other aircraft. All remaining hostages are to be taken to the Villa Buchove! We have no time to—" He broke off his sentence and cocked his ear, listening for something he had just caught a trace of. But there it was, unmistakable, stronger, closer.

"NOW!" he roared, his arms waving violently. His men scrambled to carry out his order. The Fox slapped his hands palms down against his ears as the whistle of the incoming mortar shrilled through the night air.

In the deserted baggage room, Barrabas and the other men watched the transfer begin. Four of the hostages climbed aboard the DC-9 with their guards. They were soon followed by more of the Amal. The Fox's short, pearlike figure made him easy to identify, even in the patchy darkness left by the glowing lights of the terminal buildings.

There were fifty-two hostages remaining. A dozen or so had been brought from the 727 and isolated on one side. Amal soldiers herded the rest down the steps and onto the tarmac.

From the western perimeter, the headlights of an approaching convoy glowed dimly across the dark runways. They braked beside the hijacked airplane. The first hostages who had been brought from the 727 were being forced into a half-ton truck.

"Something is terribly wrong," Bridgewater breathed, gazing through the window over Barrabas's shoulder.

The men heard the faint whistle of a mortar.

"Incoming," Sharif breathed.

There was a second whistle, and a third. Suddenly, explosions ranged along the western perimeter of the airport. A wall of orange flame lit the night, half a mile away. Already there was the incoming whistle of a fourth mortar. It hit closer to the terminal, impacting near the end of the northern wing, spraying dirt and slabs of asphalt into the air. There was a loud electronic hum from the walls, and the lights of the terminal dipped, rose brighter—too bright—and dipped low again. They returned to normal, but the electric hum continued.

A glimmer of a smile played on Barrabas's lips. O'Toole loved to do his thing, and his boys were right on time.

"Get out of here!" Barrabas commanded the men in the room with him.

Sharif and Bridgewater moved to the door that led into the terminal. The Ministry of Defense official cast a lingering backward glance at the lone mercenary.

"I have arranged for the disinformation campaign to begin immediately. The Amal will learn that the Druze attacked them."

"Just make sure your people meet up with us on the coastal highway so we can slip out of here without any publicity when it's over."

"I assure you. We will be there. Good luck."

"Luck?" the mercenary asked. "Luck has nothing to do with it."

AT THE WESTERN PERIMETER of the airport, the first mortar blew a wide section of the fence to pieces at the very moment an Amal Jeep was driving through. The welded frame collapsed in fiery cloud, its passengers instantly annihilated. Half-tons careered crazily to each side to avoid the conflagration. Soldiers leapt from the trucks, their excitement and confusion carrying to the mercs, still hidden in the forest of cedars.

"Great, we got our hole in the fence, but someone's in the way," the Greek complained.

Billy Two harrumphed, as if to say "I told you so." Trust the unexpected.

Without warning, a shrill whistle sounded above them, and almost overhead a glowing orange line marked the flight path of another missile. The mercs cringed instinctively.

"O'Toooole!" Nanos screamed the Irishman's name as if it were a curse, and shook his head after the projectile. The mortar blew forty yards away, opening a crater four feet wide and taking out a small section of the wire.

"We got ourselves a way in!" Hayes chanted. He leapt from the forest like a shadow, running toward the smoking gap.

The night was filled with whistles, golden arcs and then explosions. Successions of mortar rounds bombarded their way across the fields bordering the airport. There was a brief pause, another whistle, then a boom, and a corner of the terminal disappeared into rubble.

The mercs ran, cursing the bulletproof Kevlar vests that added weight, knowing that in a few short moments they would be equally thankful for them.

Their next position was in the sand dunes on the western side of the runway, half a mile away. Behind them, they heard the Amal soldiers cursing and yelling as they cleared the debris. With its engine roaring angrily, a half-ton bashed its way through, clearing a path for the rest.

BARRABAS RAN ONTO THE RUNWAY. Luggage carts shielded him from the airplane. From the west came the sound of more fading whistles as mortars reached the height of their arced flight and descended. The ground underneath the airport shook from the impact of the explosions. The lights in the terminal building dipped, went out for a fraction of a second and glowed again, their wattage reduced by half.

Sirens split the air. Fire trucks raced from garages along the base of terminal to the western perimeter. Orange flashes burst in the field beyond as the Amal militia returned fire from ground-based surface-to-air launchers.

Barrabas skittered across the deserted asphalt and knelt in the cover of the luggage dollies. He pulled a long black antenna from the box at his belt and checked the portable monitor cradled in his hand. A tiny red dot moved on the tiny screen, converging on the western perimeter of the airport. Nate's little invention worked like magic.

The SOBs had moved through the perimeter of the airport. Nanos and Hatton circled to the right. Claude Hayes and Billy Two angled left to approach it from the rear.

Barrabas felt movement nearby. Liam O'Toole ran to his side, still carrying the radio transmitter that had set off the automated mortar attack.

"Nice fireworks," the merc leader whispered, keeping his eyes on the movements of the red dots on the monitor.

"The party's just started, Colonel."

The Irish American, who learned to love explosives in the streets of Belfast, had taken to Beirut like a duck to water. Working feverishly from the moment the plan had been set up, he had engineered serial bombardment from secret launching sites in the southern suburbs of Beirut, and it was working like a charm.

The Amal militia had been drawn away from the terminal building to form a defense line on the northern runways. Automatic weapons sounded crazily, a nervous chatter at the edge of night.

Another mortar whined.

"This is the closest one," O'Toole muttered, instinctively crouching lower and raising his shoulders.

The missile struck a corner of the terminal's north wing. Masonry and glass blew into a fiery orange cloud, spraying the militiamen below. Some screamed and retreated. More sank to their knees, collapsing under the hail of flying debris.

The orange light from the explosion threw a long, fast-moving shadow on the runway. Nate Beck dropped beside the two mercs, panting for breath. In his hands he held a black control box with a long antenna. His fingers twisted a dial. The lights in the terminal buildings and along the runway flickered wildly.

"Now?"

Barrabas held his breath, following the tiny red dots that now were no bigger than the head of a pin. Suddenly they stopped. "Now!"

"This'll be a power surge they'll never forget." As Nate twisted the dial all the way to the end, the mercs buried their faces in their arms.

There was a sound like air escaping from a tire. Then the low hum grew in volume. The signal lights along the runways began to shine brighter, and light streamed from the terminal building. The traffic-control tower glowed eerily green.

The whining hum became insistent, deafening, droning against their eardrums. Light spread across the runways, freezing the Amal militia while their shadows fled. Hostages were caught on the stairs leading from the airplane, their pale white faces frozen in the growing light.

A whip cracked in the sky overhead. The humming stopped. Simultaneously the tinselly sound of breaking glass resonated across the airport. Overwhelmed by a sudden electrical surge, bulbs popped in the high halogen lamps. The tiny blue and red signal lights along the runway began to explode like neon lawn sprinklers. The brilliant spotlights on the terminal roof zapped out to total blackness. Room by room, the terminal building dimmed. The tower went out all at once, and a shower of sparks rose from the portable generators next to the airplanes. The Amal militiamen put their hands up to shield their eyes.

Blackness, as thick as a nightmare, followed the sudden illumination. The Amal militiamen called to each other and fired into the air in panic. Screams rose from the hostages congregated at the steps of the 727.

Barrabas and his mercs leapt forward, seeing the shadowy shapes of the militiamen flailing in the grayish dark. They fanned out and zigzagged erratically across the runway. Orange muzzle flash from their Uzi's mouthed 3-round bursts into the darkness. Death came, first from one place, then another, then somewhere else again. The Amal guards encircling the airplanes faced the bullets.

They clutched their bellies, hearts, chests. They groaned, screamed, contorted in death spasms. Some just dropped and were totally still.

Relentlessly, and with near-perfect timing, Barrabas picked one target, stitched a 9 mm vertical line, and sought a second. He aimed and fired on instinct, his eyes scanning for hostile contact, running from side to side to gain precious yards on the airplanes.

When Barrabas came up behind the portable generator, he flattened his back against it, grabbing the tiny hand monitor from his belt. O'Toole came up beside him, breathing hard, sweat glistening through the black paint on his forehead.

"What in hell's going on, sir?"

Amal soldiers were pushing the hostages into the vehicles of the waiting convoy.

Barrabas snapped open the monitor and pulled out the antenna. The tiny red dots showed that Claude Hayes and Billy Two had reached their position in the cover of a fuel truck near the tail of the plane. Lee Hatton and Alex Nanos were in the sand dunes on the other side. Nate Beck was off the board, nowhere to be seen.

Engines roared, and two half-tons rolled forward with a load of human cargo.

"One thing we didn't plan on," Barrabas told O'Toole between gritted teeth.

The Irish American spat between his front teeth. "What's that, Colonel?"

"The Amal double cross."

WHEN BECK'S LIGHT SHOW BEGAN, Nanos and Hatton took cover behind a grassy knoll in the sand dunes, fifty feet from the edge of the runway.

Automatic-weapons fire sounded in syncopated 3-round bursts. Then it was answered by a cacophony of undirected chatter. Muzzles flashed like sparks in the darkness beyond the airplane.

"Something's wrong," Lee whispered.

The plan was to assault the airplane just as the transfer had begun. Most of the hostages would still be aboard the plane, but the hijackers would be spread thinner and distracted by their operations. Now the hostages were milling about on the runway while the Amal militia herded them into trucks with brutal force. A Jeep and another half-ton pulled away from the airplane and headed back toward the coastal road.

"They're taking the hostages."

"If we go in, it'll be a bloody slaughter of the hostages," said Nanos.

"And for us, suicide," Lee added grimly. "Listen!" The gunfire died.

"It's over. The whole thing's aborted. The colonel, O'Toole—they're out there."

"Look at the guy riding on the bumper." Nanos pointed to the half-ton trucks heading across the runway into the dunes. There were two of them. A Jeep was in the lead. The backs of the trucks were tightly closed, and on each an armed soldier rode guard. A third truck pulled away from the airplane.

"I can take out the guy riding on the bumper of that last truck," Nanos explained, speaking rapidly between deep breaths. "Trade uniforms and wait in the dunes. It'll take the truck left on the runway another minute to get here. When it does, I take out the guy riding shotgun on it. Then I take his place."

"And then what? You play hero and singlehandedly—"

"Ride into their headquarters." Nanos smiled and held up the modular radio unit. "These have a range of three miles, remember? Get the colonel. Follow."

Doubt was written across Hatton's face.

"I'm dark—black hair. I look like them. I can pull it off, Lee."

She looked at the Greek. He probably could.

"Just make sure you guys are there to save my ass when I need you," he added.

Lee nodded.

Nanos clutched his Uzi and start to run.

CLAUDE HAYES AND BILLY TWO raced from the sand dunes when the light show ended, encountering minimum resistance. The jarring staccato of auto rifles danced farther off in the warmth of the Lebanese night. Hayes zigzagged toward the tail of the plane. Billy Two strode like an automaton, holding his Uzi in front of him like a toy and picking off the occasional Amal that came across his path.

Suddenly the rules changed. The convoy of trucks passed them, heading west, their headlights bobbing across the dunes. The two men made it to the shelter of a fuel truck a hundred feet from the tail of the 727.

They heard boots pounding rapidly across the pavement. Barrabas pivoted around the corner of the fuel truck to cut his running speed, his Uzi held tightly across his chest.

"It's off!"

"You're telling me," Hayes said, almost wearily. "Where's O'Toole?"

"Gone to look for Nate. He's off the map." Barrabas held up the tiny monitor to clarify. He moved to the edge and peered around the corner. An Amal officer was standing over a pile of bodies and unleashing a tirade of abuse at his soldiers. The last half-ton drove into the dunes.

"They think they killed their own men," Barrabas said, turning back to Hayes and Starfoot. "Let's go. Into the dunes to get Alex and Lee. O'Toole is heading there, too. We'll leave the back way and rendezvous with Sharif and his men."

A hundred yards into the dunes, Barrabas signaled by dropping his hands, and the three mercs fell to the ground. Someone, with quiet movements, their shape barely darker than the night, eased along the ridge of a dune.

Claude Hayes moved his Uzi into position. Barrabas put his hand out, stopping him. Noise would reveal their position. They stopped breathing as the dark shape came close enough to step on them. Barrabas grabbed an ankle and twisted, pulling the body down.

The soldier fell with a grunt. The American propelled himself forward, blocking the man's furious struggling.

Raising his arm high overhead, Barrabas balled his fist to smash his opponent unconscious. He froze halfway through the downswing. Lee Hatton gasped underneath him, her thumbs inches from the underside of the colonel's jaw.

Barrabas blinked. Escrimo, the Filipino art of self-defense. Hatton was an expert. He rolled off.

Lee picked herself up and quickly outlined Nanos's plan.

"You two go with Lee," Barrabas ordered Billy Two and Claude Hayes. He handed them the miniature monitor and the battery pack. "Take the 301 and track Alex. I'm going after O'Toole and Beck. Remember, we're to be exfiltrated from the coastal highway in half an hour."

Barrabas ran low through the sand dunes, paralleling the runway until he was in front of the hijacked airplane. The windows of the terminal glowed with the ghostly illumination of emergency lighting. Near the service hangars, regulars of the Lebanese army worked frantically to focus a spotlight mounted on the back of a wrecker. The brilliant white light spilled sloppily across the runway.

On the roof of the terminal, a man barked a stream of orders in Arabic. Amal soldiers rushed to tend to the wounded and the dead, who lay in drying puddles of their own blood. An ambulance, its blue lights flashing madly, careered across the runway toward the 727.

Barrabas saw dark outlines moving into the dunes on his left and went down, silently twisting under the cover of a ridge of grass. Two men breathing, one heaving from exertion, the other wheezing, his breathing jagged and irregular. Beck was wounded.

He lifted his head and stage whispered to O'Toole. "Here!"

The two men came over the ridge, Beck leaning on O'Toole for support. They dropped into the swale, panting to catch their breath. The electronics genius was clearly in pain.

"It's my right leg, Colonel," Beck explained. "Below the knee. Another one hit my transmitter unit. In my breast pocket. Saved my life. The leg doesn't hurt so much when I look at it that way."

"Bullet passed right through, next to the bone," O'Toole murmured after a quick examination of the bloody wound.

"Can you bind it?" Barrabas asked.

O'Toole nodded.

"You have to walk," Barrabas told Beck, looking him firmly in the eyes. He gave them Hatton's story. O'Toole narrowed his eyes and went to work, using his knife to cut the fabric away from Nate's wound. The hi-tech genius gritted his teeth to fight the burning pain when the Irish American began wrapping the makeshift bandage tightly around his raw flesh.

"We have to get to the coastal highway. Sharif will rendezvous with us there in twenty-five minutes," Barrabas told them.

"T'would be a pleasure, Colonel, to get ourselves out of this friggin' disaster area." O'Toole finished tying the bandage. He looked at Barrabas and grinned. It was not a pleasant grin. "A pleasure, indeed, if we could pay these maggots a home visit and snuff them in their nest."

THE FOX STOOD AT THE TOP OF THE STEPS, just inside the door of the DC-9. In the blackout, the stars overhead were as glittery as diamonds in the velvet black sky. The rhythmic groans of the wounded and the dying drifted to him, a somber note on the Beirut breeze.

Their blood lay like great red flowers, crimson poppies smashed onto pavement, each with a tiny man at the center, small, crumpled, lifeless or twisted with pain. Medics ran among them, soldiers with stretchers. Men screamed until the morphine hit.

The airplane was dark. One soldier inside guarded the crew and the elderly scientist. Airport workers struggled to line up a second generator with the airplane. One by one, the ambulances formed a line, cool blue lights flashing, one coming for each one going.

He was barely able to stifle his rage over the number of casualties. He did not believe that his men had shot one another in the confusion after the bombardment, as Hafoud Namoud alleged in his first communication.

An aide mounted the steps and stood stiffly in front of him. He held out a flashlight. The Fox took it.

"Namoud insists he is correct. Our old enemies the Druze are up to their tricks. They launched the bombardment when they heard that we were occupying the airport. They damaged the power station. In the confusion—"

"But thirty!" the Fox snapped. "Thirty casualties because my men were confused in the darkness! No. I do not believe it. I refuse."

"But what else—" The aide stopped meekly.

The Fox looked out over the airport. Emergency lights glowed in the terminal. Soldiers had commandeered civilian cars, and lined them up with their headlights facing across the runway. Thirty of his men were dead, and yet Namoud insisted that no one had entered the airport or attacked.

It was impossible.

What happened? the Fox asked himself silently, mentally reconstructing the events of the last half hour. The newspaper story from America. That was when he ordered the hostages taken to Beirut. The transfer never took place. They had aborted their mission.

A soft warm breeze blew in from the Arabian Peninsula. He sniffed. He caught the mysterious perfume of the cedar forests of the mountains of Lebanon. He sniffed again. Several times. There was something else there, too. An animal smell. Powerful. Dangerous.

"A team of crack American commandos," he said, almost whimsically, to his aide. The man looked incredulous.

"As for the Syrians, I think they will be most gratified to interview this scientist about his strange contraption. Put out a call to our people. We will surround the airport with a human barrier of thousands of loyal Shiite followers until we take off."

The Fox tossed the flashlight to his aide and entered the airplane.

In the cockpit of the DC-9, the exhausted crew from the 727 sat dazed and alone, a single question foremost in each person's mind. What next? Lights came on around the airport, trickling through the narrow window, throwing the geometric symmetries of the instrument panel into high relief. An arrow of light hit the handle of the fire ax.

Captain Ratcliffe looked through the open door into the cabin. Only a small amount of light filtered through the small porthole windows that ran the length of the plane. There was one guard, just beyond the door, his figure only slightly more solid than the darkness around him.

Ratcliffe stood, his eyes wide and glassy, hypnotized by the curvature of the wooden ax handle and the image of the man with his back turned toward the cockpit. The pilot reached for the ax, noticing that his hands fit perfectly the contours of the slender wood. The steel head was heavy. The sharpened edge glinted with reflected light.

Suddenly his copilot noticed and sat up. "What are you doing!" he whispered, half in warning, half in shock.

"Shhht!" Captain Ratcliffe growled. One step took him to the cockpit door. The weight pulled the head of the ax over his shoulder. When he swung, he was certain at the last moment that the darkness and the ax had tricked him.

It sounded like an eggshell breaking. The blade of the ax cleaved the guard's skull, smashing through soft matter until it struck the jawbone.

Someone gasped. It was the old man, the last of the passengers from the 727, sitting somewhere in the darkness. Captain Ratcliffe tightened his hold on the ax. The body dipped forward, slumped out from underneath the blade and spiraled, the broken cranium strewing its contents over the seats. It flopped into the aisle.

"My God, what have you done!" The copilot stepped forward, frozen in the shafts of light from outside that illuminated the cockpit, his expression utterly aghast. The flight engineer rose from his seat, uncertain of what to do.

Halfway down the plane there was a shout, and a beam from a powerful flashlight blinded Ratcliffe. Footsteps. Someone ran into the plane. More shouts. He couldn't see anything except the brilliant light and beyond the radius of its beam, blackness. He put his arm up to shield his eyes. He had to get out. The urge to escape, to be free and safe, clawed inside his chest. He stepped forward.

"Captain!" the copilot shouted, grabbing Ratcliffe's shoulder from behind and shaking him. He reached to take the ax from the pilot's hands. Ratcliffe held it away from him and they struggled for it.

A loud hum vibrated through the airplane, the ceiling lights flickering on suddenly, dimming, and starting up again. The orange glow was barely sufficient to illuminate the interior of the DC-9. The old man looked up at him from the first row of seats, his mouth open in horror.

Blood streamed from one end of the body at Ratcliffe's feet. Brains spilled everywhere. As the copilot and flight engineer tried to restrain him, he fought against them, desperately trying to pull away. Their hands clutched at the ax, forcing it from him, wrenching it from his grasp.

The Fox's aide sighted on the armed men and squeezed the trigger of his submachine gun. Nine millimeter parabellum slammed into Ratcliffe cutting red badges in a neat diagonal row across his chest. The Amal officer strode forward, flicking the gun on full auto and depressing the trigger again.

The copilot and the flight engineer caught the full load from the forty-round mag. They jerked and quivered as bullets smashed into their skulls and chests, spraying bits of flesh and uniform against the bulkhead wall. For Ratcliffe and his crew members, the nightmare was over.

The entangled bodies of the three-man flight crew teetered in the door of the cockpit, finally collapsing to a crumpled heap. Ratcliffe stared down the length of the aisle, his lifeless eyes sighting just above the pile of the carpet.

The Amal militia officer clasped the submachine gun with sweaty hands. The Fox walked up behind him, and he felt his leader's breath hot on the back of his neck.

"That was rather stupid," the Shiite terrorist purred coldly. "You've killed the entire flight crew."

11

In a dark stone cell not far from Beirut airport, a man lay curled on his side on a straw mattress. His arms were folded around his head, providing instinctive protection from the intrusions of the poodle-sized wharf rats with whom he shared his tiny damp quarters.

In the months in which he had been a prisoner there, he had made a sort of peace with them. They were fat and sleek and well fed, and for the most part could afford the luxury of ignoring him. They kept to their foul nest of straw in the farthest corner of the dank dungeon. Slipping like eels through cracks in the stone walls, they foraged in the kitchens and refuse heaps of the Amal fortress, returning with unidentifiable morsels of gristle or putrid meat for their young.

It was their fourth litter in the prisoner's time there, and he had come to feel a proprietary—almost grand-fatherly—interest in the rodents. Studying the mating habits of the rats had kept him sane.

By day, a sliver of light intruded into the cell through a narrow slit ten feet above the floor in one wall. He watched them. He gave them names and observed their quirks. He analyzed their individual traits. In the long tedium of his isolated days he began to imagine himself an expert on them. In his head, he wrote a scientific treatise about them, and lectured in thronged auditoriums the world over. But his dread remained.

Sometimes he caught them looking at him, hostility unconcealed in their dark shiny eyes, as if he were their prisoner instead of a captive of Shiite terrorists. The rats were tolerating him, and he was saddened when it finally occurred to him that to the rodents he was merely a reserve food supply should the rations from upstairs ever run out.

He heard metal tapping against metal, and his eyes opened instantly. A key in the lock. The steel door swung inward on well-oiled springs, and a man entered the cell. The rats squealed and cowered in their nest. The prisoner recognized the sound of Muammar's steel-toed boots scraping on the stone floor and pretended he was asleep.

He was aware of the guard standing over him, looking down, watching him the way the rats watched, curiosity and hostility mingling with indecision. Muammar nudged the prisoner sharply in the small of his back. He stiffened, faking the surprise of a rude awakening. It was better that they thought he slept through everything.

"Get up!" the Shiite ordered loudly in English.

The prisoner rolled over, blinking his eyes as if they were filled with sleep. In the first days of his imprisonment, he had been awakened at random intervals for the interrogations. When they were finished with him, the mind-numbing routine of captivity with its identical daily regimen set in—two meals, an hour of exercise outdoors, eternities of solitude spent in the company of rats. Now, after the slow parade of months, the midnight interruption was highly unusual. For a brief instant, his spirits warmed to the precious delusion that he might be freed. Quickly he stifled the thought. After so much time, hope was too hard on him. It was easier to assume his execution time had come.

"Finally, your fate has been decided," Muammar added ominously, waving at him with his submachine gun.

"Why? The rats are hungry?" The prisoner swung his legs over the side of the narrow bed and looked up.

Muammar was a young man, smooth-faced but intelligent and intensely serious. His dark Arab eyes smoked with hidden fury. And yet the prisoner had, at times, been able to engage him in conversation, even debates. He had been a university student before the Israeli invasion of Lebanon, and had embraced the absolute world vision of Shiite fundamentalism only lately. The fanatical creed provided him with answers to all of life's problems, answers pat enough to be used inside Chinese fortune cookies. But the thrust and parry of verbal debate still tempted him.

The prisoner had tried on several occasions to goad Muammar into explaining what their purpose was in keeping him prisoner. The guard was intelligent, earnest and intensely loyal to his leaders, the Ayatollah Khomeini, of course, and the military commander in Beirut, named only the Fox. It was the cause that made little sense. A good man in the service of some nut cases. Muammar smiled. "In Lebanon, rats are rarely hungry anymore."

"Exactly the way I feel about Islamic fundamentalism."

The guard was perplexed by the non sequitur. "God is great," he replied somewhat uncertainly.

"You say that all the time, Muammar, as if you think it's a good excuse for making everyone behave according to some literal reading of the Bible or the pronouncement of a senile old man in the holy city of Qom. I'll tell you what I think of your fundamentalist religious movement. It's like the brightness control on a television set turned down low, so you can't see anything except shadows moving through the fog. You can't see the real world, you can't understand it, so it scares you. And because you're scared you want everyone to be predictable, to follow the official pattern."

The Shiite shook his head emphatically. "The Ayatollah knows the truth. Allah speaks through him."

"Uh-uh. He knows his truth, the truth of a useless old man in an ivory tower. That truth is against human nature. A guy still likes to have a drink now and again, to get laid occasionally. So don't shove that fundamentalist shit down my throat."

"This is irrelevant," Muammar answered sharply, hooking the keys to the cell onto his belt. He fingered his submachine gun impatiently. "And we do not have time for it. Stand up. We are in a hurry."

"For what?"

"It would have gone much easier on you during the interrogations if you had simply told us what we wanted to know." Muammar smiled mysteriously. Like any good jailer, he rarely answered a question directly.

ALEX NANOS CLUTCHED tightly to the back of the truck, straining to keep his footing on the steel bumper. The half-ton bounced and jolted over the cracked and broken road as the madman at the wheel drove at breakneck speed through the southern suburbs of Beirut.

The first part of the Greek's big idea had gone perfectly. He had jumped the guard on the rear of the second truck, slitting his throat with a single neat slice of his razor-sharp Bowie knife.

Then he had pulled the dead man into the dunes and stripped him. The uniform was tight on the Greek's muscular frame, but the proportions were right. Only the *kefireh* gave him some trouble. He had barely tied the cords around his head to keep it on when he heard the rumbling engine of the last approaching truck.

Once again, he leapt onto the rear bumper, driving the sharply honed knife deep under the guard's rib cage. The Shiite stiffened, his mouth opening in a silent scream. Saliva sprayed from his throat, and he turned his head slowly sideways to look at his executioner.

"Bye-bye," Nanos said, yanking the knife out. The Amal militiaman dropped from the back of the truck and flopped onto the road.

The half-ton with its human cargo picked up speed until it caught up to the convoy ahead. They passed the sprawling refugee camps of Shatila and Shabra, and farther on, the shells of defunct industrial complexes. Seven minutes later they entered the streets of the southern suburbs. Five-story apartments lined the broad avenues, most of them bombed into ruins by the Israeli air force.

Alex Nanos had begun to question the wisdom of his actions. A question kept popping up. What next? He didn't know. He only hoped that his fellow mercs were somewhere behind him, following the signal thrown out by the modular cell in the little gadget that hung from his web belt. Until such time as they turned up, the Greek was on his own.

The streets rose in a gradual incline until the convoy came to an spot where five streets intersected on the crest of a hill. On one side, a high stucco wall ran along the street, broken in the center by a wide gate. Beyond, the red tile roof of a fortresslike villa was visible.

The stout wooden gates swung open at the approach of the convoy. Once the home of a wealthy Beirut merchant, the villa was built on the crest of a hill that overlooked a coastal highway and the Mediterranean. The merchant had fled to Paris with his family and the military had long since taken over. The walls that faced the street were topped with barbed wire and reinforced by steel girders salvaged from bombed-out buildings. Twenty-five feet inside the outer wall, a high wire fence had been erected. Doberman pinschers patrolled the no-man's-land in between.

The yard, still showing the shriveled remnants of extensive lawns and gardens, was brilliantly lit by spotlights on the roof of the villa. A Russian-made rocket launcher, surrounded by sandbags, sat in the center of the estate. A short drive led through the second gate to the front doors of the big Mediterranean-style house.

Traces of the opulence of Beirut's bygone era were still visible. Two one-story wings jutted from each side of the main house, forming a U shape around a central courtyard. The north wing was fronted by a vine-covered arcade of stately columns. On the left, there were garages and a service entrance.

The convoy of Jeeps and half-tons drove into the courtyard, circled an empty fountain and the rocket launcher, and stopped in front of the main doors. The Amal militia streamed from the villa. Soldiers jumped from the Jeeps, joining the others, their officers frantically shouting to bring order to the confusion.

Nanos hopped off the bumper of the last truck and backed away, while the Amal rushed to unload the cargo of American hostages. He scanned his surroundings, searching frantically for a place of concealment. For the moment, the bedlam was his only friend.

The frightened hostages were herded from the trucks. An Amal officer, waving his arms to direct his men, glanced in Nanos's direction. Their eyes caught. The Greek gave a quick nod and turned away, careful to keep the Shiite in his peripheral vision as he walked slowly to the side of the courtyard.

The officer stared harder, his face impassive. His gaze fell to the Greek's submachine gun. The Amal carried World War II vintage Czech-made ZK 3s. Nanos still had his Israeli-made Uzi. A dead giveaway, it occurred to him, too late. He pulled the SMG in and covered it with his arm as the Amal officer stepped toward him.

Suddenly the Shiite's attention was diverted by a messenger. Nanos backed into the arcade that ran along the north side of the courtyard. It was dark there and quiet. Double glass doors led into the villa. He flattened himself in the deepest shadows in a corner behind the doors, looking for his next avenue of escape.

In the courtyard, the soldiers pushed the hostages into three straight lines and forced them to stand erect. The Amal officer spun around, panning the compound with his eyes. The soldier with the strange rifle had disappeared.

A shaft of light fell through the glass doors into the arcade. A handle turned. The doors were thrown open, one of them almost striking the Greek. Long white curtains were caught by the night wind, and licked along the stone floor of the dark arcade. Nanos froze. Instinctively he squeezed closer to the wall.

HIS ARMS AND LEGS SHACKLED, the prisoner was led up narrow stone steps far older than the villa, slippery with condensation and worn by the passing of ages. He emerged with Muammar and the other guards in the interior of the house. They led him at a hurried pace through corridors and rubble-strewn palatial rooms, prodding him to move faster with the barrels of their rifles.

They stopped finally in a darkened room. Glass doors on one side overlooked a covered veranda to the courtyard where he exercised daily. The shouts of soldiers drew his attention to a familiar scene. Frightened civilians had been forced to stand in lines. Beirut had had another of its periodic upheavals, he thought, his mind balking at the two ominous words. Mass execution.

Muammar flicked on the lights.

They were in an office, furnished with a desk littered with papers, and several wooden chairs. The door opened, and an Arab in an officer's uniform of the Amal militia entered. The prisoner recognized him as one of his interrogators from the early months of his captivity.

The officer snapped an order. Muammar jumped forward, taking the ring of keys from his belt and undoing the shackles that bound the prisoner's ankles. He dropped the shackles in a heap on a nearby chair. The prisoner's hands were left in cuffs behind his back.

The officer spoke again. Muammar handed him the ring of keys and immediately departed. The prisoner and the officer were left in silence. They stared at each other.

"I am Mohammed," the man in the uniform said, looking over the prisoner's soiled blue coveralls. "Of course, I know somewhat more about you than you do about me."

The prisoner averted his gaze and looked through the glass doors at the civilians lined up across the courtyard.

"Hostages," Mohammed explained. "From an airline hijacking. We will use them to obtain the release of our brethren in Israeli prisons."

"Hijackings. Kidnappings. Terrorist conspiracies. You've got a regular assembly line going here, don't you."

Amusement showed in the officer's face. He walked slowly to the desk and perched on a corner of it, regarding the man intently.

"It was enough for us to know your name. Although your courage and stamina during the interrogations were admirable. But our agents in America brought us the answers we needed. It wasn't difficult. You are an outlaw there."

Mohammed lowered his eyes to the desk and lifted a sheet of paper with two fingers. It was a Wanted bulletin from the FBI. The photograph was blurry, but it was clearly the prisoner. And his name was unmistakable.

"Information about you is available in every post office in the United States. The curious thing is that no reward is offered. Perhaps they don't want you back." He dropped the poster and it fluttered slowly to the floor. "And as the Fox expected, your skills have made you useful finally—to us."

"My skills?"

Mohammed stepped close to the prisoner and spoke quietly near his ear.

"We know that you are a pilot. We have an airplane for you to fly. A DC-9. To Iran."

The prisoner felt the man's breath on the side of his face and leaned his head away to avoid it.

"And what makes you think I will do this for you?"

For a moment Mohammed didn't answer. Then the prisoner felt a key inserted in the handcuffs. The lock snapped.

"Your freedom." The officer removed the cuffs and dropped them on the desk, the key on its ring still inserted in the tiny lock. The prisoner lifted his arms and massaged his wrists.

"Know what I ask myself all the time?" The prisoner sighed wearily. He looked the Amal officer in the eyes, taunting him with an expression of defiance. "Why do you guys get to rule the world?"

"Because Allah is with us."

"Say, that sounds familiar. Yeah, it's what the Germans said in World War II. God's on our side."

Mohammed smiled graciously and shrugged. "Whatever works. Muammar, the guard you have befriended, has told me of your conversations. Yet still, he believes in the inestimable wisdom of the great Ayatollah."

He turned his back to cross the wooden floor and opened the glass doors. As he did, the prisoner grabbed the keys from the desk, closing his hand around them and clenching them tightly behind his back. Ballast for his fist. At the right moment, Mohammed would feel it—briefly—right between his eyes. There was no escape plan beyond that. If he didn't make it, at least he'd die the way he wanted—fighting.

Shouts from the soldiers and the noise of idling engines floated in from the courtyard, but the night air was fresh and invigorating. The hostages were being forced into the house.

"Muammar is a fool," the prisoner replied in a savage whisper, walking to the open door and standing close to the Amal officer. The long sheer curtains swayed in the Mediterranean breezes, wraithlike arms stretching into the night. "And so am I if I fly this DC-9."

"But you will be alive. I guarantee it."

Suddenly there was an furious pounding on the wooden door that led from the office into the villa. Without waiting for an answer, an officer opened it from the courtyard, with a party of soldiers behind him.

"There is an infiltrator in the compound," he explained. "We are searching the entire house!"

ALEX NANOS shrank against the wall when the glass doors swung into the arcade, his breathing controlled and virtually imperceptible. The long white curtains flickered back and forth in the moving air, two men framed by them. Nanos prayed feverishly that they would not venture farther. They spoke. In English. Nanos felt an eerie chill rise up the back of his head. He knew the voice!

Pounding and harsh shouts came from inside, and soldiers stormed into the room. Voices argued and demanded in rapid Arabic. The prisoner stepped onto the arcade and took a deep breath of the fresh night air.

As if on cue, the long white curtain snapped away from the window. The prisoner turned. Through his own reflection in the glass door, he saw the Greek, wide-eyed and amazed, pressed against the wall and staring directly at him.

Alex Nanos gasped in spite of himself. He shook his head, as if to clear the mysterious hallucination from his eyes. He was staring at a dead man. A man who had been blown to bits in a fiery explosion on a bridge high over the shark-filled waters of Tampa Bay. There had been no remains.

The curtain fell back, its thin, diaphanous material like a death shroud over the ghostly image. A dead man who, on that same long-ago night, had saved his life.

Geoff Bishop.

The voices of the Amal officers rose sharply, and the soldiers ripped through the room, opening closets and poking under the desk with their bayonets. Their boots thudded heavily on the bare wooden floor. The prisoner turned back to face into the room, pressing against the door and shielding the man hidden behind the glass. The soldiers ran onto the arcade, searching the shadows for the intruder.

They returned to the office, shaking their heads. Their leader ordered them from the room.

The prisoner stayed with his back to the glass, facing Mohammed, but edging slightly along the door with his arms behind him. The ring of keys was still tightly clenched inside his fist.

"And these hostages? You'll keep them in the dungeons with the rats and the stink?" As he spoke, he opened his tightly curled fist. The ring of keys lay in the palm of his hand.

Mohammed shrugged. "Perhaps later. For now they are in the interrogation rooms in the south wing across the courtyard. You will not be returning there. One way or another."

The Shiite's meaning was perfectly clear.

"Where do you want me to fly this DC-9?"

"There is a secret desert landing strip at Qu'lude, where we train the soldiers of the Islamic Jihad. It belongs to the Iranian air force. Of course, we have landing rights."

The prisoner felt the keys being lifted carefully from his hand by the man hidden behind the door.

"And then what?"

Mohammed threw his arms into the air. "Pick a city! Anywhere in the Middle East. A European capital. You will be taken there and released. You can return to your old life. For what it's worth." Suddenly he laughed derisively, slapping his hands on his knees. He kicked at the FBI Wanted poster on the floor and sent it swirling halfway across the room on a current of air. The laugh became a snicker, sinking to cruelty.

"Geoff Bishop. The outlaw. That life isn't worth much, but it's better than dead."

12

The mercs' armored car rushed through ruined residential neighborhoods, where the doors and windows of burned out buildings yawned like the mouths of blackened corpses. Lee Hatton watched the small red dot that represented Alex Nanos moving slowly across the tiny monitor in her hand. "Left," Lee Hatton instructed Claude Hayes, who slowed the SB-301 at a debris-filled intersection,

Somewhere in the night, an automatic rifle opened up, and a few lead rounds *ching*ed harmlessly against the aluminum hull of the armored carrier. The black man accelerated, leaving the anonymous fire behind.

"They live in the ruins of Beirut like rats," Billy Two murmured in the back. "At night they lie in ambush, to hunt, to kill."

In the distance behind them the rifle fire had been answered by another automatic weapon, then joined by a third. The vehicle began to ascend a shallow incline. The sound of warfare and retaliation died as quickly as it had begun.

"He's stopped," Lee said excitedly, staring at the monitor.

"Where?" Hayes braked, cutting his speed in half

"It's gotta be less than a mile from here or we wouldn't get a signal. And straight ahead."

Hayes spotted an opening that led to the courtyard of a wrecked apartment house. He slammed into rubble, shoving garbage and blackened timbers aside, and stopped. He tore the signaling device from his belt and threw it under his seat.

"So the colonel can zero in on us if he needs to," he explained.

They abandoned the carrier and ran with their automatic weapons, skulking behind gutted cars and barricades of rubble to survey the street ahead. A hidden sniper loosed a single round, narrowly missing Hatton. The mercs jumped into a darkened doorway.

"We've been spotted." Lee pressed herself against a wall, trying to pierce the gloom to ascertain the gunman's position. There were hundreds of hiding places behind the wrecked facades. It was impossible.

"Random shooting," Hayes said. "After sundown anything that moves is fair game here."

More gunfire, and bullets pinged against the portal over the doorway, dropping a cloud of fine dust over the mercs.

"Beirut used to be famous for its nightlife," Lee sighed. "Now it's night death."

"Come," Billy Two growled tersely. The red war paint down his cheeks looked like tears of blood in the gray illumination. Without waiting for an answer, the big Osage moved stealthily into the building, stepping over rubble and debris in the pitch-black interior with the vision of a cat.

Lee and Hayes looked at each other. Hayes nodded and they followed. The Indian led them with preternatural awareness down a corridor, into a courtyard, and from there through broken windows into the next building.

There they found another darkened courtyard, half filled in with slabs of concrete that had collapsed from the upper stories of an adjacent building. Without slowing, Billy Two climbed the debris and entered a second-story window.

Staying close behind him, Hayes and Hatton raced through abandoned apartments, their throats itching from the cloying odor of burn and decay. Among the scorched and broken possessions of the inhabitants who had long since fled, thousands of empty shell cases littered the floors, mute testimony to Beirut's horrendous history.

"We're very close," Lee told the others, looking at the tiny monitor. They descended some steps. Billy Two stood by a window and pointed.

The villa was an island of light in the darkened landscape. There were no guards outside the walls, but activity inside was evident. The bark of Amal militia officers issuing commands carried into the street.

"How do we get in?" Hayes asked.

Lee Hatton crowded against him to survey the intersection. Billy Two shoved his arm between them and held up his hand with his fingers spread apart.

"You give me five minutes."

"And then what?" Lee said dubiously.

"And I will open the gates from the inside."

The team's medical officer opened her mouth to protest.

"Trust me."

The Osage melted into the darkness and was gone.

For a moment the colors confused him. It was a kaleidoscope, a swirling vortex drawing him toward its center. The war zone was gone. There was a mist around him, wet and cold, dissipating as rapidly as it enshrouded him. Then yellow sunshine and warmth poured through. It was daytime and he could see.

He passed through a forest, his sense of smell assaulted by the scent of the verdure. He ran, his feet sinking lightly into the spongy ground. Surefooted and wary, he dodged the branches of trees, a boulder, jumped a stream, moving rapidly on a mysterious journey toward a goal he could not remember. He looked down. He was dressed in buckskin. In his hand he carried a bow. It was the hunt.

This part was easy for Billy Two. Hawk Spirit, the warrior god of the Osage people's ancient faith, had come to him. Sometimes the god appeared before him like a vaporous wraith. At other times Billy Two heard his voice, and debated with it, resenting the god's presence in his head. Their arguments raged sometimes for hours, driving the Osage warrior almost to the point of insanity. Sometimes, he became Hawk Spirit, transplanted to another world where he walked as a warrior in the footsteps of his ancestors.

Insanity. Is that what the others think? He no longer cared. He trusted in what he knew. Sometimes, when Hawk Spirit came to him, the god laughed, feigning ignorance. Billy Two knew better. It was a gift, the sugar coating on a bitter pill. Hawk Spirit demanded trust at times when only a fool would think to give it.

At these moments, Billy Two had no idea what was going to happen, but whatever it was, he always knew exactly what to do. It was a psychic premonition that occurred in the heat of battle. A super power. Automatic pilot. He became invulnerable, and knowing it, was invincible.

Unfortunately, the gift had an inbuilt flaw. The luck could run out as unexpectedly as it came, and with as little warning—sometimes with none at all. It could leave him in the midst of a firefight, a sea creature beached by the fickle waves. At times, Billy Two had cursed the warrior god of his people for it and called himself a fool for believing in his own delusions. But Hawk Spirit would only laugh from somewhere in the recesses of his consciousness, an indulgent father with a doubting child.

The moment of battle would continue, the instinct to survive driving betrayal from his mind. And always, he had emerged from battle whole, victorious, convinced again of his warrior prowess, and convinced also that somewhere in the spirit world, the old Osage god watched over him, smiling tolerantly at the faithlessness of mortals.

A barefaced cliff rose before the American Indian. He tucked the bow behind him and scaled it, surefooted as a mountain lion, his hands clawing at the rock, his feet digging into niches and crannies to force him up. He pulled himself over the edge. The wilderness and sunlight blinked out as abruptly as a dream ends with the awakening of the sleeper.

He was squatting in darkness at the top of a Beirut wall, looking over the Amal compound. The white walls of the Villa Buchove rose above some bomb-splintered tree trunks three hundred yards away. On the other side, there was a drop to certain death on the highway running along the coast.

He dropped, landing with bended knees as lightly as a feather. A dog barked, and he heard the soft clip of paws moving rapidly across the earth. He turned. There were three of them, black-and-tan Dobermans. They growled, eyes afire with the prospect of prey, of blood, of bones to gnaw. They scrambled on slender muscled legs, stretching to gain on one another in their race across the no-man's-land between the wall and the wire fence.

Automatic pilot. Billy Two reached out his hand.

The dogs smashed into each other in their haste to stop. Their blood lust was gone, the need to kill drained from their strong lithe bodies. They ducked their heads quickly in a gesture of deference, their tongues lolling from their mouths. One of them, the biggest, stretched out his neck and sniffed at the Osage.

The dog snorted and backed away. The other two moved forward tentatively, sniffed and looked up at Billy Two, the fawning eyes soft and friendly.

"Good dogs," the native American whispered. "Ye-e-s, that's a good dog now, aren't you?"

One of the Dobermans licked his hand. Then they lost interest and, without hurry, trotted back to the depressions they had pawed out for themselves in the soft earth near a dead tree.

Billy Two flattened himself against the wall and moved laterally down the no-man's-land toward the front gates. There was an inner gate in the wire security fence, twenty feet beyond the stout wooden gates in the stone wall. The wire fence joined the two, penning the guard dogs in the strip that ran around each side of the compound.

Two guards paced at the gate. They chatted for a moment, separated and walked on. The wind carried the sound of a Doberman's low growl. A man carrying a basket walked down the drive from the villa and shouted to the guards. One of them opened the inner gate to let him through.

Billy Two crouched twenty feet away in the cover of a buttress that reinforced the stone wall. The man with the basket chatted jovially with the two sullen guards, fiddling with a lock on the gate into the dog zone. Feeding time.

The pitter-patter of soft paws alerted the Indian to the Dobermans' approach. They galloped toward their keeper until they were parallel to Billy Two. Suddenly they stopped, sitting on their haunches. They looked from their keeper to the Osage hidden in darkness.

Go away! Starfoot urged them silently, screaming the order in his mind. And then he heard words from somewhere else, soft and persuasive as they rolled through his mind. Come here, come to me.

The dogs got up and trotted across the soft earth toward him. Thirty feet away, their keeper closed the gate behind him. He shouted to the dogs. They ignored him, sniffing their way toward the Osage. The keeper laughed. He reached into the basket and threw a handful of meat across the dead zone. The Dobermans stopped and looked at him. They growled testily, their confusion growing.

Come here, Billy Two thought, looking at them, calling to them with his silence. He pulled his knife from his sheath. The dogs came closer. The keeper called again, this time annoyed. He threw another handful of meat. It landed barely five feet from the Osage. The dogs sniffed. One bit at it and picked it up, holding it between his long yellow fangs. The other two walked into the shadows surrounding Billy Two and sniffed at his feet.

Angrily the keeper set his basket down and strode across the no-man's-land. The dog with the meat backed away. The keeper looked surprised. He spoke soothingly and the Doberman emitted a long vicious growl from deep in its throat.

The man stopped, eyed the guard dog warily, perplexed, and continued toward the other two, calling a question to them softly in Arabic. When he came around the side of the buttress, he saw Billy Two.

The seven-inch blade of the Osage's knife swooped upward like a silver bird of prey, piercing the soft underside of his chin, his tongue, the upper palate, sinuses and finally the brain. The tip of the dagger struck the inside of the skull and stopped. The force of the blow was so strong that the keeper was lifted several inches off his feet, and Billy Two stood tall, holding him like a fish on a hook. He sputtered and died instantly, blood mixed with saliva spilling from his mouth

A dog whimpered briefly, as if in sympathy. When Billy dropped the body, putting his boot to the man's chin to pull his knife out, the Dobermans sniffed at the corpse. Then Billy Two ran toward the gate, a gray blur moving through the no-man's-land.

Two guards stood near the gate. One withdrew a package of cigarettes from his pocket and offered it to the other. Billy Two slipped into the driveway, approaching from behind, stepping lightly on the soles of his feet. One of the guards struck a match and held it to the other's cigarette. A breeze extinguished it. They huddled together and lit another match.

Billy Two reached out. His hands were the size of tennis rackets. His fingers closed over the sides of their heads like steel traps, smashing their skulls together. There was a hollow crunch of bone striking bone and the two men sank in his hands, their eyes open but vacant. Blood dribbled from the mouth of one.

A muffled explosion came from the Villa Buchove, followed by scattered shouts and automatic-weapon fire. The Osage dug his hands into the collars of their uniforms and dragged them to the gate that led to the security zone.

The Dobermans perked up, their ears erect. They ran to the fence and watched, their yellow eyes alert, debating. One growled. Another answered. The spell was fading. Billy Two pushed the bodies through and closed the gate.

It was done.

Another explosion thundered from the villa, louder, closer, and the night was saturated with the chatter of automatic weapons.

The Osage checked at his watch. Five minutes was up. Hawk Spirit, his silent guide, was right on time. The Osage ran to the gate, pushing aside a heavy iron bar. From the street beyond came the sound of changing gears, and an engine revving. He pulled at the iron handle and the stout wooden gates swung inward.

THE MEN FROM FLIGHT 707 were of all ages, professions, types and sizes. They were herded like animals, shunted from airplane to truck, crowded into a prison at the hands of the most fanatical and dangerous corps of militant terrorists in the world.

The Amal soldiers were harsh, their nerves raw, the tension mounting steadily as the stakes in the deadly power play rose. They used the butts of their rifles freely to prod their prisoners, screaming for them to hurry down the steps to the cellar.

Some of the hostages obeyed, dreamlike, their eyes dazed and beyond understanding. A few put up their arms to shield their bodies from the blows. They were pulled from the line and beaten, thrown against the stone walls and kicked when they fell.

Finally the hostages were pushed into a large interrogation room, lined up into rows of eight, their hands together on top of their heads.

"Kneel!" the commanding officer shouted.

Slowly, uncertainly, the hostages sank, their eyes hovering over the line of men with automatic rifles.

Matt Chicago knelt on the cold floor. John Lorch was next to him. His eyes wandered over a pocked and cratered wall, the dried brown bloodstains splashed across them. That it was an execution chamber was unmistakable. Several dozen Amal soldiers surrounded them, their weapons aimed.

With shock, Chicago recognized Hafez, one of the original hijackers, the one he had cheated of a victim. Their eyes met, captor and captive once again, and an ice-cold chill fluttered through the American. Recognition sat ugly on the Shiite terrorist's face. Chicago cast his eyes down and lowered his head, like the others.

Hafez left his position and spoke quickly to the commander. The officer laughed and nodded. Hafez looked at Chicago and smiled vindictively as the officer walked slowly along the front line of hostages. He stopped in front of Matt Chicago, and placed the barrel of his autorifle against the American's chin, forcing him to look up.

"A troublemaker," the Amal officer stated flatly, a cruel smile tugging at the corners of his thin lips. He moved sideways and struck Chicago in the middle of the back with his rifle, knocking him flat on his face.

The American writhed in pain. A jackboot swung against his ribs, and he heard the sound of his bones cracking. He gasped for breath, holding his arms over his head for protection from the next blow.

It didn't come.

"Get up!"

Chicago rose slowly to his knees. Several of the Amal guards closed in on him, standing attentively beside their mocking superior. Chicago's eyes flickered over them as he wondered which of them would strike him next.

The officer jerked his head, motioning Chicago to step out of line. He walked forward on his knees, his hands still clasped together on top of his head.

As fast as lightning, the Shiite commander drew his handgun, slammed the tip of the barrel against Chicago's temple and cocked it.

There was a moment of absolute quiet. Behind him, some of the hostages sucked in their breath. Someone stifled a sob. Hafez stepped from the line of soldiers. He raised his rifle and struck John Lorch across the side of the head. The Marine fell sideways, caught himself, and sat up, cringing, his lips turned inward in bitter anger.

The Amal soldiers began to laugh. They jabbered, making jokes and pointing. The officer looked down at Chicago. He took the revolver away, opened it and shook the bullets into his hand. He made an ostentatious show of returning a single bullet to its chamber. He closed the gun and spun the chamber.

He snickered, looking contemptuously at the American hostage. From a pocket in his uniform he withdrew a wad of tattered paper currency and threw a handful of bank notes on the floor. Pointing the gun at the ceiling, he challenged the others. The soldiers laughed, took money from their pockets and threw it on the pile.

The Marine watched, his bruised face pale and terrible with anger.

With his foot, the officer forced Chicago's head to the ground.

"Stop it, y—" Lorch screamed in protest. Hafez kicked him in the face, knocking him backward.

The officer slammed the revolver against Chicago's skull and squeezed the trigger.

The revolver clicked. Chicago felt faint, dizzy, his head swirling into a chaos of fear and helplessness. His breath caught in his throat. He was still alive.

The Amal militiamen laughed. Several walked forward and threw more money on the pile, urging another round. The officer nodded. Again Chicago felt the boot planted squarely in the middle of his back, and the cold circle of steel pressed against the back of his head.

"No, you fucking bastards!" Lorch screamed, hurling himself across the room. He tackled the officer around his knees, knocking him to the ground with a heavy thud. The soldiers rushed at him, kicking and pounding him with the butts of their rifles.

The officer roared furiously, and the soldiers stopped. He rose to his feet, livid with terrible anger, visibly controlling his rage. He kicked the pile of money, scattering it across the floor.

The soldiers lifted the two Americans and threw them in front of the blood-spattered wall. They fell against each other, the Marine clenching his gut, his face contorted by pain.

Eight of the soldiers formed a line ten feet back from the wall. The maddened officer uttered a stream of orders. The soldiers jammed fresh mags into their automatic rifles.

The officer curled his lip and stood to one side. He raised his head arrogantly and his eyes swept over the doomed men.

"Hey, buddy," Lorch said softly, facing the firing squad. He put his arm on Matt Chicago's shoulders. "Thought we had the beginnings of a long friendship."

13

Alex Nanos remained in the shadows of the arcade until the prisoner and the Amal officer were gone. Moments later, he saw them walk from the Villa Buchove and climb into a shiny black car. It left the compound in a convoy with armed Jeeps.

His mind raced through possibilities, eliminating battle fatigue, hallucination, nightmares, returning always to the keys. He tightened his hand around the cold hard metal. They were real. Geoff Bishop was real. He had come back. He was alive. It was impossible!

A few scattered images from long ago floated through his mind's eye: a damp cool night on the Gulf of Mexico, a mysterious yacht under surveillance, the sudden missile attack, the heat of fire, the cold sting of saltwater, terrible pain, Bishop's arm around his chest, pulling him from the suffocation of the waves while the last remnants of his consciousness ebbed into growing darkness.

Later, there had been the newspaper photographs, the missing SOB attacking the death-hungry terrorist, hundreds of witnesses who saw the two men fall over the side of the bridge, who saw the midair explosion of the mass murderer's bomb, the rain of debris into the waters of Tampa Bay, the people who swore they had seen the sinister black dorsal fins of sharks.

And subsequently, ultimate betrayal. Barrabas's team always worked in complete secrecy, the mercs serving for the risk, the danger, the hell of it, the chance to put their lives on the razor's edge of a dare, sometimes for the money. It was a game, foiling Death who was always patient, who waited for the moment when the reprieve vouchers ran out.

Geoff Bishop's voucher had run out on a bridge over Tampa Bay. He had saved the life of the governor of Florida from bomb-carrying maniacs, but the witnesses got it wrong. The photos had lied. The merc became the terrorist. To clear his name from the public record would have compromised the entire team. He had died, an unsung hero branded with infamy.

Regaining consciousness in a hospital bed, Alex Nanos had tried to piece together the events of the terrible night, but only one thing was certain—before the madness on the bridge over Tampa Bay, Geoff Bishop had saved the Greek's life.

But Nanos owed him far more than that. He'd always been a wild guy, a cheeky smartass who got busted from the Coast Guard for insubordination, who had learned to be a party boy, using looks and charm to go from booze to broad to bed with never a moment's thought or reflection about anything but the pursuit of his own gratification.

When Geoff Bishop had joined the team, Nanos picked on him. He had been jealous about Bishop's secret affair with Lee Hatton. He carried a chip on his shoulder about Bishop that was as big as Mount

Rushmore, and he had let the guy know it—once by slugging him in the face in a Thailand bar. Despite everything, Bishop had come through for him. The Greek had known who the better man was. The better man was dead.

He looked at the keys for the jails of the Villa Buchove and saw that he was trembling, the palm of his hand glistening with sweat, his breath coming in short rapid bursts. He was a tease and a flirt and a joker, and he pretended he didn't have a serious bone in his body because it was the only way he knew how to be. All his life he had reacted without thinking.

It often served him well in battle. But in the regular world there were times when banging his head against a wall would have been as useful. Maybe that was why he never fit in there, why between the parties he became a mercenary. His entire life consisted of treading the razor-thin line between thrills and extinction.

He stared at the keys. Slowly a strange feeling of certainty fell over him, and with it a kind of peace. It didn't matter if Bishop was alive or a ghost, if it was mistaken identity, a bizarre hallucination or the Twilight Zone. The keys were the ticket to the hostages' freedom, and he held them in the palm of his hand.

He moved to the cover of one of the pillars that supported the roof of the arcade. The courtyard was filled with dozens of Amal soldiers guarding the walls and entrances of the villa, patrolling the perimeter of the driveway and pacing in the deep shadows of the gardens. The tension hung in the air like taut invisible wires strung through the compound. For a moment his mind worked feverishly to devise a way to cross the open space. Then he remembered—he was still wearing the uniform of the Amal militia. The gun was the problem. He flicked it on full auto and held it beside his leg, looked straight ahead and started walking.

It was something he'd learned in the gambling halls of Reno and Atlantic City. When you won big or lost big—and the Greek had done both several times—everyone checked you out when you crossed the room. You had to do it like you owned the place.

The doors to the villa were open. Two guards stood at each side of the short flight of steps. He felt their eyes burning into him, examining his face. The nearest one narrowed his eyes, moving slightly. Nanos picked up his pace, focusing on the space beyond the door. He nodded curtly without looking at them, eyes intent on the distance ahead, until he clipped up the steps and strode into the Villa Buchove.

He was in a hallway. On one side were the doors to the garages. In front of him there was a wide staircase. Four guards paced to and fro, their heels clicking on the polished wood floor. Several more sat on a bench near the door. Nanos held up the keys and dangled them from his finger. The guards nodded. The Greek headed for the stairs.

A musty smell from the cellars grew as he descended to a thick wooden door with a barred window. He used the keys, testing one, discarding it, trying again. The third one worked. The door swung into a long corridor striped by light bulbs, in wire cages, that glowed against the white-washed walls.

Derisive laughter and the shouts of men in pain echoed along the vaulted stone ceiling. He ran toward the sound, veering sharply around a corner. A single Shiite soldier stood in the corridor, staring through an open door, amused by what he saw in the room beyond. Nanos recognized the voice shouting orders. It was the officer who had spotted him earlier.

The merc gripped his knife. He stepped behind the guard, clapping his hand over his mouth and thrust the dagger deep into his kidney. The guard stiffened, every fibre straining to pull away, to scream. Nanos pushed the dagger to its hilt, twisting slowly. The vital organ was torn to pieces and toxic renal chemicals flooded into the Arab's bloodstream.

The man's eyes bugged from his skull in lethal shock. The Greek tightened his grip against the death spasms as his victim's wet tongue pushed desperately against his hand. A great lungful of air gushed from the man's mouth and he was dead. It had taken less than fifteen seconds. Nanos lowered the quivering body gently to the floor. He heard the click of mags jammed into automatic weapons, and spun into the opening. The executioners raised their rifles.

Nanos fired.

The Uzi spat its death rounds into the line of Amal soldiers. They teetered from the impact of the 9 mm bullets and dropped like a row of dominoes.

"Get down!" he screamed, striding forward with his finger tight against the trigger and pulled against the recoil of the little Uzi. The hostages cowered on the floor, covering their heads with their hands.

Nanos planted his legs wide, moving one foot at a time into the room. The Uzi zigzagged, bullets blowing chunks of bloody flesh against the stone walls and ricocheting in clouds of sparks.

The officer slammed backward, critically wounded by a row of gore holes that turned his chest into a shield of blood. A trained fighter, he reacted, pulling his submachine gun in front of him and firing with his last vestige of will. Three rounds spun past the Greek. He turned and fired, the bullets erasing the Shiite's face. His head fell back, and his body collapsed in a dead heap.

For a fraction of a second the room was still. Then hostages became aware of the sound of breathing. Their own. They were alive. Matt Chicago looked at Lorch, then at the Amal soldier standing in the door.

Nanos grabbed the checkered *kefireh* around his head and ripped it off. He threw his fist up and shouted in jubilation.

"USAAAAA! Let's go!"

The hostages of Flight 707 burst into joyful cheers, surging in confusion to encircle their rescuer.

"The guns!" someone shouted. They rushed toward the bodies that littered the bloody floor, stripping them for weapons. Nanos strode to the two men whose lives he had just saved, grabbing two automatic rifles from their previous owners on his way by.

Chicago and Lorch picked themselves up and faced their rescuer, overcome with gratitude.

"How many of you are there?" Lorch asked.

"So far, just me." Nanos pushed the guns into their hands. "Wanna get your own back?"

He grabbed a fresh mag from his belt and pushed it into the Uzi. Already boots thundered in the corridor.

Chicago looked at the gun in disbelief. He shook his head.

"I dunno how to use it."

"You'll learn. Real fast," the Marine shot back, running after Nanos.

The Greek plucked a concussion grenade from his web belt and yanked the pin with his teeth. He pressed himself against the doorframe, and counted. He always got scared at three. At three and a half he thanked his lucky stars and arced it through the door.

It spun down the corridor, exploding instantaneously, the blast thundering through the prison. The impact of the explosion hurled bodies aside like rag dolls.

Lorch pressed himself against the wall beside Alex Nanos.

"John Lorch, U.S. Marines. What's next?"

The Greek looked at the young soldier's bruised and swollen face, the dried blood that covered his clothing and the ugly purple lacerations on his skin.

"Alex," he said, reaching across his chest to shake hands.

A third man, paunchy and with graying sideburns, joined them, clenching a submachine in a professional manner.

"Ah haven't done this since Korea, but Ah'm pig-bitin' mad," he drawled. "'Nuff to fight mah way out alone if Ah have to."

More of the hostages gathered, holding pistols and submachine guns liberated from the dead executioners. At least one of them held a submachine backward. But the Greek needed all the help he could get.

"We fight our way out of here, floor by floor. You ready?"

The Marine and the others nodded.

"Mess with the best, die like the rest!" Lorch screamed with all the savagery of a grunt in battle.

He and Nanos whirled into the corridor, spraying a volley of 9 mm lead ahead to clear the way.

Two Amal soldiers running for the door caught it sideways and slammed into the wall. They slithered down the bloodstreak and collapsed.

The second door was open. Boots clattered on the stairs. Nanos reached for another concussion grenade and bit on the pin. Lorch hit the doorway, his submachine gun pumping a stream of empty casings. Return fire pinged against the iron door, and ricocheted in the corridor. Nanos hurled the grenade through and covered his ears.

The explosion reverberated off the stone walls. A body flew through the door in a cloud of debris. Nanos stepped over it and through the doorway. The Amal soldiers, unconscious or dead, lay in a smoking heap on the stairs. The SOB led the way up the mound of groaning, bleeding men.

He came up the top of the stairs, firing the last of his mag into the two men at the outside door. They flipped backward and tumbled down the steps. Lorch took up the slack while he inserted a fresh mag.

Amal militia ran toward the villa, the front line dropping to their knees and firing into the open doors.

"Close it!" Nanos shouted, running to one of the thick wooden doors and pushing it closed. Lorch and another man ran to the other side. Bullets pounded against the thick wood. The windows on both sides shattered, showering them with broken glass. Plaster exploded from the walls.

There were gunshots behind them, and choking white dust filled the room. The hostages scaled the bodies on the stairs and crouched below the level of the windowsills to avoid the rain of deadly Amal fire. Some stripped weapons from the bodies. Others finished off the jailers who still lived with coup de grace bullets to the back of their heads.

For a second the Greek considered stepping in, but he stopped himself. The Shiites had invoked these forces of destruction, and now were dying from the terror they had unleashed. He could do nothing to stop the orgy of revenge. This was not the time to search his conscience for a rationalization of rough justice. The enemy was still at the door.

"Alex!" the Marine shouted from a corner beside a window. He pointed outside.

The autofire was slowing, becoming sporadic.

The Greek threw himself against the wall beside the doors. Then he crouched and spun low across the windowsill, landing in the corner next to Lorch.

"See what I see?" the young Marine asked, breathing hard.

Nanos nodded. The surface-to-air missile launcher. The Amal militia were strapping a long needle-nosed rocket into it and aiming it for the door. Kingdom come was just a step away.

BARRABAS AND O'TOOLE HELPED BECK to the deserted coastal highway beyond the perimeter of the airport. As the merc leader expected, there was no sign of the armored carrier or the other mercs.

"Now what?" O'Toole muttered. "We need transportation."

Barrabas withdrew his portable monitor and snapped open the case. The screen was blank. The mercs were out of range.

"Colonel!" Beck called to him. The wounded man sat on a boulder near the road. He was pointing north. "Someone's coming."

Barely visible in the distant illumination of the airport lights, a convoy lumbered over the cratered road toward the opening in the perimeter fence.

"Liam! Let's take it!" Barrabas ordered, sprinting back into the dunes.

The Irishman followed. The two mercs moved in a path diagonal to the road and the convoy, coming ahead of it just past the perimeter fence. They threw themselves down behind a grassy ridge at the crest of an windblown dune. There were three vehicles—two Jeeps flanking a big black car. The distinctive green flag of the Amal militia fluttered from the front aerial. The convoy slowed at the mortar-damaged wreckage from the first convoy, pulled around it and crossed through the perimeter fence into the airport. Sixty-millimeter machine guns were mounted on the Jeeps.

"Get the feeling someone important is coming," O'Toole whispered, his eyes following the shiny black car.

Barrabas nodded. He plucked a grenade from his belt and bounced it in his hand. "I'll eighty-six the lead Jeep and slow them down. You take out the rear."

"You want the occupants of the car alive?"

"That's up to them, isn't it?"

Barrabas pushed himself up and ran laterally into the dunes, circling around until he was ahead of the lead car, close to the trail that led toward the runway. His dark fatigues and blackened face wed him to the night. He dropped to his knees in a shallow depression below a ridge. The convoy had picked up speed in its last lap toward the DC-9.

He waited, his finger holding the ring on the grenade's safety pin, until the lead car was barely yards away. The team had chosen offensive grenades for use in the closed quarters of an airplane. The steel balls and fragmentation sleeve had been replaced with an extra twenty-five grams of explosives. The blast would knock most of the soldiers in the Jeep unconscious. At the very least, they would be stunned. It wasn't the most effective weapon of choice for two men facing a convoy of heavily armed soldiers. Their best ally was the element of surprise.

The first Jeep in the convoy crossed his line of vision.

Barrabas yanked the pin from the lever and counted down the four-second delay. Then he jumped up, hurling it overhand and threw himself down into the sand again.

The grenade exploded with a thundering boom. The Amal militiamen blew into the air like bundles of rags, along with shattered fragments of the machine guns. The windshield and doors exploded outward, and the Jeep changed direction, the gears screaming as it rumbled haphazardly into the dunes.

A second explosion jarred the night, and the end Jeep met the same fate from O'Toole's deadly missive. The driver of the car hit the gas, steering sideways into the dunes. Barrabas pulled the pin on a second grenade and threw it past the out-of-control Jeep, into the path of the escaping vehicle.

The front Jeep suddenly erupted in a ball of liquid fire. The monstrous force of the gas tank explosion ruptured the metal body and sent a heat wave of destruction across the dunes, flattening the high grasses. Barrabas narrowed his eyes against the brightness and dropped to a crouch. Radiation from the wave of fire washed across him, so intense he smelled the acrid odor of singed hair. The Jeep lurched to a halt and burned, sending voluminous clouds of rank black smoke billowing into the night.

Barrabas's second grenade blew in the path of the fleeing car, shattering the windshield. The driver braked. Autofire sounded, and orange muzzle flash was visible from the front window. The mercenary set his Uzi for a 3-round burst and returned the greeting.

A man shrieked, and a rifle flew from the car window, clattering over the hood of the car. The car plowed blindly into a swale, crashed against the side of a dune and stalled. Behind it, more autofire drilled as O'Toole finished off the troops in the final Jeep.

There was silence, and the smell of cordite and burning rubber mingled with the scent of salt on the sea breeze. Barrabas cocked his ear. He heard the sounds of a frantic struggle inside the car, men grunting and grappling for control.

A single shot.

More silence.

The commander of the SOBs rose cautiously to a semicrouch and zigzagged over the dunes, closing the distance to the car. Orange flames flickering from the carcass of the destroyed Jeep were reflected on the polished black paint.

The rear door opened slowly.

Barrabas knelt and aimed his Uzi, his finger applying a slight pressure on the hair-pin trigger.

A man stepped from the car.

He was tall, sturdy, and wore baggy clothes that rippled against his body in the light winds. His dark curly hair fluttered back from his forehead. The flames from the burning Jeep flickered across pale skin, which appeared almost as white as the surface of the moon.

Slowly, tentatively, Geoff Bishop raised his arms and faced the convoy's attackers.

Barrabas froze. For the first time in memory he was uncertain. He refused to believe what his eyes saw, his mind racing to identify the trickery that placed this apparition before him. He stood and stepped forward several feet.

Bishop saw the movement, saw the darkness ahead of him take shape, and the shape become a man camouflaged in black. He sucked in his breath, unsure of his fate. Rescuer or foe.

Barrabas stared, unable to speak. In his life he had seen strange things unfold. Men had come back to him from the dead before: Karl Heiss, a Cambodian warlord, and there were others, too, evil men who somehow in its very clutches had outwitted death. They disappeared into an abyss of time and space, timing their resurrections. Then they returned for vengeance, again unleashing their destructive powers into the world.

In his countless wars, good men had died, too, many of them. Too many. But it was the evil that endured. Good men never returned from the grave. Long ago, he had accepted that as the unfair truth.

"Geoff!"

He heard the name breathed out of his mouth, a whisper. The man turned toward the noise.

Running footsteps sounded on the ground to Barrabas's left. O'Toole came toward him, helping Nate Beck.

"We've got—" The words froze in the Irishman's throat. He stared at the man from the car. Nate Beck stood on his good leg, leaning against the Irishman for support.

"O'Toole?" Bishop blinked, staring at the armed men in the darkness. He stepped forward. "Beck? Colonel!"

The mercs fell together in a tangle of arms and shouts of joy. Barrabas and O'Toole slapped Bishop on the back and hugged him, still unable to believe that the missing merc was alive.

The merc leader stood back and faced the Canadian airman. Bishop was thin, but he looked strong and healthy. His skin had the pallor of prison confinement, and Barrabas noticed a shiny swathe of scar tissue that reached up one side of Bishop's neck, ending just below his ear.

"Bishop, you're supposed to be shark food in Tampa Bay!" Nate said, hobbling toward the mercs. The mercs embraced and broke apart.

"Talk to me, Geoff," Barrabas said, still shaking his head.

"I tackled the terrorist on the Skyway Bridge just as he was about to set off his bomb. We went over the side, and the bomb blew. I don't remember because it knocked me out. Burned me, too." His hand touched the shiny skin on his neck. "But we both survived the fall into the water. The terrorist pulled me to the surface. They had another boat out there. I was in pretty rough shape and barely alive for the next few months. When I regained consciousness, I was here. They kept me in a prison cell at a terrorist headquarters here—the villa where they've taken the hostages. Said they'd have a use for me sometime. I've been there almost a year. I'm in good shape. But boy I've never been so glad to see friends."

Relief showed in his smile.

"They told me I had to fly that DC-9 over there," he added, pointing to the waiting airplane on the runway half a kilometer away.

"They want you to pilot it?" Barrabas said sharply, furrowing his brow.

Bishop nodded.

"Colonel," O'Toole spoke. "There's a convoy approaching from the south." He looked at his watch. "Our escort out of here."

Barrabas turned and saw a long line of moving headlights strung down the coastal highway. It looked like Sharif was bringing half the Lebanese army with him.

Bishop looked uncertainly at the two mercs. "The rest of...?" His voice faltered. They heard the name in his silence. Lee Hatton.

"They followed the convoy that took the hostages," Barrabas explained quickly. "Billy Two, Alex, Claude. And Lee. We didn't expect them to be dispersed. We were going to assault the 727 when they transferred the hostages to the DC-9. Now something very strange is going on. Why do they need you to fly the plane?"

Bishop inclined his head toward the car. "They told me there was an accident. The flight crew from the 727 is out of commission. They didn't get specific."

"The fuckers killed 'em," O'Toole concluded with an angry mutter.

"Come on," Barrabas said grimly. "We have work to do."

Jeeps and armored carriers with the distinctive markings of the Lebanese National Army painted on their sides rolled across the dunes. Their headlights framed the mercs, and the vehicles fanned to a halt around them. Sharif emerged from a carrier, and walked briskly toward them. The lithe Lebanese official had changed into combat fatigues and a maroon beret.

"Your covert action team isn't such a secret, after all," he snapped, handing Barrabas a newspaper. It was the newest edition of the *International Herald Tribune*. Black headlines at the top of the front page screamed: "SECRET COMMANDOS SENT TO MIDEAST—Decision to Take Hijacked Jet by Force by Calhoun Bellow."

Barrabas slowly crushed the newspaper in one hand.

"That's what changed everything."

Sharif nodded. "When this leaked out, they decided to disperse most of the hostages into Beirut. We know where—their headquarters at the Villa Buchove. The Amal have ordered thousands of their followers to surround the airport by morning. Already there are hundreds of Shiites outside the terminal. Soon we will lose control completely. They will swarm on the runway. Now the Fox is aboard the DC-9 with the flight crew from the 727 and at least one other hostage. We suspect he will try to take off. Why he waits, we do not know."

"He's waiting for a pilot," Barrabas told him. "The crew's dead." He motioned toward Geoff Bishop, who stood with the other mercs nearby, and explained.

"Then nothing will happen!" Sharif groaned. "The Shiites will surround the airport, and the Fox will simply escape. And it is dangerous now for you and your people to be here." He kicked at the crumpled newspaper. "The reporter who wrote this has already arrived in Beirut and visited me. He has vowed to find you. It would be the end of everything for you."

Barrabas shook his head, wondering how in hell the newspaper had got hold of the story. He studied the

DC-9 on the distant runway for an instant and turned back to the Ministry of Defense official.

"You said you know where they took the hostages?"

Sharif nodded. "To a place called the Villa Buchove."

"Four of my people followed. Get them for me. Make sure they're back here. I'll take care of the DC-9 and the leader of these maniacs. Tell them we're going to fly out of here in it. No one will know who's on it."

For a moment, Sharif look doubtful of the idea. "It would be a great favor for us to have the Fox eliminated once and for all," he mused, looking thoughtfully at Barrabas. He nodded once. "Yes, I believe you can do it."

14

Billy Two had barely released the bar when the mercs' armored carrier slammed into the heavy wood gate. He leapt from its path as it smashed inward. Armor plate was pulled down over the windshield, and the barrel of an Uzi hovered in the observation hatch. The 301 slowed slightly, the back door of the compartment swinging wildly on its hinges.

The Osage jumped for it, pulling the door closed and bolting it. The brightly lit courtyard of the Villa Buchové swarmed with Amal militia. More soldiers poured from the house into the yard, loosing streams of bullets into the south wing.

"He's gotta be in there!" Lee shouted, watching the position of the red dot on the tiny monitor.

"Tell me something," Hayes growled sarcastically. He gripped the wheel and floored the gas pedal, leaning close to the windshield to peer through the observation hatch. The armored car smashed through the wire gates.

Billy Two stood up, the top of his head banging into the roof of the gun turret. He opened a firing port on one side and poked the barrel of his Uzi through the vertical slot. He pumped the Uzi's trigger, pushing the gun from side to side, and drawing the attention of the Amal militia. They scrambled back toward the villa, or returned fire from the cover of the parked trucks. Bullets reverberated against the armored carrier. Muzzle flash at a sandbag barrier in the middle of the courtyard drew his eyes. The sinister projection of the rocket launcher was unmistakable. The three-foot missile was aimed for the south wing of the Villa Buchove.

"Circle right!" he shouted. "They have a rocket!"

Claude Hayes pulled the steering, hand-over-hand. Something clanged against his door. He pulled himself back from the observation hatch, his ears ringing with agony from a deafening grenade explosion. A spray of shrapnel *ching*ed harmlessly against the carrier's metal skin and bounced.

The tires tore the dusty earth as it built speed, and the centrifugal force slammed the mercs off-balance. They spun around the courtyard, bearing down on the open flank of the sandbagged rocket launcher. Horror-stricken Amal soldiers scrambled from their positions, seeking refuge elsewhere.

Lee Hatton and Billy Two tightened their grips against the Uzis' slight recoil and simultaneously loosed volleys of autofire. The line of fleeing soldiers dropped. The men manning the launcher sprayed gore, spun wildly and slumped over their death machine.

A hail of bullets pinged off Hatton's door. Lee pulled her Uzi from the front and switched to the side hatch. She jammed a fresh mag in and started over, driving the Amal militia back toward the main portion of the villa. Claude Hayes completed an arc around the courtyard. Autofire rained against the side of the carrier from dozens of sniper positions in the Villa Buchove.

"Think we can turn that launcher around?" Hayes shouted in the compartment.

"I can do it!" Lee answered.

Billy Two ducked down from the gun turret.

"I go to help the Greek."

The black man nodded, veering sharply to the left for another circuit around the courtyard. He slammed on the brakes, abruptly slowing the carrier while the back faced the bullet-ridden facade of the south wing. One of the doors sank inward, and the Greek appeared briefly in the opening. Billy Two jumped from the fender of the carrier, rolling in a somersault on the hard ground, then leaping up the steps.

A chorus of cheers greeted him inside. He looked through the floating dust and the dim yellow light from the few remaining bulbs. A roomful of dirty but enthusiastic men, covered with grit and dressed in soiled and torn clothing, whistled and shouted, welcoming another rescuer.

Alex Nanos gave the Osage a hearty slap on the back, grabbed his head and planted a big noisy kiss on his cheek.

"Man, I'm so happy to see your red skin!" Nanos proclaimed. He clutched Billy Two's shoulders. "Bishop. He's alive!"

The Greek was the Osage's oldest buddy, cool as a cocktail lounge in July. Nothing ever fazed him. But this time he sounded definitely flipped out.

"What are you talking about?" The image of the faraway figure of the parachute floating in blue flashed in his mind. What had Hawk Spirit meant?

"Geoff Bishop. He's here! He was here. They took him to the airport to fly the DC-9!"

The savage chatter of autofire shattered their conversation. Plaster exploded from the ceiling, and the freed hostages ran for the corners, holding their arms up to protect their heads. The young Marine ran to Nanos.

"Some of them are trying to get through from the villa. They're smashing through a door!"

The two mercs ran with him toward the next room. There was a loud boom and the sound of splintering wood. The submachine-gun fire ended, and hostages poured from the room, fleeing for their lives. Beyond them, flames of fire ate the frame of a smoking doorway, quickly spreading along the walls. Amal soldiers leapt from the gap, rolling and kneeling as they sent a withering fusillade of autofire at the mercs.

The American hostages dove to cover in the first room. Alex Nanos pulled another grenade from his belt. A small black object blurred low in his peripheral vision. A rock clattered on the floor. His teeth closed around the pin, then he realized it was already too late.

Two grenades skittered across the floor, spinning in their deadly orbits toward the mercs and the American hostages.

LEE JUMPED FROM THE ARMORED CARRIER before it had stopped and ran to the cover of the sandbags that surrounded the missile launcher. Claude Hayes scrambled across the seat after her. Bullets from the Shiite positions inside the villa winged harmlessly overhead, or chunked against the SB-301 with a hollow ring.

The launcher was capable of firing two rockets, Russian-made Scrim 1s, a meter and a half of sleek, deadly explosive power. Intended to pulverize low-flying aircraft in midflight, it had a two-stage motor stolen from American Redeye technology that allowed it to travel at Mach 2.5. The Amal probably got it from their friends in Syria, a Soviet client state.

Hatton grabbed the metal handlebars on each side of the mount and pressed her body against the site bars. The launcher swiveled down easily. The Villa Buchove was squarely in focus. She pulled the trigger, and both missiles vanished from the launcher.

Claude Hayes threw himself on Hatton, pushing her onto the ground against the sandbags and covering her with his body.

The world exploded into a maelstrom. The front of the Villa Buchove vaporized into a fireball four stories high, tearing oxygen from the air and feeding it into the conflagration. The sound of the inferno battered their eardrums. Debris snowed down, piling over them until they were covered with bits of wood and tiny fragments of masonry.

ALEX NANOS clenched his own grenade between his teeth and dove toward the skidding death fruit, reaching for them with both arms. They slapped into his hands like alligator hardballs.

Still sliding across the floor, the Greek flipped onto his back and hurled the grenades. They sailed over his head, back to the original owners.

A recipient screamed.

Nanos flipped again, curling into a fetal position with his head between his legs.

The grenades blew.

He felt the shrapnel spraying over his back, and digging through the bulletproof padding. His rear end wasn't as lucky. He stifled a scream and squeezed his legs tighter together. There were major arteries down there—and a couple of other items the Greek couldn't do without.

The sounds of falling plaster and breaking glass ebbed, overtaken by the slow, horrible moans of injured men. Then they heard the noise, a high decibel hiss that ended with deadening silence. A fiery blast swept through the room of the dead like a jet from a giant welding torch, and the Villa Buchove crumpled around them.

"Alex? Alex!" Billy Two pushed away plaster and splintered wood from the supine body of the Greek. Nanos flipped over and shook his head as if he was dazed. The grenade was still firmly gripped between his teeth. "Hmph." Billy Two grunted. The Greek's pants had been shredded and were drenched with blood.

Nanos opened his mouth, and the grenade dropped into his lap.

"Geoff Bishop really is alive. I saw him. Less than ten minutes ago. Right here."

"I don't believe you," Billy Two said, helping the Greek to his feet. "You okay?" Once again the image of a man in a parachute flashed into his mind's eye like an instant slide projection. Hawk Spirit was trying to tell him something. What had the Osage Warrior god said before the battle? That tonight he must trust the unexpected.

Nanos winced with his first step. "Yeah, I'm okay. Cut up pretty bad, but nothing major."

The battle was over, the sounds of automatic rifle fire gone. Fire consumed the Villa Buchove. Around the room, the hostages picked themselves up, dazed and dust covered, but all in one piece. They ran for the door to the courtyard as the flames spread.

Lee Hatton and Claude Hayes waited outside in a field of carnage. Alex Nanos hobbled toward them, bursting to tell his news about the appearance of the missing SOB. Suddenly he stopped. He turned and looked at Billy Two.

The Osage shook his head. "Not yet," he said.

Nanos nodded. Not until Geoff Bishop was right in front of them. It would be too hard on Lee Hatton.

"C'mon, we gotta get our asses moving out of here!" Hayes bellowed, waving his rifle. He ran toward the SB-301 and climbed in the driver's door.

"Alex!" Lee said with alarm when she saw his blood-covered backside.

"It's okay, really." Nanos put his hand up to fend off her concern. He winked. "I saved the family jewels, anyway."

The freed hostages crowded around, jostling one another to get a glimpse of their rescuers. They threw themselves at the battle-fatigued mercs, hugging and reaching to touch, shake hands, offer gratitude and congratulations.

Matt Chicago, John Lorch and Flight 707's purser, Mike Mitchell, pushed their way to the front of the crowd.

"Who are you guys?" Lorch demanded, a crooked smile of amazement creasing his bruised face. "Delta Force? What?"

The mercs exchanged uncomfortable glances.

"Friends," Lee Hatton mumbled uneasily.

The crowd of Americans parted to let the armored carrier through. Hayes braked beside the mercs.

"We have seven minutes left for a ten-minute drive to our exfiltration point," he shouted to them.

Nanos turned to the hostages. "You guys can return the favor, okay?"

"How?" Chicago stepped forward to speak for the others.

"Let's just say you guys found a way to turn the tables on your jail keepers all by yourselves. You don't know about us."

The puzzled hostages looked at one another.

"But that's not fair," Lorch said. "You saved our lives. You're heroes."

Lee tugged at Alex's shirt sleeve, urging him toward the carrier.

"You guys take the credit. You deserve it. You're a helluva bunch," the Greek told them, moving away.

"But—"

"Move it!" Hayes bellowed from the window of the 301.

"As a favor." Nanos climbed into the carrier. "Make up a story. Anything. You just don't know about us. You guys are the real heroes, after what you've been through. Hey, for us it's just a job. And at least we get paid for it."

Man by man, the hostages began to nod their unconditional assent. Claude Hayes hit the accelerator. The armored carrier lurched forward. The cheers of the hostages followed them through the gates and rang in their ears as they headed through the ruins of Beirut toward the airport.

THE FOX PACED THE AISLE of the 727, brooding over the night's events. He cast skeptical glances at Hafoud Namoud, who stood near the cockpit door. The bloodied bodies of the flight crew, already growing stiff with rigor mortis, were stacked in the first row of seats, ready to be pushed outside when they were ready

to takeoff. Hafoud Namoud looked at them distaste-
fully and wiped the tips of his fingers on his suit
jacket.

"The hostages had been secured at the Villa
Buchove," he said, addressing the Fox. The terrorist
leader appeared not to be listening. Namoud continued.

"The airport will be deluged by thousands of our
fanatical followers. They will form a human cordon
between the runways and these secret commando
agents of Satan." He spoke with a tone of contempt.

The Fox listened with one ear while his mind traveled again over the evening's events and a sense of
apprehension that he could not shake. Where was the
captured pilot he had ordered brought to him from the
villa? And the alleged Druze bombardment continued to disturb him. He had never known the incompetent Druze to score such accurate hits.

He stopped just inside the door and gazed at the
runways and terminal buildings bathed in yellow light.
Hafoud Namoud walked close to him. "What are you
thinking?" he asked finally.

"They are out there!" he said, furious with convic-
tion.

"Out there? Who? These American commandos?" Namoud looked almost dismissive.

"They prowl!" the Fox whispered thunderously.
"Stealthily, steadily, they are circling us. They have the
scent of my blood in their nostrils just as I can smell
them, the hounds of the Great Devil. I hear them, demons padding softly through the dunes, waiting to

pounce, waiting for the Fox!" He pressed his face up close to Namoud's. The Shiite back away, uncertain how to respond.

Several Amal soldiers laughed in the tail section, sharing a ribald joke of their own. Halfway down the airplane, Dr. Wheatley, the last of the hostages, sat with his curious leather case.

"Why is this one so important that you have separated him out?" Namoud asked the Fox.

"You have not seen the strange contraption this man carries? Our Syrian allies will be most grateful to see it."

The Fox straightened and walked down the aisle. Namoud followed. Dr. Wheatley cringed in his seat, not even daring to look up. The Fox reached out and clenched Wheatley's face, digging his fingers into his jowls and the underside of his chin.

"Look at me," he growled, twisting the scientist's head up until their eyes met.

Wheatley's light blue eyes darted back and forth in their sockets, frightened, trying desperately to avoid the Fox's gaze.

"Stand up!" the Fox ordered between clenched teeth, prying the old man from his seat and lifting with his hands. Wheatley squealed as the terrorist leader's nails dug into his skin. He rose to his feet, trembling violently.

The Fox let go of him and stepped back.

"Now the case," said Hafoud Namoud, moving in beside the Fox. "Open it." Wheatley hesitated.

The Fox pulled his pistol and pointed it.

"No! No, right away!" Wheatley exclaimed, holding up his hands.

"He thinks he can stop a bullet!" Hafoud joked, slapping the American's hands away. The terrorist leaders laughed.

The scientist undid the clasps. Slowly he lifted the lid back. The black metal helmet glittered inside.

Namoud's eyes went wide with amazement. "Take it out!" he whispered.

Slowly, carefully, the scientist lifted it from the box. The giant full-faced helmet was laced with silver wires and sparkled with tiny colored transistors and filaments of glass.

"What is it?" Namoud demanded.

Unable to take his eyes from it, the Fox raised his gun and pressed it against the scientist's temple.

Dr. Wheatley held the mask in front of him like a talisman, his eyes wandering over its contours in frank adoration. He reached into the case and pulled out a square plastic disk that he inserted into the back of the helmet.

"A virtual cockpit," he said, the satisfaction evident in his voice. He held it higher as if he were about to put it on and stopped. "Cyborg. Half man and half machine. When man and machine become one! Think of it. What you see is the beginning of the future!" He put his hand on the rim of the opening and pressed a switch. The multi-faceted bulges over the eyes sparkled with dozens of tiny lights. Optical fibers glowed. His finger slipped against a dial inside the rim. He turned it, pushing it right to the end. The lights pulsing through the wires began to move faster.

The scientist turned toward the Fox, holding the helmet out. "I inserted a simulated test program." He smiled gently, his eyebrows rising in a slight taunt. "Would you like to try it?"

NILE BARRABAS rode beside Bishop in the back of the black car. He brushed at the dried blood on the chest of the Amal jacket. He and O'Toole didn't have much to choose from in their sizes. The previous owner had given the Irishman some trouble, and O'Toole had returned the favor with his Uzi.

"We're going in, Colonel." O'Toole drove the car slowly from the sandy dunes onto the tarmac. The system of lights improvised around the terminal building cast long shadows across the runway. They flickered over the mercs' faces as the car slid toward the DC-9. The little Amal flag on the antenna fluttered, and the Shiite soldiers ringing the airplane snapped to attention. Shouts burst from the terminal building.

"What in hell's going on over there, Colonel," the Irish American murmured, glancing in the rearview mirror.

Barrabas shook his head. Hundreds of white-robed Shiites were flooding onto the runway. O'Toole braked smoothly beside the steps that led to the forward door.

The two mercs left the car and walked to the other side. They dragged Bishop and Beck from the back seat. Barrabas jammed his gun into the pilot's back and shoved him up the steps. O'Toole followed, giving Nate the same treatment.

They pushed through the door of the airplane.

"But there are two prisoners!" Hafoud Namoud cried, walking the aisle toward the mercs. "Why are there two?"

The Fox stood beside the elderly scientist and turned stiffly. His eyes met Barrabas's. The guards stepped forward to seize Bishop.

"That's him!" the Fox screamed. "The American devil!" He swatted the elderly scientist sideways over the seats. The electronic helmet rolled on top of him.

The guards looked confused. Hafoud Namoud reached inside his jacket and withdrew a pistol.

Bishop and Beck dropped to the floor.

Namoud fired. Alarm washed over the faces of the guards, and they raised their submachine guns. O'Toole opened up on them, riddling them with 9 mm death holes.

Barrabas swung his Uzi in one hand and leveled three rounds into Namoud's head. The Shiite politician's face disappeared into a gore mask, and his brains sprayed through the back of his skull in a pink cloud.

"Servant of Satan!" the Fox roared. He yanked his SMG forward, sighting on the merc leader.

Barrabas and O'Toole dove for cover behind a seat as submachine-gun fire chunked into the back of the head rest, shattering plastic and burning the fabric.

Suddenly Dr. Wheatley stood on his seat, holding the virtual cockpit electronic helmet high overhead.

He dropped it down over the Fox like a death mask. The lights and glass fibers pulsated and blinked.

The Fox staggered backward, trying to force the helmet off with one hand, but the scientist fought him, tightening a leather strap at the back of his neck. An unearthly scream, muffled by the metal apparatus, came from the man in the alloy mask.

The scientist backed off.

The Fox stood in the aisle of the DC-9, the upper part of his body weaving in circles. He screamed again. The gun dropped from his hands. He fell, writhing horribly on the floor, trying desperately to pull the mask from his head. The muffled screams came faster now. The terrorist leader kicked at the floor and clawed with his hands.

He felt his gun, pulled it to him and banged the barrel against the helmet, trying to shatter it. The metal rang with the shock. Sparks exploded, and the lights pulsated crazily. His scream became a high-pitched squeal of consuming madness. He shoved the barrel of the SMG under the rim of the helmet to pry it away. Circuits shorted, and another wild shower of sparks spritzed over the seats. The Fox stiffened, banging the helmet against a seat. His finger tightened involuntarily on the trigger of his SMG.

The gun shook violently in his hands, pumping a mag of bullets into his head. They ricocheted from the tough titanium-alloy steel casing. Trapped in a metal cage, the autofire pulverized his head. Blood, thick with gore, sluiced from the helmet. The submachine fell harmlessly from dead hands, and the Fox's body slumped on the floor, quivering with a final death spasm.

Dr. Wheatley looked at Barrabas. "Thank God you've come," he whispered. His eyes rolled up inside his head and he fainted headlong into a seat.

Bishop sprang from the floor.

"Geoff, get this thing moving!" Barrabas ordered.

The airman ran to the cockpit and took the pilot's seat, snapping on instruments and switches. From outside the airplane came shouts of alarm, and in the distance the angry chanting of a mob.

"Colonel, they didn't like the sound of what they heard," Beck shouted from the door of the airplane. He cut loose with his Uzi, knocking the first three soldiers off the stairs. O'Toole joined him.

Barrabas ran to the rear door and reached to close it. Bullets brushed past his ribs, slamming into the bulkhead. He braced himself in the door, pumping off a mag at the Amal soldiers racing toward the DC-9. They spun wildly in a dance of death, the whirling dead. Others fled back to the safety of the sidelines.

The airplane shuddered. Its engines vibrated and roared to life. The DC-9 inched forward, tearing away from the landing stairs and the generator hookup.

A tremendous roar went up from the Shiite mob streaming from the terminal building. Fueled by blood lust, the fanatics in front burst into a run, and the crowd surged forward across the tarmac like a wave washing across a beach.

The lights of a vehicle bobbed in the sand dunes. The SB-301 sped onto the runway, racing against the onrushing mob to reach the airplane.

The DC-9 gathered speed down the runway.

Barrabas slammed the rear door securely shut and ran to the front. O'Toole waited at the door, his hand resting on the handle.

"They're coming," Barrabas told him. The Irishman pulled the door open. Rushing winds swept into the cabin.

"Runway's all clear ahead," Bishop shouted from the cockpit.

The frenzied mob of Shiites screamed louder, thousands of voices melding into a single deafening curse of hatred. Automatic rifle fire sounded sporadically, the bullets whizzing past in the airstream around the plane. The SB-301 pulled ahead of them and came alongside the tail of the DC-9, slowly gaining on the taxiing airplane. The side door swung open, and Alex Nanos pulled himself onto the roof. He reached down and dragged Lee Hatton up beside him. The armored carrier came alongside the open door, driving half under the high aluminum belly.

O'Toole and Barrabas fell flat and reached their powerful arms over the edge of the airplane. They gripped the mercs' hands and pulled. Hatton and Nanos grabbed the edge and kicked their legs over.

Billy Two scrambled from the door of the carrier.

"Mother, is this guy big," O'Toole muttered.

"Do it together," shouted Barrabas over the noise of the airplane and the wind.

The two mercs stretched out their arms. Billy Two leapt for the airplane, his fingers curling around the lip of the doorframe. Barrabas's hand closed over his forearm. O'Toole grabbed the other side, and Nanos rushed forward, pulling at the Indian's head. The Osage bellowed in pain and sprang at the Greek like a coiled spring, knocking him backward. But he was in.

"Geoff, slow it until we get Hayes in!" Barrabas shouted.

The armored carrier wove crazily from side to side. Hayes was still in there, at the wheel, and slowly but surely the DC-9 gained on the little carrier. The black man gave the accelerator a final squeeze. The 301's engines revved faster, and the speedometer needle topped sixty miles an hour. It pulled ahead of the airplane, paralleling the nose.

Claude Hayes wedged his Uzi against the gas pedal and the seat. The carrier slowed slightly. Keeping one hand on the wheel, he moved over the passenger seat, steering the carrier until it was almost under the airplane.

Barrabas stood at the door of the DC-9, watching Hayes scramble to the door of the armored carrier. The airplane was gaining on it again.

"Colonel! Found this!" O'Toole handed him a long industrial extension cord. The airplane shuddered and lifted several inches from the ground, then settled momentarily.

Barrabas threw the coils of the makeshift lifeline at the carrier. The long yellow cord fell in the door of the

301. Hayes grabbed it and wound his right hand around it. Barrabas took up the slack.

Hayes jarred the steering wheel sharply to the left and let go. He swung out the side of the vehicle as it careered across the tarmac toward the onrushing mob of Shiite fanatics. The ones who saw it coming screamed and tried to stop.

It was like holding back a tidal wave.

The bloodthirsty mob surged forward, crying to the heavens to stop the escaping airplane, their brethren crushed to a pulp underneath their stampeding feet.

In the door of the escaping airplane, Barrabas and O'Toole pulled at the wire cord, feeling the tough plastic sheath burn their hands. The wheels of the DC-9 left the ground again, and the nose tilted upward.

Billy Two balanced himself precariously at the open door. His arm swooped down for the black man and plucked him from the air like a grizzly pawing a trout from running water. Hayes dropped inside the cabin, his chest heaving for air, and Barrabas slammed the door shut.

It was over. The only sound was that of exhausted breathing. The plane ascended, and the airport grew small below, an island of chaos in Lebanon's long troubled night.

15

Barrabas entered the cockpit of the DC-9, closing the door quietly behind him. Bishop stared ahead at the dark horizon of the earth, his face lit by the glow of the instrument panel. The merc leader took the empty copilot's seat and faced the airman.

For a few moments they said nothing.

"Glad to be back, Colonel." Bishop looked at him quickly and turned to the window. "We're heading west over the Mediterranean. Where are we flying this thing?"

"The coast of Majorca. Lee has contacts there. We'll ditch it in the ocean and use the flotation devices to get to shore."

Bishop stiffened almost imperceptibly at the name of the woman warrior.

"You were missed, Geoff."

The pilot didn't answer. Barrabas saw tears well up in his eyes. The man had come through hell.

"You managed to stay in pretty good shape."

Bishop shrugged. "Nothing much to do in a prison 'cept exercise." He snickered. "And study rats. Remind me to tell you what I learned about rats sometime, Colonel."

His voice was calm and even, tightly controlled.

"You know what happened after.. afterward?"

"Liam told me. Pretty fucked up." He shrugged again, and forced a smile. "I guess that's a . . . weird kind of distinction—making the FBI's Most Wanted list."

"We're going to have to build you a new life."

Bishop nodded slowly without answering.

Barrabas slapped him affectionately on the back. "You want to see Lee?"

"I'd like that."

The merc leader stood. "I'll send her in."

When he returned to the DC-9's cabin, the mercs had moved the bodies into the tail section and thrown blankets over the worst of the carnage. Still, the blood-spattered interior of the passenger jetliner looked like a charnel house.

The mercs had gathered in the first-class section. Alex Nanos was lying flat in the aisle, naked from the waist down. Lee Hatton bent over him, extracting shrapnel from his buttocks with a pair of surgical tweezers.

"Keep still, Alex!" she scolded. The Greek grunted. She jerked the tweezers and came up with another jagged piece of metal. The rest of the mercs couldn't help laughing.

"Man, that's going to cut into your action for the next few weeks," Hayes joked.

Dr. Wheatley was in the front row of seats, clutching the empty leather case. Barrabas sat on the arm of the aisle seat.

"Sorry about the virtual cockpit. Is it worth saving?"

Wheatley shook his head. "It's not a major loss. It will take time—several months—but I can rebuild it."

"What exactly happened when you dropped it over the Fox's head?"

"You know what the virtual cockpit does?"

"Like a video air-combat game."

Wheatley raised his eyebrows and nodded. "Except more real. And instead of looking at a screen, you're inside it. That's what it feels like. I had a program simulation on a magnetic disk that I put in. But I increased the operating speed. That man wouldn't have known what was going on. Sensory overload. It must have been horrible."

"Horrible enough to stop it any way he could."

"Indeed," the scientist replied stiffly. "He deserved it."

"He did," Barrabas answered. "Yes, he did."

Lee Hatton solemnly clipped the last bandage around Nanos's buttocks and packed away the gauze and tweezers.

The Greek raised himself gingerly from the floor and tried to sit. He stood quickly, sucking air between his teeth and shuddering from the pain. Hatton stood and walked to the colonel. Her face was white.

"I filled her in, Colonel," O'Toole said quietly. He turned away to leave them alone.

"You want to see him?" Barrabas asked.

"It's all right?" She was shaking. She laughed nervously. "I don't know what to say."

"You'll know." Barrabas opened the door of the cockpit. Bishop looked over his shoulder, his eyes meeting Hatton's. It was a moment of joy and doubt. The woman's face lit up. Slowly, a smile spread across the pilot's face. Barrabas closed the door quietly behind them.

"Hey, Colonel!" Nate called to him from the seat across the aisle. His leg had been bandaged, and he seemed oblivious to pain.

"How're you feeling, Nate?"

"After Lee 'Florence Nightingale' Hatton and her magic morphine injections—hey, I feel great. But I'm wondering—are we getting the eight hundred thou for this, or the, uh, kill fee, as Jessup called it?"

Barrabas laughed and pointed at Dr. Wheatley with his thumb. "If they want this guy back, the full amount. Is that all right with you?" he asked the scientist.

Wheatley shrugged, slightly mystified. "Evidently you deserve it."

"And if we each throw in a hundred thou," Hayes called from a seat at the back, "the guy who's flying this rig can share in the spoils."

A chorus of assent quickly went up from the mercs. Billy Two inflated his massive lungs and added a celebratory war whoop.

Mission accomplished. Home was just a breath away.

A BATTERED TAXI PULLED UP to the ruined front gates of the Villa Buchove. The street was crowded with Red Cross vehicles and units of the Lebanese army.

Calhoun Bellow, dressed immaculately in a light gray summer suit, with his customary fedora, stepped into the street. A tape recorder and a camera hung from shoulder straps. He flashed his press card at the soldiers blocking the gate and entered the compound.

On the other side of a high wire fence, several Doberman pinschers grappled with a bloody carcass, ripping chunks of flesh away from the bones. Bellow stopped and stared. What were they eating? It looked...

He swallowed against his heaving stomach and pushed on.

The courtyard was littered with bloodied bodies, already beginning to swell in the heat of the tropical night. The house was a charred ruin. Army regulars and officers milled about, gathering abandoned weapons and beginning the gruesome task of corpse disposal.

The Red Cross had set up a food wagon for the hostages. Several vans operated as mobile hospitals. Medics processed the Americans, treating them for minor wounds.

"Press!" he called to them, flashing his laminated card with the intimidating black letters. "American press! Who's your spokesperson? I have questions to ask."

A tired-looking middle-aged man holding a cup of steaming coffee looked him over. He nodded toward Chicago, Lorch and Mitchell. The three men sat on the running board of a truck. On their knees they balanced paper plates piled high with food.

"Tastes awful, but I don't think I've ever been happier to eat," Chicago muttered, wolfing down another loaded forkful. A shadow fell across him. He looked up.

Calhoun Bellow stood over him. In one hand he clutched a steno pad, in the other a microphone. He shoved the mike in Chicago's face.

"I want to know everything about them. The commandos who rescued you. Who were they? What did they look like? How many?" His questions came in an unforgiving torrent.

Chicago recoiled from the mike halfway through a swallow. Food choked his throat. Bellow persisted, pressing the mike closer. Chicago coughed and pushed the food out. The masticated mush dripped over the head of the microphone.

Bellow's upper lip curled in distaste. He held the mike upside down like a rat by its tail and shook the mess off.

"No one, man," Chicago answered with a broad smile. "We don't know what you're talking about."

"Haven't got a clue," Mitchell joined, concentrating his attention on his plate.

Bellow snapped at them. "I know they were here! I know they rescued you!"

Lorch shook his head and dug at his food.

"Nope. Did it all ourselves." He brought the fork to his mouth and continued eating.

"That's impossible!"

The three men looked at one another.

"Who is this jerk?" Chicago asked.

The other two shrugged.

The journalist opened his press card again and waved in before their noses. Other hostages had begun to gather to listen to the commotion.

"I'm press! I'm Calhoun Bellow! And I know you're lying! I want answers! This is the press talking!"

"So talk somewhere else," said Mitchell.

"And get your answers somewhere else," Chicago added.

Lorch set his plate on the ground. "He says we're lying." He stood and faced the reporter with the kind of belligerent expression Marines specialized in.

Bellow backed off, his eyes darting among them. He ran to another hostage and pushed the mike in his face.

"Who rescued you?"

The man shook his head and backed off.

"You!" Bellow rushed to a second man, then a third. "You! Tell me! You!"

He saw a conspiracy of silence shining in their eyes. The circle of hostages widened around the raving journalist as he spun from man to man, demanding, cursing.

They turned their backs and walked away.

Calhoun Bellow stood alone in the compound, ignored by everyone, stunned. It was unthinkable. The story he wouldn't get. He vowed he would find out, somehow and he would spread their names over the front pages of every newspaper in America.

He heard the tiny sound of an airplane and looked up. He could barely make it out, a dark shape flying without running lights, illuminated by the dim gray light reflected from the Mediterranean as it headed west.

"I'll get you," Calhoun Bellow swore, shaking his fist at the night sky. "Whoever you are."

BULLETS OF PALESTINE

Howard Kaplan

A Kaplan novel is "an edge-of-the-chair, throat-grabbing page-turner! Accurate and terrifying."
—Gerald Green, writer, NBC's *Holocaust*

His name is Abu Nidal. A breakaway Palestinian known as the "terrorists' terrorist." An Israeli and a Palestinian join forces, despite the hatreds of their heritage, to eliminate this man. Will they ensnare Abu Nidal—or trap each other in a bloodbath of betrayal?

Take
4 explosive books
plus a
mystery bonus
FREE

Mail to Gold Eagle Reader Service

In the U.S.
P.O. Box 1396
Buffalo, N.Y. 14240-1396

In Canada
P.O. Box 609
Fort Erie, Ont. L2A 5X3

YEAH! Rush me 4 free Gold Eagle novels and my free mystery bonus. Then send me 6 brand-new novels every other month as they come off the presses. Bill me at the low price of just $14.95*— a 12% saving off the retail price. There is no minimum number of books I must buy. I can always return a shipment and cancel at any time. Even if I never buy another book from Gold Eagle, the 4 free novels and the mystery bonus are mine to keep forever. 166 BPM BP7S

*Plus 69¢ postage and handling per shipment in Canada.

_____

Name   (PLEASE PRINT)

_____

Address   Apt. No.

_____

City   State/Prov.   Zip/Postal Code

_____

Signature (If under 18, parent or guardian must sign)

This offer is limited to one order per household and not valid to present subscribers. Price is subject to change.

4E-SUB-1B